KRIS LONGKNIFE
COMMANDING

MIKE SHEPHERD

KL & MM BOOKS

PRAISE FOR THE KRIS LONGKNIFE NOVELS

"A whopping good read . . . Fast-paced, exciting, nicely detailed, with some innovative touches." - Elisabeth Moon, Nebula Award-winning author of Crown Renewal

"Shepherd delivers no shortage of military action, in space and on the ground. It's cinematic, dramatic, and dynamic . . . [He also] demonstrates a knack for characterization, balancing serious moments with dry humor . . . A thoroughly enjoyable adventure featuring one of science fiction's most interesting recurring heroines." - Tor.com

"A tightly written, action-packed adventure from start to finish . . . Heart-thumping action will keep the reader engrossed and emotionally involved. It will be hard waiting for the next in the series." - Fresh Fiction

"[Daring] will elate fans of the series . . . The story line is faster than the speed of light." - Alternative Worlds

"[Kris Longknife] will remind readers of David Weber's

Honor Harrington with her strength and intelligence. Mike Shepherd provides an exciting military science fiction thriller." -Genre Go Round Reviews

"'I'm a woman of very few words, but lots of action': so said Mae West, but it might just as well have been Lieutenant Kris Longknife, princess of the one hundred worlds of Wardhaven. Kris can kick, shoot, and punch her way out of any dangerous situation, and she can do it while wearing stilettos and a tight cocktail dress. She's all business, with a Hell's Angel handshake and a 'get out of my face' attitude. But her hair always looks good . . . Kris Longknife is funny and she entertains us." - SciFi Weekly

"[A] fast-paced, exciting military SF series . . . Mike Shepherd has a great ear for dialogue and talent for injecting dry humor into things at just the right moment . . . The characters are engaging, and the plot is full of twists and peppered liberally with sharply described action. I always look forward to installments in the Kris Longknife series because I know I'm guaranteed a good time with plenty of adventure." -SF Site

In the New York Times bestselling Kris Longknife novels, "Fans of the Honor Harrington escapades will welcome the adventures of another strong female in outer space starring in a thrill-a-page military space opera." - Alternative Worlds

"Military SF fans are bound to get a kick out of the series as a whole." - SF Site

COPYRIGHT INFORMATION

investing in a copy so I can continue to earn a living at this wonderful art.

I would like to thank my wonderful cover artist, Scott Grimando, who did all my Ace covers and will continue doing my own book covers. I also am grateful for the editing skill of Lisa Müller, Edee Lemonier, and as ever, Ellen Moscoe.

Rev 1.0

eBook ISBN-13: 978-1-64211-0241
Print ISBN-13: 978-1-64211-0234

ALSO BY MIKE SHEPHERD

Published by KL & MM Books

Kris Longknife: Admiral

Kris Longknife: Emissary

Kris Longknife: Commanding

Kris Longknife's Relief

Kris Longknife's Replacement

Kris Longknife's Successor

Rita Longknife: Enemy Unknown

Rita Longknife: Enemy in Sight

Short Stories from KL & MM Books

Kris Longknife's Maid Goes On Strike and Other Short Stories:
Vignettes from Kris Longknife's World

Kris Longknife's Maid Goes On Strike

Kris Longknife's Bad Day

Ruth Longknife's First Christmas

Kris Longknife: Among the Kicking Birds

Ace Books by Mike Shepherd

Kris Longknife: Mutineer

Kris Longknife: Deserter

Kris Longknife: Defiant

Kris Longknife: Resolute

Kris Longknife: Audacious

Kris Longknife: Intrepid

Kris Longknife: Undaunted

Kris Longknife: Redoubtable

Kris Longknife: Daring

Kris Longknife: Furious

Kris Longknife: Defender

Kris Longknife: Tenacious

Kris Longknife: Unrelenting

Kris Longknife: Bold

Vicky Peterwald: Target

Vicky Peterwald: Survivor

Vicky Peterwald: Rebel

Mike Shepherd writing as Mike Moscoe in the Jump Point Universe

First Casualty

The Price of Peace

They Also Serve

Rita Longknife: To Do or Die

Short Specials

Kris Longknife: Training Daze

Kris Longknife: Welcome Home, Go Away

Kris Longknife's Bloodhound

Kris Longknife's Assassin

The Lost Millennium Trilogy Published by KL & MM Books

Lost Dawns: Prequel

First Dawn

Second Fire

Lost Days

G rand Admiral, Her Royal Highness Kris Longknife of Wardhaven stood at attention. Today, she stood her place both as a Grand Admiral in the United Society's Navy and as an Iteeche Imperial Admiral of the First Order of Steel.

Kris kept her eyes front, but soldiers for eons had learned to take in their world while looking straight ahead. The Imperial throne room was dazzling.

The massive, opulent hall was large enough to build several star ships in. However, the actual throne room stood on a massive block of rare blue marble streaked with onyx and silver. It was surrounded on three sides by twisting banners that streamed from the ceiling several hundred meters overhead. They reflected every color of the ocean. The area atop the marble platform had seemed vast when Kris presented her Emissary credentials to the Emperor. There had been only two other, very senior Imperial advisors, present that day.

Today, it was actually crowded.

The air, then sweet with the scent of incense, now stank of every possible scent . . . overlaid with deathly fear.

On a dais, approachable by six steep steps, was a large throne of delicately carved soft pink coral.

The young Emperor, barely half the size of one of the eight-foot-tall Iteeche officials, was almost lost in the folds of his regalia and swallowed up by the throne. The teenager was the All Powerful and Worshipful Emperor of All the Iteeche. He ruled nearly three thousand planets with absolute power.

He was also a very frightened puppet.

Kris felt pity for the poor boy, but there was nothing she could do about his situation. The Imperial Household controlled every waking moment of the boy's life. Except for the occasional audience, that life was hidden from all.

Kris's only job, as far as the Imperial Court was concerned, was to keep the kid alive. Oh, and serve as the First and Prime Emissary to the Imperial Court from the Human Race.

For the moment, Kris stood at an expectant attention. To her left, and two steps behind her, stood Admiral Amber Kitano. She'd brought out the United Society's First Battlecruiser Fleet that was ninety-six ships strong. They hadn't quite saved Kris's bacon, but they most definitely had ruined the dash for the exit by a whole lot of rebel leaders racing to save their own bacon.

Those leaders were the "guests of honor" at this Most Sincere and Very Complete Apology to the Emperor.

Behind Admiral Kitano were arrayed the other human admirals, both Rear Admirals Ajax and Afon who had fought with Kris in her long and bloody battle, and the vice admirals and rear admirals that had come out with Admiral Kitano.

The human delegation was the smallest; both in number, height, and weight.

To Kris's distant left stood Imperial Admiral of the Second Order of Steel Cloth, resplendent in his gray and gold uniform. His recent promotion had been earned in a hard-fought battle under Kris's command. Behind him, drawn up in several rows, stood the surviving Iteeche admirals of that battle, organized by a myriad of ranks from the Fourth Order of Cloth on up.

When you had a fleet with tens of thousands of ships and a society where every tiny bit of status was observed meticulously, the five stars the humans used to rank admirals seemed ridiculous.

The Iteeche admirals stood closer to the boy Emperor, as if they might need to rush forward to impose themselves between these two-legged aliens and His Worshipfulness. As if the humans might suddenly decide to renew the Iteeche-Human war.

Kris suppressed a smile at this thought. She commanded the Iteeche Combined Battle Fleet. She was fighting the rebels to keep the child on the throne and a couple of billion people on this planet from being murdered from space.

Still, the Iteeche measured every action of state with a micrometer accurate to nanometers.

Across from Kris stood row upon row of court officials. Usually, they'd all be crawling on their belly before the Emperor. However, so many people were present, both to observe and learn a stern lesson, that they could do nothing but stand.

Half of the mob was made of Iteeche in pure white robes, and others in every shade of green. Kris still didn't understand the full role of those Iteeche. Officially, the Iteeche had no religion. Yet the white robes seemed to commune with something transcendent, and the green spoke of philosophy as they offered conflicting advice to the Emperor.

The other half of the mass of Iteeche across from Kris wore robes of many iridescent colors, marking them as Administrators or Counselors to the Emperor. Among them were Roth'sum'We'sum'Quin, leader of the Chap'sum'We clan. Standing right behind his chooser was Ron'-sum'Pin'sum'We.

The Chap'sum'We clan was probably Kris's strongest ally in this court, if any Iteeche would truly commit itself to tie its interests to that of the still-hated humans. Ron alone had been raised to understand the strange way of the human aliens. He was the closest Kris had to a friend among the four-legged, four-armed and four-eyed aliens.

What was more interesting to Kris at the moment was Ron's dress. Like his chooser, he wore the iridescent robes of an Imperial Administrator and Counselor. He had, however, commanded one of the wings in the recent battle. He'd led a fifth of the forces under Kris's command.

As such, he should have stood among the fighting admirals.

Instead, he stood with his chooser and the political over-lords of the Empire. If Kris had any doubt that it was preferred for Navy Officers to use the servants' entrance, this told her all she needed to know.

To Kris's right, between her and the Iteeche priests, philosophers, and administrators, knelt the pathetic "guests of honor" for this apology.

These were the leaders of the rebel clans that had come with the fleet of eight thousand battlecruisers. They had intended to blast their way through an Imperial fleet badly sapped by treachery, seize the sky over the Imperial Capital

Planet, and gas every inhabitant on it. They would then bring in their own people to repopulate the planet and use its resources.

Oh, and one of them would have sat his butt down on the Imperial throne after tossing the body of this poor kid aside like a chunk of dead meat.

That, of course, assumed they didn't start squabbling and murdering each other first.

Fortunately, their plans ran afoul of a scratch fleet Kris had pulled together and been training for way too short a time. Outnumbered at almost 4:1, the battle had been brutally hard and bloody, but Kris won it and most of the 8,000 rebel warships were blown out of space.

The rebel clan chieftains, seeing their Navy slaughtered, chose to run. By blessed poetic justice, they ran right into Admiral Kitano who was bringing reinforcements for Kris.

Now they knelt naked. The gray metal manacles and chains marred the near-perfect white of their skin. Their heads were bowed; their four legs chained in iron, their four arms bound behind their backs.

They were here to make a Most Sincere and Very Complete Apology to the young Emperor.

The prisoners formed four rows. Behind each of them stood two Iteeche. One wore a red cowl so long that it covered his head and the hem dragged on the ground. Each of those red-robed Iteeche held a crystal-clear bowl with a snake that slithered within. Kris wondered if that would be the means of the "apology."

However, beside the Iteeche in red robes stood an Iteeche clothed in black. His clothes were tight, putting his bulging muscles on display for all to see. In his right hand, he held aloft a three- to four-meter-long pole with a half-meter long blade jutting from the top. Most of the tips were more like axes than the traditional human glaive they resembled. However, each was a bit different. Some had hooks on the side opposite the sharp blade. Others had spikes.

All the edges gleamed in the light leaving no doubt they had been sharpened to a fine cutting edge.

From among the administrators, Roth strode forward. He humbled himself before the Emperor, going down into a kowtow using the lowermost four of his elbows and knees.

The young boy Emperor may have given him a sign. If he did, Kris lost it in the folds of his oversize robes. Whatever it was, Roth rose and turned to the rebels.

He paused for a moment, glowering at the captives. Then Kris heard the slap of bare feet on the marble, and a naked slave ran out to humble himself before Roth. When told, he stood and unfolded a scroll for Roth to read from, lord forbid that the high lord of a clan soil his hands by holding something.

Unlike most Iteeche declarations that began with long-winded listings of the honors of the recipient and the sender, Roth jumped right into the matter at hand.

"You kneel before Your Worshipful Emperor, besmirched with the shit of your own crimes."

NELLY, DID YOU GET THAT RIGHT?

YES, KRIS. APPARENTLY, THERE IS NO LIMIT TO THE DEGRADATION THAT CAN BE HEAPED ON THE HEADS OF REBELS.

REBELS THAT LOSE.

IF YOU DON'T LOSE, YOU'RE NOT A REBEL. Nelly pointed out.

Kris went back to paying attention to Roth's diatribe.

"The stink of your improper behavior rises to the blue of the sky. The offal of your actions sinks into the depths to mingle with the chaos of the abyss. Even as you kneel before the Emperor, none of you have said a word to repent for your misguided steps. Will you now tell His Worshipful Majesty that you repent of your false ways?"

Kris had been warned that none of the rebels was getting out of here alive. She had to wonder if an easier death might lay ahead for any who voiced regret.

She need not have wasted the thought. Not one of the rebels said a word.

Kris eyed them as carefully as she could without moving her head. None of them had said anything as they'd been dragged in. Had their tongues been cut out?

That wouldn't surprise Kris. Not really. The Iteeche liked their ceremonies to go down exactly according to plan. Having rebels screaming defiance would not fit very well in the quiet space between the broad streamers that somehow managed to wave in a wind of their own creation.

"So be it," Roth said, "Let your deaths be upon your head. Let no clan seek blood for blood. Let no blood price be paid."

Kris had previously been introduced to this quaint tradition. Every head had a price on it. Kill an Iteeche, and you owed his clan a price or a life. This practice was crimping Kris's usual style since even dead assassins created a blood price.

Now Roth turned, and once more went down on his elbows and knees. Behind him, among the rebels, the snake wranglers in red knelt and lifted the top from their crystal bowls. They placed them at the feet of the prisoners and tilted them forward. Quick as any snake in the galaxy, the many-colored serpents struck, sinking their fangs deep into the soles of the feet of the condemned prisoners.

Almost every snake wrangler tipped the bowl back and the snake tumbled back into its cage.

A few snakes still had their fangs sunk deep into a foot. They held on. The snake wranglers brought down the lid, trapping the snake. Then they stood, tipped the bowl back, and let the snake fall back into its crystal prison.

One, however, failed to contain his snake.

When that one stood up, the snake twisted under the lid and threw itself at the Iteeche in red.

The snake wrangler did not cry out as he was bit. It was more like a soft sigh that escaped his lips, as if the air was being slowly let out of a balloon.

He did, however, drop the crystal bowl; it shattered into a thousand shards. The snake wiggled free even as the Iteeche in red fell to his knees.

Kris expected a mad run for safety, but nothing of the sort happened. The blade man, who had stood beside the man in red, took one step back then swung his blade down.

It rang off the marble in a clear, crystal note and suddenly there were two shorter snakes wiggling where one long one had been.

While all this had been holding Kris's attention, the prisoners had begun to writhe in pain. Muscles knotted up into huge lumps, then knotted up some more. Now, under the screams, was the horrible sound of muscles ripping bones from their joints . . . and the Iteeche had a lot of joints.

Soon, the Iteeche rebels were convulsing on the blue marble floor as their muscles continued to knot up or release, wracking them with pain.

Now, they did scream.

As ever, death was no respecter of dignity. As the rebel leaders squirmed on the blue marble, they lost all muscle control. The Iteeche showed no genitals, be they male or female. They had a cloaca that served all purposes. Now the air stank as urine and feces spilled out of them, mixing with the packets of sperm that was the usual male contribution to procreation.

At the tiniest hint of movement, Kris shifted her eyes from the horrendous scene to the young lad on the throne. He had actually recoiled, retreating farther back into his oversized throne. He had the pale skin of an Iteeche, but it was now tinged with green. Even from her place, Kris could hear the hard gulps the fellow was making as he desperately struggled to keep the contents of his stomach in place.

What a scene for such a young boy! Yet, as Emperor, it could not take place without him.

More movement drew Kris's attention to Admiral Coth and the contingent of Navy officers standing behind him. They still stood at rigid attention. Now, however, they turned their faces to the rebels, and grinned at their agony.

Of course, the rebels had intended each of those officers to die, either in battle or on some executioner's block if they failed to achieve that honorable death in battle. Possibly, the admirals would have suffered just as horribly as these rebels now did.

As much as Kris abhorred torture, she could understand the Iteeche demand for this retribution.

The Iteeche rebels and the one unlucky snake wrangler continued to writhe in pain. However, slowly the cries died down to moans. The muscles began to knot less quickly. Kris didn't need to be told that death was rapidly approaching.

Now the Iteeche in black stepped forward. They began to twirl their pole weapons over their heads. Since the weapons were longer than the space between them, this was done to perfect timing. Every other man twirled his glaive a quarter of a turn behind the man to his right. Some twirled higher, some lower.

For a full minute, the welder of these razor-sharp blades did this deadly dance without a single misstep. Then, as one they stepped forward and brought their axes down on the necks of nearly dead rebels.

Every head flew off, blood spraying from their severed necks.

Only then did one axe man step back and bring his blade down on the snake wrangler who had bungled his job and earned his tortured death while risking the same for all those around him.

The Emperor stood. His legs were barely able to hold him. Still, he stood.

Kris alone bowed from the waist to the young boy.

The poor young Iteeche paused as his servant-masters hustled him from his throne to an exit behind it. His eyes met Kris's.

Did the young man understand that Roth lay out, obeisant for all those Iteeche standing? Kris, however, bowed to him as a representative of her king, and thus, equal to equal.

The young emperor bowed his head to Kris. It might only be a nod, but it was there and it was not lost on the court.

Then his servants rushed him behind a curtain and he was gone.

Kris did a smart about face. She eyed her admirals. "Relax crew. You have all survived your first audience with the Emperor of All the Iteeche."

She glanced at the still-twitching bodies of the Iteeche rebels. "That's more than those damn fools can claim. Now, I suggest we wait a bit until the traffic jam is over."

"Or you can march off with my officers," Admiral Coth said. "No one will dare gainsay you if you are in the company of victorious Iteeche admirals."

"Aren't we victorious human admirals?" Kris asked.

"Shush. We can't let the peasants hear victorious in the same sentence with 'human.' Black water and chaos, I doubt half of our overlords are all that happy to hear it, and we just saved all of them from being gassed to free up their palace."

"Well then, you lead and we will follow." Kris said.

"No way," Nelly's translation said. "You march beside me. If your admirals will form a file down one side of our column, we will all march out together, assuming you two-legged types can keep in step with us."

"Or you could keep in step with us?" Kris pointed out.

"Oh, right. Sometimes I forget. I've got a human for a commanding officer. What is your wish, oh victorious admiral?"

"You get your guys in step. I'll get my crew in step. And I'll pay for the first round of beer."

And with that, the victorious admirals marched from the Imperial Throne Room and no one dared get in their way.

2

Kris did buy the first round of beer. Before those tankards were drained, she'd declared the bar open for all the admirals and they, both human and Iteeche, began to get seriously drunk.

The Forward Lounge, the site of this drunken debriefing, was atop the Smart Metal™ castle that Kris had caused to be constructed in the sky above the courtyard of the Pink Coral Palace that the Iteeche had provided to her for a human embassy.

It had been abandoned by a rebel clan and confiscated by the Imperium. Kris, however, was doing her best to establish that this was human soil and not subject to Iteeche search.

Thus, the human admirals marched through the outer gate guarded by Iteeche Marines, and the inner gate guarded by US Marines before taking elevators up to the Forward Lounge. The Iteeche admirals took a more roundabout route.

From the outer gate, they marched up the special

entrance to the Iteeche Navy Annex that Kris had spun out of Smart Metal™ above the human entrance to the Pink Coral Palace. From there, they took elevators to the topmost floor where a long corridor, put there to allow Kris access to their spaces, now whisked them to the towering castle. From there, they rode elevators high up to the Forward Lounge.

Kris was already there, a tankard of non-alcoholic beer in hand. She greeted every one of them and personally thanked each Iteeche admiral for his valor in battle. The Iteeche under her command had suffered the heaviest in the fight. There had been just over 2,100 Iteeche battle-cruisers and only 32 human warships.

Kris had minted a medal in honor of this fight, and she told them there would be a formal ceremony in a week to award them. Unusual for the Iteeche, Kris intended every sailor to get one. A bronze medal for the other ranks, a silver one for the officers, and a gold one for the admirals.

The Iteeche admirals were quite taken aback by this, but seemed very happy to learn of it.

Admiral Coth joined Kris, arriving last behind all his junior commanders.

"So, you're going to go through with this idea of giving every man who fought in the Imperial Guard System, a what do you humans call it? A decoration to wear on their uniform," Admiral Coth said.

"It seems only right that those who fought there and survived should be able to show everyone they meet that they risked their lives to save the Emperor," Kris answered.

"I cannot disagree with you, being a sailor myself. Still, I have fought many, many campaigns against rebels and you see no ribbons or medals on my chest like you wear. Great blue sky above, I can hardly see your uniform for all the gee-gaws on it."

"And human warriors who know what all this means, know to get out of my way when they see me coming. That, or have a nice cup of tea waiting for me."

The two of them shared a laugh.

"Well, you are right," Coth agreed. "This medal of yours will give our sailors bragging rights in every bar in the Empire."

"And, even better," Kris added, "those that have bare chests will be eager to join us for the next campaign. I assume that our single victory has not ended the rebellion."

"Sadly, it has not," Coth said. "Our spies report that the rebels have many more ships and sailors to fight in them. While many of the rebel clans lost leaders in this Most Sincere and Very Complete Apology, all of the clans have ambitious junior lords only too quick to step into the vacant shoes of their clan overlords. Now they are eager to lead their followers to victory over the hated Imperials."

"Then we must teach them the proper wisdom of Worshiping the Emperor."

"Shall we not teach them the proper wisdom of fighting these magnificent battlecruisers you humans have developed? We could not have won that battle if we fought our ships the same way the rebels fought theirs."

Kris nodded. For thousands of years, Iteeche warriors had gone into battle standing up. She had had a nearly impossible time persuading Iteeche sailors that they could better withstand the high gees of acceleration if they reclined in high gee stations. Her battle fleet had gone into the fight jinking and dodging. She'd also improved the fire control on her ships.

Consequently, fewer of her ships died and more of the enemy were blown to gas and shards of metal.

The ships might be identical when they came from the

builders, but the tweaks the humans applied to them had been the difference between life or death, victory or defeat

Now, the humans and Iteeche drank together, refought the battle together, and got to understand each other better.

Having shaken the hands of every admiral she was buying drinks for, Kris settled down at a table with Lieutenant General Jack Montoya, USMC. As Kris's husband, he'd long ago gotten used to be addressed as a Longknife. Since he'd been sucked into the Longknife legend, with all its advantages and penalties, he had no problem with people who addressed him as Jack Longknife. In honest moments, he'd even admit to himself that he half-thought of himself that way. It took a very good sense of humor as well as the fine art of dodging incoming fire to survive when you were married to a force of nature like Kris.

Also at the table was Lieutenant Megan Longknife, Kris's cousin, *aide de camp*, dog robber, and computer sensitive. She might have missed the battle, but she'd kept the home fires burning. Megan, plus some of the wait staff, were the only ones present who wouldn't be receiving Kris's battle medal.

Still, Kris would hate to have done this job without Megan to sort out the snakes that came her way.

Admiral Kitano settled down at the table.

"Damn it, woman," she said with no preamble, "once again, you leave the late arrivals with nothing to do."

"Still, I can't tell you how happy I was to see you," Kris said. Her fleet of 32 battlecruisers was smaller than the average Iteeche flotilla. Each of the five wings Kris had commanded included some 440 Iteeche battlecruisers.

Here in the Iteeche Empire, fleets numbered ships in the thousands.

Still, Kris would be very happy to add another 96 human battlecruisers to her fleet. They came with hidden virtues.

Kitano took a sip from the glass of scotch in her hand. "I'm sure you'll find a few odds and ends for us to tie up."

"You're staying?" Kris asked. This was a burning question she had not had time to ask.

"We've made a great team, what with you leading and me following. There are plenty of dead aliens to prove it. Besides, when you sent home that incompetent vice admiral you busted from command of your escorting task fleet, I figured you'd need someone to fill in and keep you from making a mess of the details."

The two chuckled. Kris had promoted Kitano from skipper of a single ship to command of almost all of the battlecruisers of her fleet, back during the battle for System X to defend the planet Alwa on the other side of the galaxy. Together, they'd destroyed 4 alien mother ships and the wolf packs they led. Thousands of alien battleships and cruisers had been blown out of space and hundreds of billions of the aliens had died.

Death was the only option. If the vicious alien raiders had won, they would have murdered every living soul on the lovely planet Alwa, sanitizing it down to the bedrock. If Kris won, they refused to negotiate and refused to surrender. They'd blow up their ships or open them to space's vacuum rather than accept mercy.

Kris had spent four years fighting those barbaric bastards on the other side of the galaxy. She'd thought her fighting days were done. When the job of first emissary to the Imperial Iteeche Court was offered, Kris jumped at it.

At the time, she'd expected to negotiate trade deals, cultural exchanges, and tourist visas. What she discovered was the supposed monolithic Iteeche Empire was riven with bitter enmity and rebellion. The Imperials needed a fighting admiral.

So, they invited in the most fighting admiral in the galaxy and gave her command of their Combined Battle Fleet. Well, sort of.

Command is a delicate fiction, made up of authority and obedience. Still, it requires loyalty both ways. Being commanded by a hated human did not sit well with far too many Iteeche.

Kris had had to earn the loyalty of the Iteeche under her command. She'd had to persuade them that obeying her orders would give them victory and keep them alive to fight again.

The victory in the Imperial Guard System had disproven a lot of the old stories from the war. Sailors on leave were already talking the fight up in the bars of the space stations. Hopefully, their delight in victory and approval of their human commander would draw more ships to Kris's command.

Unfortunately, it was also likely that rebel spies would be listening. Maybe even buying the drinks. No doubt, a lot of informative coded messages would be speeding their way into rebel space.

If Kris was going to fight, she'd have to do it soon before the rebels knew and imitated all of her best moves.

Kris eyed Kitano across the table. "I'd like you to absorb my 6th Battlecruiser Task Fleet into your First Battlecruiser Fleet. That assumes that you aren't just on loan. Who's minding the store back at Main Navy?"

"Admiral Phil Taussig should be arriving from Alwa on the next transport," Amber said. "I've recommended he take over as Battlecruiser Type Commander on Wardhaven. He's old Navy. His father and grandfather were Navy, and I'm sure they've told him where all the best skeletons are buried. He learned to be a good fighting admiral at our knees and bureaucratic infighting at his pappy's. That guy is the perfect choice for that job."

"Can he take over without you there to show him the ropes?" was Kris's main concern. The battlecruisers were her babies. She'd been there at the birth of the first and had been midwife to every class that had come down the way ever since.

"I left him my chief of staff to serve as his, as well as the two fine *aide de camps* you got us. I miss my wife, and I hope she can cut loose soon, but she'll get Phil up to speed."

Kris was glad to see Phil had gotten his fourth star. He'd been a skipper under her in the old Tenth Patrol Squadron. He'd gone with her to circumnavigate the galaxy. When they ran into the vicious alien raiders, he'd taken the *Hornet* in one direction to lead the aliens hounding their wake, so Kris and the *Wasp* could go in the other direction and bring news back to human space that we were now at war with a bunch of aliens that wanted us dead.

Dead to the last man, woman, and child.

Kris had managed to later rescue Phil and the rest of the crew of the *Hornet*, but he'd been in pretty bad shape and had missed several of the earlier battles. That took him out of the meteoric rise of some great fighting admirals that followed close in Kris's wake.

It was good to see that he had caught up.

"So, I can keep you here and not feel guilty."

"Yep. We can put the old band back together and start making beautiful music again," Amber said with a chuckle. "There are still a few rebels that need killing. Although I'm tempted to just kill the next batch and save them that apology thing we just saw."

"I know what you mean, but we're in Iteeche land and we've got to let them do things the Iteeche way."

Speaking of which, Admiral Coth was making his way to her table, a beer stein in both of his right hands.

"You know how to throw a bash," the admiral shouted as he approached. "Is that raw sook at the bar? Do you have cold slices of foo to put them on?"

"We have laid in the most delicious delicacies for your admirals. They deserve the best we can give them," Kris shouted back.

Coth eyed a female Marine in dress blue and reds, maneuvering her way through a milling crowd of Iteeche easily three feet taller than her, a plate of hors d'oeuvres expertly held aloft by one hand. She spotted his eyes on her and turned toward him.

"Would you care for a few delicacies?" she asked the admiral.

"Just leave the tray here, youngling. Does your chooser know you're out of the Palace of Learning?"

"Admiral," Kris put in, "those two medals on her pocket show that she qualified as a sharpshooter last time she shot and that she's also a trained sniper."

"You can tell that just by glancing at the youngling?"

"I told you that there were advantages to wearing these gee-gaws to warn people not to cross you."

All four of Coth's eyes grew wide. Then he turned back to the Marine. "I honor you, warrior. It is true that I have a lot to learn about you two-eyes."

"As we have to learn about you four-eyes," the corporal said with a dimpled smile. She turned and headed back to the bar for another plate.

"You require your young women warriors to serve drinks to your officers?" Coth asked.

"Say instead that we invite Marines to volunteer for extra pay. Often times, they get tips, extra money for good service. I will see that all the servers tonight get a large tip for this party," Kris said.

Coth shook his head. "I would be doing good to weasel my officers and crew an extra week's pay for surviving a fight like we just won. To be invited to share drinks with their fellow officers! To be served such rich food! Food reserved for the likes of clan leaders!"

Again, he shook his head. "You humans have a strange way of doing things."

"Yes, we do. But you Iteeche have your own way of doing things. You can learn from us and we, no doubt, will learn from you."

"Yes," Coth agreed. "You gave us your Smart Metal and the shape of your battlecruisers. We gave you the trick we have of getting more power out of the same reactors. Those were good trades," the Iteeche Admiral said, then went on.

"Still, it would be nice if you would give us the secret of this new crystal armor you sheath your ships in that makes them shine like a star instead of blowing up like one."

"I wish I could, Admiral, but the decision to release it must be made at the highest level of my government. Even then, it would be likely that a lot of different human alliances would want to have some say in the matter."

"Yes, and we will not give you the secret of our maskers," the admiral grumped.

"We are but servants of our political superiors," Kris said.

"But I sure would like to have that armor for what we must do next."

"Have you heard what our next assignment will be?" Kris asked.

"Only rumors, but they are logical rumors."

"And?" Kris asked.

"Have you given much thought to how you storm a jump point defended by an armed space station? One like you are building to defend the jumps into your planets?"

"Oh, crap," Amber said.

Kris just managed to keep her mouth shut. What she would likely have said would have been even more unprincess-like and would certainly have gotten her a lecture from her six-year-old daughter.

3

Kris found herself leaving the party early, and very sober. She adjourned to her Flag Plot. It might be in her embassy castle, but she had too much ship duty in her blood to call it a conference room. Soon, much of her team was filling up a table.

Jacques la Duke, her anthropologist on all things Iteeche, sat next to his gorgeous wife, Amanda Kutter. She was Kris's economic genius at figuring out what made an economy tick. The two had helped Kris understand both the birds of Alwa and the cats of Susquan. They had yet to get a handle on the Iteeche Empire, but Kris was confident that they would sooner or later.

Jack and Megan were, of course, there. Kris had called in Abby, her former maid, who now served as liaison between her support staff, assisting both the Navy and diplomatic side. She'd survived quite a few years as Kris's maid, bodyguard, and occasional assassin. Kris treated her input like gold.

Ambassador Tsusumu Kawaguchi from Musashi represented the diplomatic side. As a lawyer, he had saved Kris from a politically trumped-up capital charge of initiating a war with the vicious alien raiders. Kris had trusted him with her life when the Lord High Executioner was waiting in the wings, and she still did.

It was moments like this that Kris missed Captain Penny Paisley. She had known her since Kris was a J.G. and Penny was a full lieutenant. She'd been her intelligence officer when they were just dealing with the local cops and had grown into an expert on birds, cats, and the monsters that would not seek peace.

Penny had settled down on Alwa and was now giving Grand Admiral Santiago the benefits of her expertise.

Today, a new captain, Quinn Sung, sat at Kris's table. With both Jacques and Amanda, she had been studying the Iteeche. Quinn had concentrated on the military side of the Iteeche Empire. Unfortunately, just like the other two, she had little to show from her work.

At the table across from them, sat Admiral Coth with his deputy and several subordinates, all admirals of various ranks.

"Can you share with us anything you may have picked up about potential future operations that may be headed our way?" Kris asked.

"I hate to respond to you, My Admiral, with a question, but could you tell us what you know about the Empire? I need to know what you know so I do not bore you."

Coth paused to eye Kris before adding, "I also need to know what you do not know so that I may not tell you what I should not."

Kris suppressed a scowl, "I thank you for your honesty. It is clear that though I command the Imperial Iteeche

Combined Battle Fleet, I am still a hated human and potential enemy."

Coth shrugged with all four of his shoulders, "There are those who are very happy that you are here, My Admiral. There are others who are not so happy. I and my admirals must navigate the troubled waters of our Empire if we are to live to old age."

"I understand. Nelly, display the star map that we have of the Iteeche Empire."

Suddenly, a hologram appeared above the table. Bright yellow stars hung in space. The capital planet showed red off to one side. Since the Human-Iteeche War, the Empire had added a thousand planets, all on the opposite side from human space.

"We know that each of these planets is occupied," Kris said. "We know the size of the population of each planet. We know some of the planets that have human engineers assigned to them to help with the construction of battlecruisers. We don't know all of them because quite a few of the humans who have returned have no idea of what planet their spaceship building yards orbited. I don't know if that is inattention on their part or good field craft and asset management by your security services. Is this enough?" Kris asked.

Admiral Coth eyed the star map before turning to one of his subordinates.

"Is that an accurate map?" he asked.

The other Iteeche's eyes flew over the map. It was as if he had the planets of the Empire memorized. It quickly appeared that he had.

"They are only missing two of the most recently settled planets, Honored Superior."

"And you say that you know the population of each planet?" Admiral Coth asked Kris.

"Yes. Should we give you a list?" she asked.

"Please."

On the wall in front of each party, a list appeared. Some three thousand planetary names seemed to float into existence on the bulkhead. Each had a number beside it with a whole lot of commas in it. One moment, the wall was bare. The next moment, Nelly had made the entire census of the Iteeche Empire appear on it.

The vestigial gills on the admirals, long since replaced by lungs, showed yellow, a color Kris had never catalogued before.

ANY IDEA WHAT YELLOW MEANS? Kris asked Nelly.

SURPRISE, I WOULD GUESS. IT'S THE FIRST TIME I'VE SEEN IT AND WITH THE POLITICAL TYPES WEARING HIGH COLLARS NOW, I HAVEN'T BEEN ABLE TO DO A LOT OF RESEARCH.

THANKS, NELLY.

In only a few moments, the junior admiral scanned down the twelve rows of planetary names and populations. "The numbers are low," he said. "They appear to date back to the last general census with no updates. Someone gave them a lot of data on the Imperium. That someone needs to make a formal apology."

"This information was part of a mutual exchange of maps and information," Kris said evenly. "We gave a complete map of human space for a complete map of Iteeche space."

"Well, the human map has not been shared with the Navy," the admiral grumped.

Coth let his eyes rove the list for a long couple of minutes. "Do you know what you have here?" he asked Kris.

"A map of planets and jumps. A list of planetary populations," Kris said. She paused before going on. "A list of just how badly overpopulated your planets are."

"I wonder, My Admiral, if you would trust me with an answer to my next question. Will you tell me just how much you understand? How much do you know? Do you grasp the full import of what someone has chosen to share with you?"

Kris chose to turn silently to her economist.

Amanda leaned forward and said, "I would have thought that you had a solid handle on how to control the growth of your populations. I thought I understood how you reproduced. Am I wrong?"

When the Iteeche sat through her question with no response, Amanda went on. "A male is allowed to spread his sperm packets into the mating ponds. A female plucks several sperm packets while she bathes and inserts them into herself. Fertilization takes place and the eggs are expelled. Eggs hatch into tadpoles which grow into fingerlings, and in time, become smelt. That's when they become amphibious, right?"

Admiral Coth nodded.

"My understanding," Amber went on, "is that they remain amphibious while they attend the first few years of your Palace of Learning. I'm not too sure of the process of how the they become fully land-based and get chosen."

"You understand enough," Admiral Coth said, cutting off his subordinate before he could answer. "What you fail to understand is the drive we have to grow our families, tribes, and clans. The need we have to have more Iteeche in *our* group rather than *your* group."

"So, it's not that you can't control births," Kris put in, "but that social and political pressure demand you choose spawn and bring them into your association."

"Do you have a saying . . ." Coth began and talked long before Nelly translated it as, "God is on the side of the biggest battalion?"

"If Nelly translated that correctly," Kris said, "yes, we have understood it the same way. There have been times when governments felt the strongest need to encourage peasants to raise their birthrate. However, when we gained control of public health and cut the death rate, many countries took a step back. When we learned that one fully developed, educated, and healthy citizen was worth more than a dozen or more ignorant and sickly citizens, we changed our policy. Even our infantry became skilled craftsmen of death rather than cannon fodder."

Kris paused to hunt for a summation, "There are more ways to compete than raw numbers. Quality can yield a stronger, sharper edge than quantity."

Admiral Coth had been leaning forward, listening to Kris. Most of his junior admirals had been leaning back, displaying several levels of dismay. Still, there were a few that seemed eager to accept anything Kris had to say.

Now Coth leaned back in his chair and said, "Admiral Longknife, we Iteeche do not like change. Many of us are doing the same thing our forefathers did thousands of years ago. Yet, in hardly more than a month, you have succeeded in getting brave warriors to go into battle laying on our backs. Do you know how hard it was for us to accept that change?"

"Yes, I think that I do," Kris said.

"It is only because of your victory that we are willing to swallow all this change you ask of us. Victory alone has shown eager Navy officers that they want to follow in your ways. Victory alone"

"Yes."

"However, getting clan overlords to believe that a hundred of your educated and healthy members could be more powerful than a thousand or ten thousand peasants is something that will be a million times more difficult. A million times more difficult to get anyone to even try. And it will be a thousand years before anyone will agree that you are right, and they are wrong."

Now it was Kris's turn to lean back in her seat. She gave in to her nervous need to wipe her face with her palms and then rub her eyes. "I told one of my officers, 'We are in Iteeche-land. Now we must do things the Iteeche way.' I hear you telling me that this is one idea that is too close to the bone for any Iteeche to accept."

"That is correct."

Kris thought on that for a moment. "Okay, then let us go on. May I ask you a question? What are the most valuable and productive planets in the rebel camp?"

"I doubt if there are more than fifty among the thousand," Coth said.

"Why is that?" Amanda asked.

"It is that way because over nine hundred of the planets that are following the rebel clan lords can hardly feed themselves. They can barely meet the essential needs of their population. They have almost nothing left to export except what they pay to the Capital in taxes."

"And those other handful of planets are where the battlecruisers are spun out?" Kris asked.

"Yes," Coth answered.

"Then they are the planets that we must capture," Kris said, decisively. "Talk to me about them."

4

Kris Longknife had seen star maps of the Iteeche Empire that showed which planets were in rebellion and which were loyal. It had seemed like a mash-up, with rebels and loyalists all mixed together.

Now she discovered why that was.

After some serious whispering among themselves, the junior admiral, whom Kris was starting to take for an intelligence officer, began to rattle off planets. At each name, Nelly would turn one of the planets listed on the bulkhead purple and would also add a star in the star map floating above Kris's head.

When 61 had been named and their colors changed, they formed four clusters.

"Now the industrial planets of the Empire," Kris said.

That generated more whispered discussions, but in the end, the intel officer began to rattle off 116 planets which Nelly turned green.

Suddenly, the battle lines snapped into place. Except for two outliers, all the rebel industrial base was clumped into four clusters well away from the human sphere. Again, with only four scattered planets, all of the most productive loyalist systems were in 9 clusters scattered around the capital, closer to the humans.

The other planets merely gave one side or the other avenues for attack on those valuable planets.

"Can the over-populated planets feed a fleet passing through?" Kris asked.

Coth shook his head. "Not much. Not well. Every gram of food and water taken off of the planet has to be measured against a gram of manure or urine returned to the system. Why do you think we off-ship manure?"

"We wondered about that," Kris said.

"We learned the hard way to be careful to balance what we take out with what we return. Famine and cannibalism is not a pretty sight."

"We've had some close calls on those as well," Kris admitted.

"So, My Admiral, what can a Longknife do with a map like this?"

Kris stood up. Her night quarters shrank as the space was added to her flag plot. The holographic map filled the plot from deck to overhead. Kris walked among the stars, examining threat axis and lines of communication where she could marshal her forces and what her avenues of attack might be. She also examined the rebels' options to attack the loyalists.

She quickly spotted how the rebels had been able to swoop in on the Imperial Guard System without being noticed.

Here was a game of chess almost beyond comprehension.

"I need to know where our battlecruiser production is

located, as well as theirs. Oh, and show me how productive each planet is." Kris asked.

This time, the Intel officer dragged Admiral Coth out into the passageway. Kris could hear the sound of raising voices, but she told Nelly no when she offered to fill her in.

Finally, the shame-faced junior admiral stomped in and began rattling off planet names and production numbers. He was half-shouting, but just as he finished one pair, Nelly would make a number pop up next to the planet as well as add it to the list on the wall. Then, she and the admiral would go on to the next.

"Nelly, make the larger production planets greener or more purple. Lighten up the smaller production. I need to know how big the numbers are at a glance."

"Some of these planets are way above the rest. Could I make them bigger on the map? Maybe add a ring or two around the most productive?" Nelly asked.

"Do it," and Kris found herself looking at a picture of her problem. Each of the clusters had at least one planet that earned a circle around it. One rebel and two loyal clusters had several of the ringed planets and a few with two rings.

Kris began to plan a campaign to reduce those systems – then caught herself before she made that mistake.

"Coth, tell me, how would an Iteeche go about attacking this situation?"

"I am not really sure," Coth answered, scrubbing at his skull with his two of his four hands. "Our histories don't tell us of a rebellion that was this large that did not succeed. That is one of the reasons you were called for."

"Oh," was all Kris could say.

"However, the usual way for attacking a rebellious satrap is to start at the nearest planet along the edge of the rebellion and eat them one planet at a time."

"You don't go for the industrial core of the rebellion first?" Kris asked.

"The wages of rebellion are death. Every rebel is deserving of death. Why should we jump past rebels? Aren't you taught to never leave an enemy in your rear?"

That was not at all the way Kris had been taught. She pursed her lips in thought. "So, how does that work for you?"

"I have, myself, campaigned against five rebellions. All have been put down, though none were more than fifty strong and most were smaller."

"Excuse me," Kris said, "but how could a rebellion of fifty planets threaten an Empire this big?"

"If a rebellion is allowed to fester and grow, it can explode quickly."

"Tell me about those rebellions," Kris said.

Coth leaned back and used his two outer eyes to stare at the overhead. His other two fixed on Kris. "The two largest ones I fought involved squabbles among junior clan chiefs who sought to take over a satrap from its pasha. It is not unusual for a pasha to die suddenly and a younger clan lord to step in. Sometimes there is much palace intrigue involved with the transfer of power."

Now all four eyes were on Kris. "Once the political machinations are done, the new pasha offers his worship to the Emperor and all is well."

"But then . . .?" Kris left the question hanging.

"Then there are the industrial satraps that have their own Navy. They are the ones that have much of the power in the Empire. If there is a struggle for such a throne of that satrap, it may spill out into open warfare. Often, the satrap's battle fleet is split down the middle, or more of the fleet follows one or the other. When they start fighting, things get messy."

Now, all four of Coth's eyes settled on the overhead. When he spoke, his words were soft.

"Sometimes one or both of them will appeal to the Emporium. Sometimes the Emperor will bless the present pasha. Sometimes they will bless the upstart. From where I stand, it is as if they draw straws to decide who the Emperor will bless. However it goes down, some of the fleet will be dispatched."

Coth barked a harsh laugh.

"Not the toy fleet that stands ready to display its power to intimidate with its colorful uniforms. No, they send us, the ships with the last chosen. The sailors and officers that no one will mourn. It is up to us to impose the Blessing of the Emperor."

He shook his head. His beak seemed to form something like a scowl.

"It is often strange how long it takes the Fleet of Retribution to sail. How long it takes us to acquire food for our storerooms or sailors to fill up our crew. And all the time we are twiddling our thumbs, the rebel or the pasha are fighting it out. More than once, I have arrived in a rebellious system only to be told the pasha is dead and the rebel has occupied his throne and sent his most urgent worship to the Emperor.

Coth leaned forward, all four hands on the table. "One might almost think that we of the Navy were just the bottom lake along a river that has many, many lakes upstream for the water to collect and be swam in."

"We have a saying, 'War is the continuation of diplomacy by other means.' It seems like here war is the continuation of political machinations, only a bit deadlier," Kris said.

"I think you have the right of that. The few times when the rebel had not won or been defeated by his lawful lord. It is our doctrine to begin with the first planet we come to. First, we destroy all the planet's warships and defenses. Then we round up all the leaders that are in rebellion. This often involves destroying those who defend them. It's not unusual for much of a city to be flattened as the two sides fight it out. After the first few assaults, we often have a lot of help collaring the rest. Once we have control of the planet, everyone is eager to denounce all the traitors."

"Likely," Kris interjected, "even some of the innocent, assuming they have a lot of money to confiscate, they being traitors and all."

"So, you know the way of it," Coth said.

"Our history has black chapters like that," she admitted.

"After we have reduced a few planets," Coth said, going on, "the rebels are much more willing to surrender when they are given the chance. A few will be executed. Often, they are killed by their own people if they won't open the gates and walk up to the axe on their own. If they surrender quickly, they may escape a meeting with the red-clad man and his snake, and just face the axe."

Having just seen the horrors of the death that snake's bite brought, Kris could understand a certain willingness to get it over with as quickly and easily as possible.

"There was one rebellion that succeeded even after the Imperial fleet arrived. One of the women in the pasha's harem managed to slip poison into the mating pond. While he was absorbed by the pleasure of expelling sperm packets, he was soaking up poison. He never got out of the pond. I had reduced two planets and taken the surrender of three more, when suddenly, I was being told the rebellion was over and His Most Worshipful Majesty had condescended to smile upon the younger brother."

"I take it that this rebellion, though, is nothing like the others you've fought against," Kris said.

"Usually, it's a feud between two sons, or an uncle and a son. A few thousand Imperial ships. A few hundred rebel ships. Yes, a battle like we just fought was new to me entirely. My biggest command was hardly more than half the size of one wing in the recent battle, and you had five under your command."

"Do I hear you telling me that when as many Iteeche as this rise up in rebellion, it usually means a new Imperial dynasty?" Kris asked.

"There are certain books on the Empire's history that are only allowed to senior admirals. I have been reading a lot of them since the rebellion passed a hundred planets. Yes, if the Empire is this badly split, it usually bodes very ill for the one on the throne."

"Admiral Coth, it is hard for me to become excited about the poor lad that sits on the throne," Kris said. "From where I sit, it looks like too many counselors are feathering their own nest. (Nelly's translation involved stone, sand, and seaweed, but it likely carried well.) I find myself fighting for the likes of you and your men. For the simple people on this planet and maybe a few others that will be wiped out if we fail. It will be for them that I fight. Can you understand and accept that?"

The looks Kris drew from the other side of the table were nearly impossible for her to comprehend. Each one was a bit different, most involved looking at the admiral on either side and left all the Iteeche with their mouths hanging open.

The silence began to worry Kris and she wondered if she should have Nelly call in the Marines. She and her humans could hardly stand off an attack by the bigger, stronger, and more numerous Iteeche.

Finally, Admiral Coth broke the silence. "You will fight for the likes of us?"

"Yes," Kris said, pouring absolute and finality into that one word. It stood like a rock between them.

"We are told from when we were younglings, just adapting to staying on land, that we exist only to die for the pasha of our satrap. No one dies for us. We are only one step above the nothings that clean the streets and the sewers. Most of our sailors can't even call upon a clan for their defense. Our clan is the Navy. It is all we have. I cannot wrap my brain around this thought you bring."

"I fight," Kris said, "for every sailor that sails with me. I fight for every citizen in the United Society. Yes, from the richest and most powerful to the poorest and least of them all. But first, I fight for the man on my right and the woman on my left. We fight for each other and each of us matter to each other."

Kris paused to catch her breath before going on.

"I have stood up to the powerful and told them that they were wrong. I have told leaders that what they wanted was not the right way to go. I am an officer in my Navy, but that does not mean that I am any less a citizen. My uniform does not mean that I cannot confront my superior with what I think is right. Indeed, there are times when my duty is more demanding than the average citizen."

"Oh, and she has," Jack said from beside her.

"I noticed," Kris said, "that the Iteeche I call Ron commanded a wing in the battle, but when we stood before the Emperor, he stood among the Imperial counselors. I wondered at that."

"The counselors put words in the mouth of the Emperor. We Navy obey those words. There is a world of difference between us. It is for them to say and for us to die."

Kris mulled over what she'd just learned. She wasn't surprised, but she was disappointed. She was being asked to defend a badly flawed system of government. Was she prepared to do that?

She was used to telling her father or grandfather or great-grandfather to take a long walk off a short pier. They always listened, even if they didn't always change. Still, she felt loyalty from them and knew that they were loyal to her and her crews.

How did she fight to defend the likes of the Imperial Counselors?

The urge to pack it in and go home was the strongest it had been since she arrived. Yet, the wide eyes from across the table held her. These Iteeche had fought with her, and many had died. How could she walk away from them? If the present dynasty fell, they would likely all lose their heads. She owed them.

But the political system should owe them as well.

Kris took a deep breath and let it out. She took another and another. Then she eyed the Iteeche admirals across the table.

"Okay, then how do we fight for each of us?"

5

"Tell me, Admiral Coth, if you were to organize a standard Navy expeditionary force to fight this rebellion, where would you attack first?" Grand Admiral Kris Longknife asked her senior Iteeche subordinate.

He eyed the star map that Kris stood in for a long moment, then pointed with one of his left hands. "Zargoth. That is the planet where the fleet that tried to force its way into the sky over the Imperial Capital Planet came from."

"Zargoth belongs to one of the rebel clans?" Kris asked.

"Yes. A minor one. I think everyone agrees they raised the flag of rebellion only because the Quid'sum'Coroth clan did first. They rely on them for all their fine foods and goods. I think you would call that a donation from the strong to the weak to keep them in their corner."

"Yes," Kris said. "And this planet Zargoth, of what value is it?"

"Worthless. They can hardly feed themselves. Their planetary lord's palace is little more than a hovel. However, he lords it over fifty billion peasants and craftsmen. That is not a number to be sneezed at."

SNEEZED AT, NELLY?

WOULD YOU PREFER I TRANSLATE IT USING A BODILY NOISE FROM A MUCH LOWER ORIFICE?

NO. SNEEZE IS GOOD.

Clearly, these Navy officers were quite earthy. I wonder if that's just them and their low place on the totem pole, or if this is what Ron and Roth sound like when they let their hair down.

"How much trouble would you have subduing this planet?" Kris asked.

"That would depend on how much trouble the clan lords want to give me," Coth said. "They might or might not have a fleet standing by to resist us. Those two battles where both the rebels and the loyalists sent a thousand battle-cruisers were over planets that jutted toward the Imperial Capital? In one we were taking the offensive. In the other case, they were."

"So, we just have to worry about warships?" Kris asked.

"No, there are also armies on the ground. How many of the peasants have the clan lords formed into an army? Most of them will have been press-ganged into some sort of an army only with the start of the war, some maybe later. You can't take too many people out of farming without risking crop failure or a poor harvest."

"Should I assume that most of these peasants have no idea how to fight?" Kris asked.

"Maybe one quarter of them will even have a gun," Coth said. "The others are supposed to pick up guns from those fallen and start shooting."

"You're kidding me," Jack said.

"No, but they could be ready to bury you under their bodies and blood."

"Hmm," Jack said. "I wonder how one of these horde attacks would take to being sticky-foamed."

"What?" was Coth's reaction.

"It's a nifty little device we have," Jack answered. "You spray it out over a mischievous civilian population. It sticks to their skin, and then sticks to anything. Say the concrete of a floor or wall. Each other. Their arm to their leg or to the body next to them. It sticks and won't let go for several hours."

The blank stares coming from the Iteeche side of the table would have been comical if the issues weren't so serious.

"Why would you do that?" Coth asked.

"When you don't kill a lot of people, they get over losing a lot easier," Kris said. "They hold fewer grudges."

"Why would clan masters care what grudges peasants hold?"

"What if," Jack said, "after we sticky-bombed all the drafted fighters, we captured the clan lords? What if we turned the stuck fighters loose and let them say or do anything they wanted with the clan lords?"

"They would tear them limb from limb," Coth said.

"Hmm. What do you think clan lords would think about that?"

Coth stared wide-eyed at Kris. It took him a while before he started to talk, low, and slow. "Clan lords live their life knowing they could be expected to make a sincere apology to the Emperor. The death you watched was horrible, but they earned the right to it by their rank and status. To be torn to death by peasants . . ."

Words failed Coth. It took him three tries before he could finish his sentence. "It would be the most horrible death a clan lord could suffer. It would be humiliating."

Kris just looked at Coth, hardly blinking.

"I told you that we Iteeche take thousands of years to change," Coth said in a soft whisper, as if saying words no one would ever hear. "I said that it would take a thousand years for you to change anything here."

He paused to look up and down the admirals seated at the other side of the table. "I was wrong. You do this, and you will begin change, changes like we have not seen in ten thousand years. I do not know where such changes will take us, and, honestly, I fear that."

"I understand your concern," Kris said, firmly, but softly. "However, Admiral, I must ask you. Is this system in need of a change? Is it deserving of change?"

Again, the Iteeche admiral who had befriended Kris looked to his right and his left. Most of the admirals beside him had skippered battlecruisers in the two horrible battles that both sides fought to a tie and in which very few survived. They had barely avoided making sincere apologies for not dying. For the sin of living, they had been turned out to jobs that were beneath them. Humiliated.

Kris had pulled them together into an effective force and given them a chance to fight again. To fight and win. They owed their very existence to the strange ways of this human woman. Their Empire and its culture had hurled them down. Kris Longknife had raised them back up. Let them do what they'd been born to do.

That fire burned in every set of four eyes across the table from Kris.

These Iteeche did not believe in a heaven or a hell, but looking across the table at them, there was no doubt in Kris's mind that they would follow her into hell and then fight their way back out again.

6

To Grand Admiral Kris Longknife, this meeting had achieved its goals. Now she needed to close it down.

"Admiral Coth, I need for you to collect as many volunteer ships and crews as we can lay our hands on. Once you have them, modify the ships and train them up to our standards. I will assign Admiral Kitano and her fleet and General Bruce to work with you to make those changes."

"That may be a problem, My Admiral," Coth said. "A lot of ships were destroyed in the fighting around the defensive space stations in both the Guard System and the Imperial Capital System. We won the battle, but the casualties were brutal. The Emperor has already announced a draft on all the satrap navies to replenish the forces here. The word we hear around the fleet is that few pashas want to give up a ship, much less a large chunk of their fleet when the rebels could launch an attack at any time."

"Well, the rebels are minus eight thousand of their ships at the moment," Kris said, dryly. "It will be a while before they can do much of anything. In the meantime, we have ships, and we are ready to take the initiative. Pass that word to the fleet and see if that changes a few minds."

"Some fleet admirals do have some say in the counsel of the pasha," Coth agreed, "although I've never been one. I'll pass that word around and see what we get."

Kris nodded at Admiral Coth from where she stood behind her chair. "Good. While you're recruiting and training a fleet, have your staff work up a plan for an offensive that will start with the planet Zargoth and end at a double-ringed planet."

"It will be done, My Admiral," Coth said as he stood and the other Iteeche admirals came to their feet. There were sharp snaps of the hips as the Iteeche made a shallow bow in Kris's direction and the Iteeche began to file out.

Admiral Kitano made to follow them, but Kris held her back with a quick, "A word, Admiral."

Once the room held only humans, Kris signaled Admiral Kitano and her Navy staff to move to the other side of the table. Nelly shrank it and switched out the Iteeche stools for comfortable human chairs, even before they were ready to sit down across from Kris.

"Now, Amber, is the fleet battle ready?"

"As ready as I could make it on the cruise out here. I'd prefer if it was a bit faster in its drills, but that will come with more practice."

"Check with Nelly," Kris said. "We've been holding live fire exercises using our lasers dialed back to .01 percent power. It creates an honest test on a moving target and makes it very easy to score the hits."

"Lord, why didn't we think of that before?"

"Because we didn't have the crystal armor, although we've been doing it on Iteeche ships without it and just pumping in a few hundred kilos of extra Smart Metal to make up for the damage. Now, I need a few things from you,"

"I expected that you would," Admiral Kitano said.

"I want you to dispatch a division of battlecruisers to take a look at this Zargoth system. I don't want you to actually get in the system."

"Use a periscope, huh?"

"Yeah. I expect they're terrified of the retribution headed their way, but I need to know what I'm facing. As soon as they know, send the word back by one ship and keep the other three watching that spot."

"Can I ask why?"

"Because I don't want to wait forever to get a fleet moving. If there are few ships above that planet, I want to swoop in like an avenging angel."

"What if they've got a peasant army on the ground?" Jack asked.

"Yeah. We'll need to look like we have an invasion fleet. However, if all we're after is the head of government, why not just send down a drop team, find the guy and bring back his head and a few others? Do you doubt that the rest of the fifty billion won't turn their coats in a flash?"

"That's a drop mission you will not be leading, right, my beloved Grand Admiral and mother?" was not a question from Jack.

"Yes, my loving general. I can see that look you get in your eyes when you're dreaming of locking me in our cabin. Maybe with you inside to apply your special kind of torture. I will be a dutiful grand admiral and spend the drop watching the feed from my flag plot."

"Good. You might finally be getting this adulting thing down."

Kris just managed to not stick her tongue out at her husband. They were probably stretching the limits of PDA enough for this staff meeting.

"Any further questions?" Kris asked the Navy side of the table.

They had none. Kris stood, they stood, and filed out of the conference room.

That left Kris with just her key staff and Ambassador Kawaguchi.

"What can we do for you?" the ambassador from Musashi asked.

"How many ambassadors do we have left after that wild abandon ship exercise we ran?" Kris queried.

"It wasn't so much an abandon ship drill as a 'run for the hills and save yourself,' kind of thing," Abby drawled softly. "That bit of conspiracy to slaughter all us diplomats in our sleep so that SOB from Nuu Enterprises could seal the deal with one Iteeche family got the summer types out of our hair. We got a lot of junior types, some of which didn't rate a seat on the last ships out, and some of which got told to hold the fort so the bosses could run for it. As of right now, all the yellow types are still running. I hear tell that someone told the fast transport skippers not to stop until they reached Wardhaven."

"I may have mentioned a certain preference to that effect," Kris admitted, diffidently.

"I strongly suspect it was a written order," Ambassador Kawaguchi said. "I doubt many ship captains would resist orders from the great men of business and the senior diplomats if he didn't have something locked away in his safe."

"No doubt," Emissary Kris Longknife said. "Okay, you two, talk to me about the trade side of this mission."

"I was not surprised," Ambassador Kawaguchi began,

most diplomatically, "when Admiral Coth admitted that the Empire has many planets barely getting by. From what we have been able to learn, there is very little anyone is willing to swap. Most items made out of metal are in short supply. The Iteeche make great use of ceramics and glass wherever possible. Some of the artistic items may sell for their novelty, but that market will soon be glutted. We are looking into pharmaceuticals, but the Iteeche seem to be behind us in medicine and every time we talk about selling them life saving devices, some mandarin steps in and puts the kibosh on the talks."

"They can't afford to disrupt their death rate," Jacques said, putting a sociology twist to the fact. "If the clans are to reward their preferred subordinates with time in the mating ponds and the right to choose a progeny, they must have Iteeche die."

"There's no interest among the mandarin class in extending their own lives?" Kris asked, incredulous.

"The guy from Nuu Enterprises who was helping equip the uprising we quashed," Jack said, "may have been negotiating with that clan to give them exclusive access to our rejuvenation technology. Whatever he was doing, he's gone, and so are most of Grampa Al's henchmen. I have to wonder what he thought he'd get after he'd watched mobs of Iteeche slaughter the rest of us."

"From an economic view," Amanda said, "there's not much to bargain for."

"Power," Kris said. "With Grampa Al, power is its own reward. No doubt the fellow he put in charge here was of the same ilk. Acquire power at any cost."

"Well, they are gone," Ambassador Kawaguchi said. "We will continue the search for something they can trade for what we want to sell you. This is not an unusual problem. I remember a time in Earth's past when a place called China was all too content with itself. It sent forth what were misnamed trading fleets to distant places. There, they gave out huge gifts of silk, jewelry, steel, and porcelain. In return, they received gifts of skins, jewels, and animals.

"When the treasure fleets returned, the Emperor was impressed, but the Imperial Counselors managed to have the fleet destroyed and never sent out again. We think it was because they did not want to risk the changes those fleets might bring," the ambassador said.

"Later, the Europeans discovered ways to sail their own ships to China. There was a mountain of silver in one land group the Spanish had conquered. They shipped a lot of the silver to a trading post off the coast of China and swapped the silver for what they wanted. For the Spanish, that worked out fine, until the silver petered out. For the Chinese, all that new silver created inflation and other problems their Empire wasn't ready for."

The twinkle in Kawaguchi's eyes began to fade. "The next group of Europeans to attempt trade with China had little silver or gold. However, the English had captured a land where opium was grown. They introduced that dope to China, selling it for Chinese money, then buying what they wanted with that. A number of the leaders in China did not want their people becoming addicted to the English dope and tried to outlaw its import. The British brought in warships and forced the Chinese government to swap opium for the precious goods they demanded. China could not stop this robbery."

Ambassador Kawaguchi ended his tale. "Do you see how this fits our situation?"

"No," Kris said. "It's kind of like the Europeans who got my Native American ancestors to swap pelts for whiskey.

Whiskey was cheap and quickly gone. The pelts fueled a fashion industry in the lands all around the Atlantic Ocean. But in both cases, it was a more powerful group forcing something bad on a weaker group. To me, the Iteeche are our equals."

"Yes and no," Amanda said. "As far as you, a Navy officer, are concerned, they are our fighting equal. That, or close enough to it. In a few technological areas, like energy and maskers, they are our superiors. However, their huge, over-populated planets leave them very vulnerable. Let's say that one of the several pharmacology labs that came out here with you finds a drug that is like opium to the Iteeche. What happens when they offer to manufacture and import the drug? How do the Iteeche pay for it? If they take critical resources out of their bare subsistence economy to trade for it, what happens?"

"Given a choice between sugar water and nutritious food," Jacques said, "rats will literally kill themselves drinking the sugar water. If we come up with the opium or sugar water of the Iteeche, we could bring the entire Empire crashing down and God only knows what would rise up in its place."

Kris eyed her friends sitting at the table. "It could get that bad?"

The economist, the sociologist, and the ambassador all nodded their heads in silence.

Kris shook her head. "We are a potential poison to these people."

"Yes," Jacques said.

"How do we not become poison?" Kris asked no one in particular.

"Very carefully," Abby said, dryly. "Very, very carefully."

Kris took a long while to mull this development. "Okay,

keep me in the loop both about ideas our side comes up with and what the mandarins slap a kibosh on. I'm looking for a pattern, folks."

Everyone stood. This meeting was as over as one could get. Everyone filed out, leaving Jack and Kris alone.

"Good God, what am I doing?" Kris said. "Back in Earth's dark history, some outside force might be invited by one faction or another to help them win the throne. Often enough, that outsider was the one to sit his butt down on the throne, over the dead bodies of both sides."

Kris turned and folded herself into Jack's arms. "I swore that I would not be such an outsider. I swore I would help one faction. Now I've seen the kid on the throne and the rebels. I don't much care for either side, but I still don't want to wreck this culture if it means something like anarchy will replace it. Thousands of planets loaded with fifty billion Iteeche they can barely feed. What would this place look like if the Empire imploded?"

"Any encounter between two cultures always causes change," Jack said, holding her, stroking her back gently. "Let's be honest, the Iteeche superior power transfer from their reactors hasn't been without its problems among us humans."

The post-battle hum had begun in Kris's body before the meeting was half over. Between Coth and Kawaguchi, she'd been taken to a high mountain and shown a more gigantic butcher's bill than she'd ever run up against the vicious alien raiders. To date, Kris estimated she'd killed a quarter of a trillion aliens. A check of the Empire's population showed well over ten trillion, maybe fifteen.

Could a population collapse within the Empire cost the lives of a third? Half? More?

Kris had thought she was leaving a lousy bureaucratic

job at Main Navy for a nice, comfortable, manageable task as an Emissary to an Empire.

Now she knew.

They wanted a killer. Instead, they'd gotten her, a deadly poison. Somehow, she had to avoid the Iteeche swallowing her down whole.

Oh, God, help me.

7

Lieutenant Megan Longknife, Admiral Longknife's *aide de camp*, went straight to the motor pool as soon as that set of meetings closed down. She couldn't help but notice that the Intel officer, Quinn Sung, was right behind her.

At the motor pool, Megan asked to check out a car.

"Where are you headed?" the second-class petty officer asked her.

"To the beanstalk terminal."

"How long will you need the car?"

Megan considered the travel time up and down, then added in what she needed to do, and answered, "Five, maybe six hours."

"Last week I would have given you a car, Lieutenant, but, in case you haven't noticed, those Iteeche drivers out on the roads are damn near suicidal."

"I've dodged a few that seemed intent on not surviving until sunset," Megan admitted.

"We've hired locals to be our drivers. We've also come up

with a Smart Metal version of the kind of four-wheeled cars the head high muckety-mucks ride around in. That should get our people some respect. Oh, and ours have extra armor. I'll assign you one of them and a driver. When you're headed down the beanstalk, call me and I'll have a driver waiting for you at the curb."

"That sounds like a deal. Now, can I help you, Captain?"

"Is the lieutenant's car big enough for the two of us?" Quinn asked.

"Yes, ma'am."

"You mind sharing the ride?" the captain asked.

"Not one bit," the lieutenant answered.

They made only small talk while they waited for their car. Once in it, they continued the small talk until Megan said, "Lily says she's nailed the last spy bot. She's already reported the tally to Security. There was nothing new or special. We can talk now."

"Right, you've got one of the special computers," Quinn said.

"Yep. Lily is one of Nelly's kids."

"So, why are you headed up the beanstalk?" the intel chief asked.

Megan cocked her head a bit to the right and eyed her superior officer. "Likely for the same reason you are."

"That's a coy answer."

"We'll know I'm right if we keep walking together until we reach the lockers outside the drop bays."

"You have an armored space suit," Quinn said, no question at all in her words.

"I got it the first time I was assigned to Kris's staff. It's followed me around the fleet. I haven't used it yet, but there's always a first time. You?"

"I got myself fitted for one the day after I found out I'd

be working for a Longknife. I figured sooner or later I'd be doing a drop mission, though I thought I'd be doing it right behind her."

Megan shrugged, doing her best to make it cute. "You may be dropping right behind a Longknife. Just not the one you figured on."

The two of them grinned at each other.

"So, do we tell her we're going to drop onto Zargoth or not?" Quinn asked.

"I've heard her say many times that it's easier to ask forgiveness than permission."

Now the two laughed.

8

Kris Longknife now had so many irons in the fire she was amazed that she wasn't burned to a crisp.

Having sent out an invitation to every Clan leader in the capital, it behooved Kris to put together a sing-along. Abby's best efforts at figuring out what one of those involved came up with nothing. After contracting several available singing groups, it became clear that what the common people got to sing to, and sing with, was not the same as the flower of Imperial society.

Kris found herself sending a major off to visit Roth and arrange for a visit. The Marine officer returned quickly; he had arranged for a visit later that afternoon.

Apparently, Roth was not about to risk Kris crashing his party again.

Kris found Megan, for some reason, was up aboard the *Princess Royal*, so it was just her and Jack along with a company of Marines making their way to the Chap'sum'We clan's palace.

The chamberlain, in his cloth of gold garments, with an entourage of staff, met them and immediately led them by not quite the most direct route to the tree-shaded and flower-perfumed pergola on the palace roof.

THE DETOUR IS AROUND THE LADIES' QUARTERS, Nelly told Kris.

Kris failed to suppress a smile. Jack apparently got the same bit of information; he was smiling softly as well.

Both Ron and Roth were seated on pillows when Kris arrived. There were pillows for her and Jack. There were also several Iteeche seated around Ron and Roth. Since it was impossible to tell male and female Iteeche apart, what with their lack of external genitalia, the only hint that these might be females were the gossamer veils the four wore. It barely covered their faces and nothing else.

The females in the harem Kris had marched her Marines through had worn more.

Interesting.

"It is a pleasure to have my eyes fall upon your visage, Royal Emissary from our Emperor's brother ruler. It is joyful to see the face of such a conqueror. To what do we owe this visit?" Roth asked.

Kris bowed her head from the neck for a moment. "It is an honor to see such an eminent advisor to the Emperor and wise leader of such a mighty clan," she said, modifying the Iteeche greeting she'd been given. She wasn't worshiping the Emperor. Grampa Ray would never go along with that.

"Your eminent self and several other wise clan leaders have been invited to a sing-along in the gardens of the Pink Coral Palace. Sadly, those I have ordered to arrange the party have found that they are so ignorant of the fashion here in the capital that we do not know how to invite such singers to our palace."

Kris would take anything she could get from Roth. Since his clan was risking its place near the seat of power, it was best for him that Kris's embassy be acceptable to all the other clan chiefs who measured face with a micrometer.

"Oh, yes," the clan leader said. "It would be difficult for someone so new to the capital to know who to choose and who would be too common for a party of such elite."

"Yes. I do not want to offend."

"Ron, my chosen, will you take care to help our victorious admiral to throw a celebration befitting of her station?"

"It is my honor to serve you and she who commanded me in the recent battle," Ron said. The Navy may only be dirt under the feet of these powerful clans, but a victory you were part of was still something to remind your dad about.

"Yes, this must be appropriate to the status of a victor as well as an Emissary to our worshipful Emperor," Roth said, before opening his hands and adding. "I am told that my chosen has often dined with you. Will you not allow us an opportunity to share the taste of some of the best from our tidal pond?"

Kris wasn't opposed to sushi. Still, all that she could think of was eating the fish raw off the bone. The very thought was a bit horrifying. Instead, she replied, "I would be so honored."

Dinner turned out to be not quite as terrifying as she had expected. While the Iteeche reclined at small tables and ate live crustacean-like creatures from a bowl, Kris and Jack were fed the same fish, only boiled and chilled. It was quite as good as shrimp, although one small taste of the hot dipping sauce was more than enough.

The next course was a white fish. They were small enough that the Iteeche speared them live and ate theirs in two or three bites. The humans were served fish bites, fried in oil and rolled in some sort of crunchy meal. It didn't taste bad, but the white sauce provided for dipping had a rancid taste.

The main course was a flakey red fish, kind of like salmon from Earth. The Iteeche were served the fish still flapping from a kettle. They used a mallet to dispatch the fish, then filleted it right there on their plate and enjoyed eating each morsel with a fork. Kris's fish had been filleted beforehand and roasted over an open flame. The pink sauce the Iteeche poured over the fish they had cut up wasn't bad, but Kris worried about what it might do to her stomach. It and all this strange fish.

As luck would have it, Kris and Jack made it to their rides before their stomach revolted at what they'd eaten. Very quickly, they were losing it from both ends.

One of the nice things about Smart Metal™ was that you could turn at least part of your armored vehicle into a rolling outhouse. Oh, and isolate the stink and vent it to atmosphere without filling the rest of the crew compartment with the various odors.

By the time Kris and Jack got back to their palace, the entire Marine detachment, both those that had gone with them . . . and not been fed . . . and those that stayed behind, were grinning like they never had good sense.

Kris, having gone through potty training with the kids not so long ago, was inured to the situation.

9

Over the next couple of weeks, Kris found herself wishing she was an Iteeche. On their four hands, they had two sets of opposing thumbs with two fingers between, for a total of eight fingers and eight thumbs. Trying to keep her two thumbs on all the things she needed to keep them on was proving a major challenge.

Admiral Coth reported that ships were straggling into the system in flotillas and half-flotillas. Considering that close to 5,000 ships had been destroyed in the sneak attack around the jump fortresses, there was a strong expectation that these new ships would be divvied up among the 6 forts and stations.

It didn't take Kris long to find that the Iteeche did have an adage that 'he who tries to be strong everywhere is strong nowhere.' She had Admiral Coth schedule her for a long overdue appointment with the Iteeche Navy General Staff.

On the way over, she had a conversation with both Jack and Ron.

"Can I fire them?" Kris asked.

"It would not be wise," Ron answered quickly.

"Can I kill them?"

"That would be even more unwise," Ron said with a huff that qualified for a chuckle among the Iteeche.

"So, I've got to live with them."

"Preferably."

"Am I their boss?" Kris asked.

"Not actually," Ron answered.

"Hold it. I thought I had command of the entire fleet."

"You do. Well, you do command the Imperial Combined Fleet and the ships seconded from the satrap pashas."

"I command the ships," Kris said, slowly. "They command the Navy?"

"Something like that," Ron said. "You have complete command over every ship in the Imperial fleet. However, you owe proper respect and honor to the Navy General Staff. It is customary for neither of you to resort to something so crass as an order. Instead, they recommend strategies and operations to you, and you suggest things that they might do to supply and maintain the fleet."

Kris mulled that over, a frown growing on her face. "I had Admiral Coth put together a planning staff as well as a team to review and modify our training and doctrine to fit the way I fight battlecruisers. I do have that authority, don't I?"

"Of course you do, Admiral Longknife," Ron said, rather unctuously. "However, they also have a planning staff, as well as a Division for Training and Doctrine."

"Whose doctrine defines how my fleet will operate?" Kris asked.

"Yours does, of course. However, a smart Commander of

the Imperial Combined Fleet will also pay proper respect to the wise old heads of the Navy General Staff."

"And you Iteeche damn nearly wiped out the human race with this kind of a lash up?"

"It has served us well for ten thousand years, or so our history books say."

Kris wanted to mention that those history books didn't go back much further than the last dynastic upheaval, but she didn't.

"Kris, a situation like this is not unknown to humans," Nelly said. "During the great Pacific War of the early 1940's the Japanese Navy had an admiral commanding a Combined Fleet with all the warships. Above him was a Navy General Staff, and above them was a Minister of the Navy. All three had their own Office of Planning. It was not unusual for the General Staff to have operations laid on them by the Navy Ministry and then to combine those with their ideas for operations and pass them along to the Combined Fleets Commander who would then ignore them but more likely fold them into the plan he had already drawn up for his ships."

"So, everyone was polite to each other and no one was in total command. How did that work Nelly?"

"Not well. They lost the war badly. Their land was occupied and their military was abolished."

"How's that for a defeat?" Kris asked Ron.

He chose not to answer.

The meeting with the Navy General Staff was a very formal affair. It took place in a cool marble hall, not quite as impressive or intimidating as the Imperial Palace, but certainly doing its best to shrink everyone in it down to size.

Standing to one side were row upon row of admirals arranged on risers so everyone could see the victim standing in the focus of all those eyes. On the other side were members of an Imperial Navy Counselors' Association. They were dressed much like Ron and seemed to stand between the Navy and the Throne.

In this case, literally. They stood on the side closest to the palace.

The meeting was very polite. They told Kris to divide up her fleet.

Just as politely, she told them that she had trained her fleet to fight outnumbered 4:1 and win. In the recent battle, it had done just that.

One counselor asked if that might not have just been luck. Many of the counselors and admirals nodded most sagely.

Kris politely mentioned the quarter trillion murderous alien raiders that she had destroyed, along with their tens of thousands of ships.

They admitted, politely, that was most impressive, but that the Iteeche were not so foolish and the rebels were fighting with ships just as capable as her own.

Kris advised them that she had modified her warships to make them better.

One of the counselors knew about her sending her crews into battle laying on their backs. "Is such an unwarlike practice all that effective?"

"We won the battle," Kris answered back, very politely.

"But can't the rebels adopt the same methods of fighting?" another counselor asked.

Kris wanted to shoot back a fast "No," but she swallowed that answer. "I expect that all the experienced officers of the Navy General Staff would tell you that no real warrior wants to go into battle on his backside."

Kris nodded respectfully to the admirals and they nodded, somewhat reluctantly back.

"I also have other tricks up one of my two sleeves, so even if the rebels do adopt some of my new policies and practices, they will still be behind us in combat effectiveness."

The two Iteeche groups mulled that over. Finally, a counselor standing in the middle of the first row said, "Will you please share some of these ideas with us?"

"I would very much appreciate your comments," Kris lied. "Doubtlessly, they would make my improvements even better. However, such designs are yet in their nascent stage and I have not been able to test them. I do not know which of them are possible and which are not."

"I hope you will share them with us when you have."

"Most surely, I will," Kris answered, but did not add, *in a pig's eye.*

Kris waited for only a moment before she began her exit strategy. "I appreciate your graciousness in sharing your most precious time with this humble commander. Now, as I have told you, I will establish a major defense force at the station guarding the jump into the Imperial Capital's System. I will also concentrate a large force that we can use to hammer the rebels into submission. I thank you for your blessing," Kris said.

She gave them the kind of bow King Raymond would accede to a bunch of troublesome bureaucrats, turned on her heels and withdrew.

The march out of the Navy Palace, or whatever that building was called, was done at a measured tread. Once back into their waiting armored limo, the three stayed quiet until Nelly announced all the freshly acquired bots had been done away with or suborned.

"Were any of the nanos of human design?" Jack asked.

"No, sir," Nelly answered.

"Have all the niceties been met between me and my 'associates'?" Kris asked Ron.

"I do not doubt that they know that you will do, what do you humans say? 'What you damn well please.' However, you have soothed the water in their mating pond and they can make no complaints."

"Good," Kris growled. "Now, let's have Amber and Coth get the fleet ready to sail."

egan Longknife found herself dividing her time between Kris and Amber. Or more correctly, the embassy and the fleet.

Except Admiral Kitano reorganized the First Battlecruiser Fleet.

Kris had come out with the 6th Battlecruiser Task fleet. It was smaller than most Iteeche flotillas. It was embarrassing to call it a fleet, even a task fleet, so Amber changed all the names.

The eight-ship squadron was still the basic building block. They were paired into task groups of sixteen and then paired again in First, Second, Third, and Fourth Flotillas. Amber commanded the First Battlecruiser Task Force.

Flotillas were the only place where the human organization mirrored the Iteeche one.

Megan had nothing to do with the fleet reorganization. However, when she wasn't doing whatever Kris needed done, she went up the beanstalk to join Admiral Kitano for training exercises.

They weren't actually training. More often than not, the fleet went to space to perform a challenging indoctrination of new recruits.

Amber's four flotillas would be paired with eight of Admiral Coth's flotillas that had fought in the recent battle, usually with him commanding them all. Accompanying their three hundred and eighty-four battlecruisers would be a force twice their size, say seven hundred and sixty-eight. Maybe larger.

Megan got quite a kick out of watching the fleet sail out.

Once they got well clear of the space station, they'd begin a live fire fight. Of course, the lasers on both sides had been dialed back to .01 percent of full power so no one got hurt.

According to standard Iteeche fleet doctrine, a force outnumbered two to one should run or surrender with something like the honors of war. Iteeche honors of war, however, included executing the skipper of the ship . . . honorably, with a blade, not a snake.

Thus, it was always a surprise when a fleet twice the size of the other force ended up a few minutes after starting with ten hits on every ship and the entire force declared dead and the exercise over. The smaller force rarely had more than one or two hits per ship. Many ships might have none.

Consternation was a mild description of the captains and crews' reactions to this result. All of them, no doubt, had heard that Coth and that human, Kris Longknife, had outfought the rebels. Still, it was one thing to hear rumors, another thing to have it done to you.

Coth would then assign four of his flotillas to engage the other side at 6:1 odds. More often than not, the two sides fought each other to mutual annihilation.

Every Iteeche in the fleet knew well that twice now, a

thousand loyalists and an equal number of rebels had fought themselves to near-mutual annihilation. To fight outnumbered 6:1 and win a draw was a major shock to the system.

The inevitable call would come in, "How do we fight like that?"

That is when Coth would invite all the ships in the opposing fleet to open up their ship nets and let his programmers insert the subroutine that allowed every ship in the fleet to create the Level 1 high gee stations for every Iteeche on a ship. Buried deep in the subroutine was another routine. When activated just before battle, it would switch the stations to Level 2 so the crew could survive higher gees.

Level 2 was kept under wraps because no one knew which "loyal" sailor or officer was actually a rebel sympathizer.

While that was going down in public, Megan would be busy with Lily, her Nelly-level computer, making modifications to the Iteeche battlecruisers that their crew had no idea about. She, Admirals Kitano, Ajax, Afon, as well as another commodore, the people who had Nelly's kids for computers, would be deep inside the Iteeche ship systems working nearly as fast as the speed of light.

Kris Longknife had learned early on during her command of the Alwa Defense Sector that ships came from the builders with their lasers loose in their cradles. It had to do with the lasers being government-provided equipment. It wasn't much, but it didn't take a lot to send a shot wild at two hundred thousand kilometers. The first thing they did was tighten up the guns.

Second, the Iteeche fire control computers took about twice as long to arrive at a firing solution as a human computer did. However, the Iteeche couldn't relate to a human-computer interface, so the Iteeche yards replaced the human computer with one of their design. Now, each ship acquired a new, unnoticed, human-like computer. It would interface with the Iteeche sensor input, process the data, and project the solution on an Iteeche screen. It took a bit more than half the time, but the results of the next shoot were a major improvement.

With just these three modifications, Kris had brought the loyalist Iteeche fleet up to a force that could fight outnumbered 5:1 and win!

Of course, it took all the computing power of five of Nelly's brood to pull it off for nearly 770 ships in only half an hour.

Thus, Megan spent a lot of time on the *Princess Royal*, standing an underway bridge watch to keep her qualifications up for OOD, and no one was the wiser for her presence.

Eight times, the fleet sailed with a new bunch of recruits. Over six thousand Iteeche battlecruisers went through an introduction to Kris's battle tactics and upgrades, both known and unknown, to their equipment and systems.

Most of the crew came back very excited to be joining a winning team. Most, but not all.

Each time the fleet returned, there would be a long line of ambulances waiting to take some of the older officers and senior ratings to the hospital. They'd be carried off their ship on stretchers writhing in back pain or with badly strained muscles.

Kris had warned her fleet that she fought a young man's war, and after just one exercise, a lot of the older members of the crew knew it was time to throw in the towel. That created a major problem, however. The loss of their job meant not only the loss of prestige, but also the loss of income in a very competitive market. Nelly quoted to Kris a saying from old Earth. "You're taking away their rice bowl."

Amber came to Kris's rescue. "I know you've been death on fleet support, but working with Admiral Benson on Alwa taught me the importance of a decent support force. Let me handle this."

She came back a week later, a week during which none of the arriving skippers or admirals allowed any of their ships to go out on exercises in the new ways of fighting, with a major reorganization.

"The Iteeche maintain a ridiculous teeth-to-tail ratio," Amber said. "There is no central supply. Each ship captain is expected to purchase his own supplies and support. It's a mad house out there. No wonder they need so many people on their ships. I've got the officers and ratings that can't cut it with the fleet creating a supply system, as well as a full staff of support people. Personnel, training, qualification stan- dards, and, as much as I hate the idea, staff visits and inspec- tions. Intelligence is also a cottage industry."

Amber shook her head. "They say they have a Navy General Staff, but they're more like an advisory board. Old troglodytes grumbling about how things have changed since their day, and not really contributing anything to the fighting power of their fleet. This staff will do that. Oh, I'm also making sure all of them - supply, intel, personnel, all of them - get data support. Would you believe, most of them are carrying around what they know in their heads, or in a card file? God, how did these guys give us such a run for our money back in the war?"

"I'm wondering about that," Kris admitted. "But when you've got a fleet as huge as the Iteeche fleet, and can muster warriors from a population of trillions, you can just about bury us in bodies."

"Yeah," Amber snorted. "Well, I've got the staff shaking itself out. Oh, I've also created several pocket crests so people can tell who's commanding a ship and who's on staff. I don't want to demote anyone, but I think the War Fighting Qualifications badge will go a long way into keeping the high-ranking staff officers from lording it over the fighters."

"Good," Kris said. She gave Amber an "atta boy" and sent her back to work.

Now, a lot of older Iteeche transferred off their ship before it went through the grueling warfare qualifications with Admirals Coth and Kitano. Since the Iteeche had crewed their ships with 1,000 crew and the humans made do with 400, the lost fifth of the Iteeche crew were rarely replaced. More were transferred to new construction.

There was a lot of that.

There were also a lot of promotions as juniors slipped in to replace their elders, many of which had turned the bridge crew into something like a geriatric ward.

There were complaints about this whole process from the Navy Chief of Staff as well as the Council of Advisors, however, Kris just turned them over to Ron and Admiral Coth to handle. She'd glance at what they prepared for her, signed it, and sent it on its way.

She got no visits from the Navy General Staff.

Kris knew she was skating on thin ice. Hopefully, she'd get where she was headed before the cracking noises behind her caught up with her.

11

Too much of Kris's time was taken up with photo ops.

However, there was one ceremony she did appreciate. She went up the beanstalk to stand before rank on rank of ships' companies to pin the Battle Medal on the chest of Admiral Coth and his most senior admirals.

Upon further consideration, Kris had admitted that she expected a lot of battles in her future. What she needed was not a medal to celebrate the most recent battle, but one medal that could have stars added to it for the battles to come.

Once Kris had awarded the Gold Battle Medal to the senior Iteeche and Human admirals, she stepped aside. They marched smartly to their subordinates and awarded the medal to junior admirals, captains, and senior staff.

The officers in the smart gray and gold uniforms were then dismissed. Further ceremonies would take place aboard ship as the rapidly mass-produced medals went down the ranks: silver for officers not in command and bronze for all other ranks.

That, and an extra month's pay made for a lot of happy sailors, and not a few tap men and bar girls.

It was during a conversation about this that Kris discovered another thing about the Iteeche. With the proper bar girl, a male Iteeche might be made to disperse his sperm packets with much pleasure for both involved.

Nelly thought this was very informative. Kris thought it too much information, but Nelly passed the word to Jacques and Amanda, and they were just as excited as Nelly.

Kris's other major photo op was the Embassy's Formal Reception and Sing-along.

Abby did a bang-up job of bringing all the pieces together. She got the finest delicacies. She located and hired the most sought-after singing groups. She even had Mata redo the gardens, raising the castle up higher so that more of the sky was visible. The lighting for the garden was nothing short of spectacular as different colored lights shown around the plaza, then changed slowly to another color.

Ron came early and pronounced it the most spectacular sing-along he had ever attended.

Kris established a receiving line. She stood at the head of it with a long line of human ambassadors to her right. Since most of the ambassadors had fled leaving behind only *charge d'affaires*, Kris promoted them all to ambassador rank and Abby arranged to get them all the proper uniform for their new status.

Fifteen minutes into the soiree, Roth'sum'We'sum Quin,Chap'sum'We arrived with a large contingent from his clan. Thirty minutes later, some minor mandarins from the Hoff'sum'Seava clan waltzed in and ignored the receiving line. The same happened a few minutes later when minor clan officials of the Don'sum'Wo clan showed up.

Kris remembered that clan. It was the one that cooperated under the table with Dani Ishmay of Nuu Enterprises to massacre the human embassy, take Roth down, and leave the court to themselves. Whether or not Dani would have gotten a monopoly on Iteeche trade would have been determined later. Likely not to his liking, the fool.

While these junior clan leaders circulated. Ron watched them from Kris's elbow.

"They are guzzling down your fine repast with disgusting abandon, as if they had not fed in years," Ron growled. "They have no culture."

Kris had kind of been expecting a disaster. She moved the starting time for the music up. All the attending Iteeche sang lustily along with the *a capella* singers. After the second song, the other clans that had crashed the party made a show of walking out. After the third song, Roth gave his sincere excuses, but led his clan out the door.

"I'm sorry, Kris," Ron said. "With the others gone, my eminent chooser could not remain."

"I understand," she said. "Ron, would you like to stay for a bit?"

"Isn't this sing-along done? You humans cannot sing with our people."

Kris had to agree with that. Iteeche singing was horrible to the human ear.

"You are right," she said, "but I have invited some more guests."

So saying, a wide staircase opened up and led down into the garden from the Navy Staff building Kris had built over the gate. Down that staircase flooded a long line of admirals and captains, many with a female companion. They quickly joined in the next song as they circulated around the garden, finding drinks and tasting the hors d'oeuvres.

This was rich food for them, and the entertainment was several notches above what a Navy officer, even a senior one, might expect. All of them now sported their battle medal. Most had a gleaming command crest on the left breast of their uniform.

"Were you expecting this social snub?" Ron asked Kris.

"I was hoping for better," she admitted, "but I planned for the worst. I had a small party arranged in the enlarged staff lounge of my Navy Annex. If we had been flooded by clan leaders, the Navy officers would have enjoyed a fine evening. I might have even piped in the singing and allowed them to sing along. But . . ." Kris ended with a shrug.

The night went long and was thoroughly enjoyed by all. The diplomatic personnel circulated among the Iteeche, listening to their talk, gleaning what they could, maybe even asking questions that took the conversation in the direction they wanted.

Diplomats were good listeners.

At the end of the evening, Kris's commanding officers left, feeling very affirmed by this strange human commander they now served.

Kris sent them on their way, knowing she'd soon be leading them into another battle.

12

On Kris's orders, Admiral Kitano had dispatched a division of four battlecruisers. Maybe it was just an accident, but all four had proud names that went back to the days of wet Navies. Even back to the age of wood and sails. They also bore the names of well-fought battles: the *Lexington, Saratoga, Yorktown* and *Bonhomme Richard*.

The last one required an explanation from Nelly. These ships had been bought and paid for by several cities on New Eden that claimed their roots went back all the way to the North American District of old Earth.

The division arrived at the jump into the Zargoth system with no misadventures. It was as if no one wanted to be caught along the path that the defeated rebel fleet had trod.

The *Lexington* sent a probe up to the jump. A few minutes looking through the periscope showed that this jump was both unguarded and had no traffic headed for it. A second probe was formed from the first one and dispatched through the jump.

It passively collected data for an hour on the single occupied planet some twenty-four light minutes from the jump. It reported its findings only after it returned through the jump.

Five minutes later, the captain commanding the division knew what he faced on the other side of the jump. He provided a full report to Admiral Kitano and dispatched the *Bonhomme Richard* back to the Imperial Capital.

The probe was sent back to monitor things. It reported back four hours before the *Bonny Dick* jumped out of the system. A review of the data showed refinements, but no basic change in the first examination.

The update was sent to the courier battlecruiser and the other three settled down to watch a very empty mouse hole.

A week later, Grand Admiral Kris Longknife and Admiral Amber Kitano were eyeing the report.

"No warship activity in the system," Amber said. "None at all."

"Not much ship traffic either," Kris added.

"I think they're loathe to let anyone run for the exit. If they let a few get out, they'd have a mass panic on their hands."

Kris nodded. "If that message traffic is right, there are one whale of a lot of armed Iteeche on the ground."

"Almost fifty billion people on that planet and nearly a quarter of them are under arms.

"Under arms of some sort," Kris corrected. "As to training . . .?"

Intercepted messages offered no answer to that critical question.

"Nelly, ask Admiral Coth if he would mind dropping into my flag plot."

The two admirals and their key human Navy staff had

just time for a cup of tea before the Admiral trotted in, followed by his intelligence admiral and several others.

Kris took only a minute to share their data on Zargoth with him and pose her question concerning the quality of the ten to fifteen billion Iteeche under arms on the planet.

Coth barked his version of a laugh. "What planetary lord would risk his own life arming the people he rules? There is enough risk that they may wake up dead some morning thanks to a brother, uncle, or son. The thought of the peasants, what do you say, 'storming the castle,' is a repugnant reality. More than one rebellion has been quelled when the peasants took it into their own hands to bring down a planetary lord rather than risk an invasion fleet and the soldiers wading through their blood to the lord's throne."

"Don't the lords have a major bodyguard?" Amber asked.

"Of course, but you throw a hundred thousand desperate people, even if they are armed with knives and clubs and whatever they may find at hand, at a thousand guards, and you tell me how many of them will run for their lives."

Kris knew that the king's coin only went so far.

"So, most of these billions suddenly armed are lightly armed and not very well trained."

"Most of them have no training and their main weapon is likely a sack of gunpowder they are expected to light and throw at your people. Many are being exhorted to strap on the explosives and hurl their bodies at you."

"Ugh," Kris said. "This sounds like a bloody mess."

"No," Coth answered so matter-of-factly. "We just bring enough troops and plenty of ammunition and we kill them all. They're rebels."

The right way, the wrong way, the Navy way, and now the Iteeche way. God help us, Kris thought.

"We try to avoid civilian casualties," was all Kris said.

"But why? The lower the population after the rebellion, the more of your own people you can bring in. Certainly, the rebels will be spending no time in the mating ponds. In twenty years, the planet will have no loyalty but to your clan."

Kris found herself wondering if she'd been hired to oversee a blood bath.

"Why don't you just gas the planet from orbit?" Admiral Kitano asked. "They were planning on doing that to the Capital."

"Yes, but that is so inefficient. Yes, they could not trust a soul in the Capital and gassing would have to be done. Still, if you gas a planet, you have a lot of accidents. Fires can get out of control. Aircraft crash into buildings. And the machinery rusts while you're bringing in your own population. You need the captured population to keep things going."

"But with an invasion army marching through blood?" Jack asked.

"The planetary capital may be destroyed. There may be a campaign around the capital to find a weakness in its defenses. Yes, that area may be reduced to rubble, but most of the planet, maybe ninety percent of it, will be captured intact."

Kris had to make an effort not to run screaming from such cold-blooded policy. This might be the Iteeche Way, but there was no way she would go there.

"Admiral Coth," Kris said, with careful, formal precision, "please have five wings of at least four hundred ships ready to sail within the week. Admiral Kitano, I want your First Battlecruiser Task Force to be included in this fleet. Coth, I'll need enough merchant ships to carry an army of, what, half a billion soldiers?"

"That is a large force," Coth replied. "Most of the time we'd send maybe two hundred million. After all, they are fully equipped soldiers and they face civilians that hardly qualify as armed."

"Then get me enough ships to carry that many," Kris said.

"It will take some time to pull that many troops from the satraps."

"Don't you have that many soldiers in the Capital and Guard systems?

"Many times that many, but no Iteeche commander would pull them away from their present duty."

Why did Kris suspect that the army she wanted to borrow was fully committed to occupation duty? To making sure the peasants stayed pleasant to their clan overlords? The stink of this place was getting harder and harder to breathe.

"I don't want the soldiers. Only the ships. In fact, you can use some of those loaded with manure and settlers. We can send them on their way after we capture the planet."

"How will you?" Coth said, incredulous.

"If you can keep secret what is on those ships," Kris said, "I will show you how we do this."

Coth looked at Kris like she had lost her mind, but also as if that was all you could expect from a human. "Aye, aye, My Admiral," he said, and the meeting ended.

Two days after the sing-along, Grand Admiral Kris Longknife, Imperial Admiral of the First Order of Steel, led her armada out from the space station above the Imperial Iteeche Capital. Trailing behind her 2,000 battlecruisers were another 2,000 merchant ships, each loaded with manure and over 100,000 involuntary settlers for some new systems. They came from eight different clans and were destined for five different planets.

But first, they had to perform a masquerade for one risk-taking human admiral.

13

That one human risk-taking admiral needed to say good-bye to two very wonderful children.

Gramma and Grampa Trouble brought Ruth and John up the beanstalk to see the fleet sail. On the quarterdeck of the *Princess Royal*, they hit Kris like wild tornados.

"Can we see the ship?" Johnnie demanded. "Grampa Trouble said we could see the ship! I want to see the raycor," didn't quite come out right.

Kris raised an eyebrow to her great-grandfather.

"The boy is very interested in what makes a spaceship run," the old general answered.

"We've got on our red shipsuits," Ruth put in, very prim and proper for a six-year-old lady.

"Yes, you do," Kris admitted, lifting Ruth up, a process that was getting harder and harder to do these days.

Jack gave Johnnie a lift for a big hug, but it was clear that "little brother," was now the bigger of the two.

"Well, if Grampa Trouble thinks you should see the

reactor," Jack said, "the three of us ought to go down and give engineering a look."

"May I see your bridge?" Ruth piped up before she could be shuffled off to do what her younger brother wanted to do.

"I think that can be arranged. Oh, and we're having ice cream for lunch, with different flavored syrups so you can make sundaes."

That almost stopped Johnnie in his tracks, but after serious consideration, he headed for the stairway down. The ship was in Condition Able Royal, so it was very comfortable to get around in it.

Kris, Gramma Trouble, and Ruth took the stairways up to her the flag bridge. Ruth was excited at the sight of the place, but she put her hands in her pockets to make sure she didn't touch anything and walked carefully around the flag plot.

She stopped at Sensors and Comm to get instructions on what they did and the equipment they did it with. Ruth got to sit in the Sensor watch chair and even order a sweep of the surrounding space.

She was elated as, first a map of the station and the ships tied up there formed in front of her, then, under the watchful eye of the senior duty officer, she expanded her search area to cover a million kilometers around the station. Ruth was elated to see ships moving in and out of the planetary space.

"How do you know if they are warships or freighters?"

"Now you're really asking the right question," the old chief said, and explained how the passive sensors identified reactors to determine how powerful they were. She also explained how the mass detector showed how large the ship was.

"A small reactor on a big, heavy ship and you know you've got a freighter."

"And a battlecruiser?" Ruth asked.

"We know the type of reactors they use. Even if their lasers aren't on or their capacitors full, we can still tell that those eight ships over there are battlecruisers," she said, pointing at a squadron formation.

"Wow!" Ruth said, eyes wide and bright.

Her last stop was the battle board. She approached it as if it was a holy relic. "Is this your battle board, Momma?"

"That's what I use, my girl."

"Can you show me a battle?"

"How about I show you our last drill? Would that be okay?" Kris really didn't want to have her young daughter watch as hundreds, if not thousands of ships were snuffed out.

"Okay," Ruth said, not at all crestfallen.

Kris ran her daughter through a drill where 770 traditional Iteeche battlecruisers took on 360 upgraded ships.

"We're using real lasers, only Nelly has them dialed back to .01 percent power. You know when you're hit, but nothing really happens. Ten hits and a ship is out of the fight. Okay?"

"Yes," was more an aside as Ruth focused on the look of the ships moving around the battle board. Nelly had created a step under her and Ruth went from barely having a nose over the edge of the board to having the board at her middle.

Kris's young daughter looked down on the ship formations, waiting.

"You ready for the shooting phase of the training exercise?" Kris asked.

"Yes, mother," was quite formal.

"Nelly, jump ahead to just before we unleashed the lasers."

"Done, Admiral. In five, four, three, two, one. Fire!"

At five, the small force under Admiral Coth threw itself into Evasion Plan 3. By one, most of his ships had danced well away from where they were going, even as they maintained the base course.

After the first salvos were exchanged, the battlecruisers flipped ship to bring their aft batteries to bear.

Ruth studied that operation very seriously. "Momma, could you replay that?"

"What part?"

"The part where the ships swing around to bring their bow guns to bear, then flip over to bring the aft ones. I'd always thought you stayed on the same course while you did that, but you didn't."

"No, honey. The lasers can be swung fifteen degrees up, down, or sideways. We coordinate the flip ship maneuver with both the gunners and defense. That way, as we flip ship, we change our course enough to throw off the other sides' fire solution. Momma does her best not to be there when the lasers aimed at her ship arrive where she was headed."

"And they don't," Ruth said, pointing at the larger force, of which nearly half was falling out of the exercise. "Did the smaller force really get ten hits on nearly half of the larger force?"

"Yes, dear. Remember, battlecruisers fire twelve lasers in their forward batteries. If all ten hit, that's it for the ship."

"But momma, aren't the other ships dodging like your ships do?"

"No, honey, they aren't."

"Why?"

"The Iteeche go into battle standing at their battle stations."

"Why?"

Kris chuckled, and Ruthie grinned back. They both knew this game well and enjoyed playing it.

"The Iteeche are standing at their battle stations because the Iteeche have gone into battle standing up for ten thousand years, and they refuse to change."

"That's stupid," Ruth said, frowning.

"Yes, honey, but the Iteeche can learn. Every one of the ships in the large force watched how quickly they were destroyed and how few of the smaller force got hit. They all asked to have our new systems installed and to have high gee stations."

"Like my egg?" Ruth asked with the enthusiasm that only a six-year-old can bring to a question.

"Something like your egg," Kris admitted, now wanting to bring a six-year-old mind into the battle of how much tech to give the Iteeche, how much of it would leak to the rebels and how much to you hold on to.

"Now, I'm told that lunch is ready. Mac and cheese for you, corn dogs for your brother."

"And sundaes afterward!" Ruth made sure to point out.

～

Gramma Trouble watched the fleet sail away from the station and quickly form itself into divisions, squadrons, flotillas and wings. The kids watched from the observation deck at the end of the pier. The bulkhead and the deck were perfectly clear. The kids could see everything.

They watched the ships drift away quietly. Somewhere

else on the observation deck, a three-year-old was throwing a full-fledged tantrum, complete with throwing themselves on the deck and kicking it, while pounding small fists as well. "I want my daddy! I want my daddy!" was the child's battle cry.

Gramma Trouble slipped Ruthie's hand into her own, but the six-year-old followed her great-great-grandmother to where a mortified woman tried to calm her child.

Gramma Trouble began by soothing the mother. "Every time the fleet sails, there's at least one little one that can't understand. In years to come, you'll look back on this and laugh."

"How many years?" the mother answered, dejection in her words.

"Probably quite a few," the senior Ruth admitted.

Meanwhile, little Ruthie had introduced herself to a five-year-old boy who looked like he was hoping the deck would open up and let his entire family fall out into space.

Little Ruth and the older brother sat down around the little sister and slowly slid her into a hug, the three of them together. Ruth talked about going swimming in the embassy pool. Both of the kids loved that. Ruth promised them a swim when they got back, and even an ice cream treat as well.

"We had ice cream for lunch," the boy explained.

"That doesn't matter, we'll have an ice cream treat after we swim," Ruth said.

"You can do that?"

"I'm a Longknife. We do what we have to do, and you two need more ice cream," Ruth said, authoritatively.

That seemed to settle it for them, though their mother eyed Gramma Ruth in horror.

"I told you, everything would work out," Gramma Ruth

said. "Now, we've got to get these kids down the beanstalk and into the swimming pool."

The mother just nodded. Grampa Trouble arrived with Johnnie, and the seven of them began to make their way toward the station rig that waited for them. The young wife was more than a bit taken aback to board an electric cart with a blue flag and five white stars on it, but the kids didn't notice, so, for at least today, that was one thing that didn't matter.

14

Kris lead her armada into the Zargoth system. It took quite a lot of time to move over 3,300 ships carefully through a jump, especially since half of them were merchant ships that had demonstrated on the voyage out that they had trouble maintaining acceleration and their proper station in formation.

Kris had held the acceleration to 1.25 gees. That was hard on the settlers, but let the human Marines in Admiral Kitano's First Battlecruiser Task Force drill and exercise at extra weight.

Once through the jump, Kris had the warships put on 2.5 gees and headed for the target planet while the freighters closed the planet at a more comfortable .75 gees. She wanted her battlecruisers over the planet well before the rebels expected an invasion. Kris had little to build on, given that most of the Iteeche battlecruisers carried no Marines, but could only form an untrained landing force.

Being human, Grand Admiral Longknife offered the Iteeche a chance to surrender. She promised all of them their lives. That was an offer that got a lot of heat from Admiral Coth, but Kris did it anyway.

She need not have bothered.

There was no response. Kris might as well have been talking to the murderous alien space raiders.

Kris learned to keep Captain Quinn Sung, her new intel chief as close to her elbow as she had kept Penny. Between Quinn, Megan, and Nelly, of course, her brood studied everything they could get off the planet and reported it to Kris in stand-up meetings on her flag bridge as the target planet grew on the view screen.

"We've been monitoring their airwaves," Quinn reported. "Mostly, the stations are playing martial music and showing videos of courageous civilians throwing themselves on rather stupid soldiers. In every instance, the soldiers die. About half the time, civilians live through the experience."

"Don't you just hate it when the trained soldiers are so dumb," Jack said, drolly.

"Still," Megan said, "when the civilians do die, they do it gloriously and to a swelling choral arrangement."

"All the better to welcome them to whatever afterlife they expect," Kris said with a sigh at the government-sponsored lie.

"I wonder how many of the population are swallowing this bull," Kris said.

"There's no way to tell," Megan said.

"Most of our sensors have been applied," Quinn said, "to helping Nelly and her brood search for the planets' clan overlord and his court. The people of the capital are staying off the streets. When they go out, they do it furtively, quickly, and alone. No groups of more than three. Likely that's the law, but we haven't seen a lot of enforcers on the streets. The palace doesn't even have that much going on. It's like a ghost town."

"No activity at all in the place," Megan said. "No signal intelligence. No movement in or out. No energy signatures. It's a ghost town."

"I have been searching," Nelly put in, "for a site or sites, among the huddled population, where there was still activity. We have identified six of them to date."

Once the fleet went into orbit, longboats probed the outer atmosphere, swatting down surface-to-air missiles, and getting better signal intel, while dropping off drones which, in turn could be reformed into scout nanos. The six interesting sites were quickly infiltrated and mapped while the defenses were measured, and the occupants finger-printed.

"We have our first report on the six active sites," Quinn reported. "We think we've found the one with the clan elite for the planet. They're buried well underground so that lazing them from orbit would hardly raise a sweat. However, a mole in a hole can be easily isolated."

"I can think of several ways to attack this problem," Kris said.

"The challenge is which one will work best and kill the least?" Jack added.

"Lazing the entire complex from orbit might melt the mountain above the redoubt into a molten capstone over the top of it," Quinn said, "but the complex runs deep, and the lower precinct might not be touched. We have already identified several escape tunnels that lead to hidden exits miles away from the mountain. We can hit them also, but if we miss even one, they're out of there and running."

"There is also a strong suspicion among Coth's intel

staff," Megan said, "that the six redoubts might be connected with deeply dug maglev trains."

"That would turn the situation into a whack-a-mole game," Jack pointed out.

"We still haven't gotten to the lower levels of the complexes we're investigating," Nelly pointed out. "The places are a maze and it's taking a lot of time for our nano scouts to map it.

"Also," Quinn reported, "As yet, our nanos have not located the Planetary Overlord and his closest subordinates. The senior clan officials are also off the map. Clearly, there are many more layers to dig through."

"Have the long boats run more sweeps," Kris ordered. "We need to kill more SAMs and locate more of the local search radars if we intend to run a drop mission. They can also drop more drones and nanos while they're at it."

One report on intel gathered turned into a discussion of what to do when they found the local high muckety-mucks. "You remember the time we took down a space station by causing an air fueled explosion using the nanos as dust?" Jack said. "Get the right mixture of tiny partials, a spark, and WHOOP! Walls get blown out. Lungs get exploded from the inside. It's a great way to take out a large space."

That got stares from most of those on the flag bridge.

"Nelly, explain," Kris said.

"Historically, when miners dug deep into mountains to extract coal, they had to make sure coal dust was not allowed to collect. If they didn't, the dust could ignite and explode, killing a lot of miners. It still is that way with grain silos. If you get too much dust in the air and a spark, you'll be chasing pieces of silo over the next five counties."

"So, we could use nanos to actually explode the tunnels?" Megan asked.

"Yep. We'd need a lot of nanos, but we could do it."

"The question is," Jack said, "just how big is this redoubt? Also, how compartmentalized is it? Would one explosion do the trick? If not, how many?"

"I have my own favorite trick up my sleeve," Kris said, "though this one is borrowed."

"What's that?" Jack asked.

"For Ruthie's first Christmas, we actually managed to arrange for a real family get-together. Of course, to keep Grampa Al happy, it had to be at his 'Tower of Insecurity'."

"Oh, right," Jack said, scowling at the memory.

"As luck would have it," Kris said, going on with the story, "one of his competitors chose that moment to launch a real killer attack on dear old grampa. They managed to get a flock of nanos up to the top floor. First, they ate out the windows of his private quarters. Then, if we hadn't been there, they would have eaten the meat off his bones."

"It might have worked," Jack said, "but we were visiting with one cute little baby and two very magnificent computers.

Now Nelly got into the story. "Sal and I commandeered all the Smart Metal™ in the art work, office equipment, everything possible, and reformed them into defender nanos."

"It was quite a fight," Jack said. "Way too close, but while Nelly was defending us, she also managed to identify the location of the mobile command center controlling the attack. A Marine detachment closed them down in the nick of time."

"And through it all," Kris pointed out, smiling, "Ruthie giggled and cooed, showing early the proper Longknife attitude toward assassins."

"Do you intend to repeat that attack?" Jack asked.

"No, I'd rather arrange for it to be done with more finesse. How about we have the nanos only eat out the heart of the clan leaders, leaving an identifiable body to be filmed and broadcasted to the people of Zargoth? It might also be an ice breaker for the next couple of planets on our hit list. Anyone think it will be a conversation starter?"

"Eat their hearts out?" Quinn said, kind of squeamishly. "They warned me about working for you Longknifes."

"Sorry, Captain, but I'd rather kill just the right culprits and leave the rest of the people to pick up the pieces. So, keep me appraised of developments."

The apparent invasion fleet was half-way to the planet when Captain Sung and Lieutenant Megan Longknife reported that they'd fully mapped all six redoubts. Probably for political reasons, all the powers that be were in one of them, running things together with the bigger fish looking over the smaller fishes' shoulders and the biggest fish making sure no one was nibbling at his tail.

It was time to decapitate this rebel planet.

15

Or maybe not.

Grand Admiral Kris Longknife knew things had hit a snag when she got a look at the long faces on Megan and Quinn as they entered the wardroom while their admiral was eating supper that evening.

Neither turned toward the food line, but instead headed straight for her and Jack.

Kris kept buttering a roll, meticulously, and way past what it needed, until the two of them settled into the seats across the table from her.

"You two look like somebody stole your puppy and you don't want to tell your momma your favorite Christmas present is gone 'cause you know she won't like having her nice day messed with."

"Well, since you put it that way, we could always wait and mess up your day tomorrow, over breakfast," Megan offered, through false cheer.

Quinn looked at the young lieutenant as if she had lost

her mind. Megan had been with Kris longer and knew how these kinds of talks went. Quinn would learn soon enough.

"Spill it, folks," Jack said. "We really didn't want to sleep tonight."

"The boss guys of Zargoth are messing with us," Megan said. "Or, more likely, they don't want us messing with them."

"How so?" Kris said, and decided that roll might as well have a bite taken out of it. It was quite tasty, she discovered.

"They're closing up all six of their redoubts tight as a tick," Megan reported. "They're even welding the entrances shut. They've put covers on all air intakes and welded them shut as well. We've got nanos checking on the emergency exits we've identified. It will be an hour before we know for sure if they're also being welded shut, but I doubt they'll miss them,"

"It sounds like someone has let the rebels know about that little nano infestation that follows us around," Jack said, cutting into his meatloaf.

Kris tried one of the sautéed red potatoes on her plate and mulled the situation as she chewed. "I wonder who passed the word to the rebels about our nanos. The Don'-sum'Wo clan head worked with my 'loyal' Nuu Enterprises boss man to scatter nanos so they could take me down. But then, the way we marched through the Chap'sum'We clan's palace wasn't exactly subtle."

"These people aren't dumb," Jack pointed out.

"So," Kris said. "Megan, I'm sure you've told Quinn that I don't mind having my dinner ruined so long as the bearer of the lousy news also comes bearing solutions. Talk to me."

"Well, Kris, we think we've got a way around this," the lieutenant said, almost cheerfully. "All we need is a company of Marines, a platoon of Combat Engineers, and a couple of unique supplies."

"Talk to me, Lieutenant."

"It also involves me and the captain here leading the drop mission."

Kris frowned at the young woman, but Jack spoke before she could.

"Have you been drinking too much of the Longknife Kool-Aid, kid? It's taken me years to break this woman from her habit of gleefully rushing into suicidal missions. Have I got to start locking you up in your quarters?"

"Hey, that royal blood thing doesn't cover me," Megan insisted.

"Great Grampa Ray is somewhere at the bottom of *your* family tree," Kris pointed out, way too placidly. "Thus, the security chief of any activity you're attached to has the right to veto any hair-brained stunt and, if necessary, lock you up."

Megan eyed her two flag officers like they were something the cat hacked up. "You never mentioned this before," she said, accusingly.

"You never said anything about going off to get yourself killed, before," Jack shot back.

"I'd really appreciate Megan coming along," Quinn said, sounding a whole lot less sure of herself than the average four-striper. Of course, there were a whole lot of stars on the other side of the table.

"Okay, Megan. Why do you need to go?" Jack asked.

"I need to get my head into their computer system," the lieutenant answered quickly and firmly. "I expect we'll need Lily if we're going to pull off this *coup de main*. With me and Lily, it could be a walk in the park. Without us, I think the mission should be scrubbed. Without the mission, a whole lot of innocent bystanders are going to be dead by sundown tomorrow."

Kris could not count the number of times an argument just like that had been her response to Jack when he questioned one of her hair-brained stunts. Cutting down on the butcher's bill was always a winning argument. Still, it was a bit of a shock to find herself on the other side of the table from some young, optimistic, and enthusiastic Longknife so willing to race out and get herself killed.

Kris leaned forward, rested her elbows on the table and her chin on her hands. "Okay, Longknife, talk me out of locking you in your quarters and throwing away the key."

16

Lieutenant Megan Longknife and Captain Quinn Sung checked out each other's armored space suits with attached battle gear, then waited as two grizzled Gunny Sergeants double-checked them. Megan was relieved to pass muster, and, from the sigh, so was Quinn.

For the drop, they boarded separate light assault crafts. No need to lose all the command and intel assets to one unlucky shot. Of course, if Megan and Lily bought it, the whole mission would become damn near impossible to pull off.

Megan and Quinn had had their battle gear upgraded to scout suits. With any good luck, they'd be invisible to the eye, radar, and infrared. If things went the way she intended, they wouldn't have to use the extra bells and whistles a scout battle suit brought to the fight, but Kris had been adamant that they jack up their safety margins to the max.

Neither Megan nor Quinn objected to that. Not at all.

The LCA dropped away from the *Princess Royal*. For the

first time in her life, Megan found herself with space all around her. The landing craft was just a thin shell with just enough heat shielding to protect the Marines from the sky-high temperatures of reentry.

Megan was seated up front with orders to watch the instruments but not touch the controls. She did keep one eye on the colorful display, but she could hardly fail to observe the sight around her.

The canopy was clear. She had a panoramic view of the stars above and the lovely planet below. It was enough to take her breath away, and she was breathing pure oxygen.

Megan remembered that in Kris's first combat jump, her LCA had been jimmied to burn her up in the planet's atmosphere. This Longknife had gone over her LCA with a senior tech sergeant and a fine-toothed comb. She didn't expect any surprises, but she stood ready to grab the freely moving stick and land this sucker if she had to.

YOU AND ME? she told Lily.

WE COULD DO IT IF WE HAD TO.

LET'S DON'T AND SAY EVERYTHING WORKED FINE.

The thin ionized air began to give the LCA a glow. A quick glance around showed a dozen similarly glowing lights. This was the pathfinder wave. Once they had identified the drop zone and made it secure, the rest of the company and the engineers would drop from longboats.

General Montoya had wanted Megan and Quinn to come in with the second wave. Kris had gotten a kind of big-sister smile and sent them on their way.

Still, Megan knew that her cousin was watching like a hawk from her flag bridge.

So far, the drop was going according to plan. As they

came out of the ionization part of the landing, Lily projected a full electronic countermeasures display on the visor of Megan's helmet. There were several specially equipped longboats loitering over each of the six underground fortresses. They were there to spot any radar or laser that went active and call in 24-inch lasers from orbit to flatten the things before they could do anything bad. Several were also armed with anti-missile lasers of their own.

The one worry was infrared guided lasers, but so far, they had not been heard from. Still, each LCA was dispensing tiny flares to bury its heat signature in a confusing stream of high temperature targets.

Each of the LCAs had a different amount of ablative material to bleed off more or less heat. Thus, none of the landers showed the same temperature.

Three lasers shot up from three different ground locations.

Almost instantaneously, 24-inch lasers shot down from battlecruisers in orbit to turn the offending weapon into molten hell.

Fortunately, the rebel targeteers had guessed wrong. They only destroyed decoys.

After those sites got hell rained down on them, none of the others dared to go active. Still, the signature of the system had been marked and several dozen sites that made similar electronic noise were flamed. A few minutes later, smart rebel radar crews had flipped switches and there was no noise in that part of the electromagnetic spectrum.

The twelve LCAs continued their descent unmolested.

They'd intentionally chosen a bit of rough mountain terrain for their target. The LCAs could not land here, so, as the lander passed 2,000 feet over ground, they flipped over.

One by one, from aft to front, the computer popped the restraining harness and a Marine fell loose.

Megan went last. She steadied herself by spreading out her arms and legs. At 500 feet, she popped her chute and then guided it by hand to a landing spot in a small meadow where thirty-six of the assault team had landed. The other twelve were scattered in pairs, forming outposts to warn if trouble was coming.

They'd also call in hell from orbit to mess with the trouble.

Once the site was secure, Megan and Quinn kept close to the single engineer who had dropped with them. He was deploying sensitive monitors and making narrow holes by jamming a sharp steel rod into the ground. After filling them with explosives, he'd step off a safe distance and set off the tiny explosion.

On Megan's helmet a subterranean map began to form. They quickly spotted the escape tunnel a couple of hundred meters below them, but it was not as clear as the textbook Megan had skimmed through.

"Is there a problem, sergeant?" she asked.

"One very big one," the tech sergeant answered. "There's an old stream bed between us and the tunnel. If I didn't know better, I'd say they dug the damn tunnel exactly under it intentionally. Our nanos are going to have a bitch of a time gnawing through that."

"Why?" Quinn asked.

"A stream bed has a whole lot of cobblestones. You know, the nice rocks that make comforting sounds as the water rushes over and around them? The problem from where I stand is that those stones have been washed down river from a whole lot of different mountains. We got granite. We got basalt. We got flint. From the sound of things, this damn stream would be a treasure trove for a bunch of geology undergrad students. Me, it just means I need a whole lot of different nanos. I've called in my results, but the next jump is already on its way. It'll be two hours or more before we can get the stuff we need."

"And we'll have made three landings around this fortress," Quinn added. "We might as well send out engraved invitations."

"Could the nanos be low-dropped by a longboat? A tiny package?" Megan asked.

"Do you want to risk that bunch of eating nanos getting loose without adult supervision?" the Marine said. "I mean, I know we jarheads ain't known for our niceness, but at least we'd know to kill those things if there's a risk of them getting loose in the environment. No, Lieutenant. A Marine drops with that package."

Megan had spent enough time in the Navy to know when a Marine sergeant had respectfully and politely told her that she was one dumb-ass officer. "Thank you, Sergeant," was her proper reply.

The engineer stayed busy, not wasting a second. Since the Marines would be rappelling down into the escape hole, he would need to widen the hole sooner or later. Now, he used many of the nanos to widen the hole as far as he could. Other nanos ate and wiggled their way through the sand around rocks, drilling a tiny corkscrew hole through them and then headed straight down for the main target.

He already had his first scout nanos in the escape tunnel when the second drop arrived.

Things got rather crowded around the hole as more engineers added both diggers and scout nanos to what was going on below. Megan took a step back, but not too far. She and Lily would likely be needed before too long.

The scout nanos in the tunnel were busy mapping the situation and checking for any monitoring devices or nasty surprises. They were not disappointed.

The tunnel was studded with sensors. There were both passive listening microphones to detect noise and active sonic devices to spot movement. There were also lasers to back those up. If that wasn't enough, there were cameras monitoring the place as well.

All the stuff they found in the tunnel weren't nice polite sensors. There were auto cannon nests every two hundred meters ready to swivel in any direction. If 20mm exploding cannon shells weren't enough to ruin a visitor's day, the wall and floor showed explosives: both claymores and large mines.

Oh, and there were gas canisters. Canisters that carried no markings on their red exterior.

A second order was put in for scout nanos that could sense any gas residue on the outside of the cans and identify their contents.

For now, they were assumed to be deadly.

"You know, if I didn't know better, I'd say these folks are paranoid," Megan drawled to Quinn.

"I don't think they like us," she answered, catching on to the Longknife way of facing death and dismemberment.

"Now," Megan said with a happy grin, "Lily and I get to work."

Quinn eyed Megan through her face mask. "Work?"

"The combat engineers aren't the only ones that brought nanos to this gun fight," Megan said as she tapped a belt and satchel at her waist.

"Help me get my left glove off," she told Quinn.

Once Megan was bare-handed, she stroked a finger

along the belt. Instantly, a thin cloud seemed to waft from it. "Lily, get them to work," the lieutenant ordered.

For the longest time, all Megan saw through her helmet visor was her and Quinn getting her glove back on. For a long minute after she was buttoned up, Megan saw nothing.

Then her faceplate came to life.

"My nanos are down there, now," Megan said. "We've found the comm lines and I've borrowed a few of the engineer's nanos to bore holes in them. Oh, I'm in. Give me a few minutes. I think I'm going to be quite busy."

Megan and Lily seemed to be plastered to the wall of a tunnel. Lots of weird animals flowed in one direction. Only a handful of different, but just as weird critters moved in the other. The two of them began to brand each of the animals as it went by with a tiny sigil. Inside the brand were enough nanos to read the contents of the beastie as well as take control of it.

Megan left a supervisory nano to continue that task and punched through to another data stream. One after another, she took control of the data flow through a dozen different streams. By the time that was done, the scouts had located another data cable and Megan and Lily set about gaining control of that one as well.

About the time the third drop brought in eater nanos for the river stones, Megan had control of all the reports flowing back to the redoubt and any orders headed out into the tunnel.

They also had problems.

Two of the observation posts reported traffic headed up to what looked like a fire road through what didn't look at all like trees, except they were tall and had branches.

Kris had spread the fleet out in orbit so there were always two battlecruisers close at hand.

In eighteen seconds of stutter fire, the convoys vanished in a hellish fire.

Unfortunately, the trees also caught fire and the observation posts started a quick retrograde out of that area.

Drones were rapidly knocked together in the orbiting longboats to drop down and provide solid coverage in all directions to assure that the next interloper might be spotted sooner.

Megan couldn't help but notice the red of the forest fire being reflected onto her helmet. She picked up the pace just in case this team needed to be underground before the fire got to them.

Despite having what she thought was total control over the data flow, the tunnel suddenly started to fill with gas. Not only gas but also different colors of smoke. Some of the smoke particles managed to collide and stick to a few of her nanos and drop them to the deck, but most of her nano army seemed unbothered by the change in their work environment.

Lily took control of all the scout nanos in the tunnel and assigned them to finding another data flow. Clearly, they'd missed one.

They resorted to entering an auto cannon and following its connections. There were the two identified fiber optic cables, but well down the line, one of the cables spun off a tiny, single thread that plunged down before meeting up with a third major cable that was buried under the floor of the tunnel.

Five minutes later, Megan had control of that bunch of animals carrying information back to the central control site.

Of course, the Iteeche had to know they were down here.

Megan doubted that anyone with half a mind would be trusting anything coming from the sensors here.

Still, when the engineers reported they had a hole a meter wide open all the way down, it was Megan who volunteered to go, head first, down the rabbit hole. She didn't so much rappel as she was lowered.

There was no way that she could be lowered directly down the center of the hole. She found herself shoving off, first from one side, then the other. When her backside bumped into the wall, she'd have to use her butt to move, since both her legs were in a harness.

Oh, and Megan discovered she was a bit claustrophobic. Maybe it had something to do with being lowered head first and feeling the blood rush to her head. Still, she was nowhere near panic, but this was a very tiny hole, and not perfect. Especially when she passed through the stream bed.

There were nice, rounded river stones poking out from the wall. Megan called up and they did slow her down, so she wouldn't bang herself too much on them.

Finally, she approached the end of the drop. The nanos reported everything under control, but Megan still waved a small flag before she risked her own fair body in what the builder had intended to be a target gallery.

Nothing fired at her flag.

She risked a hand.

Nothing.

She waved it about.

Nothing.

She had herself lowered very slowly until enough of her head was out that she could actually see the tunnel.

The walls and ceiling of the tunnel had been coated with some sort of concrete that gave it a reddish hue. The deck was a pleasant blue. There was a rail for the maglev running down the center of the deck, large and ready.

That maglev was now Megan's main concern. They might have disabled the auto cannons and already tripped the gas and smoke, but once her troopers were in the tunnel, a train racing at several hundred miles an hour could really ruin their whole day.

Now it was time for Megan to set up her own communications network. Lily spun out more nanos from the 5 kilos her human had dropped with. They took off in both directions. First, they sought out trouble, but at a certain distance, one of them would convert from a wandering scout to a static repeater. It would stick to the overhead and send messages in both directions using either laser, microwave, or radio.

The scouts continued to report the tunnel empty in both directions, but Megan couldn't risk more troops in the tunnel when there was any chance that they might be turned to human soup by a rampaging maglev train.

The maglev track was not a surprise. This escape tunnel had been specifically chosen in the hope it would have one. It was known that the overlord of this planet would want to flee from one redoubt under attack to another one that was still safe. They needed a fast way to get away.

Thus, the maglev.

Megan spun more nanos off her satchel. These were different, but really very simple. They could take large bites out of high quality steel, spit it out, and take another bite. A maglev needed a magnetic track to repel off of. Megan intended that any train headed their way would find a large hole in its track. The young officer smiled at the mental picture of a hurtling train shooting out onto a couple of dozen meters of track that weren't there. It would nose dive right into the track at the other end of the break.

Nothing like using the system against the system.

Since a train might come from either redoubt, Megan had to send probes in both directions.

That done, Megan ordered them to lower her the rest of the way into the pacified chamber.

Megan ended up lying on her back. A quick release got her legs free. Cautiously, she stood up, the M-14 carbine she'd drawn for this mission at the ready.

Nothing moved as far as she could see, which, admittedly was not far, what with the swirling smoke and gas. Just as importantly, nothing within range opened up on the intruding Navy officer.

Taking a few steps, Megan tested the deck and found it hard concrete. It stretched out unblemished in both directions. It was the same with the wall. There was no hint of the explosives hidden in the deck or bulkheads. They were well concealed to hide their sudden death.

Of course, if you had hidden destruction in those walls, you'd want them to be nice and perfectly hidden.

A Marine lieutenant rappelled into the underground chamber, followed by a Gunny, then a quartet of trigger-pullers. As soon as they'd set up a base of fire, the engineers began to drop, mixed with more sharpshooters. Somewhere in the mix, a medic showed up. Only after the Marines had things well in hand did Captain Sung get to drop down.

"Next time, I go first, and you can wait in line," she said, darkly.

"Hey, I'm the Longknife. We always go first."

"And hog all the fun."

Megan tried to shrug and discovered that was one of several things you can't do in an armored battle suit. "Really, it's been a bore down here, waiting for all of you. Now the fun can start."

"Yeah, right."

Marines were already advancing down the tunnel in both directions. An attack was possible from either end. The Marines wanted to put quit to any assault early.

Then the Iteeche rebels pulled their own surprise out of their hat.

17

"We got a problem developing up here. I'll relay you the take," was calm, belying the havoc the words conveyed.

Immediately, Megan's faceplate filled with the information.

On the surface, the hostiles had launched half a dozen small rockets, really not much larger than fireworks. However, before any fire could be directed at them, they exploded, scattering a cloud. That cloud quickly proved itself made up of a mixture of countermeasures. Infrared, lasers, and radar sensors got hashed along with line of sight.

It was, however, a very small cloud, well away from the redoubt as well as the landing. Nothing to worry about.

Seconds later, more rockets shot out of the cloud. Some climbed higher for two or three seconds, then exploded while others extended the cloud.

Every couple of seconds, another wave of rockets would pop out, expanding the blind spot like ripples on a pond. Try as the longboat could, their fire controls could not acquire the rockets and direct laser fire at them before they exploded.

"It's a problem," Admiral Longknife said on net, "but it won't last long. What goes up always goes down."

Megan was glad to know that she and her team were foremost in Kris's attention at the moment.

Except the admiral didn't seem to be correct in her assumption.

The cloud did not dissipate. If anything, it got thicker!

Then one of the longboats discovered why.

It spotted a tiny flying drone. It was no more sophisticated than what a school kid might knock together for a sixth-grade class on Wardhaven. It had a long thin wing with a long thin body powered by a tiny engine. That looked to be all there was to it. However, upon further examination, the drones were spotted pouring fog out both in front of and behind them.

This one drone was spotted when the front nozzles failed, and it cruised out of its own cloud. It was allowed to keep flying for half a minute as it was studied, and an electronic signature was taken off of it.

Or not.

The drone was so dumb that it made no noise. It appeared to be operating completely on mechanical guidance.

"Talk about low tech," Jack muttered on net.

"Still, a sharpened bamboo stick through the heart can kill you just as dead as any bullet," Kris said.

Then she started snapping out orders. "Gunnery, identify the location of each of the outposts. Mark it clearly. Outposts, prepare to identify targets by range and bearing from your position. We'll have to base any fire plan on offset from our Ops.

"Aye, aye, Admiral," came back at her.

Megan sighed; she'd hoped that the destroyed reaction force was the sum total of what the hostiles had for a mobile strike force. Now it looked more like they'd only destroyed the eager beaver who'd jumped off immediately to his destruction.

Now, apparently, the planet overlord was coming at them with malice aforethought.

Megan needed to get serious about her situation down here in the tunnel. She might have to bring her entire team down here and block the hole they'd dug. She'd given some thought to just this tactic, but she'd hoped to keep a line of retreat.

The enemy seemed intent on wiping out her exit strategy, as well as her team.

Many of the digger nanos were expanding the hole, smoothing out the kinks. Megan decided to slow that down and divide up her nanos.

At the moment, the maglev trains were her major concern. There was no way to tell if there was only one train running around the six redoubts, or if they used a different train between each one. Also, Megan would not bet that, when the overlord decided on a chicken run, that there might not be several trains following in his wake.

Nope, she'd have to stand ready to cover threats from either direction.

Now, she had Lily spin off more nanos from her satchel of Smart Metal™ . These were standard carriers, rather than complex devices. Each could lift off a chewer from the hole's wall, and glide down to the tunnel, then off in the direction of the far redoubt.

Several kilometers from their entrance hole, Megan had chosen a twenty meter stretch of track for destruction. It was in the middle of a gentle curve, so if the train lost levitation, it would not only fall, but race ahead a critical few centimeters off from the track ahead. The wreck would be spectacular as bodies in motion at three hundred klicks per hour suddenly tried to come to a dead stop.

The emphasis would be on dead.

Megan had chosen the site for her sabotage well away from their hole because she wanted more space for a fighting withdrawal. No doubt, after the first train spilled its guts and a lot of Iteeche guts as well, a second train might come up slower, stop earlier, and launch its own attack force.

Megan felt like a juggler, busy keeping a dozen screaming chain saws in the air at all times while trying not to lose a hand or arm.

Of course, she could always blow that end of the tunnel and seal them all in. And maybe seal them all in a tomb if their advance led them nowhere.

Megan shivered at that thought. Around Kris Longknife, she'd faced death a few times.

She'd been there when little toothless Ruthie was held hostage. She'd let Jack and Kris take the kill shots while she dropped her automatic and dove to catch the infant as it dropped from dead hands.

And what she'd done to keep Kris alive when she visited the Grand Duchess Vicky for her wedding hadn't been a walk in the park, either.

Still, this was the first time she'd actually walked up to the lion's mouth and put her head in amongst the teeth with malice aforethought. This was her first time to choose to put her life on the line and have to live with it minute after long minute, for what looked to be several hours.

It was exhilarating.

It was terrifying.

It was what Longknifes did.

Welcome to the legend, girl.

"Lily, give Captain Sung and I a status report."

"Iteeche communications have been interrupted. We now are feeding them a picture of you wandering around the tunnel, checking things out. You are still alone as far as they know."

"Assuming they trust their video," Quinn said. "I know I wouldn't."

"For now," Megan said, "let's assume they're gullible and inexperienced in dealing with Longknifes and their insane followers."

The two turned their helmets toward each other and managed to exchange grins. Whether they were eager or resigned, Megan couldn't decide.

"We have begun to destroy track on the far side. In fifteen minutes, we should have a major break. I suggest that we double it to add a safety margin."

"Agreed," Megan said.

"I will keep the electricity flowing through the track. They won't know what we've done to it."

"Good, Lily."

"As far as communications is concerned," Nelly's daughter went on, "there is no change in the flow of instructions to this section of the railway. There has been no effort to detonate mines or claymores, nor have they popped any more gas or smoke. They seem to be content to let you wander around in the tunnel."

"Fine, Lily. Let's let them see some more Marines down here. Pass them the take from when I got reinforcements, then let me know if we get any reaction to that."

"Megan, before I dropped, Mom and I did some artwork.

We projected that the cave would have claymores. They'd be good to clear out invaders without destroying the track. We have some really cool video of your team being wiped out by one, two, or three claymore mines. If they trigger the claymores, can I send them that video?"

Megan found herself smiling. Lily sounded as eager as a kid to show off what she'd done at school today. Quinn was still looking in Megan's faceplate. The Navy captain looked kind of poleaxed. No doubt, she wasn't used to a computer being two thousand steps ahead of her. Oh, and artistic as well.

"Sure, Lily. I almost hope they do trigger the claymores. Just make sure we have total control over those detonation comm lines."

"Megan, they were the first thing I seized, and I check them every two nanoseconds. Please."

Now Megan laughed. It was never wise to hurt a computer's feelings. Still, there was way too much hurt human pride in that reply.

"Why are you laughing?" Lily demanded.

"Because, Lily, you sound just like I would have if my mom had nagged me about something I'd never miss doing."

"Oh. Yes. Someday I would like to meet your mom."

"First, we have to survive this. Major?" Megan called to the Marine in charge. She needed to change the subject.

"Could you move out a combat team in both directions? The ones going down the tunnel," here she pointed in the direction away from the redoubt they were interested in, "need to be prepared for a defensive action. You'll need to send a Marine engineer with programming skills. I've assigned a portion of our nanos to destroy track there."

It was always a delicate proposition when a Longknife

tied the chain of command in knots. Megan knew Kris had effectively told admirals what to do when she was but a lieutenant commander, one promotion up from where Megan now stood. Still, it was best to ask very politely for something you needed rather than say anything that might be mistaken for a command.

Kris had been careful to school her distant cousin from Santa Maria in the delicate art of getting people to cooperate with the Longknife legend without getting pissed at it.

Today, Megan seemed to be doing it right.

"I'll send a platoon to cover that direction," the major said. "Do you think a squad of engineers will be enough?"

"Likely. Tell them to expect a train some time in the future. The present break in the track should take care of that. After that train wreck, I'd appreciate it if they could advance a good distance down the track and set up another ambush. How far do you think they should go to surprise a train full of reinforcements?"

"Can you tell us if there's a train on the tracks?"

"As soon as it leaves that other redoubt, I can let you know." Actually, Lily would be the one announcing "The British are coming," whoever they were.

"Good. If your nanos don't have the time, we can always blow the track the old-fashioned way. There are few things in life that the proper application of excessive explosives can't solve."

Megan and Quinn allowed the major a chuckle at his ancient joke.

"I'll send the other platoon up the tracks toward the target. Same size as the other?"

"I think so," Quinn said. "We'll be going with them and I suspect Lieutenant Longknife will have as many nanos as she can lay her hands on, ready to chew up track when we need to."

"I'll split my reserve platoon between here and above ground."

"I wonder why they haven't attacked us yet," Megan said.

Megan was just a lieutenant, and she knew she had a lot to learn, but did the next learning experience have to stampede toward her just after she said something so stupid?

18

"Outpost 12, I have traffic approaching my position. It's damn close, so whoever gets this fire mission better be right on the coordinates I'm passing you."

"Outpost 12, my squadron flag, the *Dauntless*, is coming up on your position in fifteen seconds. Send me your range and bearing to target and we will smoke them."

"This is Admiral Longknife," came on net. "*Dauntless*, fire one laser, quarter charge, to verify your target."

"Aye, aye, Admiral."

Megan held her breath while troopers several hundred meters above her head and a few kilometers from her hole held theirs as well.

"OP 12 to *Dauntless*, your fire is short. Add half a click, fifteen degrees north of your ranging shot."

"On its way."

"OP 12, *Dauntless*, your aim is good. Fire for effect."

Megan would not want to be on the receiving end of what was headed for that bunch.

"OP 12, *Dauntless*, check fire. Check fire! I do not have the target under observation. There is a major forest fire where the target was. Oh, and that fire is headed our way. Request permission to withdraw from my position if it gets too hot around here."

"This is Bird Dog 6 actual. We have your location registered. If you withdraw, we cannot reregister your position. Hold position."

"Bird Dog 6 actual, this is Admiral Longknife. Be advised that I trust your OP Marines to withdraw when, and only when, they can no longer serve their mission. OP 12, use your discretion."

"Understood Admiral. Bird Dog 6 actual, we are holding our position and praying for rain."

"OP 12, Bird Dog 6 actual understands you are holding your position for now and praying for rain."

"Admiral Longknife here. OP 12, rain dances are authorized."

Megan shook her head. How did her cousin manage to pull things like this out of her hat? No wonder her troops were ready to march through hell without map coordinates for that woman.

"OP 7 here. I have displaced one observer forward to verify what I took for action on our front. I have a long convoy of troop transports stopped in the middle of the road. It appears that the troops have dismounted. They may be infiltrating through the forest. I do not have any of them under observation."

"Bird Dog 6 actual, how hot do the transports appear to be?"

"Forward Observer. They're warm. I'd call it ten, maybe fifteen minutes cooling."

"OP 7, can you provide firing coordinates?"

"Negative."

"OP 7, this is Forward Observer. I can range on the target. You can range on me."

Megan knew what that young woman had just done. With a range and bearing from OP 7 to the forward observer, and a range and bearing from her to the target area, they could bring hell down.

However, this fire mission would not be targeting a convoy of trucks on a road. Now, the targets were a lot of infantry advancing along a broad front, moving from cover to cover. Whatever battlecruiser got the fire mission would be aiming for a lot of land.

The Forward Observer could not be all that distant from those targets. Indeed, the chance she could come through this fire mission alive were slim to none.

Still, she had given the recommendation for how the fire mission could be run that would likely kill her.

There was a short pause on net. Likely, everyone was hoping that the Grand Admiral, herself, would stick her nose into this again, and either approve or cancel this fire mission.

Kris Longknife stayed silent on net.

A moment later, OP 7 provided range and bearing to the young woman Marine. A moment later, she provided the range and bearing to the lead parked truck. Bird Dog 6 recommended a wide spread half a klick to two full klicks out from there.

"This is *Dauntless*, we are ready to execute fire mission."

"This is Longknife 1, execute fire mission," was crisp. Dry. Deadly.

Again, Megan was glad to be underground. She might be storming the gates of hell in an hour or so, but what they faced up there was the worst fiery pit of hell with a whole lot of pissed off demons.

Megan broke from the tragedy playing out above her head. A platoon of Marines, not on the command net, and ignorant of what their fellows were facing above, had advanced forward of her position.

"Embrace the suck," Megan said to herself, and she and Captain Sung followed the Marines forward, advancing on the one guy on this planet who deserved to die.

19

MEGAN, THERE IS NOISE ON THE TRACK COMING FROM THE DISTANT REDOUBT. Lily reported on Nelly net.

"Back Door, you may have company coming fast," Megan reported on net. "Lily, can you give me an ETA?"

"Negative. We haven't tracked this before, but I'd estimate ten minutes. I've got scouts out fifteen klicks down the line, so I can assure a five-minute warning."

"Lieutenant, you copy that?"

"On it."

With their rear covered, Megan switched to Nelly Net.

IS THERE ANY NOISE AHEAD OF US?

THE RAIL IS GENERATING NO NOISE. NOT ONE DECIBEL.

LILY, LET ME KNOW THE MOMENT YOU GET A PING. ANY PING.

ON IT.

As Megan advanced slowly behind cautious Marines, over her head, a battle was running its bloody course. OP 12 was falling back slowly as the forest fire advanced on them. They maintained sporadic observation of the trail.

There was no traffic.

OP 7 was minus their Forward Observer. She had not been heard from since the laser salvos from orbit. They also were evading now, both the forest fire and sporadic weapons fire.

The reserve platoon had sent two squads into the woods. They were advancing to contact and expected to engage survivors soon.

Despite regular requests from battlecruisers in orbit, no one on the ground could identify any targets worthy of a 24-inch laser, even one at a quarter power.

"Bird Dog 6 actual," Megan called on net. "Have you considered retreating down our rabbit hole and sealing the thing? We can't afford to have all the air sucked out of the tunnel by a forest fire."

"We're all in space suits," the major pointed out.

"Yes, sir, but if this goes long, we might have to risk going to local atmosphere. I've disabled all the gas canisters I've come upon."

"I'll keep that option in mind. So far, we have half of our perimeter unengaged. I'd prefer to retreat above ground."

"Yes, sir," Megan said. She'd done what she could. She could understand why a Marine major might not want to be caught in a tunnel with no corners to hide behind and only two ways out.

Then matters changed again.

20

"**O**P 3 here. We have activity on our front. Well-dispersed infantry are advancing across a meadow. Bearing and range to follow." The fire mission called for a wide spread of laser fire. Someone wanted to kill a lot of infantry they couldn't see.

There went the major's avenue of withdrawal.

"This is the *Implacable*, I have your fire mission.

"This is Bird Dog 6 actual, you are authorized to fire."

A long minute later, OP 3 reported. "We've got quite a bonfire here. Bird Dog 6, we need to pull back."

"This is Bird Dog 6 actual. I understand you need to withdraw. Identify any hostiles on your front and maintain contact if you can."

"Roger. This is OP 3. Since we forgot to bring the hot dogs and marshmallows, we are moving."

While topside had been getting rambunctious, things also got interesting down the rabbit hole.

"This is Lily 1," Megan's computer said on net. "Back Door, you have hostiles five minutes out."

"Understood, Lily 1. We will engage them one minute out."

After serious consideration, involving a lot of input both from the deck and orbit, the break in the track had been set up three kilometers away from the first Marine fire team. Closer might have been better, but the shock or air wave traveling ahead of the maglev train was a major concern.

Most human underground maglev trains operated in a vacuum. The Iteeche models did not. They'd tried it several thousand years ago and had an incident where several important people, along with thousands of not important people had suffocated when an accident halted a train. Now, there were vents along the tracks to shoot air from the front and suck it out behind the train.

Sensors had done their best to discover the vent holes, but to no avail. There had been no traffic, and the vents had stayed unobservable. Reports from orbit now were tracking the approaching train by the venting air before and after it.

Now that it was not necessary to know where the vents were, they were being mapped easily. Such was the way of war. Still, Megan set up some fans at the bottom of the vents to blow air up. That got a breeze coming down the main rabbit hole and started clearing the smoke and gas out of the tunnel.

As planned, the track break had been arranged in the middle of a gentle curve. That meant the LT's helmet camera had a good take of the break but saw nothing further down the track.

"Two minutes out," Lily said. She never got to say, "One minute out." The LT's camera handled that announcement perfectly.

The train came in sight around the curve, racing toward them. Then, in less than a blink of an eye, it shot off the track. The lead car kind of disintegrated against the wall of the tunnel, then careened forward, propelled by both momentum and the cars behind it, to spear itself on the other end of the track break. In a moment, the train was nothing but a heap of small fragments, crashing together, bouncing off the deck, bulkhead, and overhead. Large pieces became medium pieces, and those were soon reduced to tiny bits of metal.

Somewhere in all that mess, were likely Iteeche bodies. However, with all the flying metal, the flesh and blood was reduced to an insignificant amount.

All of this passed in a second or two while everyone on net was too shocked to breathe.

"Lily, could you slow the video down and run it again?" Megan said as the dust of what had once been a moving structure began to settle.

Now, the horror ran on the command net in slow motion. The LT's camera had been enhanced to 120 frames per second, well above what the human eye could track. Now it was played back at 12 frames per second. The 3 second crash now took half a minute.

Megan still found it hard to breathe during it.

"Bird Dog 6 actual to Back Door. Extend your perimeter at least three more clicks. Look for a good place to cut the track."

"Aye, aye, sir."

Thus ended the first battle of Back Door. No doubt, there would be more.

"Lily, do you have sensors on the other side of the track?"

"Megan, I'm getting reports from fifty clicks down the track. There's another curve nine clicks farther out. Should I begin cutting the track there?"

"We'll need an hour and a half to get there," the LT said.

"However, if your computer says it's a nice curve, I'd suggest that we use it. Hitting the wall at three hundred klicks an hour really does a number on these things."

"Lily will begin the cut," Megan said.

"They're on their way. We should have a solid cut in fifteen minutes," her computer reported to the humans on line.

"This is Bird Dog 6 actual. Do we need to go nine klicks back? Could we do it closer?"

"That depends on what you'd do if you commanded a follow-up strike team, Sir," Megan said. "You know the first team went off the air suddenly. You have no report back from it. When would you slow the train and possibly deploy your troops?"

The major chewed on that question for a while. "You say you can have the cut in fifteen minutes?" he finally said.

"That includes travel time and time for the nanos to chew up the track," Lily said. "I have them working to chew a wedge out of the track first. That way, even if we haven't got a full break, the train will take a nose dive into the track ahead. We should have that in eleven minutes, including travel and initial destruction."

"Very good. Proceed. Bird Dog 6 out."

SOME BOSS'S TOES GOT STEPPED ON, Lily said.

WE WERE BOTH GOOD, TACTFUL LITTLE SUBOR-DINATES, Megan answered.

I DON'T LIKE BEING DOUBTED.

DON'T TAKE IT PERSONALLY. HE WAS DOUBTING ME AS MUCH AS YOU.

I'LL TALK TO MOM ABOUT GETTING YOU A PROMOTION.

NO, LILY. I'VE STILL GOT TWO YEARS IN GRADE AS A LIEUTENANT. I DON'T WANT ALL THE EXTRA BOSS

TIME I'D HAVE TO SPEND IF I WAS A LIEUTENANT COMMANDER. REMEMBER, KRIS HAD A SQUADRON WHEN SHE WAS THAT RANK.

OH, RIGHT. STILL, YOU SHOULDN'T HAVE TO ANSWER TO KNUCKLEHEADS LIKE THE MAJOR.

DIDN'T HE HAVE A GOOD POINT?

OF COURSE. I WAS ALREADY DOING IT.

SO, YOU WERE BOTH RIGHT, AND WE DIDN'T WASTE ALL THAT MUCH TIME MAKING SURE WE WERE RIGHT. LILY, THE NAVY LIKES TO CHECK AND DOUBLE CHECK STUFF. IT'S JUST THE NAVY WAY.

YEAH, YEAH. THE RIGHT WAY, THE WRONG WAY, AND THE NAVY WAY. MOM IS ALWAYS SAYING THAT.

The idea that human foibles were a regular topic of conversation between the Magnificent Nelly and her kids brought a smile to Megan's lips. She often wondered how this symbiotic relationship between super computers and Kris Longknife's command team was going to work its way out.

With luck, she'd be around to see all the fun.

Meanwhile, Megan had a battle to track ahead of her. So far it had been quiet.

Then, suddenly, it wasn't.

21

"**W**e have noise on the track ahead of us." Lily reported on the command net. "I make it a maglev warming up in the target redoubt station."

"This is Bird Dog 6 actual. Initiate rail cut three klicks ahead of our advanced position."

"This is Lily 1. There is a small curve at four klicks. May I recommend it for the break?"

"Bird Dog 6 actual. Affirmative. Go ahead with the break four klicks out. Front Door, advance one more klick, then . . ." there was a pause as the major reconsidered ordering the team to dig in. "Establish defensive positions."

"Aye, aye, sir," came back from the platoon's LT.

"Captain Sung, how close to the fun do you want to get?" Megan said on a private channel she selected for just the two of them.

"Megan, your guess is as good as mine. How close do you want to get?"

Megan hefted her M-12 carbine. Below the 4mm rifled

barrel was the gaping maw of a 25mm grenade launcher. If push came to shove, Megan wanted to be as pushy as she could. Still, her job was to command an army of nanites. She and Lily also had to keep control of the Iteeche communications net. If they slipped up, those autocannons could become very nasty.

"What do you say we stay two klicks back. It may not be as much fun, but it may let us put the most hurt to our beloved Planetary Overlord."

"I'm all for that," the captain said, agreeing with the lieutenant.

They advanced cautiously. Problem was, in a tunnel with solid concrete all around and just one large magnetic rail in the middle, there was not a lot of places to be cautious behind. The rail stretched forward, as far as Megan could see without increasing the amplitude of her faceplate.

Clearly, if it came to a fire fight, it was going to be a short and bloody affair.

"Lily 1 here. From the noise I'm getting from the rail, a maglev vehicle has departed the station in the target redoubt," the computer reported on net.

"Any idea how soon it will get to us?" the major asked.

"Ten minutes at most. Longer, depending on how long it takes them to get up to full speed, assuming they don't keep their speed down."

"A lot of variables," Megan added. She didn't want the major coming back with some crack about her computer being indecisive.

"Understood. The situation topside is getting a bit warm. The OPs are falling back to the base. I'm moving non-essential personnel down the rabbit hole. Do you have plans for closing the hole?"

"Ask the engineers if they dropped with enough Smart

Metal. I can use nanos to collapse the walls of the shaft, but it would be best to do it slowly, and have a solid dome down below to catch the rubble and stop any explosives that come our way."

"This is Eager Beaver 6 actual. We're ready to plug the hole. We're dropping down now and will prepare that effort when we're down there."

"Thank you, Eager Beaver," the major said to all his engineering platoon.

Megan was beginning to be curious about her situation. "Back Door, was your train preceded by wind and over pressure?"

"Affirmative. I noticed dust coming my way even before the train came in sight."

"We're not getting any of that," Captain Sung remarked.

"Nope. I think our train is advancing with a lot more caution than the last one."

"We don't want that," Quinn said.

"Nope." Megan trotted over to the wall and leaned her forehead against it. She knew the Iteeche data cables were just a few centimeters away from her helmet, but she was getting no feel for the net.

She chipped off a few nanos from what was left of her Smart Metal™ belt (her satchel was long gone), and had them drill through the wall to the comm line.

Still no access.

"Captain, will you help me get my helmet off?"

"Are you crazy?"

"No. I'm just a Longknife," Megan said, with resignation in her voice.

When the Navy captain didn't move to help her, she added. "I've got to do what I do best, and that means getting my helmet off. Please?"

The officer looked at her like she was crazy, but she did as Megan asked.

As soon as they popped the helmet seal, Quinn hit Megan's neck with a broad-spectrum antidote for most known gases that disabled humans.

Meanwhile, Megan was tasting stale air and smoke. She coughed, and her eyes teared up. One of the extra modifications she'd had done on her suit was an additional oxygen line leading from her suit. She settled it against her nose and put the cord over her head.

Now, at least, she didn't have to breathe that stink, although it still seeped in through her mouth no matter how tightly she kept it closed.

She coughed, again. Likely she'd be coughing a lot.

Now, Megan leaned her bare forehead against the smooth, cool concrete and let her mind, or maybe just her imagination, wander. Her first image was of many segmented insects, skittering through a midnight landscape.

She blinked twice, both to work the smog out of her eyes, and to change her vision.

Now Megan was in the data stream. Lily was quickly converting the Iteeche data into something that a human could understand.

In another blink, it all came into focus.

Now Megan could see through the Iteeche cameras scattered up and down the tunnel. Lily overlaid the input from the human nanos and the picture jelled into one seamless vision. Another blink and the picture highlighted the auto-cannons as well as the claymores. Everything that Megan controlled was there for her to use.

She spotted the train, still well down the track and out of view of the Marines.

"Longknife 2 here. The train is coming," Megan reported

on net, and got the taste of metal, acid, and crap for her reward. "It's coming a lot slower than the last train. Wait one."

For fifteen seconds, Megan tracked the train. "It's slowing. They aren't going to go slamming off the track a second time."

"Bird Dog 6 actual. Roger. Front Door, prepare to receive an infantry assault."

"Front Door. Roger."

The train went into the curve at a speed that still sent it off of the track and slamming into the tunnel wall. This time, however, there was no smashing into little tiny pieces. Instead, the lead car just slid along the tunnel wall, screeching like the devil's own fingernail on hell's chalkboard. When it reached the other end of the break in the track, it quickly came to rest.

Just as quickly, troops began to pour out of the train. Officers gave orders, NCO's shouted commands, and the infantry formed up into squads and began to cautiously make their way toward Megan's Marines.

There was no cover. No cover for either of the forces. If they got into a fire fight, there would be blood all over the place. The side with the deepest reserve would be the one to win.

From the looks of all the troops dismounting that wrecked train, the Iteeche had brought a battalion to fight her small platoon.

"Front Door, this is Longknife 2. May I suggest that you fall back a klick from your present advanced position?"

"Bird Dog 6 actual. Longknife 2, you want to explain yourself?"

"The force on our front appears to be battalion strength. They are shaking out into what looks like three companies forward, with one well back. I intend to engage the battalion when they are all fully committed and advancing toward us. Until the reserve gets away from the train, I can't effectively engage them."

There was a bit of a pause on the net while several Marine officers mulled over what a Navy lieutenant had just told them. That this lieutenant was a Longknife probably weighed heavily in their consideration.

"Bird Dog 6 actual. You sound like you intend to wipe them out all by your lonesome."

"Longknife 2 here. That is exactly what I intend, sir."

There was only a brief pause before, "Bird Dog 6 actual to Longknife 2. Proceed."

In one part of Megan's visor, the humans withdrew. Unfortunately, withdrawal did little to provide them cover. The tunnel stretched long and straight both in front and behind them.

In the distance, armed Iteeche in light blue field dress began to work their way around the curve that their train had not been able to complete. They moved at a low crouch.

The range was almost three klicks, a long shot even for a trained sniper. Iteeche NCO's ordered trigger-pullers to keep advancing. They gave a quick kick in the butt to any young private that went to ground.

On the human side, the NCOs walked backwards slowly, making sure this retrograde did not turn into a running route. The professionalism of the human soldiers showed. They, too, walked backwards. At least two-thirds of them did. The other third was facing to the rear, eyes open for any unexpected surprise.

Back at the train, the last of the troops had dismounted. They formed up behind a pair of rocket launchers. A driver brought the wheeled vehicle forward at the pace of the infantry. Mounted behind his head were two stubby rocket launchers. Gunners sat beside each launcher, sighting them down the tunnel. Between the launchers, a vehicle commander sat on an upraised seat, peering down range, hunting for a target.

If Megan let either of those rigs get around the bend in the tunnel, their rockets would slaughter her force.

Megan began to plan her attack carefully. She had auto-cannons under her control as well as claymores. Which weapon would get rid of this threat most effectively and most efficiently?

Megan chose the claymores. She also chose only those on the right side of the tunnel. She had a hunch that that would give her an advantage.

The battalion commander was a pretty savvy guy. He had his troops spread out, both across the width of the tunnel and well back. His main body was spread along a lot of the tunnel.

However, whoever built the defenses of this thing had not spared on cost. There were a lot of claymores.

For the main force, Megan chose two daisy chains. One started aft and moved forward. The second started forward and moved aft. They met in the middle. The poor sods there would know what was coming for them. They would have time to scream, but not much more.

For the reserve, including the two rocket launchers, Megan activated four claymores all at once.

The claymore darts were much more crude than those used by humans. Megan only lost ten percent of the nanos she had in the blast area. The same could not be said for the Iteeche.

The heavy darts slammed into flesh and bone. They crushed, slashed, and smashed. The left wall of the tunnel became a horrid modern artwork of blood, gore, and chunks of bleeding flesh. Here and there, a skull hung nailed to the wall.

Only a psychotic serial killer could have taken pleasure from this macabre work of art.

Megan wanted to puke.

"Megan," came a soft, almost motherly voice. Not what Megan would ever have expected from Kris Longknife. "Is this your first time?"

"Yes, Admiral," the lieutenant managed to get out as she struggled to swallow down what wanted to come up.

"You likely need to throw up. Go ahead. Your helmet is off, isn't it?"

Megan tried to answer "yes." However, her mouth was too busy emptying her stomach. Said mouth had no spare time for talking, even to give an admiral an answer.

While Captain Sung pulled Megan's air line out of the way, as well as her hair, the lieutenant just let her stomach take control of her entire body. She retched from the tip of her toenails to the longest hair on her head.

She'd gotten sick from being drunk just once in college. She'd sworn never again. Now she had the vomiting without any of the fun of the partying or drinking.

It didn't help that her nose piece had come loose, and she was breathing in the acrid smog of the tunnel. That smog that was now heavy with the sharp tang of explosives, the stink of ripped bowels, and heavy with a mist of blood.

She vomited until she had nothing more to bring up, and still her stomach retched.

"Does it look worse than you expected?" was again in the soft voice so unusual to the princess and admiral.

"So much worse. I never thought of how it would stink."

"If you're finished throwing up, you might want to put your helmet back on."

That command seemed to have been shared with Captain Sung. Maybe the captain was included in all of this. Certainly, she'd been included in the horror Megan had made.

A nearby Marine provided a canteen. Two swigs from it that were spit out were followed by one that managed to stay in Megan's stomach.

No sooner than she handed back the canteen, than her helmet was quickly back on and locked down in place. The air in her helmet stank and left her coughing. Megan toggled her oxygen and quickly vented what was around her face out to what passed for atmosphere.

It still took her several deep breaths and quite a few sips of water before she could quit coughing. Megan would have liked to vent her helmet once or twice more, but her oxygen load was small. The CO_2 scrubbers were supposed to recycle her oxygen and save her from having to lug around big tanks. However, the standard equipment was not meant to work in this situation.

A combat engineer motored along the maglev track in something that looked like a miniaturize version of what lay wrecked farther down the track. The engineer controlled it; this was no time for trusting automatic controls. There were seats for twelve marines facing out from a storage area that ran down the center of the contraption. It was picking up troopers as it moved forward.

When it approached Megan's position, it slowed down. A Marine grabbed a fresh oxygen cylinder from the stowage rack, dismounted, and trotted to set it down next to the two Navy officers. Then she dashed to catch up with her ride.

Back aboard, the gal gave Megan a cheery wave, then turned her attention to what lay ahead.

Megan drained her helmet three times, using up much of her old oxygen supply, then Quinn detached the old one and inserted the new one.

"I'm showing oxygen flow and full green," Megan said.

Behind her, the captain checked the backup readout on the bottle. "I show it full green also."

"Megan, before you head up the tunnel," Kris Longknife said gently, "I want you to know that you did not kill those Iteeche. Yes, you pulled the trigger, but every officer between you and I would have given you that order. We all carry the responsibility for that horror painted on the walls of that tunnel. They probably were good people, but they were serving bad leaders. They got between us and the guy who deserves to die. It's sad, but it has happened many, many times during my time in the Navy. It will happen many, many times in yours."

"I understand, ma'am. I'm better. I'm ready to do the job I came here to do."

"Very good, Lieutenant. Carry on."

A transport sped toward their position. Megan stepped away from the wall and waved it down.

The engineer slowed the vehicle. Eager Marines filled the first few seats. Megan and Quinn took the two rearmost seats and the rig sped up.

There were more fights ahead.

22

The battle topside was rapidly being won . . . by the forest fire. The humans withdrew ahead of it. What flames did to the Iteeche was not something to think about.

With the fire fast approaching, the reserve platoon was sending more and more of its troops down the rabbit hole. The last two to rappel were the LT and the platoon sergeant. As soon as they were down, the engineers set about sealing them in. They plugged the rabbit hole with a dome of Smart Metal™, then had nanos collapse the tunnel above them.

The Iteeche would not be dropping explosives down that hole.

Of course, that left other holes. They now had a map of just where the vent holes were along the train track. The engineers sent their own nanos up those holes to find the lids and weld them shut. They were complex valves, meant to both let air in or out. For now, they could not open for anything.

Nonetheless, Megan set up nano observers. If any vent was approached, she wanted to seal it deeper down.

By now, all of the Front Door platoon was on the far side of the train wreck.

"Bird Dog 6 actual to Longknife 2. Have you got any activity further down the tunnel?

Megan stretched out her vision as far down the tunnel as she could . . . and found herself looking at the station below the target redoubt.

"Bird Dog 6, I've used opposition video to check the track up to the train station. It shows everything clear and no activity. However, I emphasize I'm using their video. If they're using our video, this tunnel is empty."

"Understood. How far down do you have actual oversight?"

"I have nanos half-way to the target."

"Front Door, this is Bird Dog 6 actual, initiate Cobra."

"Aye, aye, sir."

Two of the small maglev Marine taxis sped down the track, picking up troops and pushing them to the front. The third one pulled up beside Megan and Quinn. "You want a ride forward, ma'ams?" a Marine asked. "I'm told they want you closer to the front."

No one had told Megan, but then again, Cobra was equally unknown. However, considering what she'd done to the advancing Iteeche battalion a ways back without telling anyone in the chain of command above her, she really had no right to complain.

"I'm guessing we missed a staff meeting," Quinn quipped.

The two of them boarded the taxi. It moved forward, adding more Marines until it was full, then it sped forward.

Two or three klicks farther down the tunnel, they came

upon a squad of Marines humping their gear forward. They moved as if they had nothing to fear. Megan didn't usually see Marines so optimistic this close to hostile forces. She leaned a bit off the taxi.

Ahead of her and her vehicle was a different kind of rig. Likely this was a reconfiguration of the two taxis into a completely different type of vehicle.

It still had room for twelve troopers, although they were packed in tighter on a narrower body. The front of the taxi now had a shield covering most of the distance to the bulkhead and overhead. The driver was now flanked by two Marines. They each had a hand resting on the butt end of something that probably looked a whole lot deadlier from the other side.

The armored rig glided forward, not as fast as Megan's taxi was approaching, but a lot faster than a Marine could walk.

Now Megan realized why she was needed forward.

Her nanos were 15 klicks farther up the tunnel, about half-way to the target's train station. The question was, what was between here and there? As the taxi caught up with the front, Megan called for a stop.

While Megan waited for her nanos to punch their way into the upper comm line on the right-hand side of the tunnel, the taxi offloaded its Marines and began to back up, picking up speed as it went. The Marines, now on foot, started hoofing it after the slowly advancing armor.

As soon as the nanos had tapped into the line, Megan tried snaking a Smart Metal™ line in and attaching it to her commlink.

This time, it worked. She didn't have to take her helmet off and lean her bare forehead against the wall.

Quickly Megan found herself in the alien data stream.

She followed it forward, taking a peek using the tunnel cameras. For the first twenty klicks, things went fine.

Then she hit a brick wall.

She made several tries to breach or climb or dig under the wall, but there was just nothing there. Her best guess would be that the line had been physically cut.

That left Megan and her Marines a good ten klicks short of the station. Very likely, those ten klicks were under total Iteeche control. Any humans who ventured into that space would face autocannons and claymores.

Megan frowned. "This is Longknife 2 to all commanders on this channel. The hostiles seem to have acquired data dominance over the last ten klicks of this tunnel. If we have to force it, we'll have to fight for every centimeter of it."

"This is Bird Dog 6 actual, roger that. Front Door, advanced up to the twelve-klick mark as quickly as you dare. Cautiously advance after that to the ten-klick mark. Wait there for further orders. Longknife 2, can you check the track ahead of our advance?"

"I've got my scouts out as far as I can. I'll need four or five minutes to cover the distance to the ten-klick mark."

"Front Door, slow down when Longknife 2 tells you to."

"Aye, aye, sir. Longknife 2, am I still in safe territory?"

"You've got about ten klicks that I have under positive observation. You may advance as quickly as you think safe."

"Advancing."

Being lightly loaded, Megan and Quinn were able to walk faster than the Marines. They caught up with them, then passed them. Megan had expected a few quips as they passed the heavily loaded gravel crunchers, but the Marines were either too tired or too wary to joke.

The taxi, fully loaded with Marines, shot up the tunnel, but slid to a halt beside the two Navy officers. Two Marines got off, the two Navy types got on. The taxi took off with a rapid pace and ten minutes later, they were on the tail of the battle rig. It was slowing as it approached the fifteen-kilometer mark.

"Longknife 2, are you ready to check out the front?" the platoon leader for Front Door asked.

"My nanos have the next three klicks under observation. They can see farther, but I'm not counting anything as fact until I have a nano over it." When this advance had started, the nanos were way ahead. Now, with the maglev rigs, the troops had caught up.

"I like your attitude, ma'am." the platoon leader said.

Two marines dismounted from the rearmost seats. Megan and Quinn boarded it, and the armored rig began to cruise forward cautiously.

On her helmet faceplate, Lily projected the visual reports from the forward scouts. Everything looked quiet, but Megan knew how deceiving that could be.

At the twelve-klick mark, the armored rig slowed to a crawl. The Marines dismounted. Two of them on each side edged around the armored shield. They began a cautious walk ahead of the advancing rig. They kept well away from the snout of the rocket launchers.

Indeed, two of them carried rocket launchers of their own.

Apparently both Megan and the platoon leader were glad to have their front under observation by human eyeballs.

For a long minute, they made their way cautiously along the single rail.

Behind them, Megan heard the slight whine of the taxi arriving. Soon, another twelve Marines were walking along behind the shield. Several of them were engineers. Four of them pulled small two-wheeled carts loaded high with gear that Megan had no idea what to do with, but looked deadly, nonetheless.

As they came up to the ten-klick mark, Megan dismounted.

Again, she had her nanos snake through invisible cracks to find the comm line. Once they had patched into it and other nanos had enlarged the cracks to allow a gossamer comm line to snake in, Megan tried looking up the line.

"Bird Dog? Front Door. We are still downstream from the break. May I suggest we advance another hundred meters?"

"Roger that. This is Bird Dog 6 actual. Front Door, advance at your discretion."

The armored rig began to move forward at the speed of a slow walk. The eerie silence from farther down the track set the hackles on the back of Megan's neck on edge. The Iteeche had to be up to something. Two wrecked trains were a flaming datum that could not be ignored.

Still, the view up the track seemed to show nothing. They reached a hundred meters beyond their last stop. The Marines walking ahead of the vehicle went into a prone firing position.

Megan again had her nanites drill through the wall. Again, she found the cable. Again, she tapped into the line.

This time, there was no line to tap into. No comm line at all. It was as if whatever had been there had been pulled out, leaving nothing but an empty conduit.

Quickly, Megan advised higher-ups of her situation. Even as she talked, she stooped down to drill for the lower communication conduit. Again, the passage was totally empty.

Now Megan had nanites drilling for all four of the

remaining conduits: one buried in the deck, one in the over-head, and two in the opposite wall.

At the same time, she sent nano scouts down the two conduits she'd examined to see what they might find.

One after the other, each of the four conduits came up empty.

"Longknife 2 here. They've stripped out their comm lines. I would assume that that means they have no comm access to the autocannons and the claymores. However, I would not bet money on that."

"This is Bird Dog 6 actual. Anybody got any ideas about this?"

The net offered back only silence.

23

"Okay, here's what we're gonna do," said the major on net. "Longknife 2, can you identify the locations of the autocannons and claymores as well as gas cylinders?"

"Yes, sir, I have them mapped."

"Front Door, get a couple of your engineers with rocket launchers out in front, and when you have a line of sight on one of those, have them blow it out of the wall."

"Aye, aye, sir."

"Longknife 2. You have any idea what you can do?"

"I've scouted all the way to the break in the line. It's at the train station. I'm infiltrating nanos into the redoubt. I'll start hunting for our Target Number One, the Planetary Overlord, and see what I can do to change his mind about resisting us."

"You do that. Okay, everyone, let's move out very cautiously."

So, the Marines began a slow, wary advance. Megan had

Lily keep one eye on the Marines, checking to make sure every identified threat was neutralized.

Meanwhile, Megan got busy marshalling her nanites. Scouts spread out from the beachhead she'd established in the train station. She had transporter nanos pick up the eater nanos, and sent teams down the line. No telling what she'd need in the fortress.

She and Lily also put together a dozen command drones, a large construct of nanos with more computing power than most. If Megan lost control of the invasion force for any reason, these command drones would take over control of the scouts and eaters and conduct a systematic sweep of the redoubt.

Although Megan didn't like the idea, if she did not have positive control and these drones identified the primary target, they were authorized to take him down, along with most of the people around him.

Megan had about ten percent of her forces inside the fortress when the Iteeche changed the game.

Suddenly, the conduit that Megan was sending her forces through got blocked. From the reports back, it looked like sand had been dumped in the hole and was being forced further down it.

Megan sent scouts to wind their way through the particles, however, on the other side they found a wet slurry of concrete mixed with fly ash.

"Someone doesn't want us in there," Megan grumbled. "Lily, send everything we've got up any of the conduits we can and move them past the train station and into the fortress."

"Doing it, Megan."

The computer sent every nano they had down the five remaining openings, but quickly, every one of them was blocked. Meanwhile, Lily had sent repeater nanos down the tunnel to establish a comm link between herself and the train station. It was just going operational when the last conduit got jammed up.

Now, Lily pulled every nano they had in the different conduits and sent them down the tunnel as fast as they could fly.

However, that soon met with a brick wall as well.

The exits from the station into the redoubt were close, locked, and welded shut.

Megan and Lily were now cut off from the several thousand nanos that were spreading inside the fortress. The Navy lieutenant would have liked to infiltrate more, but she had to settle for only 25% of what she had available.

If she wanted more in there, chasing after the great man, er, Iteeche, she'd have to blow those doors.

However, the Iteeche had no intention of letting the humans get anywhere close to those doors.

24

"This is Longknife 2, Bird Dog 6, we've got defensive activity just this side of the train station. They're putting up a sand bag wall and fronting it with sheet metal."

"You know, Longknife, I don't think they like us."

"I'm getting that same feeling, sir."

"Front Door, tell your fire support to let those hostiles know that they've hurt our feelings."

"Message on the way, sir."

A moment later, smoke filled the cavern as two rockets left the launchers on the armored maglev train. A few seconds later, two more hand-held launchers sent rockets trailing after the first two.

The Iteeche likely did not think such an attack was possible. Between the two opposing forces, there was a gentle curve in the track. There was no way to see around it.

Except for the fact that the human missiles were self-guiding. They made a turn in the gentle curve and arrowed straight for their target.

Through her scouts, Megan had a ringside seat for the fun. She had Lily send the visual stream to both Bird Dog and Front Door.

The first two rockets hit the barricade, pierced through the thin steel sheets, and buried themselves in the sandbags before they exploded. When they did, shards of steel and sand flew in all directions.

The cloud of sand had hardly begun to settle when the second pair of rockets flew into it. Then, they flew right out of it. Without hitting anything, the two rockets exploded, first one, then the second, showering deadly flechettes up and down the tunnel.

Those who had been far enough away to not be blown to pieces by the first two rockets died almost instantly as the fog of needle-thin flechettes stripped the flesh from their bones.

Those farther up the tunnel suffered worse. The tiny needles were not concentrated enough or had slowed down too much to kill them instantly. Instead, the tiny metal darts buried themselves in the flesh or sensitive places like eyes . . . and the Iteeche had four of those. In pain beyond imagination, they crumbled to the ground. Shock quickly drove them to convulsions and then death.

Those deaths, however, involved a lot of screaming in agony.

Those screams bothered Megan, but she had other problems at the moment. "Ah, Longknife 2 here, crew, before you send another batch of rockets downrange, give me a heads up. I lost some nanos in your fun and games."

"Sorry about that," came from the LT. "We'll keep you in the loop next time."

Clearly, there was going to be a next time. In the tunnel, the Marines continued to advance as engineers and rockets knocked out autocannons from the overhead. They also dug out claymores and gas canisters from the walls.

Ahead of them, the tunnel began to fill with smoke and rubble. The humans were all in armored spacesuits, so the air quality did not bother them. However, the lowered visibility was not greeted with enthusiasm. Megan had to thicken up the shell of the scout and repeater nanos to keep positive observation of the rail path ahead of them.

Meanwhile, the Iteeche set about building another sandbagged position, exactly like the one the Marines had just destroyed.

The troops came to the curve in the tunnel. They continued blowing up Iteeche threats. However, about halfway through the turn, a Marine sniper took up a position tight against the wall. He squeezed off two rounds before fire drove him back from his position.

Ammunition seemed to be no problem with the Iteeche, so now, a lot of bullets flew at and around the humans. The bullets ricocheted of walls and pinged off armor.

The advancing teams withdrew behind the vehicle's shield. It was time to rethink the situation.

The protection on the armored train reoriented itself. Now the right end extended forward, and the left end bent back. It effectively created a thirty-degree angle with the right wall of the tunnel. With the shield at the angle of ricochet, any bullet hitting it would not only face armor effectively twice as thick, but also hit it at the perfect angle to bounce it off.

Again, the sniper advanced. This time, into the tight angle in front. A small hole formed in the armor plate, right next to the tunnel wall, and the sniper leveled his gun.

One shot. Two shots. Three shots. The protective armor in front of the train showed dents, but only temporarily.

Immediately, the dent flattened out. Meanwhile, from the other side of the plate came the sound of bullets ricocheting off the armor, then the left wall, then whining as the badly deformed round wobbled back the way it came.

The fire didn't last long as the sniper responded to fusillades with single shots. With a final noisy volley, the din from downrange ceased.

"No target up," the sniper reported on net.

The train began to advance again, this time at a crawl. Now, the rockets fired to knock out the autocannons and dig out the problems in the walls were from the two rocket launchers on the train.

The fog in front of them got thicker and thicker. Tests showed that some of the cloudy gases had Sarin in its deadly combination.

Again, for the Marines, that was no problem. They had no skin exposed. However, that didn't turn out to be the situation for the Iteeche soldiers defending the new position outside of the station.

At least two of them were seen to struggle and fall over their parapet. Several bolted for the station and only got a few steps. Closer examination showed that the Iteeche had breathing masks, but their uniforms provided no protection against skin contact with the droplets of deadly gas now floating in the air.

"How do we run a decontamination for our own people when we force our way into the station?" the LT asked on net.

You could hear the crickets in the silence.

"Longknife 1 here. We don't. If we find some showers, use them. If we don't, that's their problem. They're the ones that set out the damn gas."

Megan remembered that Kris Longknife had once tried

to have a friendly, family talk with Grampa Alex, only to have him gas several floors below his penthouse to kill her if she didn't give up the uninvited intrusion.

The admiral did not like Sarin gas.

With no further fire from the station, the pace of their advance picked up. Now the fight was more Megan's than anyone else's.

Indeed, if Megan could get to the primary target, they might very well not have to fight their way through all the corridors of this labyrinth.

25

With poison gas swelling all around her, Megan concentrated with Lily on reestablishing communications with the nanos she already had in the fortress. That and reinforcing them. They needed to get the guy before he made his escape.

The hill above the redoubt had been lazed hard and heavy. Exits that way were rather thick with molten stone.

A maglev train pulled out from a side track. It didn't get very far before a human rocket wrecked the thing.

If the planetary overlord intended to escape, his options were rapidly evaporating.

Rather than mess with the thick metal hatch and the door that was welded shut, the nanos found a weakness in the wall that they could exploit faster. Soon, there was a hole barely a quarter of a micrometer wide. Nanos streamed down it and through the steel reinforced concrete to begin spreading out inside the fortress.

It took Megan a minute, but soon she could report, "I'm

back in contact with the command drones I sent through. They've established contact with the nanos that got left behind when they sealed the fortress. The first seven levels of the redoubt have been mapped. There's a lot of nothing up there. I've got the reinforcements that I'm sending in looking for some place below the level of the train. I'm guessing this guy has jumped in the deepest hole available here and pulled the mountain over the top of him."

"That is a good guess," came in Kris's voice.

"I'm having Lily put together some more command drones. I want to keep an eye on the other side of this wall. Oh, yeah, I most certainly do."

"A problem?" the major immediately asked.

"Yep. A problem. Someone is walking a large satchel toward the door. I think they need a brain aneurysm," Megan said, and sent fifty or so nanos up the Iteeche's beak.

The nanos included anything that was close at hand. Several of the nanos were transport nanos hauling eater nanos. Suddenly, teeth designed to break down rocks and stones were chomping on someone's nasal passages.

Blood began to trickle from his nose. He just had time to pause in his tracks and touch one finger to his beak before blood began to gush. He dropped his satchel and began running back the way he'd come.

"Lily, cease the attack."

"Done, Megan."

Still, no more than a dozen steps farther and the big Iteeche fell, sliding along the floor, smearing his blood in a trail behind him. Someone ran out to try to help him.

"Longknife 1 here. Leave that one alone. Medics aren't targets," Kris ordered.

"Yes, Megan," Captain Sung half-shouted.

"If he takes off running for the satchel, he's a target again," Megan said.

This was a good thing, because after a moment, the bleeding Iteeche went into convulsions and bled out. Someone, likely an officer, started bellowing for the lifesaver to get the bomb to the door and pull the tab.

"Kill him," Megan ordered Lily.

This fellow didn't make it as far as the other guy. He spotted the first hint of blood flowing from his beak, turned, and raced back toward the sandbagged barricade where the officers huddled.

Said officer now was waving a sidearm at the poor fellow. The guy refused to turn around and the officer shot him down, then ordered another Iteeche soldier, at gunpoint, to start walking toward the explosives and the door.

"Megan, I think that officer just won himself a death warrant," Kris said.

"Do it," Megan ordered Lily.

The soldier was backing up slowly, his hands up, keeping his eyes on the threatening officer. He paused to point as the first trickle of blood trickling down his superior's beak.

The officer checked and stared, all four eyes wide, at the blood on his finger.

He threw down his weapon and fled. With the sandbags in place, Megan missed when he went down. However, a scout quickly furnished a picture of the scene.

The officer was down, begging for someone to help him as he crawled, blood streaming from his beak.

No one paused to help him. His soldiers were busy throwing down their guns and running away from their position. Some tried to race down the tunnel. Others threw themselves against the doors that were welded shut.

Finally, several of them raced off to a series of business offices well to the side of things. There, they barricaded themselves in and sat huddled together, as non-threatening as a seven- or eight-foot tall Iteeche could be.

"You know, you have to wonder how stupid an officer can be," Kris Longknife said on net. "We're drilling tiny holes to keep that witch's brew of poison out of the bunker's main air supply. That idiot seemed hell bent on blowing the fortress wide open to that junk."

"No accounting for smarts," Jack answered.

"I'm taking control of all the possible avenues from there to here," Megan said. "I want to stop the next stupid senior officer just as dead as this one."

"Don't go developing a sour attitude toward superior officers, cousin," Kris said.

"How could I possibly do that, being a Longknife and all?" Megan answered back, her voice all saccharin and high fructose corn syrup.

While the command drones conducted a search of all nine floors identified in the bunker, Megan took charge of the search above, beside, and below the train station.

Above them, she found a pair of Iteeche pushing a four-wheeled cart full of what sure looked like explosives. Behind them was an officer, his sidearm out.

He had on a gas mask. However, it didn't take Lily long to infiltrate his breather. When he developed a nose bleed, he ripped the mask off, glared at the blood in it, then bolted for the nearest door out.

He didn't make it.

However, the two privates did.

Lily took care to figure out where the detonator was,

disabled it, and posted observers in the room to make sure no one chose to do mischief here again.

Below the station were only service and maintenance tunnels. The eating nanos went to work on the hinges of those doors and locks. Soon, they were too sabotaged to open.

Nanos also went down the track to make sure a train from the next bunker couldn't surprise them. The ships in orbit were looking for any evidence that a train was shooting air out ahead of itself or sucking air back in behind it.

None showed. Still, Megan wanted to know it herself.

Meanwhile, Lily was devoting at least half of her attention to the search for the next level or levels down.

There were no stairs. There was no elevator that went down from the station's floor.

Neither Megan nor Lily believed that to be true. The simple fact that they had not found any of the fifty important targets that they had on their list certainly seemed to prove that.

It was the analysis of carpet wear and dirt that finally identified a trail that led to a panel that opened to an elevator.

That led them one floor down to a rather large storage area. It was no surprise that the storage flood had no exit except the elevator down to it.

This time it took a more meticulous search effort. Since the floor was concrete, the nanos went over the walls, looking for any crack. It took fifteen minutes, but they found a section of concrete on the opposite wall that was designed to swing aside.

Now the nanos found an escalator that led down a floor.

And trouble.

This floor was as large as the storage area above.

A fire sprinkler system was filling the air with a fine, but heavy mist.

This would be death to nanos.

"Well, I guess we should have known this was coming," Kris Longknife drawled on net.

26

"This was not unexpected," Nelly said, now on net. "Lily, you know what you need to do."

"You bet, Mom," Megan's computer said, as cheerful as any daughter given a chance to show off in front of her mother.

The nanos, most of which measured only a dozen or so nanometers in size, began to coalesce into larger and larger blobs until they were hovering in the air; they became a collection of small rotary wing craft. As they reached a complete state, they'd guide themselves out into the large expanse of misty but empty space. The first one wove its way erratically across the befogged room.

When nothing shot at it, the next few used a straighter line, but still zigged and zagged to reach the far bulkhead.

Still, no shots were fired.

The helicopter form, however, proved to be just right for the moist conditions. Water formed on the rotors and was quickly slung off by the whirl of the blades. None of the tiny choppers failed to make the crossing. Once there, several of them converted to smaller craft and aimed their sensors at the wall.

It took a while, but it slowly became clear, the access port was not on that wall.

The bastard had changed his practice.

The flying sensors on the far side began to work their way back along the two side walls. Meanwhile, on a hunch, Megan converted the last batch of nanos to glide down the escalator into smaller searchers and sent them out to scout along both sides of the wall with the escalator.

Ten meters off to Megan's right, she found what she was looking for.

Nanos quickly infiltrated the cracks to find an elevator with buttons ready to push. Even one to open the door.

Megan had learned long ago that if you walked too close to Kris Longknife's shadow, someone was likely out to kill you. While the Marine LT and one of his squads was eager to head down, Megan held up a cautious hand.

"Give me a minute to check this out."

She was glad she did.

Two minutes of searching and she discovered what she expected to find.

"This is Longknife 2. I've got an elevator that looks ready to go, but I've also found explosives rigged to the buttons. I'm sending out a nano to see how you really get the door open and moving."

Behind her, eager Marines took a step back. Several took several steps back and sat down on the elevator risers, taking a load off. Smart jarheads.

Before too long, Megan found what she was looking for. In the back wall was a panel superbly hidden that only opened when the right fingerprint was placed in just the right spot. Megan's nanos managed to simulate that finger, and the panel opened.

A moment later, so did the elevator door.

The troops were up on their feet immediately, but again Megan waved them back.

"I don't think we should ride that elevator ourselves. Let me get some scouts out first."

The dive into the elevator shaft turned out to be a very long dive, indeed. The shaft sank a good hundred meters deeper into the mountain before it came to a door. The shaft went deeper, and there were three more doors below the first one.

Lily had the nanos begin to explore everything behind all the doors.

The first door opened into a guard room. Dozens of heavily armed men stood ready while many more lounged about playing games, gambling, sleeping, or enjoying the comforts of some very willing Iteeche females.

Lily and Megan left some killer nanos around but sent more scouts lower.

The next floor was full of pale-skinned male and female Iteeche, many at communication terminals, talking, listening, taking messages, and sending them down a pneumatic tube to the next lower level. There were a few alert guards watching the elevator doors as well as the bureaucrats, but much fewer than on the floor above.

On the third floor down, there were a few comm stations as well as a desk where the messages from the second floor were analyzed and passed along. However, most of the space was taken up by luxurious quarters for 40 of the major political figures on Megan's hit list. Them and their bevy of lovely girls.

Away from the elevator, there were 40 luxurious apartments. There was even a restaurant for fine dining.

There would be no suffering or deprivations for these guys during this little war.

Of guards, there were only four. Apparently, the rank that had its privileges didn't want the guards too informed about those privileges. There was no access except the elevator to this and the fourth floor. Those armored elevator doors had controls that locked them shut.

Those with rank and privileges did not want to be disturbed.

No surprise. The bottom floor proved to be spacious to the point of palatial.

Here was the Planetary Overlord with ten of his closest hench-Iteeche. Oh, and three or four girls for every one of them.

Of guards, there was only one. He was a massive Iteeche. You could tell by the color of his robes that he had been in service to the overlord since he was a child. There had been several attempts to suborn the guard. All had ended badly for those who tried it. This was shown by proudly displaying stripes on his sleeve.

That guard had the one machine pistol on the floor. The only automatic swung from the hips of the overlord. Beyond those two, the rest were at their mercy.

Of course, now all of them were at Megan's mercy.

"Longknife 2 here. Longknife 1, I need some advice."

"I'm listening," came back, soft as a mother's kiss.

"I can take out the number one target. I can take out all fifty-one of the fifty-two major targets, or I can take out any mix of that number. I feel that the final decision is way above my paygrade."

"It is, but how would you do it if the hot potato was in your lap?"

"Clearly, the Overlord must die and deserves to die. Probably, all the men on that bottom floor also deserve a death sentence. There are a few women that seem older. I can't tell if they are sex toys or confidants. I'm divided between sparing them and including them in the execution."

Megan paused, but Kris did not comment so she went on. "As for the third floor, many of them strike me as high-level clan functionaries. However, I don't know which of them have ambition and would be delighted to take a vacuum at the top as a God-given invitation to grab for the purple."

Another pause. The grand admiral still held her silence. "I've been checking over the second and top floor, and I think I've spotted a couple of power brokers. Two of them are at the desk that send down the messages. I think they consider themselves cock of the walk. I also found a couple of officers on the top floor that might be only too willing to make a grab for the crown if they had a chance."

Megan paused before summing up her opinion. "Despite my preference for killing as few as possible, if you left this in my hands, Kris, I'd go for the wide cut. It's better to decapitate this entire command team than risk this place turning into a nursery for tyrants."

"You have good instincts, Lieutenant. I, Her Royal Highness, Grand Admiral Princess Kristine Anne Longknife, order you to execute the decapitation mission as you have defined it."

Megan felt goose bumps all over her body. She'd been around Kris Longknife for going on five years, but she'd never seen her come the full royal princess/grand admiral before.

She was kind of glad she didn't have to stand too long in that presence.

"Aye, aye, Admiral. Our mission is go."

It didn't take Lily long to arrange eighty-nine killer squadrons of nanos. She held them in waiting until she had a deadly swarm for each of those chosen to die.

"I am ready now," Lily announced on net.

Megan waited for two seconds to see if Kris would give the order. Before the silence could go long, she filled it. "Execute the decapitation of the planet Zargoth's political and military command and control personnel."

"The order is given," Lily replied.

It didn't take long for the results to start showing up.

The bottom floor only had nineteen targets, eleven men and eight women. Lily hit them with enough killer nanos that they hardly had time to realize they were dying. The men, with four of the women, were standing around a broad map table, looking at what they knew of the battle for their planet. They seemed content with the situation.

Suddenly, blood began gushing from their beaks. They stared at each other, transfixed by what was happening around the table. Then, almost as one, they collapsed to the floor or sprawled across the table. Blood spread on the maps, marking the end of their rule.

On the third floor, there were more men, forty, marked for death along with nine women. Some were in meetings, others eating. A few of the men were cavorting with women. Two of the women were in bed together with one fellow. Their assigned swarms were smaller than those used on the fourth floor. It took them a bit more time to die. Still, as one, they fell, bleeding and screaming.

Their screams were mingled with those of the female courtesans as they panicked and added to the confusion. That only grew worse, when the four guards also panicked and began spraying automatic weapons fire wildly around the floor.

"Lily, put them down."

It took a long minute to get enough nanos up their beaks. Many of the nanos that had been used were wet with blood and needed time to recover before they could fly.

They got even more vicious as they began to bleed, firing at anything that moved. Over half of the women were dead or seriously wounded before the guards bled out.

The situation on the second floor was less confusing. Fewer people died. Still, the guards panicked and started shooting up anyone close to them or, if they happened to be near someone who died, they shot up anyone around the dying Iteeche.

There were fewer nanos available on the second floor, and it took Lily more time to muster an attack on the gun-wielding guards. Still, in time, they fell, and the more that died, the worse the survivors became. It wasn't as bad of a blood bath as the third floor, but there were still a lot of dead scattered around the different work, food, and rest areas.

Megan turned to the guardroom last, expecting things to be better under control. After all, there were hundreds of soldiers and she only targeted a dozen or so officers for execution.

It didn't work out like she expected.

Many of the officer's dying breaths held orders for one company to attack another. Each officer assumed that one of his fellow leaders had marked him for death.

Soon, one faction was fighting it out with the other. It

was like shooting fish in a barrel. The wall partitions on this floor were thin; they hardly slowed down a bullet, much less stopped one. Somehow a four-way fight developed. The rattle of automatic weapons fire didn't fall silent until there were only five left alive.

Still, those five stalked the others through the carnage. First one, then another, would be found and killed. It ended, fittingly enough, with the last two shooting each other.

"Megan, are you recording this?"

"Yes, Admiral."

"I left Jacques back on the capital. He's going to want to see this." Megan could almost see Kris shaking her head. "This is a part of the Iteeche culture I would not have expected."

"No, ma'am. Neither would I." A shiver shook Megan's entire body, powerful as an earthquake. "I wanted to spare their lives. I really wanted to."

"You did," Kris said. "You did. What they did, they did to themselves. Can you get the elevator working?"

"I think so," Lily said.

"Take the courtesans off the fourth floor first. Keep an eye on them. There may be one that dreams of the purple and becoming a new Empress Theodora."

"Understood, Admiral," Megan said, and personally oversaw the process of bringing the women up the elevator and into the mist-filled room where human guards moved them upstairs.

They were a pretty bedraggled bunch, and after passing through the sprinkler mist, they looked even worse. At the broken escalator, many threw off their sodden, gossamer gowns . . . now totally transparent . . . and walked forward to face their new world naked.

"Megan, can you get me on speakers on every floor of the bunker?" Kris asked.

"The quality won't be so good on the second and third floor of the deep bunker, but the rest of the redoubt should hear you."

"I'm told we've hacked their entire planetary comm net. Let's see how this works."

27

"This is Imperial Admiral of the First Order of Steel Kris Longknife, Royal Highness of the United Societies, Chosen Battle Commander of King Raymond Longknife," Kris said. She knew the Iteeche went in for long names. She wasn't about to short change herself.

"I command the Imperial Navy's Combined Battle Fleets, as well as the battle fleet over your planet, Zargoth. I command the invasion fleet only hours away from orbit," she went on.

"The proper fruit of treason is death, and I have executed your planetary overlord for said treason to his worshipfulness, Your Emperor. Along with him, I have executed his band of mis-chosen clan chiefs and those who served them. Dead as well, are your military commanders that stood ready to obey such treasonous orders."

Kris paused. They now knew who she'd killed. They knew the threat hanging over them. Now to offer the carrot. "All those who are deserving of death are now dead. It remains for you, the living, to choose if you will return to the service your Worshipful Emperor or choose to die. Aboard the invasion fleet are leaders from the clans on your planet, Zargoth. These fine Iteeche are from the faction of your clan who have not raised their banner against their lawful and worshipful Emperor. If you submit to them, you will not be harmed."

This time Kris paused to let that thought sink in. All around this planet, people who had been counting themselves as dead for the last minute or so needed time to realize that life was an option. "If you do not submit, our invasion fleet will destroy your cities and kill you where you stand. Your army has lost its leaders. It cannot help you. If you resist strongly, we will laser your defenses from orbit and melt the rocks into your flaming tombstone.

"The city leaders have two hours to announce their surrender or I will begin destroying your cities from the inside out. Choose wisely. That is all."

Kris eyed the comm unit above the main screen. When it blinked from green to red, she still asked Nelly, "Am I no longer transmitting?"

"The net is now dead," Nelly replied. "We have blocked communication among cities. They still have their local net to check among themselves to see what they want to do, but they can't get any word from city to city to organize resistance."

"Good," Kris said, then turned to reinforcing her ultimatum. "Megan, have you identified any leaders on the second floor of the overlord's private bunker?"

"I can send down the LT with a few rifles to see if anyone will offer up themselves."

"You do that. I'd like to have a few familiar faces backing up what I've just announced. Take five or six of them on a tour of the third and fourth level. Be sure to get some good pictures of the dead with faces easy to identify. Also, don't skimp on panoramic views of those palatial digs. From what I hear, belts have been mighty tight of late."

"Will do, Admiral. Show that the dead are dead and that they've been feasting while everyone else starved. I think I can retrieve some video of the courtesans being led away, as well."

"Move quickly. I've given them two hours. It would be nice if this got out an hour from now."

"I'm on it," Megan reported, and cut the connection.

Kris turned to her key staff. "Well, we seemed to have pulled that off well."

"We got the fifty-one high value targets we wanted," Jack summed up, "and held the rest of the killing to a minimum. Except for that self-inflicted blood bath, we kept it clean."

"Possibly too clean," Kris said, and turned to two of her advisors attending the meeting on screen.

The first one was beaming, as much as an Iteeche could beam with their beak. "No bloody invasion. It's fine by me," Imperial Admiral of the Second Order of Steel Coth said. "This planet is barely skimping by. You turn loose several hundred thousand soldiers and you'll wreck the place. There would be starvation and even more deaths in the invasion's wake. No. When the pictures of how the Planetary Overlord died gets around, I suspect you will find the other city lords and clan leaders much more willing to listen when you offer them the opportunity to surrender."

"I like your logic," Kris said. "It is mine as well. However, logic is not always the way to go. Ron, what's your take on this?"

Ron'sum'Pin'sumChap'sum'We was the other Iteeche still on his flagship and attending this confab by net. He was Kris's first Iteeche contact, and she considered him a friend.

That alone allowed her to get away with calling an Imperial counselor Ron.

The counselor today was dressed in full, multicolored, shimmering regalia. If a surrender could be arranged, he would lead the official delegation. While he commanded a fleet wing under Coth, at such civil ceremonies, the admiral would walk in his wake.

Kris, of course, walked in no one's wake. Well, no one but King Raymond the First, and whatever title the young Emperor used that didn't take fifteen minutes to yell out.

Ron was not smiling.

"I do fear that your success will be like ash in the beak of several clan leaders. It could be less, depending on some things. How many lower clan leaders do you intend to have offer Sincere Apologies to the Emperor for their treason?"

"How many?" Jack asked, raising a quizzical eyebrow.

"In a normal invasion," Ron explained, "the army would be tasked with digging out all the clan leaders, down to the most junior level. Them and their chosen mates."

"No wonder you mess up the place," Jack said. "I don't imagine they come willingly."

"No. Usually they and their armed retainers will put up quite a fight. To avoid being lazed from orbit, they usually do it within a very built-up area."

"So they use the common Iteeche as both hostages and shields," Kris said.

"More likely than not. However, once all those traitors are rooted out, there are many clan leadership positions open for junior sons. They, and the retainers that follow, are usually allowed to choose liberally from their spawn. There are usually quite a few opportunities to slip their spawn into skilled crafts and management positions in the newly conquered world."

Kris exchanged a telling glance with Jack. More and more they were discovering uglier aspects about this Empire they'd been led to first believe. There was no question they'd respect King Ray's assigning them to do what the Iteeche wanted. It had, after all, been the price of the chance to open diplomatic and trade relations with the Empire.

Still, the more and more they learned, the less and less they liked.

Kris faced Ron. "To me, as a human, we have cut off the head of the rebellion on Zargoth. Those who chose to rebel are dead. Those who were merely doing what their superior clan leaders chose for them to do have not earned capital punishment. Does it really serve the Empire for a planet to be racked with destruction?"

Ron eyed Kris with all four of his large eyes. "To anyone who looks at it that way, yes, you are right. However, there are those who look at it another way and see it as their just deserts for staying loyal to the Emperor. For those who see their family and clan advancing over the dead of a rebellious clan, there is also a logic. And please, my Eminent Admiral and Princess, remember that if the rebels win, they will slaughter the population of entire planets so that they may bring in their own people and repopulate it."

That was the grim reality of how the Iteeche played this game of loyalty and rebellion. The rebel rarely won, but when they did, they ruled the Empire for a thousand years.

Kris mulled over these two different objectives. One would get her the quick surrender of this planet. The other would mean a long slow slog, tying her battle fleet up in orbit for months if not longer. That, of course, assumed that she could find an army to invade this planet in less than a month.

"Do you have an army that we can use to take over this planet, brick by brick?" she asked Ron

"No, Your Royal Highness. Neither my clan, the Chap'-sum'We clan, nor their allies have been able to muster the million soldiers needed to reduce this planet."

"Then you may inform the clans that, lacking an army, I will capture this planet using the ways of my people. Once you can muster the required army, I will be glad to let you reduce a planet by your custom."

Ron made a strangled sound, which Kris had learned was an Iteeche laugh. "It is wise of you to offer my clan superiors a chance to do it their way when they can muster the forces. Since they have not, you are merely doing what you can. This will play well among many of the younger clan leaders. Let their elders play their games and kill each other. Why should those who gamble for such low stakes have to pay the ultimate forfeit?"

"Good," Kris said.

"So tell me, Your Royal Highness," Ron went on, "If your battle fleet is not to spend the next few months lounging here in orbit, what will you do with this force?"

"How about win the war?" Kris replied.

She'd never heard an Iteeche gasp. She found herself watching as two different Iteeche, from completely different walks of life, an admiral who had worked his way up from the deck plates, and an Imperial counselor who often stood in the presence of the Emperor, showed her just how an Iteeche responded to shocking news.

28

An hour later, the pictures from the Planetary Overlord's private suite in his bunker, along with those from the third floor were broadcast to every location on the planet, along with a renewed demand for their surrender. From dirtside, questions circulated about what might happen to junior clan leaders if they did surrender.

Kris offered them the chance to live.

An hour after that, city ruler after city ruler was falling all over themselves to offer their formal surrender. Of course, anything the Iteeche did had to be done formally. However, since no one had ever formally surrendered and survived the experience, the opportunities for ceremonial creativity were wide open.

Two cities, however, refused to surrender. Apparently, the local clan princes did not trust a Longknife. After all, she was just human.

Kris had both city palaces lazed from orbit and gave

them one more hour to reconsider their choice. "The next time, we will not limit our lasers to just the governor's palace."

Within the hour, two minor officials were on the net begging Kris to hold her fire and informing her that not only the city governor was dead, but also a whole pile of middle-grade clan leaders.

Kris called up Ron. "Will that make some more of the clan leaders happy?"

"Possibly," he said, cagily. "It will at least clearly show that you meant what you said and backed it up with fire from the sky."

"Good. Can you advise the new incoming clan leaders that I need them on the ground pronto? You can take the surrender of the old clan leaders, but I want to get this change of command over and done with as quickly as possible."

"The bi-pentareme with the clan lordlings and junior officials has been accelerating ahead of the merchant fleet. They should be here by tomorrow."

"Then we shall schedule the official surrender for tomorrow."

"So, tell me," Ron said. "You have rushed the reduction of this planet. You have a fleet of two thousand battle-cruisers at your command. What do you do next?"

"I am waiting for reinforcements," Kris said. "When they arrive, we'll see what options we have."

"You are not very forthcoming," Ron said. "One would almost take you for an Imperial counselor of the first order."

"Ron, we humans have been intriguing for a long, long time. Unlike the Iteeche Empire, we've done our intriguing, power against power. You have court intrigue. We have intrigues that cover hundreds of planets. I sincerely doubt you can teach us much. I will not claim that I can teach you any new tricks. However, my tricks will have the advantage of being new and different. Let us wait and see."

The Iteeche gave Kris a shallow bow. "I shall await your surprises with interest."

29

It turned out that it took two days to arrange for the surrender. The armed yacht with the arriving clan lordlings didn't make it in on time and it took more time for all the city governors to fly to the capital.

It also took the Marines all day to secure the surrender site.

The Emperor Hedoto Civic Amphitheater was the chosen site. It could hold close to 150,000 Iteeche. To allow for Marines to be stationed strategically around the arena, seating was cut down to 130,000.

A large stage, in the human fashion, was erected at one end of the vast playing field. There, Kris and the new clan leaders would sit. The surrendering clan leaders would also be seated, though in the front row below the stage.

The arriving clan leaders would be permitted an appropriate number of axe men and snake wranglers . . . all located behind them and well away from those surrendering. Those clan officials were permitted only a single axe man for status, and no snakes.

Kris made sure that Ron passed the word to the arriving leaders. If there was any attempt to harm any of the old clan officials in any way, she'd have a Marine sniper shoot down like a dog, both the axe man, snake man, *and* their lordling.

Ron actually managed to raise his eyebrows at that, but he said nothing to Kris and the looks she got on stage from some of the new clan lords told her that quite a few were not happy with certain aspects of the ceremony they had been invited to participate in.

Kris opened the ceremony.

"The planet of Zargoth was the base from which eight thousand rebel warships launched themselves into the heart of the Empire. I and the ships of the loyal fleet met and defeated them, outnumbered, almost four-to-one. Everyone expected that we would face defeat. Instead, we annihilated the rebel fleet. Many of the sailors and officers guarding this stadium were victors in that battle. They deserve your appreciation and respect."

The applause went loud and long. The population wanted their new overlords to see them as loyal worshipers of the Emperor and weren't taking any chances that their response might be called weak.

Kris went on to say nice things about the rosy future of Zargoth in the Empire, knowing full well that these people were aware that unless more resources could be found, this place had no future at all.

While she smiled through another long bout of cheering, a thought struck Kris.

NELLY, WHAT KIND OF ASTEROID BELT DOES THIS SYSTEM HAVE?

A FAIRLY DECENT ONE, KRIS. WHY?

IS ANYTHING BEING DONE TO USE ITS RESOURCES?

Kris Longknife Commanding 179

WE DIDN'T SEE ANY ACTIVITY IN THE ASTEROID BELT WHEN WE WERE ON APPROACH TO ZARGOTH.

NELLY, DON'T LET ME FORGET TO ASK MORE QUESTIONS ABOUT THIS. WHY ARE THESE PEOPLE DIRT POOR WHILE THEY'VE GOT ALL SORTS OF WEALTH ORBITING A COUPLE OF HUNDRED MILLION KLICKS ABOVE THEIR HEAD?

Thank heavens Nelly was able to help Kris get back on track to finish her speech. Done, she stepped aside and the important activities of the day for the Iteeche began.

Ron came forward, and in his position as Imperial Counselor to the Emperor, announced the name of the new Planetary Overlord the Emperor had ordained to bestow upon them. That he was of the Chap'sum'We clan spoke volumes. From here on in, this planet belonged to that clan.

The named Iteeche left his comfortable seat and strode to where Ron stood.

Meanwhile, a naked slave appeared from out of nowhere with a large red box which he held open for Ron. The Imperial Counselor withdrew a heavy golden chain composed of links of every different shape, all showing many precious jewels which made it shine with every color of the rainbow. Ron placed the chain around the new ruler's neck, and he then bowed respectfully to Ron.

Then the crowd went wild for at least five minutes.

When things quieted down, Ron called forward the ten new chiefs of the clans on Zargoth. One after another, ten slaves produced small, richly-painted, caskets. From them, Ron pulled forth chains of office that were also bejeweled gold, though the colors were fewer and the shapes more limited from chain to chain. One had red rubies decorating gold circles and rectangles. Another alternated triangles with the points up or down, all inlaid with turquoise. There were rarely more than three or four types of jewels on the links or three or four shapes in the chain.

When Ron finished, they stood beaming as much as Iteeche could while there was another long round of applause.

Ron finally raised his hands and the applause cut off like a light going out. The new ruler and clan lords returned to their seats and now seventy-nine lordlings marched out from the seats arranged at the back of the stage. Each was accompanied by a nude slave who did his best to shrink into the floor.

The lordlings stood, all four arms folded across their chests, all four feet spread wide apart in a power stance and glowered at the crowd. In the front row, seventy-seven lord governors of the largest cities on the planet, and two junior stand-ins, shuffled their way around to one side of the stage and began to climb the stairs up to it. They filed across it. When they came to a specific lordling, they went down on their knees before him.

For a long moment, the stadium was silent, more silent than Kris ever thought over 120,000 Iteeche and humans could be.

Ron spoke commandingly into the silence. "Surrender your chain of office."

Each of the kneeling Iteeche raised a complex silver chain of disks and plaques from around their neck. The naked slave slipped forward, eyes down, never meeting the kneeling man's, to accept the chain of office. They then turned, eyes still down, to hand it off to the new lord governor of the city.

Those governors now lifted the chain over their heads and placed it around their own neck. Hurriedly, the slaves arranged the chain in place, then melted into the background.

Now, 130,000 Iteeche exploded in cheers and applause.

GUN! came tersely over Nelly Net.

Kris took three steps back as a shot rang out. A large caliber bullet whizzed by, just in front of her. She felt the wind of it.

Three sharp shots snapped out as rounds from smaller caliber rifles answered the first.

Kris could read the story in the shots fired. One large Iteeche rifle had spoken her death. Three smaller human rifles responded.

There was no second bark from the larger rifle. No doubt, the Marine snipers had done their job.

The stadium, awash with shouts of joy and applause a moment ago, was silent. Not one person so much as breathed.

Into the silence, Kris shouted commandingly. "The traitor has paid the price for his treason. Long live Chap'-sum'We! Long live Zargoth!"

That must have translated fairly well. Of course, Kris also backed her words up by clapping her hands. Ron immediately followed suit. In a moment, all those on stage were applauding, and a breath later, the stadium rocked with shouts and applause.

"Anyone see any other guns?" Jack said on the general comm net.

"We're watching for them. Nothing yet, General."

"Keep it up," Jack said, as he came to stand beside Kris.

Kris smiled. No doubt, if he could, he would have put himself between her and any possible gun. However, the stadium wrapped around the stage in a full 360 degree circle. He could have ordered Marines to surround her, but he knew, after all these years, not to try that.

This time, the applause went long, and no one made any effort to cut it off. The former city governors slunk off the stage, and the ninety new lordlings of the planet moved around the stage waving at their new . . . whatever. Were they slaves? Peasants? Cannon fodder?

Kris didn't know enough about the Iteeche Empire to know what those in power considered of those below them on the last few rungs of the civic ladder. That was something she needed to learn, and likely would want to change.

She had to suppress a smile at that thought. The Iteeche powers that be had made a deal with the devil, or rather the humans . . . the same thing from their viewpoint. They were losing a civil war with the rebels. If Kris could not pull out a Longknife miracle, they'd be all be dead soon. If she could, they'd likely rule for a thousand more years.

That was what they wanted.

What they didn't want was the flip side of the coin. The humans were chaos from their perspective. The humans caused change. Iteeche hated change, at least those at the top did.

Kris had no trouble with change. Indeed, the more she saw of this place, the more she wanted to change things. Change things a lot.

Once this rebellion was over, there would be a lot of pressure from the clan lords to roll things back to the way they were. If Kris was to pull off half of the change she wanted, she'd have to do it while the fight was still on.

She'd done some of it right here, today. The planet had not been wrecked. There had been an almost orderly change of clan ownership.

Now, how to make some more changes?

Kris eyed the lordlings on the stage, and the Iteeche in the stadium who seemed afraid to slow their clapping. Now Kris began to see a problem.

The Iteeche had four arms and four hands. As she watched, people in the crowd would switch from one pair of hands to the other. Humans had to stop clapping sooner or later; their palms could only take so much. The Iteeche could switch off.

It looked like this could go on forever.

NELLY, LET'S TALK ABOUT ASTEROIDS. ARE THEIR ANY GOOD ASTEROIDS CLOSER THAN THE BELT OUT THERE?

AS A MATTER OF FACT, KRIS, THERE IS A VERY NICE METAL ASTEROID NOT ALL THAT FAR FROM THIS PLANET, APPROXIMATELY ONE HUNDRED AND SIXTY KILOMETERS IN LENGTH. IT HAS SEVERAL BILLION TONS OF IRON, NICKLE, AND OTHER INTERESTING RESOURCES.

IS IT DANGEROUS?

IN A COUPLE OF MILLION YEARS, IT MIGHT HIT THE PLANET. IT'S IN A CRAZY ORBIT.

WHAT WOULD IT TAKE TO CAPTURE IT?

YOU COULD DISPATCH A TASK FORCE, SAY SIXTEEN BATTLECRUISERS. I'D SUGGEST HUMANS, THOUGH YOU MIGHT INCLUDE A FLOTILLA OR TWO OF ITEECHE. UNLESS THERE IS A MAJOR FAULT IN THE STRUCTURE, YOU COULD HAVE IT HERE IN A WEEK.

CUT THE ORDERS, NELLY. HAVE ADMIRAL KITANO PICK HER BEST SHIPS FOR THIS JOB. ASK JACK TO ASSIGN HIS BEST ENGINEERS, AS WELL. TELL COTH I WANT FOUR FLOTILLAS.

I'M ON IT NOW, KRIS.

THANKS, NELLY.

Zargoth was a worthless planet. It was barely able to feed its people and meet their most basic needs. The clans had wanted her to slaughter a couple of million peasants so they could choose more of their own spawn to fill in the vacancies.

To the Iteeche, everything was a zero-sum game. If I got a bigger slice of the pie, you got less. That was the Iteeche way.

The human way was to increase the pie. Maybe even bake two or three more. Humans had the resources, Iteeche didn't.

It was time for the humans to teach the Iteeche the benefits of consumerism.

Kris continued waving back at the applauding masses. They didn't know it yet, but before Kris boarded the shuttle that would lift her back to her flagship in orbit, 144 battle-cruisers would be already breaking orbit.

They'd come to Zargoth prepared to slaughter millions from orbit. Now, they were off to bring billions of tons of resources to orbit.

Zargoth would never be the same.

Having captured a planet, and installed a new government, it was up to Kris to make sure the rest of the transition went smoothly.

Each of the newly installed officials had brought with him a number of civilians to help them manage their new fiefs. All of the clan princelings had armed clan retainers that stood ready to protect them with their life.

Of course, there were also armed retainers left over from the city lordlings who were now dead or unemployed. Kris strongly recommended that the new kids on the block offer those retainers jobs in their own guard force.

To back up Kris's "recommendation," she included at least one company of U.S. Fleet Marines with orders to work with a battalion of Iteeche Fleet Marines to keep things going smoothly.

It worked, with one exception.

A firefight broke out. It was a massacre, if you believed the locals, or a sneak attack, if you believed the new arrivals. Kris believed neither, but the Marines saw to it that no massacre occurred, nor did the attack succeed. Peace was restored quickly, and the message got out to all the cities, violence between the new and old teams would not be permitted.

Kris did accept Ron's suggestion that the newly installed leaders might like to move some of the old team to jobs elsewhere in the Empire. Ron was soon back with a moderate list from both the new planetary overlord, the replacement clan chiefs, and the present city governors.

Kris and Ron fired off a memo under both their signatures asking the senior clan chieftains at the Imperial Capital to provide both replacements and a list of vacancies available for the displaced bureaucrats.

Over the next two weeks, Kris got replies back, both with replacements and offers for jobs widely scattered around the loyal planets of the Empire. Very widely scattered. Two weeks later the replacements arrived on a fast bi-quadrireme and a few days later, the replaced were on their way to the capital, and from there, to their new jobs.

However, Zargoth was already busy changing.

A week after the transfer of power, an army of 100,000 Iteeche soldiers arrived in orbit, escorted by nearly 500 battlecruisers. The Imperial troops were distributed among the existing army, one battalion for every three locals to form an expanded regiment. There were several demotions among the locals, but never more than one pay grade. Artillery and armored vehicles were locked down tight and placed under guard.

There were a few incidents of fragging. Jack checked into them and discovered that the last government had installed a lot of "political officers" into the ranks of the army. Some of those political types had been rather liberal in hanging traitors. The fraggings were regular army types getting back at the worst of them.

Kris got a list of all the army's political types and offered them jobs off planet. They eagerly volunteered and were shipped off to the capital for those there to figure out what to do with.

Ron doubted their employment prospects were very good.

Most of the so-called invasion fleet of freighters loaded with sewage and refugees from the Imperial Capital had been sent on their way. Kris had rearranged the passengers to extract tens of thousands of craftsman and artisans, all from the clans represented on Zargoth. While 1,990 freighters headed out for four distant planets, 10 lingered in orbit.

The passengers did not have long to wonder why.

Eight days after the transfer of power, a huge asteroid was carefully and smoothly slipped into high orbit, just below Zargoth's protective Vanguard Allen belt. Some combat engineers began making the place livable, while others began herding nanos to mine the metals from the new moon.

Within the week, iron was being smelted and converted to steel. Sheets and I-beams were soon flowing to the space station above Zargoth. The station had not been considered large enough to build anything. At least, anything large. It was, however, large enough to repair a battleship.

The workers in the yard were soon laying down 10,000-ton freighters. No sooner had the first one finished trials, than it was headed out to a large asteroid, loaded with miners who had optimism in their hearts, even if their stomachs were a bit queasy.

Ron invited himself over for supper the afternoon the

first ship took off for the asteroid belt. Their dinner conversation revolved around how quiet things were going, "for such a recently pacified rebel planet."

"You catch more flies with honey than vinegar," Kris pointed out.

"Yes, a most interesting turn of phrase for you humans, and very helpful in situations like this," Ron agreed while spearing a small fish and lifting the still-wiggling fingerling to his beak.

He swallowed before going on. "So tell me, is this expedition to the asteroid belt honey or vinegar?"

"Actually, neither," Kris said, happy that all the beating around the bush was over. Clearly, this was the question at the root of this dinner invitation.

"First," Kris said, "how is it that the resources of the asteroid belt have not been exploited?"

Ron eyed Kris as if she had two heads. Since he was using four eyes, it was quite a look.

"How could we? We ship out settlers with just enough resources to get them started. They have to use what the planet has. Usually, we're dumping more settlers on a planet before the first wave has even caught its breath. Then, there are their own choosings and, if a planet is not rich in resources, there is little left to go wasting them on rooting around stone rocks millions of mu away."

Ron shook his head. "I know that you lucked out with this close-in rock, finding iron and other important minerals. Still, there are few chances that those that you have shipped out to the asteroids will even find enough fuel to bring them back. I have gotten some rather strong complaints from their clan leaders that you are wasting fine workers."

"I fully expect that the asteroid they're heading for will

pay off for them," Kris said. "There are also a few dirty ice rocks not too far away that they can use for fuel. That is not a suicide mission. Tell me, Ron, don't you know how to identify the asteroids that have minerals in them? We just run a spectrometer over them and look for the right colors."

Ron shook his entire body. "There are so many stories among our people of ships that went off to explore these asteroid belts and the crews ended up eating each other. These places are worse than the deepest, darkest pits of the ocean. Some of our older planets do use their asteroid belts. The asteroid belt of the Capital System has been just about mined down to bare rock. However, it is rare that a planet is rich enough long enough or has a close enough belt that they risk a mission to it."

Ron paused to consider his own words. "I must admit, however, that the strongest, most productive planets are usually those that are able to exploit those tiny worlds."

Again, Ron paused. "It was not by accident that you sent flotillas of battlecruisers out to capture that rock and move it to orbit here, was it?"

"No. We call it priming the pump. Your planet desperately needed new resources. We brought it here, but I'm insisting that the first flower of its production goes to finding more resources. We have a story of the Red Queen. In it, you have to run as fast as you can just to stay where you are."

"Because someone with large teeth is running just as fast behind you, right?"

"You got it, Ron."

"So many of our planets are running as fast as they can just to stay in the same place. You are trying to help us get enough ahead of those chasing us to get a breath. Grow stronger."

"Right."

Ron cocked his head over, something that involved much of his body. "And what will this do to us, my human friend?"

"You will grow stronger," Kris said.

"And what will we do with this strength?"

"Tear yourselves apart? Build yourselves a better world?" Kris asked with a shrug.

"Human, why do I think that you two-legged, two-eyed aliens are more trouble than you are worth?"

"Because you never know when going into a wave of change just how you will come out, and who will be on top when it's done," Kris answered slowly.

"That is so. That is just so."

Kris chose to have dessert delivered. Chocolate was a beloved taste for the Iteeche. Ron ate his chocolate-covered grasshoppers, or something like it, with a very pensive air about him. He was still quiet as Kris escorted him to his barge for return to his flagship.

Kris said nothing, letting the silence speak for itself. Yes, she was bringing change to this Empire. Forcing change down its throat. She'd done it to this one planet. Someone had still tried to kill her for this, but, as usual, they failed. Now, the question was, could she continue down this trail, or would she be stopped?

Kris returned to her quarters, looking for Jack and distraction, but knowing she needed to get things moving before those with power stripped her of her power to bring change to the lives of those that deserved something better.

31

K ris had a lot of projects to juggle. If she wanted this fleet to strike a blow for the Emperor, she needed to get it battle ready. She now had five hundred more ships that were initiated in her way of fighting and, were as yet, unmodified.

She dispatched Admiral Coth with fifteen flotillas of his ships on a training cruise to test, modify, and train the recently arrived flotillas. With only three of Nelly's kids with Kitano's fleet, Kris had to send along Megan to speed up the process. Clearly, an early, below-the-zone promotion to lieutenant commander didn't get her out of any scut work.

Why was Megan not surprised?

The training cruise went faster than expected. The new ship captains were needing less and less persuasion to adopt high gee bunks and let strange computers mess around inside their ship computers. With all the boxes checked off quickly, Coth was headed back when Kris found herself in urgent need of her flag lieutenant.

The transportation net in one major city had suffered a

catastrophic failure. If it wasn't fixed quickly, Iteeche were going to die.

Was it an accident, poor maintenance, or sabotage?

Whichever it was, Megan and Lily drew the assignment. She reported on the run immediately to Kris as soon as the training fleet returned to the station.

"We have a problem?" Lieutenant Commander Longknife asked Grand Admiral Longknife.

"Maybe. Maybe not. Whatever we have, we need someone to fix it right away. As soon as you can change to dress whites, I'd like you to please drop down and get a good look at it. Take along a couple hundred kilos of Smart Metal."

"That much?" From the look on Megan's face, it was clear the size of that limited resource told her just how big the problem was.

Kris nodded. "People are out of work because of this mess. Now it's in one city, but it could spread to more. Take my barge. Prepare to create a palanquin or other fancy ride. You can never put on enough show with these damn squids."

"Are you having a bad day?"

"Megan, things were going so smoothly, now we have this. Get to the bottom of it."

"Can Captain Sung come with me? She likes to be there when we're working with the Iteeche."

"By all means. Tell her I want her there."

"Aye, aye, Admiral."

egan found the Admiral's Barge several steps up from her usual longboat ride. The seats were more cushioned and looked to be in red leather. The carpet on the floor was plush. There were actually curtains framing the fake windows that now showed the space around them. No doubt, it was all Smart Metal™.

Captain Sung arrived right behind her and the two of them strapped in. A moment later, the barge fell away from the *Princess Royal* and began its descent. Atmosphere being no respecter of rank, the ride down in the admiral's barge was bumpier than most.

They were headed for a city with a long name that basically meant some guy with a very long name and his clan's "Beautiful Red Sunset."

Most people just called it "Sunset."

Kris was right about sending them down in her best barge, there was a greeting party that stepped on board as soon as the aft hatch opened. The new city lordling was a bit on the older side, but he proudly wore his full regalia of many colors and his silver chain of office. He was followed by several local clan chiefs decked out with less color and less fancy chains.

The high muckety-muck announced his full name, every word of it, and his office, that needed a lot more words than city regional governor, and finished with, "We are honored to see so respected a subordinate of such an eminent chosen one as Imperial Admiral of the First Order of Steel Longknife."

If Megan was right, Kris had just gotten short-changed. However, Megan had been working on her own introduction.

"I am Lieutenant Commander Megan Longknife of the clan Longknife of Santa Maria. I am Flag Lieutenant and *aide de camp* to Her Royal Highness, Grand Admiral Kris Longknife, Imperial Admiral of the First Order of Steel and personally named by the Emperor as Commander of the Imperial Combined Fleet. She is the personal Emissary of King Longknife of the United Society and chosen war leader of that republic. She is the slayer of alien space raiders and the protector of the populations of the planets Alwa and Susquan. I am her fixer, kindly take me to your problem."

I WAS WONDERING IF YOU'D EVER GET AROUND TO THE REASON WE'RE HERE, Quinn quipped on Nelly Net.

I HAD TO HAVE A LONG NAME AND JOB TITLE, OR I'D GET DISRESPECTED. BESIDES, THIS JOKER SERIOUSLY DISRESPECTED KRIS WHEN HE SHORTENED HER TITLE. I COULDN'T LET THAT HAPPEN.

YOU MOST CERTAINLY DID NOT. LOOK AT THAT FELLOW. HIS BEAK IS HANGING OPEN.

"If you will come this way," he said, only after closing his mouth with a hard click.

Megan and Quinn followed the Iteeche out of the barge. There, waiting for them on the tarmac were several sedan chairs and two seriously decked out palanquins carried by a dozen porters.

LILY, LET'S PUT ON A SERIOUS SHOW.

GOT IT, had a serious grin attached to it.

Behind Megan, a large block of metal in the barge's aft cargo bay sprouted eight wheels and rolled down the ramp. However, as it descended, it began to morph. By the time the last wheel rolled onto the tarmac, it was a large, most decorative palanquin with sparkling jewels set in a golden body that flashed in the sun.

Several Iteeche now needed to close their beaks.

"If you will care to board," Megan said to the governor. "It is our custom that the juniors enter first."

"Oh," the governor sputtered as he and his lordlings reorganized themselves and mounted the offered escalator that now took them up to this luxurious moving palace. When the last Iteeche was aboard, Lieutenant Commander Longknife invited Captain Sung to board before her.

WHY NOT? YOU'RE THE LONGKNIFE.

I APPRECIATE YOUR UNDERSTANDING.

In the large enclosure, there had been a long U-shaped couch around the front of the litter and nothing along the rear. Now, with the Iteeche seated all together, two golden chairs rose from the floor of the litter even as Quinn and Megan began to sit down.

PERFECT, LILY.

THANKS.

"Now, I understand that you use a mode of transportation we have not seen on the Capital planet."

"None of the rolling roads are allowed within five hundred miles of the palace," the governor said, elbowing the Iteeche beside him to get more room. Those on either side squished together.

"Do the rolling roads provide good service to you?"

"They have worked for Zargoth since it was first opened for the People. We have never had this problem with them before."

"Very well," Megan said, and leaned back in her chair. It began to massage her.

Around her, the palanquin rocked along, borne by those who had come to carry the other two.

"Your view from up here is quite nice," the governor said, "but do you really want everyone gawking at you?"

"But no one can see us to gawk at us," Megan said. "The material lets us see out, but no one can see in. Would you prefer they could? Lily?"

In a snap, the luxurious moving box was flooded with brighter sun light.

"To make it one way requires us to reduce the light. I always like it lighter, don't you?" Megan said.

"I would prefer not to be seen," the governor said, quickly. "All of us cannot be so lucky as your Admiral."

"Ah, yes. Lily, return us to our previous state."

"Done," said the computer at Megan's throat.

There was more beak-dropping as shade returned to the cabin of the palanquin.

"So, shall I assume that your sensitivity to snipers is based upon a fear that these rolling roads have been sabotaged?"

"It is a distinct possibility, although we have not caught anyone in the act, and there is no explanation for some of the things that have made the problem worse."

"Well, we shall see."

By now, the fancy palanquin was swaying out of the

space port. There was a small parking lot with a few of the three- and four-wheeled vehicles in it. A few looked like limos, but the lordling did not suggest they stop and dismount.

Megan soon found out why.

They were carried up a few steps with their ride being anything but level. Then, Megan got a view of these rolling roads.

Now it was her turn to make sure she kept her mouth shut.

In front of her was a large expanse. She had to blink several times before her eyes took it all in. At the moment, they were being carried onto a sliding walkway. The porters balanced them well; those that got on the road first quit moving forward and only sidled sideways until the last of those on the far side had managed to get aboard.

This slideway was just wide enough for a palanquin as large as Megan and Lily had built.

To their left were more slideways, each one stepping up the speed as you went in that direction. About half-way to the far edge of the slideways, see-through air fences started to sprout. At first, there was a windbreak every ten meters or so, then less distance as the speed of the rolling road picked up until at the far side, they were about every two meters.

This system was repeated in reverse on the far side of the road, only it was going the other direction.

Four or five meters above the fast lanes there was a freight lane. At least, Megan thought at first that it was. Containers a good ten or twenty meters in length zoomed by, going the same speed as the most distant lane. There were two of these elevated lines, one going in each direction.

Suddenly, one container zoomed by with windows. It

was gone in a flash, but Megan was left with the distinct impression of Iteeche looking out at her.

"This is a very nice system you have," Megan told the governor.

"Thank you. It is when it works."

"And it doesn't work?"

"We will show you."

Megan sped down the rolling road. To each side were buildings of ten and fifteen stories high. Their design was repetitive, just concrete and glass, every corner squared, every surface flat. There were always flowers in boxes outside the first floor, but nothing to break up the monotony as the building rose higher.

Ahead, opened to Megan's view by the wide expanse of rolling road, she could see skyscrapers that rose five hundred meters or more into the dull gray sky. They stood like soldiers, each in the same uniform, shoulder to shoulder, back to front.

How many Iteeche must live in this city? A million? Ten million? A hundred million?

The slideway carried them into a strip of destruction and construction. The buildings still standing were five or six stories tall. Many of them were built with different materials and to different designs. Here some were brick or stone. There was little concrete and glass.

Yet, those buildings were all being torn down. Next to the destruction, a new building would be going up. From the look of the crane, it might he headed for five hundred meters of concrete and glass.

The older buildings that could hold fewer people were being replaced with skyscrapers where a hundred times that many could be crammed in.

And all of those people would ride the rolling road.

So why was the passenger load on this line so light?

Megan found out rather soon. She was thrown forward in her chair as her palanquin slowed quickly. Then, it rolled to a stop.

The rolling road ahead was not rolling.

"Let's walk around a bit," Megan said as she stood. She led the parade down the escalator then turned slowly to look around.

Behind her, the road moved, although most people seem to have exited well back from the sudden stop. The buildings to either side were blockish skyscrapers, all reaching to the same 500-meter level.

It was what lay ahead of her that made her frown.

Someone had spent a lot of skull sweat figuring out how to design an interchange that merged one slideway going east to west with another going north to south. In front of her was just such an interchange. Her rolling road went one way. Another rolling road crossed before her, heading in its own direction.

Her sidewalk merged six or eight lanes into four slower one. That lane rose high in the air and then fell smoothly to match a lane in the north-south road. There were plenty of arriving lanes to let the east-west passengers merge onto the north-south road.

Except the north-south rolling road was dead in the water.

"Lily, give me a picture of this layout."

A moment later, a holographic map floated in front of Megan. It covered a lot of territory. However, it was easy to see the wide expanse where the rolling road lay. There were a lot that went east and west. There was only one that went north and south.

Haven't these folks learned about the dangers of single-threading?

Of course, these roads took up a lot of real estate that seemed to be in short supply. At the fringe of the map, green agricultural lands could already be seen running right up to the sad gray of the city.

It took a lot of land to feed fifty billion Iteeche.

"So, your main transportation backbone is broke."

"Yes, Lieutenant Longknife. The People can travel from one part of their route to the beginning or end, but none of them can transfer to any other road. Neither food nor equipment can move along it either. We are only days away from starvation breaking out in some pockets of this city."

"You can't use those three- and four-wheel trucks to move food?"

"We can move some, but we don't have nearly enough."

Megan nodded. "Show me where this breakdown is. By the way, is the guy who oversaw this road before we landed still here?"

"He is now serving the Emperor and his clan somewhere else in the Empire."

"So, who is the most senior man left from the old regime?"

"I will have him meet us at the break," the governor said, not actually naming the technician. "Now, we must backtrack to where my vehicles are waiting."

Megan did not like the idea of wasting time backing and filling. "That won't be necessary. Lily, please make transportation for us. It doesn't look to me like there's much traffic on the dead slideway."

33

In a moment, the palanquin had converted itself into an open eight-wheeled roadster with comfortable space for ten . . . and the bearers were galloping up the road. The other senior Iteeche looked like they'd love to follow them, but they held off . . . barely.

Megan offered the passenger side seat to Quinn and then walked around the snub nose to the driver's side, assuming any driving was necessary. The Iteeche piled into the three back seats. The governor sat directly behind Megan.

As the roadster accelerated to a sedate thirty kilometers per hour, Megan had her seat swivel around to face the governor even as she said, "Lily, let me know if you need my help getting us there."

"Very well, but Megan, where are we going?"

Megan raised an eyebrow to the governor, then thought better of it, since the Iteeche did not have much body hair. "Where is this breakdown?"

"I am not sure. I have not been to it."

"Could you please order that senior technician to meet us on the road where the break is?"

The governor turned to one of his toadies. He took a radio from his belt that was about as big as a shoe and spoke rapidly. He quickly got an answer. "Sak will be there."

They sedately motored north, with Megan hoping they would not have to turn around and go south. She had no idea what the range was for this roadster and she really didn't want to walk.

After five minutes of driving along the dead rolling road, they were coming up on another interchange. Lily announced, "I see five Iteeche about three kilometers away. We should be there shortly."

"Very good, Lily."

Six minutes later, they pulled to a stop next to a group of five Iteeche in brown jerkins and britches. All of them had a utility belt of one sort or another around their hips.

They went down on their knees and bowed their heads.

"How may we serve your Eminence?" the one with the most complex belt and the fewer large tools said.

"Lead us to the place where the rolling road has failed."

"I am always happy to serve your Eminence," the lead technician said as he and his team came to their feet.

The governor fell behind as Megan and Quinn were led over to the side of the road, then to a metal stairwell that took them down into a utility corridor. Off to Megan's left was what looked like the cranky underbelly of the road. At least, there was a lot of heavy machinery and none of it was working.

"As you can see here," the technician explained, "the rolling roads are not one single treadmill. Few treads are more than a kilometer long. Many, especially at junctions, are even shorter. It is at a junction where we have the problem."

They walked through this service tunnel for about a quarter kilometer. Looking up, Megan could see daylight coming through some skylights where there wasn't any road. Then, the orderly machinery became a disorganized mess.

"What happened here?" she asked.

"That spindle turns flanges. The spindle appears to have burned out when its lubricant failed and the entire spindle fell out of its place."

"Can you replace the spindle? Are the flanges damaged as well?" Megan asked.

"The spindle and the flanges are the least of our problems," Sak said. "It is the controller boards that the flanges hit when the spindle fell that has brought the roads to a halt. See?"

The spindle still lay where it had fallen. Flying off of it were flaps coated in hard rubber. Some of them looked scorched. All along the line of the spindle were burn marks.

Megan stepped close to one of the burned spots and found herself looking down at a square printed circuit board. Something like that only showed up in the History of Technology text books, and, likely, only on Santa Maria where things like this were still in use from the Times of Isolation.

She glanced up. Across the line in front of the fallen spindle there looked to be twenty or more of these burned out boards. Apparently, the flanges had flapped hard against the boards a few times and knocked off several transistors . . . if that was to be believed.

Megan, with Quinn looking over her shoulder, studied four of them that were in easy reach. The burn points were both the same yet different. Most had burned in three or four places. However, none had burned in the exact same place.

These circuit boards had found lots of different places to fail.

Even if we can find a way to scavenge different parts from different boards, we'll have trouble matching them all up.

Megan doubted she'd find anyone skilled with a soldering iron. Most of those boards were just printed, if she remembered correctly.

"What spares do you have?" Megan asked the tech.

"Our inventory records say we should have forty of this version of the board."

"It says so. What do you actually have?"

"The storage rack is empty. We have not a one."

"And why would that be?" Megan asked.

"I don't know."

"Okay, let's try that again, what other uses could that board be put to?"

"There are few places on the roads that these particular boards could be used. This is a junction where two roads are merging," he said, then went on much slower. "However, these boards could be used in automated flying machines for their remote control."

"As in drones spewing junk to blind our sensors in orbit?" Megan growled.

"Yes, sir."

Clearly the Iteeche lacked a name for an in-charge woman, but that could wait for later.

"So, it's likely that someone walked off with these boards during the recent unpleasantness and they did not enter their removal in your ordering system."

The Iteeche gulped. "During the preparations for an

invasion, anything that might be a weapon was requisitioned. Such requisitions were often informal."

That closed that door and blew it up quite well. Okay.

"Can you order in replacement parts from another city?"

"I have sent requests to every city that uses rolling roads. All have declined to send me any. They all fear that if this is sabotage, they will be next. Also, I think some of them may have also had their supply expropriated. It was hard to tell from the different replies, but it would not surprise me."

Megan walked up the belly of the road. A few hundred meters brought her to another spindle with its flanges and boards intact.

"Could you use these boards?"

"No. These boards control the inflow of a section going into the interchange. They are unique."

"Unique? There have to be other interchanges."

"Yes, sir. There are others. However, this is a very heavy-duty section of road. It controls the inflow of traffic. There are few examples of interchanges with traffic this heavy."

"Still, there must be some nearly as heavy."

"One or two. However, it is policy that we do not shuffle boards around from one location to another. Pulling a board, moving it, and reinstalling it could damage the board and destroying critical transportation items is a firing offense. Please understand, to lose one's job can often lead to a person and any dependents being thrown out of their quarters and very likely starving to death in an alley."

That was more information to pass along to Jacques. From the frozen look on Captain Sung's face, it was news to her, too. So much for a social safety net among these fish.

"However," Megan said, pointedly, "if you were ordered to take that risk and assured that any misstep would not be counted against you . . .?"

She looked around, the governor had not followed them below ground. He was still at the street level.

"Understand, there is a good reason for the policy," Sak said. "Pulling boards is risky. Some boards have been seated so long that their connections have corroded. They will work fine for a long time if left in place. If they are moved, however . . ." Now it was the technician's turn to leave his sentence hanging.

"For the purpose of conversation, where might you find a board to scavenge?"

"We have eight feeder lines into this main artery. I would go to either the last one or the first one. That would mean that one of the feeder lines would be disabled. Everyone north of that feeder line would also be left afoot."

He paused, then added one more thought. "Remember, this is one of the most heavily traveled exchanges. It may well be that those boards can't carry the load."

"And if they can't?"

"They could burn out quickly."

"And would the system be any worse off?"

The Iteeche thought for a long moment. "No, not really."

"Then we need to talk to your new governor."

"I will listen. I hope you will talk."

"Is there a problem?"

"We still have the stink of rebellion on us."

"What was your attitude toward the rebellion?" Megan asked.

"Do I look like a clan lordling? I do my job. I live my own life. I have no interest in what those above my station do or don't do."

"Smart man," Quinn said.

"Yeah," Megan drawled.

They climbed back up into the light. The governor was

now seated in his own limo, behind bulletproof glass. "What have you found? Sabotage?" he demanded after Megan approached him and he lowered the window

"There is no evidence either way," Megan said, having to bend over to talk. She filled the governor in on the situation below. "So," she said, finishing up, "We need to scavenge parts. That is against policy. I need for you to waive all punishments for those that work to move the boards from the northern most interchange to fix this one. Once it is rolling, all seven of the eight feeder roads should be back up and running."

"However, moving a board could destroy it."

"Yes."

"And whoever sabotages it should be punished as a traitor."

"They are not traitors, and they don't intend to sabotage it. However, the boards are used and potentially could fail when we move them. We either risk moving them or the road stays dead."

"I could order them to move the boards."

"Without a promise that they won't be punished, they are more likely to be nervous and make a mistake."

"You are again trying to flood us with your human ways and customs."

"And you are intent on starving your people. Your city is grinding to a standstill around this blockage. If you wish, I can return to Admiral Longknife and report this situation to her. Do you think the Planetary Overlord will respond to this report in the proper Iteeche way?"

Megan knew the proper Iteeche way probably involved loosing snakes and axes flashing in the sunlight.

If it was possible for an Iteeche to blanch, this guy did. Megan distinctly heard the guy gulp. Twice.

"There is no need to let this matter rise above our station," the governor said, his words tumbling out of his mouth so fast that Lily's translation fell behind.

"I shall grant advanced pardons and amnesties to all the craftsmen and laborers who participate in this effort. Everyone who successfully removes a board and carries it to its new place and installs it in working order shall receive authorization to become a chooser, even of choosing who swims in the mating pond with them. There will be a pension provided to raise the chosen to adulthood and a craft apprenticeship shall be opened to him. Thus I have spoken, and thus it shall be."

"Lily, you have that recorded?"

"Done, Boss. I'll have three copies printed off in the roadster and you can get the necessary signatures."

34

Megan felt like she'd won another major victory for the Emperor . . . and for Human-Iteeche relations. Of course, she likely wouldn't get much love from this city's governor in the future, but she doubted the two of them had much of a future anyway.

Megan had done her negotiations bent over, talking into a limo window with the boss guy seated like his lordling self. Now she stood up and turned to Sak. "Please get a warrant from my vehicle," she said, pointing at their temporary ride.

The Iteeche sent one of his team. All five of them seemed very shocked to find three pages of documents sitting on the seat of the roadster, but the junior Iteeche hoofed it back quickly to Sak, and he passed it along to Megan just as quickly.

Megan presented the agreement, pardons, amnesties, and rewards to the city governor for signing. This was one Iteeche that hadn't learned to wear a stiff collar. From the looks of his vestigial gill slits, he was furious. Still, he had one of his flunkies produce a writing instrument, signed each of the copies with a flourish, and handed them back to Megan.

The human Navy lieutenant commander also signed the three copies, before handing one back to the governor, another to the tech, and the final to Captain Sung.

"Are we done here?" the governor snapped.

"I do believe so," Megan said.

The limo drove off without another word from the big Iteeche lord. Apparently, his guard in the front seat knew his master's wishes and told the driver to leave.

That left Megan standing by the curb.

"So," she said to Sak, "who are your best men to do this work, and how do we get them some practice before they handled the really critical pieces."

While Sak organized his work force, Megan put a call in to Kris Longknife. The admiral answered it immediately.

"How's it going?"

"Not too bad," Megan said and briefed her boss on her day.

"So you got it signed and copied," Kris said at the end.

"Yes, ma'am. And ma'am, I'm going to be staying down here until this is all finished. I don't trust this guy not to renege on this agreement."

"He sounds like a real asshole," Kris agreed.

"Could you send me down some clothes and maybe a meal or three? Quinn and I are in our dress whites and we'll be working in a hard hat and overalls area."

"I'll see what I can do about getting you a Marine detail and a mobile command post. Maybe even a cook wagon."

"Ma'am, the Iteeche around here are awfully thin. I think they'd have better luck handling this delicate work if their stomachs weren't rubbing against their backbones."

"It's not just armies that move on their stomach. I concur. We'll have a support staff down the next orbit. More the following one."

"Much appreciated, Admiral. I don't know why they call us folks 'damn Longknifes'."

"You are just catching me on a good day," Kris said with a chuckle.

"Longknife 2, off."

"Longknife 1, off."

Megan went to let Sak in on the word that a nice, raw fish meal was on its way for his work crew. "Let me know how many are coming to dinner," she said.

It took him a while to close his beak.

"Would you mind if I had one craftsman work each board? The next two in line could watch the first one work out the board or install it, then do it themselves."

"And if something goes wrong?"

"We stop, figure out why it went belly up, then try it again."

"If you lose too many boards . . .? Megan asked.

"Then we disable the feeder road across from that one and a quarter of this city is without food."

"You do your best," Megan said.

That afternoon, Sak had twenty-eight craftsmen in, each with a helper, and they examined their situation. They went a kilometer up the road to a joint between two sections and worked the boards loose from that one. They successfully removed 23 out of 24. The last one just kind of crumbled.

A check of the records showed that that particular board had already lasted twice its planned useful life. A new one was drawn from stores. That particular mod of the board they had spares of, so they could replace it.

"Do you have any idea how many ancient boards that we

might be scavenging?" Megan asked Sak.

"I'm checking on that."

The command center had arrived, but Megan had no time to change. As they were waiting for word back on the age of the boards they'd be trying to finagle out of their place, the cook wagon arrived. Megan offered the first seating to Sak and his crew.

Apparently, the meal provided was quite above what the workers were used to. Several of the smaller fish were still wiggling on their trays and the other fish were freshly filleted and wrapped in seaweed.

Megan and Quinn locked themselves in their command center and quickly changed from somewhat besmirched whites to blue ship suits and yellow hard hats.

When they returned in working clothes, they got a cheer from the gathered craftsmen. Oh, it was also likely a cheer for the meal.

The two Navy officers drew their meal from the Marine cooks. The Iteeche eyed their meatloaf, rice, and mix of corn and string beans, all dead, and blinked several times.

"Are you giving us a better meal than you are eating?"

"Likely," Megan admitted. "We're eating what all the troops are eating. The food we brought down for you was what we had in stores for any banquets we might have to throw for visiting Iteeche."

"Who are you people?" the senior technician whispered.

"I serve Kris Longknife," Megan said. "I make things happen that she wants to happen. Your roads aren't rolling. We saw this from orbit and asked about it, right, Quinn?"

"Yes. We keep track of things from orbit. No traffic on a major artery and we started asking questions. We have a major intelligence section in the part of our fleet that are

Imperial Iteeche battlecruisers. They told us this was bad and here we are."

"Direct from the Imperial Admiral of the First Order of Steel," he whispered. "That someone that high would notice something this low."

"That's what we do, Sak. Just like I knew your people needed food to do their best on this tough assignment. If you're a leader, you take care of those that make things happen."

"I'm glad you're here," he said. "I'm glad you won your battle. I'm even more glad that you did not have to fight your way to city hall to replace our last governor. If you think the problem of this road breakdown is bad, imagine the entire city as rubble and fire."

"That's why we went into the bunker and dug out the Planetary Overlord. He was the rebel, not you."

"I have been told since I was a youngling that you humans are murderous and dangerous and would destroy us if you could. Now? Now I am looking at a human and what I am seeing is nothing like what my chooser and his chooser told me.

"I'm glad we can be of service to you, and you can help us keep this planet working."

"There are rumors that you intend to mine the sky?" one of the other technicians asked.

"We have brought an asteroid rich with iron, aluminum, copper, and other resources into your orbit. It will be a while, though, before those resources begin to show up down here."

"Why?" Sak asked.

"We're using the original production to build ships to extract more minerals from your asteroid field. There's a wealth of resources out there. If we succeed in doing that, everything will change."

"Change," a young helper said. "You humans say change a lot. My chooser says change is horrible and hurts many Iteeche."

"Look around you. Would you like to see change?" Megan asked.

The Iteeche around her let her question drop like a hot potato.

They finished their meal. Megan looked at the fifty-three Iteeche around her as well as herself, Quinn and a squad of Marines and turned the problem of getting them all to the chosen site over to Lily.

A moment later, the mobile command center stretched its eight tires out and slurped up the roadster. All that Smart Metal™ converted itself into a bus for Megan and the Iteeche. The cook wagon still kept its kitchen, but added enough room for the Marine rifle squad to ride.

Megan stood aside as the Iteeche boarded the bus. Each of the helpers carried a large toolbox. Each of the technicians carried a much smaller case. The pairs sat side by side on either aisle of the bus. Megan waited for her Marines to mount up, before turning to the bus.

The bullet knocked her flat on her face. The second round bounced off her helmet.

35

Megan rolled right. The next round hit the sliding walkway too close to her nose. She kept rolling, then stopped. The fourth bullet hit where she would have rolled to.

The Navy officer got her legs under her and bolted for the other side of the bus.

Whoever was shooting at her was good. The next round hit her right in the butt and sent her sprawling again. She hit the deck and started rolling.

There was no sixth shot. The Marines had been in their own transport. With a sergeant yelling, "Go! Go! Go!" the Marine sharpshooters poured out of their ride and began searching for the assassin.

It took them more time than usual to identify the shooter's position. There were a lot of roofs and windows around them. One finally shouted, "I've got him."

The four Marines beside her turned, slaved their rifles to her fire computer, and got the same sight picture she had.

As one, they locked in on the assumed position and waited for the next muzzle flash.

The shot that knocked Megan on her ass was the last thing that Iteeche would ever do.

It took Megan a moment to realize she could quit rolling.

For an unbelievable moment, there was total silence. Then, the cook wagon driver broke it by saying calmly on net, "Shots fired. Officer down."

"Officer is fine," Megan snapped back on net.

However, the alarm had gone out. The net quickly filled with responses.

"Medical reaction team headed down in five minutes."

"Full Marine security team headed down in five minutes."

"Crime site security and forensic team headed down in ten minutes."

"Belay the Medical team. My spider silk body armor did its job, okay, folks?" Megan insisted on net.

"Are you sure you're okay?" was in Admiral Longknife's mothering voice. Had she been following Megan on net?

"I was hit in the back and butt. I'll have Captain Sung look me over, but I think the armor did its job. I can still feel the way it hardened around the bullet strike to spread the energy."

"Megan, I want a visual validation of your claim," said Kris.

"Aye, aye, Admiral," she said, then howled, "Quinn!"

"I'm coming if you'll have Lily unlock this box."

Megan took her first serious look at the bus rather than seeing it as something to get behind. At the first shot fired, while Megan was scampering for her life, Lily had turned the bus into an armored box. Windows and doors had been transformed into a solid gray wall.

"Give us the bus back, Lily," Megan drawled.

"Yes, ma'am," Lily answered, as the block for Smart Metal™ sprouted wheels and windows again. Quinn tumbled inside from the door that was suddenly created, and headed for Megan.

"Could you use a hand up?" the captain said.

"Please," the commander answered.

Once Megan was back on her feet, Quinn glanced around. "You want to drop your ship suit right here in front of God and every damn Iteeche?"

"I've adjusted the cook wagon to allow for some privacy," Lily informed them.

"Good," Megan said and began limping for the much-modified cook wagon.

"Ma'am," the eager Marine sergeant said, "do you want us to secure the shooter's site?"

"I don't think we've got the resources, nor any idea how to get from here to wherever there is. Lily, can you raise the governor for voice?"

"I have him on the line. Wait one while he's handed the walkie-talkie."

"Yes, who is this and why are you calling me on this private line?"

"Governor, this is Lieutenant Commander Megan Longknife of the U.S. Navy. I've been shot at in your lovely town and I require police to secure the shooter's site."

"Are you being shot at now?" he demanded.

"Nope. The shooter is dead, a frequent result of trying to kill a Longknife. Fleet investigation and forensic teams are on the way down here. You will likely need to have them met at the space port and assisted in arriving here at the crime scene. Please do not have your police disturb that crime scene, I'd like to have our people go over it for trace elements."

"Of course. Of course," the governor sputtered. "Police are on their way," and the governor rang off.

"Megan," Lily said, "while you were talking, I chipped off some scout nanos. I have located the dead sniper. If you want, we can dispatch a fire team of Marines to secure the site."

Megan tried to ignore the throbbing that was starting in her back. Yes, the armor was good, but those were big honking Iteeche rounds that had been playing knick knack on her back.

"Lily, show me the scene," she said, then raised her voice, "Sak, I need some help."

Immediately, a holograph of the room with the dead sniper appeared in front of Megan. The inventory, in order, were one honking big Iteeche rifle, one table to support same, and one dead Iteeche, hopefully the sniper, and very likely from the way the body was sprawled over the weapon.

"Sak, can you loan my Marines one or two people to help my Marines make it up to that room?"

"My assistant and another of the men who met you when you arrived would be perfect to assure that your men see what they need to see."

"Sergeant? Two of your best," Megan called.

In a moment, the four men, two Iteeche senior techs, and sober-looking Marine corporal, and an eager private first class, had their orders, had been assigned a guide by Lily, and were jogging toward one of those concrete and glass monsters to Megan's right.

Now it was time for Megan to see after herself.

Captain Sung herded a reluctant Lieutenant Commander Longknife up the stairs into a much-expanded and modified vehicle. In a matter of minutes, it had been transformed from a cook wagon to a Marine transport, and now into a change room with medical possibilities. They were joined by a Marine with a large bag marked with a red cross.

"Okay, are you going to take that ship suit off," Quinn ordered, "or do I?"

"I'm doing it. I'm doing it," Megan snapped back and began unzipping her full body suit. The blue ship suit was a comfortable blend of cotton and wool, with a few synthetics thrown in to make it fire retardant, comfortable, and keep it looking good after two days of hard damage control.

Two days of sitting in a high gee station in one would usually leave both the suit and the wearer rather bedraggled, if not constipated.

Megan pulled her arms from the suit and let it fall down to her thighs. The Marine medic joined Quinn in examining Megan's back and butt. With the upgraded spider silk armor hardened around the hits, it was impossible to strip out of the armored body suit.

The Navy officer studied the blank bulkhead in front of her while fingers began to feel around her back. Megan hoped they were the medic's; he was kind of cute.

"The armor did its job," Quinn announced on net. "There are two holes in her shipsuit, but the spider silk is undistorted. The second layer expanded and hardened as advertised and is slowly returning to its liquid state. Megan, could you take off the spider silks?"

"I'd rather not." Megan wouldn't mind getting naked in front of the cute Marine. Her problem was getting back into this armor again.

Now someone was pulling on the spider silk somewhere close to the bullet strike.

"This is Corporal Duniquin, trained battlefield life saver. I've lifted the spider silks as much as they will allow. I don't see any bruising on the lieutenant's body."

He could have at least said "delectable body." Is there no poetry left in this world?

However, Megan had been cleared for duty, so the medic left, and she pulled her ship suit back on. In a moment, she rejoined a worried Sak and several of his senior techs or craftsman.

"Are you all right?" Sak asked.

"I'm fine. I'm fine," Megan said, to calm the big fellows. "We humans have tough skin."

"Tough skin my eyes," one tech said. "It was magic. The blackest of magic," and he spat on the road. He did, however, turn away from Megan to do it.

There was a rumble from the other Iteeche, whether in support of him or Megan, it was hard to tell.

"I'm wearing body armor," Megan said. "I'm a Longknife. People try to kill us. We piss them off by surviving."

That got a laugh, weak, but a laugh.

Megan was of half a mind to pull out the edge of the spider silk so they could see it, but her silks now ran all the way up her neck to where Lilly circled it like a bejeweled torc. Also, her personal armor had just saved her life, and Kris regularly benefitted from it, too. The fewer Iteeche who knew about spider silk under armor, the better.

"Actually, we wear body armor that protects us. I've got two holes in my ship suit, including one right on my behind, but no holes in me. It's not magic, just a technology we have," Megan watched the Iteeche as she spoke. She was no expert on reading Iteeche body language, but she strongly suspected that her words were meeting a brick wall.

It was no easy thing for an Iteeche to believe a human

might be better at something than they. Yes, at the top, this dismal fact was sinking in, but down at the bottom of the social pyramid, the common people were still being fed a pabulum that, if it didn't encourage hate for the two eyes, it certainly fostered superiority over them.

"This is Corporal Cortez. We've found the room," came on net. "One body with four rounds in it. One rifle. We're securing the scene."

"Very good, Corporal," Megan answered. "The local police are on the way, as well as a team from the *Princess Royal*. Let me know if there is any difficulty in working with the locals."

"Aye, aye, ma'am."

"Megan, how about I head up there?" Captain Quinn said. "A Navy captain who reports to Admiral Longknife might get a bit more respect."

She'd also likely be more politically astute than a Marine corporal in a situation that was rich in political land mines.

"I think that's a good idea," came on net from Grand Admiral Kris Longknife.

"I can detach another pair of Marine rifles, ma'am," Megan said.

"Very good. Hold your position until reinforced," Kris ordered. "I know we want to fix this mess as soon as possible, but security is paramount now that we know you're in a shooting gallery. By the way, Megan, I've got a call out to all the city governors, both from Ron and through the Planetary Overlord. Some of them are confessing that they might have one or two available circuit boards if we need them. Why don't you see what you can do, and I'll see what I can do. Maybe we can have the entire thing up soon."

"Thank you, Admiral. I figured there might be more give

when a Longknife pushed rather than when a fellow governor begged."

"Yeah. We've got to do something to get these people to solve their own problems. I know it wouldn't take a lot of Smart Metal to fix this, but I need all the Smart Metal I've got for armor. We're headed for a fight and every kilogram may count."

"Yes, ma'am." Megan knew that when push came to shove, and the devil was demanding payment, her cook wagon and bus would likely be somewhere out on the *Princess Royal's* hull trying to stop a laser from burning through. That was just what you did with Smart Metal™. And while you could send out a truck and bring it back, if you started donating armor to some civilian need, there was no telling where that would end.

Megan watched as Quinn, with two Marines and a tech guide, headed toward the ugly block of gray concrete and dull, unwashed glass. She looked around at the high rises around her and realized, she must be a perfect target.

"Sak, let's get back on the bus. We can talk until my security detail can be expanded."

The senior tech glanced around, too. He seemed to hunch his shoulders as he agreed. The two of them boarded the bus. From the outside, it looked like a gray box on wheels. Inside, however, there were windows and decent stools for the Iteeche craftsmen and their helpers.

"Is everything okay?" someone asked from the middle of the bus.

"Everything is fine," Megan answered. "We will be waiting here a while. Somebody took a potshot at me. You will notice that I'm alive and talking. I can't say the same for the very dead shooter. Now, I have orders to stay here until a larger security team can arrive and another team can get here to look at the crime scene. Longknifes like to know who's shooting at us. We especially like to find the folks that gave the order. So, while we're waiting, do you have any questions?"

"Is it true that you humans murdered the Planetary Overload by magic?"

"I was personally there," Megan said, "and I can assure you that there was no magic in use."

The response showed a serious lack of belief.

"Lily, give me a large monitor up here in the front of the bus and get a few scouts wandering around the bus."

A moment later, the front windows turned into a huge monitor, a second later, it split into six different screens. Each showed rough boots and legs.

"Okay, so whose boots do we have here?" Megan said.

"Mine," came from one old grizzled Iteeche.

"You see anything around you that could take those pictures?"

Quickly, a half dozen large Iteeche were peering at the deck or looking under the seats.

"I don't see nothing," came from several.

"Well, now your ugly mugs are on the screen," Sak said, as he barked a laugh.

Heads popped up, but Lily had wisely frozen that transmission.

"Col! You could see us, but I didn't see nothin'."

Another screen now showed the inside of a tool box.

"By the dark depths of chaos," one youngster exclaimed. "That's the wrench my old man passed to me."

He lifted up the tool box and rested it on the seat in front of him while he unlocked it. When he opened the lid, light poured into the box. For a second the view turned to white, then it returned to just a bit lighter than it had been when the box was closed.

"How you doin' that?" came from several voices.

"We are able to make scouts with cameras that are tiny. Much tinier than one of your whiskers," Megan said. "They are so small that they can slip through the cracks into a tool box. Slip through a sealed door. Find an Overlord who has buried himself deep underground and kill him. I did just that a few days ago."

"You killed them all," was but a whisper.

"I was the fist on Admiral Longknife's arm, but yes, I was there when those rebels died so that you wouldn't."

The Iteeche craftsmen and helpers sat back in their stools. They looked at Megan with a blend of respect and awe, if she was reading their gill slits right. They whispered among themselves. Most of it boiled down to them believing what they hadn't believed before.

They waited for the next thing to happen.

36

Megan was not surprised when four sonic booms shook the bus. She'd figured on maybe a company or two. When her count of double booms went past twelve, even she began to get edgy. When it finished at twenty-four, she figured she'd drawn the attention of some really big elephants.

That was never a good thing for a junior field grade officer. Particularly for a fresh Longknife lieutenant commander.

To give herself some warning, she tapped into the overhead imagery. Each lander seemed to be disgorging two or three armored vehicles. The first six formed up, then, with lights flashing and sirens blaring, they headed out of the airport and down the most direct street route to exactly where she sat.

Fifteen minutes after they landed, a company of Marines were forming a perimeter well away from her bus, and a squad had headed up to reinforce the crime scene team.

So far, nothing had been heard from the local constabulary.

"Shouldn't we have some police here by now?" Megan asked Sak.

"We rarely see the crushers in our neighborhood," he answered.

"And we're happy for every second we don't," one of the old craftsmen said, darkly.

"What happens when you do see them?" Megan asked.

"Nothing good," Sak said, and left it at that.

The full extent of Megan's elephant infestation became clear when an eight-wheeled armored infantry fighting vehicle rolled up the street that led to her section of the road. It had a red flag with three white stars painted on its side.

"Oh, God, I've drawn Lieutenant General Montoya himself," she breathed. Or prayed. Both were needed.

"Sak, you're with me," she said, as she opened the bus's door and marched to meet Kris Longknife's security chief, Marine commander, oh, and husband who was the father of her children.

He also had, by royal decree, the authority to lock any Longknife of blood up in her cabin if he considered her in danger over her head.

"Sir," Megan said, saluting, "I didn't expect to see you here."

He returned her salute. "Someone has chosen to make this a major test of our ability to keep a planet running. It seemed well worth some flag officer attention, don't you think? Oh, and Lieutenant Commander, why aren't you in full space armor?"

For the first time, it dawned on Megan that the general,

and all the Marines around her, were wearing full play clothes. They even carried their own oxygen supply.

Megan licked her lips and decided to push her luck. "General, this is Sak, he's the senior surviving transportation manager in Sunset. He's rounded up fifty or more Iteeche craftsmen or helpers to get the roads running again. You'll note, he's not wearing armor. None of his men are."

"Yes, Commander, but none of them have been shot at. A bullet to the back of the neck would have met no armor."

"Yes, sir, but if you'll excuse me, I feel compelled to lead from the front. I'm in front of Iteeche who have nothing on but their shirts. I can't look like a trembling clam."

"Longknife," he muttered, but he smiled at her as he did. "Alright, carry on, Commander. We will conform to your movements."

"Ah, that might be a problem, sir."

"Oh?" sounded like she had about one minute to explain.

"These roads normally roll. These big fellows walk on, stand, and then walk off. I'm not sure the roads can take one of our vehicles with its excessive ground pressure."

"Good point. Sal," the general said to his own computer, "modify the fighting vehicles to equal the ground pressure of an Iteeche vehicle."

"We can increase the number of wheels and tires, sir," a voice said from the general's neck. Unlike Lily, there were no jewels on his, only a Marine Corps crest. "We'll still be a bit heavy."

"I could use some of the extra metal," Megan put in. "That bus is mighty thin."

"Do it, Sal," the general ordered.

Immediately, the general's ride lengthened and sprouted two more axles. Each of the six axles soon had two tires on each side. As that hunk of heavy metal was changing, so were six others.

Lily, not to be outdone, began to do the same to both the bus and the cook wagon.

Even Megan found herself with her mouth hanging open for what happened next.

The general's rig spun out a length of line, then whipped it back and forth, as it grew longer, like some fly fisherman. Then the line snaked out to fall across the cook wagon and land on the bus. As soon as the connection was made, the line began to thicken up until it was a solid rope, pulsing with metal moving through it.

Six other armored vehicles had tossed lines from one to the other until the farthest one was hitched to the general's ride. Soon, they began to pass metal along, lightening themselves and giving Megan's rigs lifesaving armor.

All this was done in about five minutes.

"Very good, sir. I'm going to be going up the line to where we hope to scavenge some circuit boards."

"Circuit boards?"

"Yes, sir. Very old school. Could you detach a platoon to race up there and put it under guard? I would have if I'd had half a chance, but I've kind of been making this up as I go along."

"Major, send first platoon up to the last interchange. Have them secure the road, both above and below."

"Sak, you want to ride along and tell them what needs to be done?"

"Thank you, very much, yes."

"We need to keep this location secure, sir, as well."

At that moment, three of the Iteeche who had led Marines and Captain Sung up to the crime scene walked back into view.

Sak shouted at two of them to help the humans protect the intersection, they nodded and stood, waiting for further orders. Megan sent the sergeant who had been with her since she landed to coordinate with the two Iteeche and a company commander who now commanded at this location.

They had hardly started talking when seven rigs began to roll down the road, headed north.

Now it was time for Megan to get her own team together and moving.

"General, I'd like at least a platoon to escort my bus north. Could you include anti-air as well as anti-surface capabilities?"

"I think you definitely deserve some escort," the general said, and smiled at something behind Megan.

She turned to see Lily's latest innovation. She'd sucked a lot of metal from the Marine rigs and she'd put it to good use. Where one blocky bus had previously stood, now four sixteen-wheeled rigs in the spitting image of the Marine armored rigs sat ready to roll.

"Thanks, Lily. No need to have all my eggs in one basket."

"I thought you might prefer this, Megan."

The Navy officer boarded the first bus. Fifteen Iteeche, their mouths still wide open, sat staring at her. She glanced around, found a hatch that was for real, and popped her head out of the rig. Behind her, Marines stood in the hatches of her other three rigs, as well as the fifteen that looked ready to roll.

There was only one problem. They all had large helmets and she wore a yellow hard hat. Lily fixed that, even changed her ship suit from blue to regulation camouflage. It would take a very good eye, and one pretty close up, to spot the difference now.

Megan lifted her arm. "Let's roll," she shouted.

Two Marine rigs rolled out. She slipped her vehicle right behind them. The rest of her specials were merged into the Marine column. Then, they began to play games. One rig would fall back, another speed up, and soon three rigs would be rolling along side by side. Then they'd shuffle themselves and change their order as they fell back into line.

The drivers did this the entire time they were rolling up the road at a sedate twenty klicks an hour.

Then, life got more complicated.

"This is Roland 1-6. We've arrived at the target site. Be advised, it has been booby trapped. Repeat, our bomb sniffers report explosives and we've spotted what looks like booby traps among the machinery."

Someone really didn't want the people of Sunset City to eat dinner tomorrow.

37

All Megan could do was just shake her head. Someone really enjoyed messing with her day. She was rapidly getting tired of this crap. She might be a Longknife, but she really didn't believe that she deserved any of this.

"Have we got a bomb team down here?" she asked on net.

It took longer than she wanted before an answer came back, and it was from the colonel commanding this rump regiment from back at the airport. "This is Stonewall. We have several technicians capable of doing some bomb work, but we have no one with a bomb suit or the necessary kit to go at this."

"Longknife 2, I understand. Please get what assets we have moving to the target location. Longknife 1, could you get the necessary team headed for my location?"

"They will drop in fifteen minutes. We're not at the right place in our orbit where we can make a drop."

"Thank you, ma'am. Do I have permission to observe and survey the situation when I arrive?"

"Survey and observe only, Lieutenant," was not in Kris Longknife's motherly tone of voice.

"Understood. Don't blow up what we need to salvage."

"What do you know, a Longknife that can learn," was about what Megan expected from her cousin who sported five stars.

They rolled up to the interchange. It was well posted, if thinly. Megan ordered three of the buses to slow down well away from the target, but kept hers rolling right up to where Sak stood. There, she dismounted.

"We can get down there," the tech told her. "However, if we try to get anywhere close to the actual road machinery, there are all sorts of booby traps."

Megan wondered if the Iteeche word for booby trap was anything as simple as the human word.

IT'S SHORTER, MEGAN, AND IT HAS A HINT OF TRAITOR, Lily answered.

"Lily, get me some nano scouts down there. Map the place and give me a look at those booby traps."

"Aye, aye, Commander," her computer replied.

Poor Sak's eyes grew wide but he stood, steady on his four feet, beside Megan.

Less than a minute later, a holographic image began to form in front of her. It showed her the support corridor under the roads. With the exception of a few of Sak's workers and Marines in full battle rattle, the corridors had nothing in them except silent machinery painted in bright, primary colors.

Then the imaging zoomed down on a very particular bit of gear.

There was a small packet, well hidden behind a large

pipe and stuck to a gear box. It was painted the same bright red of the machinery it was slapped on. However, even at a glance, it clearly didn't belong there.

Again, the image zoomed down. Now they were in the packet. There were wires, all of the same gray color. Humans always marked their wires with red, green, blue, and yellow colors. Whoever did this didn't want anyone knowing which wire might do what.

Megan scowled at the vision before her. "It looks like this is going to be harder than I expected," she said on net, as she transmitted her take.

"Crap," came from somewhere on the net. "No colored wires. We'll have to trace each one of these damn booby traps one at a time."

"Let us know how deep you want to go into the wiring," Megan said.

"Don't get too carried away. Wait until we get there."

"Only too glad to wait. Lily, get more nano scouts down there. We need to map this place as finely and as far as we can until we're sure we have all the explosives."

"On it, Megan," and a lovely kind of rainbow was visibly spawned off their bus and flitted toward the entrance. The lieutenant raised an eyebrow. She could rarely see her nanos in actual flight and never had seen anything this spectacular. Lily must have millions of the tiny things headed for the underground.

For the next five minutes, the nanos mapped the service corridor below the roads.

Then suddenly, they didn't.

Megan heard the muffled explosions before she felt the ground tremble beneath her feet.

Something was definitely wrong.

38

"Get out of here! Grab an Iteeche and go! Go! Go! Go!" was either a Gunny or a Marine who learned well from one and was close to the head of the line to fill one's shoes.

"Masks down! Masks down! Go to oxygen!" came in another commanding voice.

In a blink, Megan lost half of her hologram. The half she still had showed jets of water shooting up from the deck below the road's service corridor.

Even as she watched, she lost more of her coverage. Someone had come up with a way to defeat the human nanos.

That someone was also killing the Iteeche road techs she'd sent into harm's way.

"Get troopers over there to help them out of the stairs," Megan shouted.

Behind her, the three other buses with Iteeche techs gunned forward. Near the exit stairs, they screeched to a halt and big Iteeche poured out the doors with an agility Megan would never have expected.

In a moment, they surrounded the stairwell. One took command and ordered two down but kept the stairs from being blocked.

Now, Megan could hear the roar of rushing water. It was as if she stood on a rock above a long stretch of white water rapids. She stayed where she stood, letting the Iteeche take care of their own. Hopefully, in the flooding tunnel below, Marines were helping where they could.

Megan had never been in harm's way when water was doing its best to slam her against a wall, a pole, or a sharp bit of machinery. On net, she could hear heavy breathing, and an occasional order to get this or that Iteeche up topside. Mostly, the Marines worked silently to save those that their grandfathers had struggled to kill.

What a change a hundred years could make.

Now, bedraggled Iteeche began to stumble up the stairs, supported by one of their co-workers. As some came up, more were sent down.

"This one's not going to make it," a Marine growled.

"Pass him along," another said.

"Can we make a breather for these Iteeche?"

"Lily?" Megan ordered.

Smart Metal™ began to spin off the closest buses. Quickly they snaked lines into the stairwell, while other chunks formed compressors that began pumping cylinders full of atmosphere. As one was filled, it would snake its way down the line, down the stair and out to wherever it was needed.

A moment later, "Got one, thanks," came through. Then another thanks in a woman Marine's voice. Megan could only hope that they'd gotten that moving fast enough.

An Iteeche was hauled up the stairs, unconscious. One of the Marine corpsmen began pumping his chest while another held an oxygen mask over his beak and slowly pumped gas in and out of flooded lungs.

With a cough that spewed water and that delicious meal all over the oxygen mask, the Iteeche rolled over and vomited up more water. It looked like that one would live.

By then, there were already two other wiped out Iteeche being cared for and another was being lifted from the stairwell.

"We've found three Iteeche gasping for air in a pocket," a Marine reported on net. "We need some breathers so we can get these big guys out quick. This air won't last long."

More lifesaving cylinders snaked down into the sunken depths. Megan prayed they'd get there in time.

"It would be nice if we could do something about this rushing water," came from below on net.

"Lily." Megan ordered.

"On it," and drones began to spawn off of the armored rigs and wind their way out in all directions, looking for stairwells so they could convert to fish and go looking for where all the water was coming from.

"Sak, who do we talk to at the waterworks?"

"I don't know."

"Longknife 2 to Longknife 1, could you get the head honcho from down here on the line and get him to cut off the flow of water to this break? We don't know how bad it is, but all the water flowing by this junction needs to be stopped at the source."

"On it," came in Kris Longknife's decisive voice. Megan sure didn't want to be in some boss man Iteeche's shoes.

Meanwhile, below, it took a few minutes, but Megan was soon watching as drones with wings formed into drones on treads and worked their way down half-flooded stairs. At a distant place in the tunnel, Smart Metal™ that had been spooled off the buses and formed into a pipe began to slip underground. There, they formed cofferdams that started to restrict the rushing water, then closed down the tunnel entirely.

"We're flooded down here, but at least the water isn't moving as much," came from below. "We're ready to move these three Iteeche. Get ready to receive them above."

"We'll be ready," Megan said, and got three thumbs up from her three medics.

It took a couple of minutes for the bedraggled and gasping Iteeche to start stumbling up the stairs, but they were breathing and alive.

Sadly, not everyone who had been below had made it. "We've got three dead Iteeche. Is it clear to bring them up?"

"This is Longknife 2, bring up your dead. Also, I don't see a need for Marines down there. If you're clear, come out as well."

"No, ma'am, I don't see anything more we can do. Someone sure made a mess of this place."

They'd also cost Megan a lot of nanos.

"Longknife 2 to Longknife 1. I know you don't want to give up any armor if you can avoid it, but whatever happened down there, we're going to need Smart Metal to set it right. At least set it right now and not in six or twelve months. You don't replace big water pipes in an afternoon."

"Longknife 2, Longknife 1 here. I agree. I'll have Admiral Coth drop a couple of thousand tons of Iteeche Smart Metal on your location. Coth, are you monitoring this?"

"Yes, My Admiral. If you will have your Nelly send me the designs for that lander you used to drop your embassy castle from orbit, I will see that a much smaller one lands close to your cousin. Then I will dispatch a flotilla to the nearest manufacturing world to appropriate ten thousand tons of that magic metal of yours. We should have known that it would come in handy and we can't expect you to expend metal from your own production."

"No. We try to keep different sources of the metal separated," Kris said. "So far we've had no problems, but you can never tell."

"Yes. Coth out."

"Megan, does this take care of your problem?"

"Yes, Admiral. I'll send probes down to find the leaks and we'll start plugging them as soon as the 'magic metal' arrives."

"Longknife 1, out."

"Longknife 2, out."

A minute later, scouts, shaped like tiny fish, were released into the dark waters. The currents were now down to just troublesome, not the twisting rapids of half an hour earlier. The fish sank deep into the tunnel and soon found smaller ladder wells that allowed access to tight spaces below.

There, they found a conduit filled with pipes and cable runs. The local constabulary arrived, complete with someone officious, as well as a pair of more knowledgeable Iteeche who had risen through the ranks based on merit, not birth.

"Yes, you are right," one said as the busybody in fancy clan robes looked on, clearly upset that the human was not talking to him. However, Megan had given him the first chance to answer her questions and he'd proven totally ignorant. Now she talked to an Iteeche in plain brown jerkins and pants.

"Below the road maintenance and access corridor is a

lower access tunnel. It has water and sewage pipes and Information Transfer Assistant Director Kun's conduits for cable runs for both voice and data."

Beside the speaker, another Iteeche in lighter brown togs, now identified as Kun, nodded his head.

"Are you getting anything downstream from here?" Megan asked.

Kun answered first. "We have lost all traffic both north from here as well as on this east-west lateral line. A good quarter of Sunset City doesn't even know what time it is. But my problem is not half that of Assistant Director Jin."

So, at least on this planet, everything was networked, even the clocks. Megan shook her head. "And the water supply department?" she asked the other one.

"The Water and Sanitation Department," Jin corrected her.

"Water and sanitation?"

"Yes, your eminence. There are two levels of tunnels beneath the road access corridors. The top tunnel has eight 1.22-meter pipes. Each pair of pipes carries water for roughly a quarter of Sunset City. As it stands now, all those pipes have been breached and all have been cut off at the plants. To be precise, in my words, half of Sunset City cannot fill a glass of drinking water."

Megan thought of several nasty words but said none.

"Below those pipes are a second set of tunnels. Much larger. In the middle set are eight 1.88-meter pipes that carry what we in the trade call brown water. You might call it shit."

"I got it the first time," Megan said.

"On either side of that tunnel are two equally large viaducts that carry rain water out of the city. If matters are bad enough, we can flood the middle one, and pray the brown pips are not broached. Only once in the last thousand years have we had to flood the upper tunnel as well. There is nothing in our recorded history of the transportation access corridor being flooded. Do you understand me?"

"So, you have no good idea about how we dewater the transportation access corridor," Megan said.

"Yes," said Sak, Kun and Jin together.

Shit, was not said by Megan.

"So, if we can open drains from the corridor and the top water tunnel into the storm drain system, we could empty this mess."

"Yes, we could, but the mouse is more likely to bell the cat."

LILY?

SORRY, MEGAN, BUT THEIR IDIOM WAS JUST SO PERFECTLY A MATCH FOR BELLING THE CAT.

OKAY, I JUST WANTED TO MAKE SURE I HAD IT RIGHT.

"Longknife 2 to Longknife 1. I'm going to need all the engineering support that you can send my way."

"Longknife 1, it's already dropping. Some is at the space port waiting for your call."

"Thanks. We've got to drain this tunnel and do it fast." Megan filled Kris in on what she'd found out.

"So, they not only have sabotaged the roads, but the water, sanitation, and communication systems as well."

"Which explains why I have yet to see any police, and the only people I have here are those that you demanded be sent here."

"Yes, having a command radio net can come in handy sometimes," Kris said drolly.

More vehicles began to roll up to her location. They were well-spaced apart, and all showed sixteen or even twenty-four wheels. Megan soon found herself in a multi-way conversation with the Iteeche civil service and her combat engineers who were only too delighted to swap out for the day to be real, honest-to-God, civil engineers.

Of course, since this job might involve blowing shit up, they were about as happy as a Marine engineer could be.

"Please. Please," Jin and Kun begged. "Do not blow up our tunnels. It will take us forever to set things right."

"It won't do my roads no good either," Sak added.

"I assure you," the brigadier of all of Kris's combat engineers told them, "when we are done, we'll give you back your facilities not only not broken, but back in working order."

"But it will take us a year to straighten up this mess," said Jin of Water and Sewer.

"More for me," added Kun of Info Transfer.

"I assure you, by sunset tonight. Well, maybe midnight at the latest, we'll have this all shipshape and Bristol fashion."

The Iteeche eyed the brigadier leaving Megan to wonder how that idiom translated.

The commanding engineer, however, took the time to keep his Iteeche clients well-informed. That left the Iteeche with their beaks hanging open a lot of the time.

The fish scouts continued to map the three levels of tunnels beneath their feet. As it turned out, the Iteeche did have bulkheads in both the water and sewage tunnels. Only a few kilometers of either had been flooded, and some of the upper tunnel was already slowly draining down into the lower.

The fish scouts, being Smart Metal™ were able to switch back to airborne form so they could scout the unflooded spaces. The fish had to switch to nano size to survive the ride next door to the storm drain. They were closed off by thick doors, but there wasn't a door the Iteeche had invented yet that could keep out a human nano.

In an hour, the entire stretch of pipes, lines, tunnels and mess were mapped, and the engineers were looking for ways to drain both the road work spaces and the lower water and data tunnel.

"The access from the upper tunnel let the lower tunnel flood, but they aren't enough to quickly empty the top one. We need to establish some drains down from the roads and data/water tunnels to the bottom, right, and left tunnels."

"There aren't any." Jin said. "Maybe if you could open the doors from the sewage tunnel to the drain tunnels . . ."

"Too slow. We'd still be waiting for it to drain next week. Nope, we want it gone now. Okay, I'm going to send engineers down to punch holes through the tunnel walls every ten meters along both sides of the top tunnel."

"How do you intend to punch all those holes?" Megan asked.

"Just a wee bit of plastic explosives will do the trick."

"Explosives!" came from three Iteeche.

"Wee explosives. Nothing big. Just enough to punch the hole and singe the dirt between the two tunnels. We don't want the water tearing out the ground beneath our feet, now do we?"

"How about we have some Smart Metal standing by to reinforce those wee holes your wee explosives will put in the tunnels?" Megan suggested.

"Oh. Yep. We can do that, too."

The three Iteeche turned to Megan. "You said that you would have everything working again by sunset," Sak said. "Midnight at the latest."

"Yes, I did."

"But now this warrior is speaking of blowing up our tunnels."

"Yes, he is."

"We will never get our systems fixed if you go blowing them up."

"You may be surprised how careful Marine combat engineers can be when they blow stuff up."

"May the wide blue sky protect us from your chaos," Sak muttered, and the three of them turned away.

As they'd talked, combat engineers in full battle armor had been making their way down the access staircase into the dark waters.

Megan called her doubting Iteeche managers back to watch her holograph as tiny Marines half-walked, half-swam along the walls of the top access tunnel with its eight huge water pipes and squared-off cable runs stacked one on top of the other going down the middle. There was just enough space for an Iteeche to crawl though.

Each engineer would stick a few soft pellets of explosives into the corner of the tunnel floor. Then, he or she would place a bit of Smart Metal™ cloth over it, and run their hand along the edges, sealing it to the wall as well.

"That is how they are going to blow holes in the wall?" Jin said. "Something that small won't even scratch the paint."

"We shall see," Megan said.

About that time, a large sonic boom shook the rigs, and likely the buildings alongside the road.

"I think our ten thousand tons of Smart Metal just arrived," the brigadier told Megan.

"Good. Will it be used to reinforce the water pipes and data conduits?"

"That, Commander, will be the first use we put it to," was

a polite way of telling a Longknife to get her nose out of his business.

Megan took two steps back, but kept watching.

In the murky waters, Marines kept laying down four long daisy chains, one on each side, one from each direction. Megan wondered if the four daisy chains would be broken up into several more, but she swallowed the question.

She didn't need to be put in her place another time.

They were still working below when a convoy of large-wheeled, crew-less rigs rolled up under the escort of a dozen more armed Marine infantry fighting vehicles. They'd come directly from the airport, driving the immobile rolling road the entire way.

An engineer and a programmer worked with the lead rig for a few minutes, then a long line of Smart Metal™ began to snake its way down the access stairwell. A pair of Marines in battle rattle moved below working alongside the snake.

More metal flowed below, and more Marines went with it. One after another, the fifty big rigs would move forward, toss a line to the big-wheeled metal transport ahead of it, and begin feeding metal down even before the first one finished emptying itself out. It was amazing to watch.

"What are you doing?" Kun asked.

"As much as we are doing our best to keep the explosions as small as possible, and direct the force of the explosion down, and away from the water in the tunnel, we know there will be blowback. This magic metal is to reinforce your conduits. We've checked, and there's water in your conduits. We don't want any pressure transferred onto them. The same with the water pipes. Especially the water pumps. We don't want to damage them."

Megan was happy to see that the Iteeche were happy

learning that the humans weren't totally set on leaving their city unlivable.

"We're putting armor around everything we think might be damaged. Oh, and we're also plugging the holes in the pipes. As soon as you make sure the water is ready to flow, you can turn it back on."

"Why did you humans not annihilate us during the war?" Sak asked, his lower beak hanging slack.

"My great-great-grandfather Raymond Longknife didn't want anyone annihilated," Megan said. "You were very good fighters. He knew if we kept that war going, the bloody wreckage when it was done would leave no one the victor."

The three Iteeche looked at Megan.

"You are one of those Longknifes?" Jin asked.

"That is both my honor and my curse."

The three of them did that chuckle that Iteeche do deep in their throats.

39

"We've got all our explosives in place," came over the net.

"Clear the tunnel," the engineering brigadier at Megan's elbow ordered.

Marines in armored space suits began to climb up the stairwell from the flooded spaces below. They quickly moved to form loose ranks. They raised their helmet face plates and stood around joking. Marines and Iteeche got food and warm drinks from the cook wagon, and spirits rose.

A captain was last up the stairs. He eyed the troops in three formations and ordered. "I want a full count from each platoon."

A moment later, a Gunny had each of the groups counting off. With the final number, the Gunny and his LT put their heads together, then the young LTs took the total to the captain. Only when it was clear that all were present or accounted for did the captain trot over to report to the brigadier.

"You may blow your daisy chains when ready," the brigadier said.

"Gunny," the captain called. "Blow this place."

"Fire in the hole," boomed in a voice it took years to acquire, and all around Megan, people looked ready to run. Especially Iteeche.

What followed was disappointing.

The original explosions that had started the mess came with a roar and shook the ground. These explosions were muffled and could hardly be felt. However, every five or ten seconds, there was another one, then another one.

"What's happening?" Megan asked the brigadier.

"We've got four daisy chains. Call them A and B on one side, right and left, and C and D on the other side, right and left of the exit we've been using. We're starting at the far end of each chain. A goes first, then D, then C, and finally B. Then we repeat, walking the explosives up closer to the stairwell. If things go as we planned, by the third or fourth number in each chain, water will be emptying down into the storm drains. There won't be much water pressure on the last couple of charges close to the stairs."

Megan nodded. She'd known the engineers knew this place did not need to look like a war zone when they finished. Sure enough, it wouldn't.

In between the soft explosions, the roar of water could now be heard coming from the stairwell. Megan turned to the three Iteeche bosses she trusted. "Did you get all that?"

They nodded.

"I'll have nanos down there as soon as the last explosion goes off. We still need to clear the explosives we spotted."

Over the next two hours, work moved at lightning speed. The engineers set up blowers to force air into the mainte-nance corridors to drive the remaining water down into the storm drains as well as empty the middle brown water tunnel.

As soon as it was safe, Marine engineers and demolition teams went below and used nanos to probe each of the threatening charges. It was quickly apparent that all had come from the same bomb maker and were to a common design. Once that was figured out, a weakness in the design was identified and the nanos began turning the bombs into inconveniences for the demolition teams to carefully remove.

Only then were the Iteeche craftsmen and technicians allowed below to do their own survey of the damage.

Thanks to the borrowed Smart Metal™, the potable water lines came up first. They were followed quickly by the brown water lines. Now Iteeche could get a drink of water and flush their toilets.

Draining the communication conduits was a bit slower, and water had damaged some delicate equipment. Again, however, with Lily, Megan, and Smart Metal™ handy, replacements were quickly installed and more and more of the communications net came back on line.

That left Megan walking over with Sak to look at the circuit board they'd come here to scavenge in the first place.

"I think the situation has changed," Megan told the Iteeche.

"How so?"

"We now have Smart Metal that we can use for the replacement boards you need down the road."

"We don't need to pull these boards?"

"Maybe one so that Lily and I can study it. Can you have your people look at the boards here and see which one might be the easiest and safest to take out?"

"Yes. Of course."

A number of craftsmen went down the line of boards and studied them all. Finally, they agreed on the best one to extract. They grounded themselves with care, then with equal care, removed the board and immediately set it to rest in one of the metal cases they had brought. There, it rested in a bed of foam, as precious as any human baby.

"Now, Lily and I need to have a look at that thing," Megan said.

There was now a lot of unneeded Smart Metal™ lines, cables, and coverings laying around. No doubt, in time, it would all be collected, but that time was still in the future. As the Iteeche watched with amazed eyes, several fine filaments of what they insisted on calling 'magic metal' proved to them again that there was magic here. They wove their way from where they were over to the circuit board. Other ends wrapped themselves around the torque at Megan's neck, connecting Lily to the board.

For several long minutes, Megan stood there as her mind infiltrated the board, accompanied by Lily, and to a lesser extent, Nelly and Sal, Kris and Jack's computers. Together, they assessed the working of the board, what it did, and, inevitably, because they associated with humans, how to make it better.

Finally, Megan nodded. "I think we have your design down. Now, do you have any testing equipment?"

Sak barked an order and three of the craftsmen had their helpers bring their tool boxes. They pulled various parts and assemblies from the three boxes and put together a large, rather clunky-looking test bed.

"Please test the original."

They did, and found it in working condition.

"Now test that one," Megan said, pointing to a new board that was extruding itself from a sheet of Smart

Metal™ that had been used as armor to protect part of the road from the pressure of explosions.

The Iteeche had been startled by the humans far too much today to show any surprise at finding an apparent copy of their circuit board dangling from part of the road. They collected it, studied it for visual imperfections, then plugged it into their test rig.

The rig hummed and the needles on a number of meters rose until they hung right on the dot of the recommended results. Their own board had showed deviations, but all within acceptable parameters.

This board was right in the middle of each meter.

A lot of beaks ended up on the floor. Still, the senior craftsman took the new board and carefully laid it in the cushioned bed of a second box.

"You can reinstall the sample," Megan ordered. "We can make the twenty-five you need."

"Why did you not do this when we first found this problem?" Sak asked, his four eyes wide.

"We had no sample like this working model we just examined," Megan said. "Also, this is Smart Metal that we're using here. What you see here was taken from the armor of one of the Iteeche battlecruisers in orbit above your heads. Some Iteeche crew is at greater risk now than they were this morning. Admittedly, the risk is small because we spread it out over a large number of ships. Still, my commanding admiral was reluctant to accept that risk."

Megan glanced around at the damp walls. "Then this happened. Someone made it a battle of wills to see if the people of Sunset City would go hungry tonight."

Megan grinned. "Never enter into a battle of wills with Longknifes. You will lose every time."

"That is the sky's honest truth," Sak said.

"Now, good friend, is this section of the road ready to roll?"

"It will be by the time we have the other section up."

And the Iteeche spoke the truth.

By sunset over Sunset City that night, all the roads were rolling.

40

Grand Admiral Kris Longknife let Megan stay below for the night. It seemed she had promised all those who had worked for her a spectacular banquet. Them and their families. It looked like she was making a major draw down on the fleet's supply of fine Iteeche food, but Kris did not gainsay her lieutenant.

She'd been through a challenging day, and the Iteeche who managed to keep up with her deserved whatever the Navy would grant them.

One of Zargoth's largest cities was back up and running. Other cities were posting guards at all critical failure points and a few saboteurs had been apprehended.

Kris had used her influence to get her military interrogators dirtside fast to have a talk with these Iteeche before the local constabulary began their kinetic counseling. Given a choice to talking versus screaming, several had become quite good conversationalists.

A few claimed to have been in the wrong place at the wrong time. Some stories checked out and the humans managed to cut most of them loose with a detective tail to see where they went.

Some of the talkers turned out to be liars. When upon verification, their information was shown to smell of untruth, they were turned over to the Iteeche police. That didn't work out very well for them.

The humans began to fill a media archive of those who talked, those who lied, and those who didn't talk. They began showing these videos to Iteeche waiting to be interrogated.

It was a great warm-up gig.

Once they had seen these videos of Iteeche being interrogated, then being fed by humans, or tortured by big Iteeche cops, the number of Iteeche talking grew exponentially.

Marines, both Iteeche and human, got to bash down a pleasing number of doors in a manner that was not pleasant, for either the doors or those behind them.

That sweep increased the number of Iteeche to talk with, which lead to more visits, and the conversations soon began to involve a better quality of Iteeche as the take went up the clan hierarchy.

By noon the next day, several hundred senior clan officials were making full and complete apologies to the Emperor, with snakes involved. They were doing it on live media for all to see.

There were no further failures of city infrastructure.

Kris ended up shaking her head. "They could have just applied to their clans for transfer off planet. Why did they have to take us on?"

Jack shrugged. "I guess they thought they could. Remember, Kris, the Iteeche are of two minds where we're concerned. They half-hate us, and half-fear us. Half want to believe that they won that war, yet some feel like they lost it. Some of them think we humans are three feet tall, and others think we're ten."

"And all of those feelings are bouncing around in the exact same skull," Kris said, ruefully.

"Yep. But are we humans any different?"

Kris remembered the Iteeche War vets she'd known over the years. Grampas Ray and Trouble had definite respect for their former enemies. However, among the average vet, they felt like they had both beat the Iteeche and almost been annihilated by them. They were sure the Iteeche were ten feet tall . . . and stupid.

That was a very strange combination on both sides.

Kris's problem was not how the Iteeche and humans felt about each other. No. She needed to make a radical change in the way this war was being fought.

Before she was given command of the Iteeche Combined Fleets, the rebels were well on their way to winning. Indeed, if she hadn't succeeded in winning the Battle of the Imperial Guard System, it would have ended with the young Emperor dead and the Imperial Capital planet gassed, leaving it empty for the winners to come in and give away to their followers.

Kris didn't much care for the way the Iteeche played this game of power. However, it was her job to see that the rebels lost, and the loyal side won. Maybe she couldn't prevent a bloodbath, but what she had just observed through Megan's experience in Sunset City was that just because you won, didn't mean the opposition was willing to give it up.

She needed to talk to the Iteeche she trusted. Tonight, she'd laid on a supper for her and Jack with Ron and Admiral Coth. It was time to decide on her next move. Those two were the only Iteeche she really trusted.

Dinner began with a soup. For Kris and Jack, it was a seafood chowder. For Ron and Coth, the soup was waterier. Of course, they had little fish and crab-like things swimming around in the bowl. Instead of a spoon, they used thin silver spears.

"So, Ron, do you think we have fully pacified Zargoth?" Kris asked as she filled her spoon.

He raised a small wiggling fish, bit its head off, chewed it slowly, then added the rest of the fish and chewed some more while he thought. That gave Kris time to enjoy her first taste of chowder.

"This is a very different situation from any that our history books tell us," the Imperial counselor said. "The planet is not half in ruins. A quarter of the population is not dead or wounded, homeless or starving. In your own strange way, you have left a lot of people alive and going about their business as if nothing had happened. There is nothing in our books that would allow me to counsel the Emperor or you on what to expect next."

"I have driven you entirely off the map," Kris observed.

"I was just as unsure of my surroundings when you had me on your ship on the other side of the galaxy," the big Iteeche counselor agreed.

That drew smiles from the humans and a bark of laughter from the Iteeche admiral.

"So, is my admiral often in strange waters?" Coth said.

"Often, and I suspect that she has called us here to talk about going even deeper into uncharted water. No?" Ron said, eyeing Kris.

"I admit that I am looking for a way to strike a blow for the young Emperor that might bring the bloodshed of this war to a halt sooner rather than later."

"How so, my Admiral?" Coth asked, holding a small squirming crab on a skewer just short of his beak.

"The situation below on this planet bothers me," Kris admitted. "I have proven that I can beat an enemy fleet, even if the odds are four to one. However, what does it mean if I cannot convert my victory in space into possession of the factories in orbit and on the ground? Especially, shall we say, if I am to seize a major production hub with many mines and smelters scattered among an asteroid belt."

"In our history," Jack said, "we have often called this winning the hearts and minds of the people."

"The people are like these wack," Ron said, holding up a tiny speared fish. "They go where their clan chiefs tell them to go."

"Was that how it went yesterday, at Sunset City? Where were the clan chiefs when Megan was using the trained technicians to make the roads roll?"

"Are you saying that we should respect the workers and their supervisors?"

"Yes," Kris said.

"The clans will never go for that."

"And if the clans find that they are not needed anymore?" Kris asked.

Ron put down his silver spear. "If the clans think that you would send them into the deep black chasm, they would do everything they could to put you down there first."

Kris really wished Ron had not adopted the recent Iteeche court style of a high collar. She very much would like to know what Ron's vestigial gills were showing. Was this a thoughtful discussion, or was he seeing death ahead for someone?

"Thank you for that advice," Kris said. "I will keep those words close to my heart."

"I hope so," Ron said, picking up his spear and stabbing viciously at a crab. He crunched down hard on it.

Kris decided on a different tack.

"Good Admiral," she said, "is it known among the common admirals and ship commanders, both here and among the rebels that we humans have ways of making long jumps? That we can appear where no jump exists?"

"Yes, my Admiral, that is known to most every Iteeche who commands a warship, and many clan lords that command them. It is very frustrating that we cannot discover the secret of this way of vanishing and reappearing. I know that my ship followed one of your ships into a vacant bit of space, and before I knew it I was hundreds of light years from where I started. I neither saw the jump as I went into it, nor did I see it after it spit me out. How do you do that?"

"Regretfully, I cannot tell you that," Kris said. "However, if our battle fleet were to appear deep in rebel territory, it is likely the rebels would be surprised, but not shocked."

"Yes, the local commander would not like the surprise of your arrival. No doubt, he would curse his luck and fate, but still, he would prepare to fight you."

Kris mulled that over for a short time as she finished up her chowder.

The second course was a white fish. For the Iteeche, it was fresh from being filleted. For the humans, it was baked and served in a Béarnaise sauce.

Both took a moment to sample their fish and praise the cook. The third class petty officer serving the course said she'd be sure to pass their words along.

After a few bites, Kris was ready to return to her planning session.

"Good Admiral, have you gathered the information I asked for?"

"I have. Your Nelly now has it," he said, stripping flesh from the raw fish's backbone and swallowing it down. "Your cook has done something special to this fish," he said.

"We call it marinade. It lets a delicate flavor seep into meat or almost anything," Jack said.

"Nelly, what can you show us?" Kris asked.

"Here are the ten most powerful and productive planets in the rebellion," Nelly said, and a star map appeared above their heads. Most of the stars were just white ghosts. Ten stars, however, were large and flashing red.

"Where are we?" Kris asked.

A gold star appeared.

"So tell me, Nelly, if we used the fastest combinations of jumps, any jump available, how many jumps would it take to get to each of those planets from here?"

Numbers of four and five appeared in white beside the stars. One had a six.

"Tell me, how many of those stars we'd be passing through have Iteeche colonies that might notice a fleet of three thousand ships zipping through at high speeds and acceleration?"

Ones or twos appeared in red beside the blinking white stars. The one exception was the one that took six jumps. It was the one farthest away, and deepest in enemy territory.

"Hmm," Kris said. "Thank you, Nelly. Tell me, Admiral Coth, how is our training program going?"

"Hold it, Kris," Ron interjected, "what do you intend to do with this?"

"As of right now, nothing. I certainly can't do anything if my fleet isn't battle ready, now can I, Admiral Coth?"

"I don't know what you would do, from any moment to

the next, My Admiral," the Iteeche officer said, then barked a laugh. "No one does, eh, Jack?"

"I never do," Jack admitted.

Ron did not look like a happy Iteeche. "Do you intend to go off and lead this fleet out to battle without telling us a single word? I know our fleet is known to leak, both the loyalist and the rebel side, but Kris, don't you trust us at the table?"

"I trust everyone at this table," Kris said, then glanced down at her plate, "except for the fish. I assure you, Ron, I will play my cards very close to my chest this next move, but this fleet will not sail without you and my Good Admiral knowing where we are bound for."

Ron seemed only half mollified. "I should hope that I would be in your counsel when you are deciding the future of this fleet."

"I would expect so, as well, Ron. I may fear that this Navy leaks to the rebels like a waterfall, but I trust those of us at this table. I will need the help of everyone at this table to pull off our next strike."

Kris paused for a moment. "I'm assuming that we all agree that we do not need to keep the fleet in orbit around this planet. Am I right?"

Kris was surprised that she did not get a quick reaction from her two Iteeche.

"So I am not, huh?"

Ron and Admiral Coth exchanged looks. For once, the Imperial counselor waited for the admiral to move into the void.

"That is not as easy a call as it might appear to you, my human admiral," Coth finally said.

"How so?"

"This is the planetary system that the rebels used to

launch their strike at the Imperial Capital planet. It is only two jumps from the honored presence of His Most Worshipful One. Many would think that it was foolish that we did not take this system before. Now that it has been used, many more would think we must guard it."

Kris frowned. "Battlecruisers are meant to be a mobile striking force. Not a bunch of chained guard dogs."

"I can see your point, but we still have many battleship admirals. For thousands of years, we have viewed our fleets under your theory of a fleet in being. So long as the fleet remains in being, it is a threat everywhere. If it is thrown away in battle, it is no longer in existence. In being, if you will, but a destroyed fleet can no longer threaten."

"Has the Iteeche fleet become a carved stone lion growling on the doorstep of some library?"

"That does not translate very well for us, but I think I understand your meaning. How do you think that you humans engaged an Empire as large as us and did so much damage in the early days of the war? Most satraps held on tight to their fleets. Your first fight was between only your united people and a fraction of us. Even once we realized that we needed to hurl more of our fleet at you, so many held back, afraid that to lose ships to you would weaken them in the eyes of their neighbors."

Admiral Coth shoved his plate away from him.

"Even now, there are hundreds, no thousands, of ships detached in dribs and drabs protecting this and that planet. Why do you think so huge an Empire as ours can only muster three thousand ships for your fleet? Maybe there will be five hundred more before we sail, but still."

"It would seem to me," Jack said, evenly, "that this is as much an opportunity as a problem. We have a saying, he who tries to be strong everywhere is strong nowhere. If your forces are deployed in dribs and drabs, then you risk defeat in detail from whomever can muster a mobile strike force."

"And you have seen the rebels muster just such a strike force," Coth said, "and you defeated it in the Imperial Guard System. However, getting that strike force together was a major success on their part. There is a reason why you had to fight outnumbered four to one. We could not gather as many ships as they."

"But, let's assume for a moment," Kris said, letting her words roll slowly off her tongue. "What if we were to take this battle fleet and a million-soldier landing party and race around through jumps to surprise that most distant system? How many ships would the rebels have guarding that system?"

"Likely fewer than our three thousand," Coth answered.

"So, we could sweep in, destroy, or better yet, capture their fleet. Once we controlled the space, it would be easy to capture their planet, maybe using similar methods to how we captured this planet. Finally, we land the landing party and occupy the system."

"And then you die deep in hostile territory," Ron spat. "It would be suicide."

"I think not," Kris said. "Not if we do it just right."

"How so?" Coth asked.

"A long time ago on old earth," Kris said, "there was a general. Sherman or something like that. He captured a city, a major supply center. He could have kept his army in supply there for however long he chose. Instead he burned the city."

"Why do that?" Coth asked.

"Because he wanted to march a hundred, maybe a hundred and fifty miles to the sea, burning everything as he went. He was kind of like one of your commanders invading and taking over a planet. He intended to feed his army off the land and destroy everything he passed through."

"That sounds like a good way to wage war," Ron said, wise Imperial counselor that he was.

"Actually, everyone told him he was crazy. You see, this was in the age of horse-drawn wagons. He could carry only enough food for a few days. It would take him ten or fifteen days to reach a port and reconnect with his supply line."

"That is risky?" Coth said.

"Yes. You have to understand, not fifty years before, another general had tried just that move, and ended up having to retreat. Retreat through the same land he'd pillaged on the way in."

"Could he not travel alongside his former path?" Ron asked.

"Yes, I suspect he thought he could when he started, but his enemy burned everything around his marching line. They left a scorched and denuded land, and his army starved."

"And everyone expected this general's army to starve as well," Coth said, drawing the right conclusion.

"Precisely," Kris said. "Everyone assumed the enemy would burn their crops, destroy their farms, actually, large plantations held by those of wealth and political power. Everyone assumed he was dooming himself."

"But he didn't?" Ron asked.

"No, he didn't. It seemed he knew the wealthy plantation owners better than his naysayers. He fully expected that they would not burn their crops and homes. Rather, they would hope that their plantation would be missed, or be off the march of his army. Instead of burning their homes for the common good, they held their breath, hoping their own property might be saved from the ravages of war by pure luck."

"And how do you think you could apply this to our distant target?" Ron asked.

"Let's say that I can defeat the fleet there. Maybe even persuade them that it is better to surrender than to fight. Okay, now let's say that I capture the planet without burning it down. Okay?"

"I do not see where you are going next." Ron said.

"Let's say that I take along junior clan leaders from the clans that are already present on our target, junior clan leaders from the same clans, but from the loyalist side."

"Yes." Ron said.

"Then let's say, for conversation's sake, that I rig much of the production facilities and wealth of this planet with high explosives. That I leave a clear order that if anyone tries to retake the planet, they are to blow up everything of any worth. Reduce this productive and wealthy jewel in the clans' crowns to nothing. Smoking wreckage."

Kris paused to let that sink in, then eyed Ron. "Would you order an attack on that planetary system?"

"If it was in the hands of my clan brother?"

"Yes," Kris said.

"Would I reduce the planet to rubble, destroying my clan's investment, in order to take it out of your hands?"

"Yes, Ron."

Ron leaned back on his stool and his eyes lost their focus. Then he blinked and sat up. "What is to keep those clan members you have imported from merely surrendering the planet back to their rebel co-clan members?"

Kris chuckled. "Let us say that not all the officers in the million Iteeche army I deploy to the planet are drawn from those friendly clans. Let's suppose that some are drawn from the clans that would love to see a major planet of their opposing clan in ruins. Let us say that those people would have access to the destruction switches."

"You are playing a deep game, Longknife," Ron said. "I still think that your wheels inside wheels will come off the axles."

"No doubt, if the war drags on long enough, this will happen. Our need is only that this hold together long enough for me to swing the battle fleet from this planet to the next, and, likely the next ten or so planets. If we can gut the rebellion of half of their warship production, do you think the rebels will not open negotiations to resolve the war?"

"Negotiate with traitors?" Ron snapped. "Never."

Kris and Jack glanced at each other and rolled their eyes at the overhead.

"Don't tell me," Kris said. "Civil wars are fought to the death."

"Of course." Ron snapped.

"So, of course, they are long, bloody, destructive, and leave only wreckage in their wake."

This time's Ron's "Of course," was slower in coming and nowhere near as absolute.

"You see the problem?" Kris asked.

"You humans," Ron said ruefully. "You have only two eyes, so how do you see the world in so many, many different ways?"

"It's just our curse. Also, Ron, we ornery humans with our fractured governments have been fighting each other and our brothers for so long, we've made just about every mistake in the book, and come up with every trick in the book to profit from the other guy's mistake."

"Slippery human," Coth whispered.

"Yes," Kris agreed. "And I'm worse than your average human. Good Admiral, I am a Longknife."

That drew a grunt from all three at the dinner table.

"So," Ron said, "let us say that your fleet sweeps in and seizes this system on the farthest side of the rebellion. What then?"

"Nelly, list me those nine remaining high production systems. How many jumps are they from Target 1?"

Nelly posted numbers, both white and black. One of the systems in the middling distance had no occupied planets involved with the voyage from Target 1.

"Mark that one as Target 2. Ron, we'll need to have an invasion fleet of a million ready to ship out and sail. Is there any place we could get reinforcements that is close by Target 1?"

"Actually, there is one close at hand. This is one time when the crazy patchwork quilt of our planets being mixed in together works for you. You could use your fast transports that dropped off your army on Target 1 and lift another army off a rather minor, but over-populated planet and get them to Target 2 right about the time when you need them."

"Once we have two of their most productive planets, Admiral Coth, what do you think they will do? Strike back at these two lost planets or defend their existing strongholds?"

"They will concentrate their forces to defend every major system that they fear losing."

"So, their forces will stay scattered and defensive."

"Well, My Admiral, calling six or seven thousand battle-cruisers and battleships a scattered force is not exactly what I'd call a small force you can defeat in detail."

"You mentioned battleships, though."

"Yes, in many cases, we will be dealing with battleships, some dating back to the Human War."

"How will they fare against battlecruisers?" Jack asked.

"Not well. Not at all well."

"So?" Ron asked. "What do you want from me?"

"I need a million Iteeche army under a good commander, not an asshole, not an inflexible fool lusting for battle glory. I need an assault fleet capable of lifting a million Iteeche Army at accelerations of 2.0 to 2.5 gees. I need clan lordlings that can take over several planets. It's possible that I may borrow clan lords from nearby loyal planets, but I need at least some senior lordlings appointed by the clan chief lords here at the capital."

"Yes, you do. Very wise of you. Okay. I believe I can depart with just my flotilla. I'll see what we can do about being back here with a million-soldier army and as many more battlecruisers as I can lay my four hands on.

"Before you leave, I'd like to send an updated report to my king for my embassy to pass along. I'll do my best to have it to you in an hour."

"That should be soon enough. Will you have an officer courier traveling with me?

"I hope you will allow one."

"Of course. Well, Your Highness, Grand Admiral and all the rest Longknife, I am beginning to think that my chooser was very wise to have chosen you for my initial contact with you humans. Very wise."

"I think my great-grandfather may have been wise to bring me along through all the assignments he gave me. Although there were times I doubted I'd survive his meddling in my life."

"Don't you hate it when those old graybacks are proven right?"

The four of them enjoyed the shared laugh. Kris watched Ron go, wondering what the Iteeche word that came through as "graybacks" was actually translated from.

She turned to see Coth still seated at her table.

"I know. I know," the Iteeche admiral said, raise all four of his hands as if to ward off a physical assault from Kris. "I have a battle fleet to train up. Still, you promised me a dinner, and I'm hoping you have some of that double chocolate silk pie for desert. We really must begin growing cocoa trees on our worlds."

"I'll see if some cocoa plantations can be arranged," Kris laughed. "Of course, we have pie. I had it made just for you."

"Then bring on the pie!"

41

A month later, Kris took her battle fleet out of orbit around Zargoth. Less than a day earlier, Ron had brought out an invasion fleet. It, and the 500 more battlecruisers to reinforce Kris's 3,000, were boosting for the jump Kris intended for her fleet to lead the way through.

The reinforcements were welcome, but it was the invasion force that was critical to their next mission. So, the 200 transports for those soldiers received a lot of scrutiny.

The soldiers were on battleships, only not at all like the Iteeche battleships Kris would have expected.

What the humans had come to call an Iteeche battleship was a large sphere. Along its equator could be four, six or eight reactor pods, but usually six. They provided plasma to the rocket motors at the rear of the pod and electricity to the weapons in the forward half, usually four lasers.

Those six pods mounted a total of twenty-four lasers, ranging in power from 14-inches to 18-inches when compared with a human battleship's lasers. Many of the smaller laser-armed death balls dated back to before the

Human/Iteeche war. The 18-inch lasers came out toward the end of the war.

The large sphere provided accommodations for the crew, and an Iteeche battleship carried a huge crew, well over 5,000.

Now, however, the death balls were no longer spheres.

"What has happened to those death balls?" Kris muttered in surprise as Ron's two hundred obsolete battleships followed his additional five hundred battlecruisers through the jump. "Sensors, compare that bunch against the death balls in our database."

"Aye, aye, Admiral," was followed a few minutes later by, "I think we have something for you, Admiral."

"Put it on screen, Sensors."

Half the forward screen in Kris's flag plot switched from the scenery in orbit above Zargoth to a schematic of a standard 18-inch death ball. Below it was what they were seeing now.

Instead of a nice, round sphere, these ships looked something like a teardrop, assuming nature allowed a teardrop to be streamlined a bit in front. Where there had always been a perfectly circular bow on them, these had noses that stretched out before narrowing and ending in a well-rounded bow. It was the same aft, only it was longer, tapered more gently and ended in a more narrow but rounded stern.

"How many troops do you think one of those can carry?" Jack asked Kris

That, of course, was the million-dollar question. Or rather the million-soldier one.

"Sensors, what's the volume and displacement on those modified ships?"

"It's hard to tell, ma'am, but it looks like they're at least double the internal volume of the original, maybe slightly more. Our mass detectors don't show that much additional displacement, however. Excuse me for this guess, but I don't think those death balls are carrying their ice armor."

"Thank you, sensors. Keep me appraised as you learn more about those," Kris said. The Iteeche had started the War with thin-skinned warships. Lots of guns, but not a lot of defense. They'd learned from the humans the advantage of ice armor layered on under a reflective coating of aluminum.

"It looks like these battlewagons are traveling light," Kris muttered to Jack.

"If that's what it takes to carry, what, five thousand soldiers and their supplies and battle gear, I'll settle for thin-skinned transports. It's your battlecruisers' job to keep the rebels away from my army," Jack answered.

"We'll just have to see what Ron has to say."

Ten minutes later, Ron did have something to say. "Hello, my Royal Grand Admiral and Imperial Order of Steel Admiral, how does your human joke go? 'Look what followed me home'?"

He laughed at his own joke. It sounded like someone was strangling a parrot.

"Not only have I acquired another five hundred battlecruisers, all with 24-inch lasers, but I have an army of two million soldiers, along with their armor and artillery. No doubt, you will find someplace good to use them. Hidden somewhere among all those old death balls are a half-dozen bi-hexaremes just loaded to the gills with eager young clan lordlings, all ready to take over the running of a major planetary system. Not all of them are young and junior, either. You have the third chosen of the Clan Chief of the Chap'sum'We. He's been promised a overlordship of a planet. One of my own chooser's senior chosen is also with us. Having won this planet, a lot of loyal clan branches are seeing a bright future for themselves."

Ron paused to look off screen.

"Right, now that you know what we have here, do you want us to drop down to the planet or head for a jump out of here? We do not need to refuel. We did so in the last system. If you will tell us what jump you want us to take, we will head for it directly."

The message had taken several hours to get to Kris. The response would take almost as much time to get back. Kris, however, was ready to issue her orders immediately. She sent directions out to Ron, then alerted her battle fleet to prepare to sail in four hours.

One flotilla would stay behind. If the system was attacked by three flotillas, it would engage. How to respond to four flotillas was left to the commanding admiral's discretion. If five or more flotillas showed up, his orders were to run like hell and report back to the capital.

In the meantime, the first fruits of the asteroid mine in orbit were starting to glide down to the planet. The first miners sent out to the asteroid belt had found both water and metals, and were setting themselves up for the long haul, and quite a few of the new clan lordlings were starting to think they might have been given something more than an overpopulated mud ball to rule.

There were a lot of happy groundlings, and not only had there been no more sabotage, but no one had been turned in for trying to attempt one.

Kris wondered if the Iteeche would take a lesson away from this. Beating the hell out of a planet wasn't such a good idea and using your battlecruisers to help spur an economy could get you a whole lot more than using them to blow shit up.

To Kris, it was a clear lesson. To an Empire that was ancient when we humans were discovering how to hammer flint to get sharp edges, it likely wasn't.

At the moment, it didn't matter. Kris had a mission. For the first time in her career, she was taking the war to the enemy. She'd won a lot of battles, defending this place or that. Taking Zargoth hadn't involved any fighting in the space around it.

Kris could not expect her luck to last forever.

She was not disappointed.

42

The voyage to Target System 1 involved six jumps. The first jump was a standard one out of the Zargoth system. They accelerated in the next system and hit one of Nelly's fuzzy jumps. They shot through three more four jumps at high speeds and high accelerations with spin on their hulls.

Each jump, a few Iteeche ships missed the jump for one reason or another and had to go back around, get herded together by a human battlecruiser assigned that job, and then trail the main battle force as they tried to catch up.

Also at each jump, a few Iteeche ships would hit the jump wrong. Since the fleet went through the jumps with four battlecruisers lashed together as a single unit, and all following one after another, the problem was most likely someone blowing the last moment acceleration or the rotation.

Despite everything Kris did, twenty-four Iteeche battlecruisers and two assault ships wandered off in sour jumps. Hopefully, their skippers knew enough to retrace their steps.

If not, they'd likely wander the stars until their oxygen ran out.

Space was not kind to the stupid or clumsy.

Kris took the time during the long voyage out to drill her crews. Much of it was ship drill for the crew, but three times she allowed the fleet to go to a one gee acceleration and drilled them as a single unit.

Evasion tactics meant having the ships zig and zag, bounce up and down, as well as throttle back or zip ahead. If that was all the ship had to do, it would be fine. However, warships didn't go to space just to keep their crews alive.

Each warship was meant to destroy other warships, preferably at a ratio of better than 5:1. For battlecruisers, that meant swinging their bows toward the enemy, so the forward battery could fire. When they were empty, the ship then flipped to bring the aft guns to bear. That all had to be done while continuing an evasion plan.

The evasion plan was programmed into the helm; aiming the battlecruiser was done at the captain's order by the helmsman. That was not at all easy, and took practice.

As Kris discovered, most of her ships had little time in space; they'd spent most of their time tied up at the pier. There was a fear among the Iteeche admirals that they might wear out their ships.

Kris cleared up that wrongheaded notion very quickly.

So, while their ships shot across the heavens on their way to war, both human and Iteeche crews sweated and trained, then trained and sweated some more.

They were probably the best-trained Iteeche fleet in millennia when they jumped into a system that was an easy, old-fashioned jump from Target 1. In this system, Kris's entire fleet spent most of the time decelerating.

They would be going through the jump into the Artiecca

system at a sedate 25,000 kilometers per hour and with no acceleration or rotation on the ship. Kris would likely arrive this time with the same number of ships she had in the last system.

That would be nice, considering the last system was unoccupied and Target 1 was potentially full of hostiles.

Right on schedule, the one Nelly had drawn up before they left Zargoth, Kris's fleet began to pour into the Artiecca system.

It was expected to be undefended. After all, it was about as far from the Imperial Capital as you could get and stay inside the Empire. There were not any loyal planets close by which had any sort of offensive significance.

Why would anyone have a battle fleet parked in orbit around this planet?

If Kris ever got the chance, she'd have to ask the admiral commanding the ten thousand rebel battlecruisers moored at the piers and dock of the four space stations above Artiecca 4 just exactly what he was doing there.

43

"**B**ring the fleet to Battle Stations," Kris ordered. "Inform all arriving ships that we are at battle stations."

"Aye, aye, Admiral," Comm said.

"Really?" Jack said, under his breath.

"Putting the fleet at battle stations, even if we are this far out, will let even the eternal optimists know that the cake walk has been canceled because someone forgot to bake us a cake."

"Yes. I do believe they have." Jack agreed, dryly.

Kris studied her battle board; she needed to get familiar with the terrain. The Artiecca system was a very busy place. Artiecca 4 was important enough to have four major space stations spaced around its equator, each one with its own beanstalk.

Most planets couldn't afford one. This one had four.

There were also production facilities on its moon as well as Artiecca 3 and 5. Admittedly, none of those planets had much of an atmosphere, but they did have minerals and other resources. Artiecca 4 had gotten them up and going. Artiecca 5 even had a beanstalk of its own and a shipyard turning out small to medium ships for the local trade, allowing the four major shipyards around Artiecca 4 to concentrate on the Navy's needs.

"Intel, what's the Navy production on Arti 4?"

"According to the reports from returning human engineers and programmers, they're producing four times the number of ships Wardhaven is making."

Kris scowled. "And none of them are likely to be obsolete battleships. I really did need to have a little conversation with Grandfather Alex about the folly of wasting resources on second-rate ships. Preferably, with a baseball bat in both hands."

"Can I sell tickets?" Jack said, through a grin. "I know a lot of people who'd pay good money to see that 'conversation'."

Kris allowed herself a chuckle. They were going to be few and far between this week.

Behind her, lashed together in groups of four, battlecruisers began popping into the system every ten seconds. Their Smart Metal™ allowed them to latch on to each other, binding themselves together with a force as strong as any atomic molecule. That made for a lot less risk when you set out to cram a huge fleet through a tiny jump.

As soon as the battlecruisers exited the jump, they split apart and put distance between themselves. Even coming through in quads, her entire battle fleet would take close to two hours to get through; several more for the ships to get reorganized into a fighting formation.

The 200 former battleships, now fast attack transports, would need over three hours to make their jump into the system. Made of old-fashioned metal, no one was willing to risk attempting to lash them together.

Reports had come in from Alwa that the murderous alien raiders had taken to doing this. It merely verified for Kris that the fear and hatred the aliens had for any other intelligent life in the galaxy was driving them to take risks no sane or rational commander would take.

But then, Kris had considered them crazy from the moment she met them.

Given eight hours, Kris would be ready to fight.

It was very unlikely that she would have to.

At one gee, it would take her four days to reach Arti 4. While she intended to seize all the industrial assets in the system, until she defeated the battle fleet orbiting Arti 4, her fleet would not spare a single ship for those other distractions.

So, it was to Arti 4 that Kris looked.

The sensors were reporting 10,000 battlecruisers, give or take a few thousand!

"Sensors, can you get me a better estimate of how many battlecruisers we face and what their types are?" Her last battle at the Imperial Guard System, the rebels had brought 8,000 battlecruisers. Five thousand of them, however, had been obsolescent ships armed only with shorter ranged 22-inch lasers.

That battle had proven that a 22-inch laser could not stand in the battle line against ships armed with 24-inch lasers.

Every battlecruiser in Kris's battle fleet carried the 24-inch lasers. Twenty of them.

"Admiral, we've been working on getting a better answer for you since we jumped into the system. As of right now, I know there are no battlecruisers, or any other warship anywhere else in the system. As to the four stations around Arti 4, I know each one has about the same number of reactors and capacitors, but, ma'am, there are so close together that at this distance, they all merge into just one noise signature. We can't count individual reactors. All I've got is so much noise that I'm estimating that each has about twenty-five hundred each."

"So it could be three thousand each, or two thousand, huh?"

"Yes, Admiral. It's just a huge blob of noise. The biggest block of noise I've ever heard of. I mean, the eight thousand ships we fought last time were a lot closer to us and spread out in battle array, with five thousand klicks between ships. These ships? Ma'am, all I know is that there are a whole lot of them."

"I'm assuming that you also can't tell if those reactors are powerful enough for 24-inch or just 22-inch lasers?"

"Yes, ma'am. There's way too much noise to get any granularity in the data."

"Tell me, Commander," Jack said gently. "If a battlecruiser was swinging around the hook on one of those stations with its reactors powered way down and its capacitors empty, could you separate it out from the noise you're getting?"

The gulp from the young woman was audible all through flag plot. "No, General. If they've got ships with no more than a trickle in their reactors, I wouldn't have anything showing on my boards."

Jack exchanged a look with Kris. It was the kind he reserved for her when she was about to stick her neck into a lion's mouth and floss its teeth.

"Yeah," was all that Kris would say.

She turned back to her board.

"If we need to make a U-turn," she told Jack, "we could make it around Arti 5? It's fairly close to our course."

"Isn't it awfully close to Art 4?"

"Yes," Kris admitted.

"Haven't you used a planet in that position to loop around and get you headed back toward the planet you're protecting?"

Kris ran a worried hand through her hair. She was letting it get long. Maybe she needed to cut it back.

She was diddling.

"Yes. If that commanding admiral has read the book I haven't gotten around to writing yet, he knows I'd use that planet to get myself on a parallel course."

Kris gauged the distance and scowled. "We'll have a long and vicious running gun battle."

"That's what I thought," Jack said. "Is there any way to turn around once we get up to speed?"

Kris shook her head. "We're too low on fuel for that," she admitted.

"Maybe we should do something about that first?" Jack's question was more of a suggestion.

Kris widened her survey of the system. Arti 7 was a large gas giant. It would definitely provide a refueling stop for her fleet. It also had the advantage of being much further back in its present journey around their sun. If she swung over to it, the option for her opposing commander to use Arti 5 as a loop around would be much diminished. Not eliminated, but it would certainly cramp his style.

"We refuel," Kris ordered. "Comm, send to Coth, the fleet will refuel around Artiecca 7 before we close on Artiecca 4."

"Aye, aye, Admiral." There was a brief pause, then Comm announced, "Message is sent and acknowledged."

"Very good," Kris said, as much to herself as to her bridge crew. She frowned at the board. She'd have more time to figure out her opposition. More time to figure out his tactics and develop her own.

More time to train her fleet and make sure they were ready to fight, very likely outnumbered 4:1.

And, if worse came to worse, she could flip around the gas giant and head right back where she came from. Or maybe somewhere else.

The rebels couldn't have ten thousand battlecruisers or more around every major industrial planet, could they?

44

The journey to Artiecca 7 took them about a tenth of the way across the system. That gave them a solid baseline on the noise being generated from Arti 4.

It also gave the enemy time to warm up any ships that were either incomplete or in reserve. Kris now had a count.

Jack shook his head and scowled. "Four-to-one. Almost exactly four-to-one. With a few left over. On their side."

Kris had to agree with him. Sensors was quite sure of the count. Three thousand four hundred and eighty-eight battlecruisers had successfully made the complete voyage with her. Of the remaining 32, some might straggle in, but none had during the long dogleg to Artiecca 7.

Kris was also missing two troop transports; she didn't expect to need the missing 20,000 troops. The thought, however, of what it would be like on those two transports if they couldn't find their way home haunted Kris's nights. This gambit of hers had better be worth it.

Of course, if she was honest, a lot more than twenty thousand sailors were about to die in this coming battle.

During the cruise from the jump to the gas giant, Kris exercised her ships. Again, she used lasers at extremely low power to count the hits on her ships. The ships that had been with her since she sailed for Zargoth were getting quite good. The last arrivals had been modified during the voyage out, and then had begun to exercise with the other ships.

In other systems, while accelerating at 2.5 gees on her way here, she had drilled her crews in evasion tactics. First, she'd had to persuade the new arrivals that going into battle lying down was not unmanly. Or was that un-Iteeche?

Once they were in high gee stations, she worked them up into more and more radical evasion maneuvers.

Most of the Iteeche crews were up to Evasion Plan 4 or 5. So far, no Iteeche had been able to reach Plan 6 and match the human battlecruisers. Kris was just not willing to create an Iteeche design that equaled the effectiveness of the human's high gee station eggs.

Kris needed to win this battle. However, how long would it take the rebels to learn what her Iteeche sailors knew? How soon would she be facing her own designs in battle?

Kris shook her head. Fighting a civil war with a Navy that leaked like a sieve was no fun. If only the rebel fleet leaked as well. She again glanced at the estimate of the rebel forces arrayed against her. "Yes, it would be nice if the damn rebels would leak their forces and distribution a bit more."

"Have you decided whether someone leaked your attack and they reinforced Artiecca?" Jack asked. "Or do you think this is just a secure rallying point for them to organize, train, and prepare this force to take us on somewhere else?"

Kris shrugged. "I have a hard time thinking that this leaked."

Jack raised an eyebrow.

"Okay," Kris said, "I don't want to believe this got leaked. You, me, Coth, and Ron were the only ones at that planning dinner. Nelly said the room was squeaky clean of bugs. So, that doesn't leave any good choices. Either the Iteeche can evade Nelly's security measure . . ."

"Not going to happen," Nelly pointed out dryly from Kris's neck.

"Or Ron and whoever he had to talk to get us a two million strong Iteeche army and the last fifteen hundred battlecruisers spilt the beans."

"Have you talked to Ron?" Jack asked.

"No. Never ask a question you won't trust the answer too."

Again, Jack raised an eyebrow.

"If Ron is turned, we're dead. If his chooser Roth has turned on us, we are just as dead. The Chap'sum'We clan is the closest ally we humans have in the Empire. Okay? If, however, someone that they talked with, or someone overheard them, or some human has sold us out and is providing nanos to spy on us . . ." Kris paused to shrug, "The list goes on and there is no benefit to asking Ron if he's a turncoat. It would be worse to ask him if he thinks his chooser is."

"So, what do you intend to do?" Jack asked

Kris chose to ignore the question and ask one of her own. "Sensors, can you tell me anything more about that hostile fleet?"

"We've managed to isolate individual ships. With us having a bigger baseline, we're getting more granularity."

"So?"

"About six thousand of the battlecruisers are the Iteeche

version of our twenty-gun cruisers with 24-inch lasers. Allowing for slight variations in programming and material, their reactors and capacitors are right there in the button. The other nearly eight thousand ships are an interesting question."

"How so?"

"They have the same three reactors that you'd find on a battlecruiser with 22-inch guns."

Jack raised his eyebrows. "After what we did to their smaller cruisers in the Battle of the Imperial Guard System, they can't be putting those fellows in the line again."

"I don't think so," Sensors said. "We can't get anything off their lasers yet, but they do have their capacitors at full load. Most of the time, we use two capacitors to a laser. That would mean the aft battery, with eight guns would have sixteen capacitors. We're counting eighteen."

"Eighteen?" Kris asked.

"Yes, ma'am. The forward battery of twelve guns has twenty-four capacitors. However, that would also be a match if you have eight lasers using three capacitors each.

"So, you think the enemy has up gunned a lot of their 22-inch battlecruisers to load out eight forward and six aft? Fourteen guns total?"

"Yes, ma'am."

"We were working on converting our newest 22-inch battlecruiser lasers to 24-inchers with about the same number," Megan reminded Kris. It seemed like it was years ago that she was running the battlecruiser desk at Main Navy. It really had been less than a year.

Kris studied the battle board long and hard. Slowly she shook her head and got back to answering Jack's question. "I wish the odds weren't balanced so perfectly on the edge of a knife," she muttered. "If it was worse, I'd turn and run, or duck out and try another of the industrial planets. If it was better, I'd lay on with a will and see this battle and invasion through with a will."

"Why not try some place else?" Jack asked.

That gave Kris pause. Then, again, she shook her head. "My basic mistake may have been not sending out scouts to recon the enemy situation. I just didn't think we could get away with running scouts around in enemy territory without them getting picked off or giving away our intent. Next time, I may try that. I just didn't expect to find a force this large, this far out."

"So, we attack them here," Jack said.

"Yes. We attack them here," Kris said, with finality.

They began refueling as soon as they made orbit around Arti 7. The battlecruisers spawned pinnaces to make runs into the gas giant's atmosphere and load up on reaction mass and any water available.

While they did that, Nelly and her kids manufactured a pair of maskers for each of the 3,500 battlecruisers in Kris's fleet. They also set in place the seeds to spin out foxers, complete drone replicas of each battlecruisers, two per ship. Between the maskers and foxers, the rebels would have a very confusing targeting problem.

Both the maskers and drones were created using the 60,000 tons of Smart Metal^{TM} that they appropriated from the closest industrial planet to Zargoth. Kris had asked for 10,000 tons, but the admiral commanding the flotilla sent to fetch it managed to talk the planetary overlord into a lot more. Little had been needed to replace the human Smart Metal^{TM} used in Sunset City's pipes. Now, the metal was coming in very handy where both maskers and foxers were concerned.

Kris might be outnumbered 4:1, but the rebels would have to target a force that they only outnumbered 4:3.

With every ship topped off to capacity, they began a 1.0 gee acceleration toward their target.

Shortly after they made their move, the rebel commander made his. His ships formed up, headed for Kris, but fifteen degrees off her course.

"Is he running?" Jack wondered.

"No, he's smart. Too damn smart," Kris growled. "He's keeping his acceleration down to half a gee. He doesn't want to get too far out here. If I'm not reading him wrong, he's going to flip ship when we're about a quarter of the way there. That should put him dead in space when we flip to begin decelerating. While we're doing that towards Artiecca 4, he'll be accelerating until we match velocities. That's when he'll start decelerating right alongside us. My only question is, when will he haul in range and start the battle?"

Kris paused, then added, "Or we haul in range of him?"

"Won't that use up a lot of reaction mass?"

"Yep. About as much reaction mass as we'll be using to cover the exact same distance. It takes a gutsy and smart guy to be willing to fight it out side by side with us when neither one of us knows who will be the winner. It's not like he or I can tack away and break off the action. Have you ever heard of a crazy bunch of nut cases that liked to tie their left arms together and then fight it out with knives in their right hand?"

"I thought I'd heard of every damn fool stunt in the book. Tell me, were they Longknifes?"

"Very funny, Security Chief."

"I thought you'd find it that way, Grand Admiral."

A day later, as they approached their flip point, Kris organized her forces into the traditional five wings. They formed a cross with vanguard, center, and rearguard forming the long axis and a top and bottom wing forming off the center. Each wing was evenly balanced with 22 flotillas, except for the rear guard that was shortchanged by a single ship.

If any of the stragglers showed up, they'd join the line there.

The fast attack transports were organized into four task forces of fifty ships each and deployed well away on the unengaged side.

The rebel admiral also deployed in five wings. Each of his wings had 87 flotillas. Kris studied the structure of each wing. The flotillas were stacked eight high and ten or eleven long. Hers were only four high and five or six long.

By all rights, the rebel commander should be able to envelop every one of Kris's wings from the top, bottom, front and back. Kris's formation should have looked suicidal from his flag bridge.

Kris kept her ships at the same interval of 5,000 klicks as the rebel commander did within his flotillas. She kept the same distance between each flotilla: 15,000 klicks.

However, Kris had two tricks up her sleeve. Before the fight started, she'd shake out her ships to double the distance between them, 10,000 klicks. She'd also doubled the distance between flotillas. This would give them plenty of room to dodge and jink in and her fleet would cover as much front as the rebel fleet.

The other ace up her sleeve was the human ships. The 4 flotillas leading the second column of the vanguard had 128 human-built and crewed battlecruisers.

These crews had the high gee egg stations that held them tight in deep cushioning. They could take higher gees and knocking around in evasion maneuvering that would leave an Iteeche crushed with sprained muscles all over his body.

The lasers in the U. S. battlecruisers had been tightened down in their cradles. Far too often, the shipbuilders delivered the lasers loose in their cradles. Kris made sure her ships had them tightened down and bore-sighted as well. Also, the human ships had better and faster fire control computers.

Kris had done all she could to pass along these two advantages to every loyalist Iteeche battlecruiser under Admiral Coth's command. Their lasers were now tight in their cradles and human computers had been inserted into their fire control systems. Still, converting data from Iteeche to human and back to Iteeche slowed them down.

They now had a two second advantage over the rebel ships in targeting a hostile ship and getting a salvo off.

However, there was one big advantage to the human battlecruisers.

Each one was coated with a crystal armor that covered its skin ten centimeters deep. Those crystals captured laser fire, slowed the light down, just the way quantum computers did, but in huge amounts and for a longer time.

Kris's crystal armored ships glowed under laser fire as the armor distributed that destructive power all around the hull. They radiated that laser energy back out into space instead of letting the concentrated power blow the ship to atoms.

The humans had that. The Iteeche badly wanted it, but, the tech was embargoed. It didn't leave human space.

If the rest of Coth's fleet could hold the rebels in place, Kris intended to use the concentrated firepower of the nearly invulnerable human battlecruisers to roll up the rebel line.

Of course, there were a whole lot of rebel ships and only 128 human ships. It was a tall bet.

Without a flinch from either force, the two fleets maintained their courses, not yet on a solid collision course, but rapidly headed for one.

45

Karl'sum'Ton'sum'Go qu Chap'sum'We, fourth chosen son of the Pasha of the Golden Flying Fish Satrap, Admiral of the First Order of Steel, studied the deployment of the loyalists on his battle board.

By all rights, they should have run away. By all rights, outnumbered 4:1, they should be coming forward to surrender to his superior force. But Karl knew that no Iteeche commanded those ships. No one with half a mind to follow in the traditions of the Empire, to act proper and correct, walked the bridge of his enemy's flagship.

No! A human commanded there. Humans brought in their wake chaos and disorder. They dredged up the black chaos of the deep abyss and fired it, as if from a fire hose at all the Iteeche that even came close to them. The humans were a plague that needed to be expunged from the Empire!

Even worse, the human commanding the forces against him was the Longknife human female. A female! What chaos allowed a female human to walk freely among men and, worse, act as if she could command warriors in battle.

What true Iteeche warrior would allow themselves to listen to the words of a woman? A human woman who strutted about in uniform and claimed the right to command!

Karl stood up tall and took a few steps away from his battle board. He strode around his flag bridge, catching his breath. His chooser had told him that he should not allow himself to be worked up like this.

"We will wipe the humans from the planets of the Empire, my chosen! We will burn out and cleanse all that they have touched! We will return the Empire to its True Path. I know you hate this Longknife human female, but you must also study her. Get to understand how she thinks. Know what she is thinking before she even knows herself. Only then can you set the net that she will swim into herself. You will trap her with her own fins. Then you can filet and chop her into chum," his chosen had said as he laughed.

So, Karl *had* studied this Longknife human woman. His eyes fell on the shelf of readers that he had read so many times that he had committed much of her words to memory. He had every one of her after-action reports, even those going back to when she had but one ship.

He also had a report from the Battle of the Imperial Guard System. No commanding officer or admiral had returned to the Alliance after that fight. No doubt, the Longknife human woman thought she had destroyed anyone from among the rebels who saw and comprehended what took place there.

However, the Alliance were not all as foolish as that idiot Donn'sum'Zu'sum'Nam qu Hav'sum'Domm. Karl's own chooser had seen that an innocent merchant ship, following close behind the invasion fleet had aboard it one of the greatest tactical minds in the Empire. Sidd was low born, but his mind was as sharp as any Pasha. His chooser had spotted this anomaly in the spawning pools and lifted the youngling up to greater training than even many of his own chosen.

Sidd watched the battle develop in the Imperial Guard System. He saw the mistakes that Donn made. He saw the mistakes and brilliant moves that the Longknife human female made. Sidd's after-action report on that battle held primacy of place among those other readers with that human female's ramblings.

He eyed the readers. Each after-action report had its own tablet. Each of them could not be accessed or access any system on his flagship. Karl did not trust the humans. Too often, these small people with their confused minds found ways to wiggle their way like tadpoles into places they should not be.

No, whatever the humans touched, could not be allowed to touch anything proper and Iteeche.

Karl had not wanted to read those tablets, to be tainted by anything human. Still his Pasha and chooser ordered him to and he had. He even journeyed to the Imperial Capital to talk with his most distant cousin Ron'sum'Pin'-sum'Chap'Sum'We, the ambassador to the hated humans and the one Iteeche that could most see into the chaos of a human brain.

Ron had also accompanied the Longknife human female, both to see her king and to explore the galaxy. He had been there when the crazy humans began a war with the vicious alien raiders that had been sniffing around the Empire.

Karl had to give the humans credit for that. They had drawn the threat to the Empire far away, keeping them focused on a dot of no significance on the other side of the galaxy. There had been no more alien scouts probing the Iteeche Empire, and none of the daring Iteeche explorers recently had failed to return from their voyage of exploration.

He would not begrudge the humans that. They were keeping the Empire safe from one enemy. Still, they were themselves an enemy to everything the Empire stood for. Everything it was.

The New Path for the Empire didn't want to destroy the humans, it merely wanted to build a wall against them. As a youth, Karl had been told that such a wall already existed. He had believed what he was told.

Now, it was clear that the wall had only been mostly there. Clearly, some Imperial counselors had kept a few cracks in the wall that they used to listen through. A few cracks to give and take information back and forth.

Ron himself had admitted that his chooser had specifically trained him to comprehend the human way of thinking, to understand a mind that was alien. Ron had been honest with Karl. He still failed to grasp so much about the humans, but Ron, an Imperial counselor of the second order, was trying.

That was the problem. The Empire could not afford to comprehend the chaos of the human mind. That mind had to be hurled back, away from the gates of the Empire.

This Longknife human female who styled herself as Human Emissary to the Imperial Court must die.

"And I will be her death," Karl said out loud. "I will certainly be her death."

He returned to his battle board.

This Longknife human was known to throw her ships around hard. She let each ship move, as if by jittering like a water bug, it could avoid laser fire. Everyone knew that lasers moved with the speed of light. Everyone knew that even with the 300,000 kililu range of the new 650 millilu lasers, it only took a second before the beam was slashing through a ship. No, there was no sense in bouncing around.

Still, Sidd's after-action report showed that the loyalists had suffered fewer casualties in the first exchange of salvos than the ships of the Alliance for the New Path. They'd continued to suffer vastly greater casualties until they began to zig and zag about. More and more as the battle went on, they jittered, but never as well as the loyalists. Never even close to as well as the humans. Even to the end, they suffered more losses in each salvo than either the loyalist or the human battlecruisers.

How could that be?

"Sidd, attend to me," Karl ordered.

Captain Sidd, his Number 2 Staff Officer, was immediately at is elbow. "Yes, My Lord Admiral."

"You have the most experience watching the humans and this Longknife female. Observe this battle array and comment upon it. Is it different from what she used when approaching the defeated and dead Admiral Donn?"

"In the Battle of the Imperial Guard System, the Longknife human had less than half of the ships she commands today. You, My Eminent Admiral, have a force over half again as large as the late and unlamented Admiral Donn."

"I can see that. I can also see that our battle array should be able to swallow them up, like a Sonta flower engulfs a Tagga. But then, with five times the forces, Donn should have been able to play the same game. Why did it not work?"

"The Longknife human female orders her ships to maintain twice the individual interval between them. This allows them to jitter about without fear of ramming each other. They also have more space between each of their flotillas."

"She doesn't now," Karl pointed out.

"We are not close enough for her ships to need it. If she acts anything like she has when engaging the two-eyed alien space raiders and when she fought Donn, she will shake out her ships only when she is nearly in range of our lasers. We will be facing a Tagga that is too big for a Sonta flower to even nibble."

Karl did not like that. He had heard that the Longknife human female bragged that she could fight outnumbered 4:1 and win. No one fought against those odds. You surrendered when faced with those odds. That was the way he had been trained.

That was just the proper and correct way for an admiral to behave.

"How does she succeed when her ships are so scattered?" Karl asked his intelligence officer for aliens. "Her ships are so widely dispersed that their fire cannot be concentrated. We could order each of our divisions to concentrate their fire on one of her ships. It seems as if she wants to lose this battle."

"She fought her last battle the same way and it was not Admiral Donn who claimed the victory."

"Then tell me, Captain," Karl said, holding his temper in all four hands, "what is the magic that she uses to win? How did she defeat the dead and unlamented Admiral Donn?"

There was a long pause before Sidd answered his admiral.

"My Lord Admiral, I have ruminated on this for many long hours. Days. Weeks! I have no answer that I would sell you for a bag of gold coins. However, I do have a few jewels that I have found. I do not see how they give her such victories, but they certainly make her different from every victorious Iteeche admiral that I have studied."

"Speak on. Do not dally," Karl snapped. He knew what a staff officer who was afraid to speak his mind sounded like. He would never have taken Sidd for such a flaw.

"Yes, My Lord Admiral," Sidd said. "It is said that she drills her crews constantly. She drills them until they are dreaming in their sleep of what to do at their battle station."

"What good is that?"

"I do not know. All I know is that she does it and wins, and we do not and lose. Is this why, or is this just some lucky totem, like a lucky buba's foot that she rubs for luck? I do not know."

Sidd paused, then went on slowly. "What I do know is that she has her ships fight each other. Even using lasers at a near infinitesimally low power rating so that they can judge their shooting. For those crews that shoot well, she awards a E for excellency and they can paint it on their lasers. It is very coveted among the ships' crews."

"How does she reduce the power of her lasers to a level that does not eat up the armor of her ships?"

"I do not know. It is said that the Longknife human female has a familiar, a voice that speaks to her and those around her. They claim that it is a tiny computer with more computational power than even the ship's main computer. It is claimed that the tiny computer has taken on a life of its own."

"Is this witchcraft now rejected by the loyalists?"

"No, My Lord Admiral. The humans insist that this is not witchcraft but superior technology."

"Has the deep abyss taken all the brain cells of the Emperor's Imperial Counselors?"

Sidd risked no answer.

"But this witch's familiar," Karl said. "You say it can weaken the lasers so they can strike a feather blow to the opposing ship in their training exercises?"

"Yes, My Lord Admiral."

"Or at least they claim that is how they do the modification to the lasers."

"Yes, My Lord Admiral."

Karl spotted something that made even less sense. "Every ship has had this modification?"

"Yes, My Lord Admiral."

"Stop that My Lord Admiral shit or this conversation will take all day and half the night."

"Yes, Admiral. And yes, every ship computer has been given just this modification."

"The loyalists have inserted human subroutines into their computers! What else have the humans done while they were rummaging around inside the guts of those computers?"

"That is impossible to say. However, My Admiral, I know that there is at least one other program the humans have added. Your high gee bed? We have programmed them and keep them beside your battle station. That is not the way on the loyalist ships. We have heard that they now have fewer crew and larger quarters, not as wastefully luxurious as the humans, but they sleep in bunk beds rather than hammocks. When they go into battle, their beds will melt into the deck and they will spin their high gee stations out of metal from those beds."

Karl shook his head. "For soft beds, the loyalists have let the human shark into their school of younglings!"

"It is not soft beds that let the loyalists shoot better than our ships. It is not roomy quarters that let the loyalists suffer fewer casualties. Yet they do, My Lord Admiral. There is something that they do that we do not. Something that they know, that we do not.

"Don't prattle on about what we do and do not know. My chooser has raised you up from the lower decks because you are supposed to know things. Don't tell me what you don't know. No, the loyalists are fools. They are the little fish, trailing the human sharks, eating the crumbs that fall from their mouths. They will certainly lose! Communications, steer two points closer to the enemy. Let us get this battle joined and the victory ours."

"As you command, so has it been done," Comm shouted back.

Admiral of the First Order of Steel, Karl, set all four of his hands on his hips. He would close with these humans and blast them to dust.

The human female Longknife had only hours to live.

～

Captain Sidd did not allow himself to show any expression. He was merely a lowborn sailor, useful to the clan lords. Whether they listened to him or not, it was no skin off his knees. Still, if this worthless spawn of a Pasha's mating pond, this pompous gray uniform dripping with gold would not listen, it might very well be the death of them all.

The lowborn Sidd suppressed again the sigh he so often had to swallow. He had told this spoiled lordling that the loyal ships under the human Longknife shot better than their ships. He'd told them that dodging about could save them losses. He'd told him all that rebel intelligence knew, and the things that he wished they knew but didn't. Yet, all he heard was bunks rather than hammocks.

Maybe it was best for the old Iteeche Empire and its strutting clans to die. Sidd drank beer with lowborn spawn that were just as smart as he was. Much smarter than his admiral, or any of the clan lords he had been pet to.

Let them die.

I just hope they don't drag us all down into the abyss as they go to their rightful hell.

46

G rand Admiral Kris Longknife listened as Nelly whispered in the back of her head that the data on her battle board was changing, but Sensors had not yet reported it.

START A TIMER, NELLY.

DONE, KRIS.

The enemy fleet off their starboard side had entered a course change. Nelly had that data coming direct from the sensor array to Kris's battle board. It was not unusual for Kris to know before the rest of her fleet knew.

The question was, how long did it take other admirals of the fleet to learn what she had learned? So, she waited to see how long it would take Sensors to report to her.

"Admiral, the enemy fleet has altered course to steer eleven degrees closer to us," Sensors reported before the timer in Kris's head passed fifteen seconds.

That wasn't too much of a delay.

"Very good, Sensors. Keep me appraised of any further changes."

"Aye, aye, ma'am."

"Nelly, project their new course with ours."

The battle board showed that the rebels would be in range of Kris's 24-inch lasers in twelve hours.

"Somebody wants to get this battle over with fast," Jack muttered.

Jack stood beside Kris. On the other side of the battle board stood her Chief of Staff Titania Tosan and Intel chief, Quinn Sung. Lieutenant Megan Longknife had held back, but Kris had ordered her to join them around the battle board. She stood at Kris's other elbow.

Kris worried her lower lip. "It does seem that our enemy has gotten eager for battle," she admitted. "Since we flipped at the midpoint and started our deceleration, I've had us steering five degrees ahead of the course we'd need to make orbit around Artiecca 4. At the Battle of the Guard System, when we needed to get to the jump, they did their damndest to crowd us off of our course by closing on us. If our long-range gunnery proves to be better than theirs, I want room to wear away if they try to charge in."

Those around her nodded their heads.

"We have a problem," Kris said. "We sail the same ships, built with the same technology. They have the same lasers with the same range as we have. By every right, four of them should be able to blast one of us out of space before we can blast four of them."

Kris looked around her the faces staring with her at the battle display. "If they trade two or three of their ships for one of ours, we lose."

"There have been times like this where the same fought same. I had Nelly research it. She found a fascinating example. Nelly?"

"In the first decade of the 1800's back on old Earth,"

Nelly began, "every nation used basically the same technology for their navies. Wet water navies, I might add. They built their ships out of wood. They propelled them by means of sails that caught the wind. They had cannons that had the same power and range. Despite sailing basically the same ships, the Royal Navy of England beat the French Navy time after time, usually against greater odds."

"Because?" Kris said.

"The Royal Navy blockaded the French Navy. The ships of the Royal Navy would sail back and forth, outside the ports, day in and day out, in fine weather or stormy, and, remember, these ships were powered by the wind. If the wind blew the wrong way, a ship could end up on a rocky shore. So, the French stayed at anchor, and the English sailed back and forth.

"But the Royal Navy didn't just sail around. Their crews had to practice changing the sails. Their captains had to become more and more skilled at taking advantage of the wind, and, below decks, they trained their crews to load and aim their cannons so that they were twice as fast as the French gunners. That often told the tale in a fight."

Nelly paused for a moment, something she was doing regularly now, then went on. "There was one more thing. The French tended to start firing their cannons at extreme range. At that range, their cannonballs rarely hit, and if they did, they had lost most of their energy, so they did little harm. Firing and loading not only used up ammunition, but it exhausted the gunners. The Royal Navy waited to fire their first broadside until they were at close range, a range where they would not only hit, but do horrible damage."

"Nelly told me there was a joke at the time. 'The royal sailors drank their grog, but the French, they kept to port.'"

No one laughed at Kris's joke.

"Ah, grog was drunk by the sailors of the Royal Navy," she explained. "It was a blend of lime, sugar, and rum. It helped prevent scurvy."

"Scurvy?" Titania asked.

"Never mind. Lousy joke," Kris knew she should stop, but she tried to finish her explanation. "The French were known to like a fortified wine called port. The English considered it effete. So, the Royal Navy drank their grog, while blockading, and the French kept to port. Port wine, ships in port? Get it?"

"Yes, Admiral," Jack said, not even trying to hide his smile. "They got it."

"I think you should keep your day job, Admiral," Megan said.

There was only slight intake of breath, still it was noticeable. Lieutenants laughed at admirals' jokes, no matter how bad they were. Of course, she was a Longknife. Both of them.

The admiral pouted for only a moment and muttered, "Well, at least my children love me."

Then she was back to business. "So, this is our problem. If we've trained and squeezed the most out of our weapons systems, like the Royal Navy, we have a chance. If they've gotten better, we're in trouble. If that happens, we'll talk about an exit strategy. For now, we concentrate on how to annihilate those poor bastards."

The bridge fell silent except for the whispered conversations between this or that watchman. Kris went on.

"By now, the enemy knows we fight in a loose formation. I see no benefit to delay going to it. When we haul within a million kilometers of each other, I propose that we go to battle stations and get the crew in their eggs. Ten minutes later, we go to Condition Zed. Twenty minutes after that, we open the formation up to fighting intervals. We will fire by squadrons for Iteeche ships, divisions for human, at least initially. Again, try to target two or three lasers for the same place. It may mean fewer hits, but those that do hit will pack a wallop. Any problems?"

"If they park nine hundred thousand klicks off our engaged side?" Titania asked.

"We'll blow up that bridge when we come to it," Kris said. "Somehow, I doubt this fellow is going to delay coming to grips with us. He seems to be quite eager from the last course correction he ordered."

"He was already closing at ten degrees. Now, twenty-one degrees," Jack said. "Yep. Does seem a bit eager. Tell me, Admiral, you want to fight at extreme range, don't you?"

"I think we have an advantage there, yes, General."

"If we want to keep the option to back off and keep the rebels at arms' length, shouldn't we be closing them, if for no other reason than to give us more space to back in to?"

Kris pursed her lips in thought. "I didn't want to aim too far ahead of the planet's orbit. If we close too much with him, we could miss the planet" she said slowly. "Still, you're right. We can always slow down to let the planet catch up. And you're right, Jack, if they do get frisky and try to charge us, the more room the better."

Then Kris let an evil grin loose on her face. "Besides, I'd like to see if he backs off when he sees us closing too fast on him. Let's take the temper of his backbone."

"Comm, advise Admiral Coth to steer the fleet eleven degrees closer to the enemy."

"Sent."

A moment later, Comm reported. "He is ordering the fleet to steer two points closer to the enemy."

"So," Kris muttered, "eleven human degrees equals two Iteeche points."

"Nice to know," Quinn whispered to herself, softly.

Three minutes later, Kris's entire fleet of nearly thirty-five hundred ships were steering a course eleven degrees closer to the enemy. The rebels were steering a closing course of twenty-one degrees. There was a bit more than a thirty-degree angle between their courses.

They would be in range within a few hours.

Kris and her team watched as the two fleets closed along this tight course. Seven minutes into it, the rebel commander swung away by six degrees.

"Comm, send to Coth, wear away one point."

"Message sent."

Two minutes later, the loyalist fleet took a point off its course. Now they closed at twenty-one degrees. The battle would have to wait for a few more hours.

"Interesting," Kris said.

"Admiral, excuse me for asking," Megan said, "but how did anyone win a battle when they are all even? Yes, you mention training, but was there a tactic?"

"Nelly?" Kris asked.

"The greatest and most decisive naval battle of the age took place off of Cape Trafalgar," Nelly began. "The combined French and Spanish fleets outnumbered the Royal Navy by slightly less than four-to-three. Still, Admiral Nelson of the Royal Navy won because he did not follow the normal tactics of the age."

"And those were?" the chief of staff asked.

"Most battles were fought much like we do. Form the ships into a line, sail along a near parallel course, and shoot away. Usually, the losing force could just wear away and the battle was over with few ships destroyed or captured. Admiral Nelson chose to violate the rules."

Again, Nelly paused. Kris was proud that her computer was learning to make her pauses just the right length. Time for the humans to catch up, consider, but not long enough for anyone to grow bored.

"Nelson divided his twenty-seven ships into two lines and aimed them at the allied fleet. Due to their poor seamanship, the French and Spanish ships were in a loose and scattered line. Nelson and his deputy hit the allied line and cut it into three parts. They engaged the two aft parts, and ignored the vanguard."

"How'd that work, the vanguard?" Jack asked.

"Again, due to poor sailing skills and weak wind, the forward third needed a long time to come about. By the time they might have engaged the Royal Navy, it looked like the battle was lost and they turned about again and fled for the nearest port. Nelson took or destroyed twenty-two of the thirty-three allied ships, including most of the largest ones. There have been few more decisive battles at sea."

"However," Titania said, "Nelson won by charging his ships at his enemy's fleet. We want to keep the battle at a comfortable distance where our better fire control can do more damage to them, and our evasion tactics cause them to do less damage to us. I don't see how this applies."

Kris thought for a moment, and then spoke slowly. "I think I see a way that Nelson would have solved our tactical problem. Let's take a look at what happens if we do this."

Everyone stared as Kris outlined a battle that Lord Horatio Nelson would have been proud of.

∿

Admiral of First Order of Steel Karl eyed his battle board. The two forces had just crossed the million-kilometer line. He was steering two points closer to her, she, one point closer to him. The two courses crossed well before they reached the orbit of Artiecca 4. At this rate, they'd cross the orbit but not get anywhere near the planet.

No doubt, they'd be adjusting their courses a lot between here and there. Suddenly, as one, the ships of the loyalist ships shrunk down to less than a quarter of their previous size.

"Captain Sidd?"

"The loyalist ships have gone to what the humans call, and the loyalists have adopted, Condition Zed. All the magic metal that the humans use for comfort has now been converted into armor for much smaller ships. Since their crews are less than a third our size, they now have a much smaller ship with more armor to cover it."

"And Admiral Coth's Iteeche ships?"

"All of them have given up many of their older officers and NCOs. When a ship jitters around like these do, it is hard on the back and knees of the older officers. Others have been transferred off because their duties are no longer required, such as runners or officer boatmen. I understand that gunners now keep their own work spaces clean. The same with engineers."

"She has no respect for tradition," Karl snapped.

"It makes her ships smaller targets, My Lord Admiral."

"Do you think this dishonorable way is good?"

"I did not say good, I said effective."

Karl shook his head. "Must we become no better than these humans to defeat them?"

"I do not know, My Lord Admiral."

"Is there anything that you do know, Staff Officer Number 2?"

"I have told you all that I know."

"Then you are worthless to me. Maybe there is a longboat somewhere on the boat deck with your name on it. Why don't you go?"

"Maybe there is such a longboat, but I will stay at my post to answer your questions as long as you ask them."

Karl waved the staff officer off and Sidd went to stand next to his high gee bed.

Alone, the Admiral of the First Order of Steel studied the battle. It was developing very much the way he intended it to. Before too much longer, sailors would begin to die. Let them be, those loyalist dogs.

Karl stood, all four legs spread wide, supporting him like a tree with four trunks. He was the fourth chosen son of the Pasha of the Golden Flying Fish Satrap. No human could defeat him and the forces arrayed around him.

The battle was practically won.

47

Grand Admiral Kris Longknife lay in the firm embrace of her high gee station. The egg had cocooned her as if she were a caterpillar. The ship might lurch from side to side, acceleration or deceleration might try to squish her or slam her forward, but the egg would hold her tight, absorbing all that energy and converting it to power that got fed back into the electric grid. This was the latest version of the egg and it was even better than the former model Kris used in the last battle.

Admiral Kitano had brought this new design out with her battle fleet.

Consequently, Kris had seen to it that the high gee couches on the Iteeche battlecruisers also got a makeover. Now, all her battlecruisers, human or Iteeche, were better able to handle the hard gees and evasion plans.

Kris wondered how much her opposite number had improved their beds.

Iteeche warriors had gone into battle for thousands of years standing on their own four feet. Kris had the devil's own time getting the Iteeche under her command to lie down. When they did, she had to put up with a lot of grousing but the more the gees increased on acceleration, the more their heads didn't get knocked about as their ships zigged and zagged, the more the Iteeche liked their high gee couches.

She'd spread her ships out in a loose formation. The rebel ships were 5,000 kilometers apart. Hers were now 10,000, the better to evade. That meant that one of their divisions of 8 ships was 40,000 klicks long. Hers was 80,000 klicks.

Between each flotilla, the rebels used a 15,000-kilometer interval. After serious analysis, Kris was also using the 15,000-klick interval. They both used a 50,000-klick distance between wings.

Each of Kris's wings was seven or eight flotillas long and 425,000 klicks in length. The opposing rebel wing was eleven or twelve flotillas in length and was usually 20,000 klicks shorter than Kris's line.

Top to bottom, though, it was a different matter. Kris's three stacks of flotillas, even with 30,000-klick intervals between them, only managed to cover 90,000 kilometers. The seven stacks in the opposing wing stood 125,000 klicks tall. If Kris was careful to keep her wing centered on the middle of the opposing wing, she'd only be overlapped by 17,500 clicks at top and bottom. Still, four of the enemy flotillas could target each of hers.

Kris faced a major problem, but then, fighting 4:1 odds meant you ended up facing a lot of major problems.

The two forces continued to close. They passed the 500,000-kilometer mark with no surprises. The 400,000-mark was just as quiet. Hardly a word was spoken around Kris.

She listened to the soft hum of the blowers circulating air throughout the ship. She took in the scent of ozone, lube oil, and human sweat with each breath. The feel of the ship's hum beneath her feet was gone, absorbed by the egg.

Since they were only at one gee, Kris sat up in her station so she was still able to see her key staff. All of them had gone into their high gee stations naked. If they had to spend days in them, the elimination system worked best without clothing. There was also the problem of how black and blue a zipper left human flesh at four gees acceleration.

At the moment, Jack was bare chested. The breasts of the women around him were covered by the high gee stations, not out of modesty, although someone somewhere might have ordered it, but so that two certain delicate feminine items were supported and cushioned if things suddenly became rowdy.

I wonder what the kids are up to? Kris asked herself. It would be terrible to orphan them in just one afternoon watch.

Kris shook herself, straining against her restraints. She focused her mind on the board and only the board.

What's that other poor son of a squid thinking?

❧

Admiral of the First Order of Steel, Karl'sum'Ton'sum'Go eyed the distance between the two fleets. Battle would come soon. Very soon.

This was the moment he had been chosen for. It was for this that he was schooled, trained, and had trained others. Still, in the pit of his stomach there was a strangeness.

He had never faced battle before.

None of the sailors or officers in his fleet had ever faced

battle.

All would be tested in the next few hours.

It might have made a lesser man fearful.

But Karl was not a lesser man. He was the fourth chosen son of the Pasha of the Golden Flying Fish Satrap. It was he who had been given the honor of fighting this Longknife human female and blasting her and the entire fleet that followed her to mere dust scattered among the stars.

He had a battle to win.

"Sidd, attend me."

"Yes, My Lord Admiral," the intelligence officer said, coming away from his as-yet-unneeded high gee bunk to stand beside the admiral at his battle board.

"The Longknife human female and her fleet just passed the 450,000-kililu mark. Has she any more surprises up one of her two sleeves?"

"In the Battle of the Imperial Guard System, she had two maskers on each of her ships."

"How did they produce that many maskers? We don't even have enough for half our ships here. So, what value are two maskers on a battlecruiser?"

"The humans made drones that they used for target practice. They were just flat silhouettes of one, but it had enough power to behave as one. They modified those target drones into what they called 'foxers.' Apparently, in their tongue to 'out-fox' someone is to fool them."

Karl did not know where this rambling was going, and he had little time for it, anyway. "And the foxers did what?"

"The unlamented Admiral Donn found himself suddenly facing three times as many visual targets and two masker targets. His gunners had to blast one or two of the dummy targets before they managed to kill one battle-cruiser."

"Why did they not discern the fake from the real?"

"I had some of the best sensor equipment on the ship I was riding in. As much as I tried, I could not distinguish the two."

"One fired lasers, the others did not," Karl snapped.

"Unfortunately, My Lord Admiral, all three fired lasers. The foxers had been rigged with low power lasers that gave off the same evidence of lasers being fired as the actual ships did."

"Could they not identify them by the radar return, noise from the reactors, heat, on infrared?"

"The radar, when it wasn't jammed, showed a solid target. The reactor noise was all jammed. As for infrared, the foxers were just as hot as the real ships."

"So, you say that while we have four ships for every one of hers, we will have to wade through two decoy ships to kill one real one."

"Yes, My Lord Admiral."

"Have you any suggestions I might consider?"

"The foxers do not have any armor. One hit may well send them spinning out of control. The loyalist ships under Longknife's command took to waving their lasers around the target area, like a firefighter waves a fire hose at a burning building. This gave them a better chance of hitting and damaging a battlecruiser. If we did that, our lasers could cover more area and increase the likelihood of a hit on a thin-skinned decoy."

"Number 1 Staff Officer."

"Yes, My Lord Admiral?"

"Our Staff Officer Number 2 has just told me something he should have told me last week. We may be facing thin-skinned fake warships. Instruct the fleet's gunnery officers to swivel their lasers when they fire them. We want to cover as much of the targets down range as possible. Our objective is to destroy the fakes quickly. Then we shall concentrate on our real enemy."

"It shall be done," and the Number 1 staff officer was gone.

"I thought you told me everything you knew?"

"The drones were in my report, My Lord Admiral. I thought you knew." *And would not want me to waste your time,* Sidd did not add.

Admiral Karl turned his back on his number two staff officer and the man retreated back to his bunk along the aft bulkhead of the flag bridge. Karl had read Donn's after-action report on the Guard System battle. Now he remembered the section about the maskers and even remembered reading about the strange foxers.

If Karl was the type to be embarrassed, he might have been, at that moment in time. Instead, he let his anger grow that a man of Sidd's rank had let this problem slip by.

Again, Karl walked around his battle board, hunting for an advantage.

Then he saw it.

"Sidd, attend me."

Immediately, the low-born officer was at his side.

"Does not the Longknife human female like to hit ships where they are the weakest?"

"Yes, My Lord Admiral."

"Then I think we shall hit her where she is the weakest. Number 3 Staff Officer, prepare to issue orders."

"Yes, My Lord Admiral."

And Karl began to speak the orders that would hit this Longknife woman the most where it was her custom to hit others.

48

Grand Admiral, Her Royal Highness Kris Longknife watched as her battle board began to change and her day began a rapid descent into hell.

"Nelly, is this right?"

"Yes, Kris," her computer answered softly.

Kris worried her lips, considering her options while the data made its way through the necessary human buffers before the information got to the senior commanders.

Thirteen seconds later, Sensors reported, "The enemy vanguard has changed its power vectors, Admiral. They are now directing half their power toward closing with us and only half to decelerating."

"Thank you, Sensors. Keep me appraised of any change."

"By dropping below us, he's going for our weak unarmored sterns," Admiral Tosan said.

"Yes," Kris answered, "I do think he's aiming for the one

place on our ships that we can't armor, our rocket motors aft and the reactors immediately forward of them."

If the rebels could get their ships below Kris's, they could blow her ships up as quickly as balloons got popped at Johnnie's last birthday party.

"Comm, send to Coth, 'I'm taking the vanguard out of the line. The enemy vanguard is attempting to get below us. We're going to do the same. You have tactical command of the other four wings. You may initiate Battle Plan Nelson at your discretion. Longknife sends.'"

"Order sent, ma'am."

"Comm, send to Admiral Kitano, prepare orders to the vanguard to cut power to match the course adjustment of the enemy. Do not close any faster but reduce deceleration."

"Order sent," Comm reported.

Kris eyed her board. Kitano had sent the instructions to the vanguard, now Kris paused for only a second before ordering, "Adjust deceleration now."

Within a second, she felt butterflies fluttering around in her stomach as she went from one gee to half that. A moment later, her body had adjusted to the change.

Kris went back to studying her battle board where it was reflected in front of her. On the screen, the two vanguards were quickly galloping ahead of the main force. The rebels were now closing on her at almost a fifty-five-degree angle. They would be in contact soon enough.

That, however, would create a situation she didn't want. If she initiated Battle Plan Nelson against the enemy, the surprise would be lost when Coth and the main force initiated it later. No, she needed to do it all together.

"Comm, send to Coth. 'Steer six points closer to the enemy. When you reach maximum range, maintain it."

"Sent. He acknowledged your order."

A moment later, all four of the loyalist wings behind Kris turned their sterns from ten degrees away from the enemy to forty-five. Now the two main forces were charging across the space between them at the same sixty-six-degree angle as the vanguard. That, and Kris's main battle force was falling forward faster, moving into a firing position that put it in a perfect position to shoot up the rebel's unarmored sterns.

Kris allowed herself a grin. "Let's see how you handle that, my fine rebel friend."

~

Admiral Karl had smiled as his vanguard fell away while charging fast toward the Longknife human female's own vanguard. "Let's see how she likes it when she has to eat what she likes to jam down other's throats."

Then that Longknife unchosen female cut the deceleration on her own vanguard. She didn't edge closer to Karl's ships as they shot toward her, but it did drop across their bows as they swept as far ahead of his force as his vanguard was now.

Karl was about to order his vanguard to adjust its course when the entire enemy main force swung around and applied the same vector to their ships as he had applied to his vanguard.

The loyalists' four main wings were charging at his main force! Oh, and they were hot to get below him and shot out his vulnerable stern!

He snapped off an order to the four wings still in his formation to cut their deceleration in half and prepare to receive the charge. He would be ready for them.

49

K ris looked at a crazy game of chase. The enemy vanguard was chasing her. Her main force was chasing the rebel's main force. Either way you cut the cards, the two forces were rapidly closing to within 300,000 kilometers of each other.

First, Kris ordered all ships to initiate hull spin. In olden times, ships had three to six meters of ice armor spun around their long axis. It was hoped the ice would ablate and cool the ship's hull when a laser hit it. The spin would move the damaged part of the hull away from the laser beam and swing new, fresh ice in its place to absorb the hellish heat. However, fighting a ship while you're being spun around as if in an amusement park ride did not help efficiency.

With Smart Metal™ the battlecruisers didn't carry thousands of tons of ice and they did not spin the ship. Instead, the outer hull of the ship spun around the inner hull. There was a thin, top-most layer of reflective material, then a thick layer honeycombed so that cool reaction mass could flow through it. When hit, the metal opened to space and the reaction mass vented out, causing the beam to bloom and dissipate. The reaction mass close to the hit heated up. It took that extra energy into the reactors and gave it up there, where the temperature of a sun's surface was the norm.

Still, nothing but the crystal armor could totally protect a ship from multiple lasers hits, especially from the new 24-inch lasers. The designers had gone for more energy per beam, and only added 30,000 kilometers to the range.

There was a reason why the Iteeche wanted the crystal cladding on the human ships, and why the humans did not want to share it.

With the battlecruisers as ready to protect themselves as they could, Kris eyed her battle board with eyes gone hard. It was time. She activated Battle Plan Nelson.

Locked inside her egg, she crossed her fingers. She hoped that her crews were trained well enough to pull off this unpracticed maneuver.

For the flotilla closest to the orbit of Artiecca 4, the order meant nothing. For every other flotilla in the fleet, it meant throttling back on the deceleration, and a delicate juggling of its position in the wing.

The distance between ships in a squadron stayed the same, 10,000 kilometers. That was needed to dodge and weave. However, the 15,000 kilometers between flotillas dropped precipitously to 5,000. Kris's wing shortened by almost twenty percent.

The biggest change was in the distance between the three different columns in a wing. It dropped 30,000 kilometers to 10,000. Suddenly, the 90,000 kilometers distance from top to bottom of a wing was only 50,000.

Kris targeted the 22 flotillas of her shrunken vanguard at the top front 22 flotillas of the vanguard's 87 ships.

Behind her, Coth had directed his forces towards just as tight a formation aimed slightly up from the center of the rebel formation. Now it became clear. He was shrinking not only the distance between flotillas, but also between wings, dropping the interval from 50,000 to a mere 10,000. A loyalist fleet that had previously spread over some 370,000 kilometers from the bottom-most flotilla of the bottom wing to the top-most flotilla of the tip wing, now extended over only 170,000 kilometers.

Furthermore, this whole concentration of firepower was aimed at the top rebel wing.

With a grin, Kris Longknife ordered the fleet to activate jammers and noise makers. Suddenly, radar became hash, and any listening devices lost all ability to discern reactors or any other noise on the electromagnetic scale.

Half the fleet's sensors were worthless.

Next, Kris ordered the activation of maskers and deployment of foxers as they crossed the 280,000-kilometer line. First, the battlecruisers turned bow-on to the enemy fleet. Then, one image of a battlecruiser appeared to form on the side of another. Or was it the other way around? Then, a second image formed. Suddenly the three images separated and two heavy masses appeared on the delicate atomic laser, showing two 75,000 ton masses, none of them near the three visual targets.

In a matter of seconds, the only sensors that could be trusted, that could be relied upon for targeting, was the Mark I eyeball, be it of the two human-eyed or four Iteeche-eyed variety.

However, where before the rebels faced not quite 3,500 battlecruisers, they now were confronted with over 10,400 targets.

Between the way the loyalist ships had concentrated

themselves well away from the rear and lower wing, and the multiplication of visual target, any fire plans the rebels had developed beforehand was now worthless.

Admiral Karl gaped at the battle board. A moment ago, he had taken delight in what he had done, and at the confusion he must have sown in that Longknife human female's battle plan. Deep black abyss, but he had grinned as most of the loyalist ships charged at his main force. It didn't even bother him that the vanguard was turning into a tangled shark fight.

He saw static for a moment on his battle board.

"What is happening?" he demanded.

"The humans and loyalists have activated their jammers and noise makers," Captain Sidd answered. "Our radar and signal intelligence will no long work. Theirs won't work either."

"Why would they do that?" Karl snapped.

Then the forces opposite him began to shuffle themselves all around, and there were suddenly a lot more of them than there had been a moment ago.

"What is this?"

"They have now deployed their maskers and foxers," Sidd said, maddeningly calm.

"We cannot let the Longknife human alien concentrate all her fire on just a few of our ships. If they close up this tight, part of our fleet won't be in range of them. Number 1 Staff Officer, order the fleet to close up."

"It will be done."

"Ah, My Lord Admiral, what do you mean by close up?" Sidd asked.

"That is a stupid question. Close up the ships. Close up the ships!" Karl screamed at Number 1 Staff Officer.

"The interval between ships, or the interval between flotillas, or maybe between wings? Which do you want to shorten, My Lord Admiral?" Sidd asked softly, as a low-born staff officer should when questioning the fourth chosen son of the lord of a satrap.

However, the damage had already been done.

Orders had gone out to five wing commanders. With the enemy about to come in range, and now under orders to reorganize, each commander issued orders to his own 87 flotilla commanders, who, in their haste, may not have understood the intent of the words they received.

A lot of captains began to move their ships closer to the ship ahead of them, but not everyone. Some flotilla commanders began to close up with the next flotillas while their ships were busy closing up with the ship next to them, or the one behind them. It was not clear which direction the columns were traveling. They were backing down, decelerating toward Artiecca's orbit. Their bows were pointed away. Which direction was which?

Many of the flotillas were operating with ships from different satraps. Many of the flotillas had never maneuvered together.

The execution of Admiral Karl's order did not go smoothly. Not smoothly at all.

Sidd began wondering if that longboat was still available for his use in the launch bay. There were a few of his friends he might want to take with him.

50

Admiral Kris Longknife cringed as her fleet made a hash out of implementing Battle Plan Nelson.

As the flotillas compressed the distance between each other from fifteen thousand kilometers to five thousand, they began to stack up or stretch out. Some closed up immediately, while others took their time. The eager ones risked rushing in and eating up the five thousand kilometers that they were still supposed to keep between flotillas.

At least three flotillas ended up mixing their forward-most ships in with the aft-most ships of the next flotilla, and had to hastily back off. Some of those backing off ended up getting mixed up with the flotilla behind them.

Thank any merciful god, there were no collisions.

The more cautious flotilla admirals took their time closing up, leaving gaping holes in the battle line.

The course set by the bottom wing to move both closer to the head of the enemy line, and the top wing was a particularly wild traffic jam with some admirals having to steer their flotillas out of the line to avoid running into the one ahead.

Battle Plan Nelson might have looked like a brilliant plan on Kris's battle board. However, with a battle force that had only been together for few months and had never attempted anything like this, it was nowhere as brilliant in execution.

Kris watched her forces try to sort themselves out as they closed the last few thousand klicks to bring them in range of the enemy.

The range finder on the battle board was rapidly counting down the remaining kilometers until the 24-inch lasers could reach out 270,000 kilometers and melt somebody.

"Kris," Jack whispered in his egg beside Kris, "take a look at the bungle that rebel admiral has made of his battle array."

Kris tore her eyes off of her own problems and found her jaw falling open.

The rebel commander had responded to her own Battle Plan Nelson with an on-the-fly order for his fleet to do the exact same thing. From the looks of the mess on Kris's board, it was a total disaster.

Likely drawn from different satraps, some of the flotillas fell apart. Other flotillas jammed together, their commanders apparently thinking the order meant shorten the interval between ships as well.

Kris watched as two ships rammed each other, then another two. One of that pair exploded, taking the second ship with it. There were flotillas wandering all over the place with some pulling out of line to avoid merging into the one ahead of it.

It was at this point, that the two fleets crossed within

range of each other.

"Admiral Kris Longknife here. Execute Evasion Plan 2. Execute prepared fire plan. Open fire by flotillas. Now!"

Kris's fleet might be in some disarray, but each ship began jinking within its own 10,000 kilometers of space. A moment later, each of them flipped to bring their forward battery to bear. A split second later, over 42,000 lasers beams flashed toward the enemy line.

The vanguard fired a hair faster than the rest of the fleet. Seventy-two loyal Iteeche squadrons targeted 84 rebel ships. Rebel ships that were on a steady, predictable course. Engaged by 8 ships with 12 forward lasers each, 70 ships just vanished.

The 24-inch lasers burned through the hulls and destroyed reactor containment fields. The ships were eaten by their own power plants. In a split second, where a ship and crew had been, there was only superheated gas.

The four human flotillas engaged by divisions. They targeted 32 ships. Every one of them died equally fast.

Under Coth's command, his 87 flotillas engaged 348 rebel ships. Three hundred and twenty-five evaporated.

It was shocking that 427 rebel ships that had been there one second were gone five seconds later.

There was no pause to celebrate. The gunners of the forward batteries immediately began to recharge their capacitors. It would take twenty seconds for massive amounts of carefully measured and monitored power to have their laser capacitors charged and ready. Other gunners watched the temperature of the lasers and let more or less reaction mass flow around them to cool them off. Technicians checked for any sign of a malfunction in any of the myriad of systems needed to make these huge lasers perform flawlessly. Where necessary, a backup system was engaged and a new part was programed from Smart Metal™.

Meanwhile, on the bridges, orders were being given. Almost as one, all up and down the human battle line, the ships flipped. As they had practiced so many times on the way out, the helmsman rotated the ship along it midpoint, swinging the forward battery away and bringing the aft battery of eight guns to bear.

Again, 452 ships were targeted. Again, the ships were dumbly following a course, straight and true. This time, with only two-thirds as many guns in the aft battery, more managed to escape the network of 24-inch laser beams that crisscrossed the space around them. Still, in five seconds, 328 ships were gone.

In seventeen seconds, the rebel force had lost 755 ships. More than five percent of its total strength, over 196 were from the vanguard. The rest were from the top wing.

Nelly had set up a counter on Kris's battle board. Her force still counted 3,488. Her enemy still showed 13,229.

Kris eyed the two battle lines as her ships returned to their base course. Coth was holding his fleet just inside the 270,000-klick range of the new 24-inch lasers. While 270,000 klicks was a long reach, Kris was confident that her tightened gun cradles and improved fire control computers could handle it and that the rebel ships couldn't.

The enemy vanguard, however, was still trying to close with Kris's vanguard.

"Comm, send to Admiral Kitano. 'Wear away from the enemy vanguard. We want to keep them just inside 270,000 kilometers.'"

"Sent and acknowledged," came back only a second later.

The vanguard began to adjust its course almost immediately.

Kris checked the re-arm clock that had been started the moment the forward batteries fell silent. It took twenty seconds to reload the 24-inch lasers. The bow batteries had been reloading while the aft batteries were firing. Ten seconds after the aft lasers fell silent, the fleet would swing their bows around to bring the reloaded forward battery to bear.

Kris was in her high gee station, but her fleet was only using one gee to decelerate and edge the ships closer or farther from the enemy. They were jinking about, juggling the deceleration a bit, but holding at Evasion Plan 2.

Again, she studied her battle board. The two fleets were spread out. Her fleet had fired two salvos. So far, the rebels were silent. Her ships were almost reloaded. She would hate to be in her opponent's shoes.

~

Admiral Karl stared at his battle board, his jaw slack, his mouth gaping open.

"That's impossible," he screamed in shock.

"No, My Lord Admiral," Captain Sidd said. "Our ships are on predictable courses. The visual sensors on the human and loyalist ships capture where we have been and are, then their fire control computers predict where we will be. Since we are staying on the same course, they are slaughtering us. We need to jitter, My Lord Admiral. Jitter and open fire."

Karl stared at the staff officer who had spoken without being spoken to. He heard his words, but it took him a moment to understand them. Finally, he shouted, "Fire! Fire! All ships fire!"

"It is done as you say, My Lord Admiral," Comm answered back.

A moment later, his flag ship swung around, bow-on to the loyalists, and Admiral Karl had to grab an overhead bar.

In those few seconds he stared in shock, another 438 of his ships disappeared. As his fleet swung around to bring their lasers to bear, 318 ships were added to the scroll of ships lost with all hands.

Finally, his fleet began to fire. At least the wing commanders reported they were firing. As Karl watched, he could see no effect on the enemy ships. Here and there, a ship from the other battle line might fall out, blasting toward the unengaged side. One ship blew up, leaving a blotch that quickly disappeared.

"Why aren't we doing anything?" Karl screamed.

"The helmsmen have had little training on how to bring their bow around and aim it at a target, My Lord Admiral," Sidd answered softly, then added, his gentle voice dripping with sarcasm, "Remember, My Lord Admiral, your crews didn't need any training. You refused to train them and now your fleet can't hit the broadside of a Longknife battle line."

"Off my bridge, you incompetent, improper mal-chosen spawn!" Karl shouted at Sidd.

"As you wish it, it shall be done," the captain said with a bow, and stormed off the bridge.

Karl turned back to his battle board. He stared in horror as more of his ships vanished in another salvo from that Longknife human female. "What must I do?" he muttered to himself in panic. "What must I do?"

"My Lord Admiral," the Number 1 Staff Officer shouted, "should we not be jittering our ships like the enemy is doing?"

"Yes! Yes! Start jittering! Start jittering and firing!"

"As you say, it will be done," the senior staff officer shouted and raced to the comm desk.

Then the bottom dropped out of the bridge as the ship flipped to bring its aft battery to bear. The Number 1 Staff Officer grabbed for a chair, missed it, and was halfway to the overhead before the ship came to a halt and he was slammed down to the deck. He stumbled painfully to the comm officer and shouted out the admiral's orders.

"It is sent," Comm shouted.

"Good, good, good," Karl muttered.

His ships were still struggling to bring their forward and aft batteries to bear. Now they began to jitter up and down, right and left.

The next salvo from the loyalist fleet only blew away 297 of his ships.

For a moment, he couldn't believe what his board was showing him. Because of the way that Longknife human woman had crunched her fleet up together, his rear guard was too far in the rear to fight, either to engage the enemy or to be engaged by them. He realized that most all of his casualties were coming from the vanguard's top and center wing, with a few from the lower wing and none from the rear guard.

"Comm, order the rear guard to close up with the center. Order the lower wing to do the same."

"As you say, it has been done," Comm answered.

Number 1 Staff Officer was limping back toward Admiral Karl. He moved carefully, moving from one overhead handhold to the next. He did not seem to mind that his admiral was issuing orders directly to the Comm unit.

Karl swayed as his flagships jittered around him. Ha! The weak humans made their Iteeche lackeys into weak warriors. Karl stood at his post, held on to the bar over his head and watched the battle evolve.

Again, his flagship flipped. He didn't know whether it was to fire its forward or aft battery.

Again, hundreds of ships disappeared from his vanguard and top-most wing, although some of the upper flotillas in the center were also being raked.

Karl began to identify a pattern. That Longknife human female would have her ships concentrate on a flotilla. Twice they would fire their forward battery, twice the aft. Twenty-five or so of the thirty-two ships in the flotilla would vanish. Then they moved on to another flotilla.

Karl watched as they did this twice. Ninety-one of his 438 flotillas were reduced to remnants. Many of the surviving ships were slipping away, decelerating and aiming well away from the enemy.

"Number 1 Staff Officer, order the ships that are fleeing to reform into flotillas and return to the fight."

"As you say, so it will be done," the staff officer shouted, but he made his way carefully, from one overhead handhold to the next, to the Comm unit.

Karl studied the battle line of loyalist ships that submitted to the so-called orders of the Longknife human female. Where he had gaping holes in his battle array, especially in his vanguard and top wings, he saw few of the loyalists either blowing themselves to atoms or limping out of the line.

Certainly, no great number were fleeing. Not like his hundreds or thousands.

This mere human could not be doing this to an Iteeche Admiral of the First Order of Steel, fourth chosen of the Pasha for the Golden Flying Fish Satrap! She just couldn't!

51

Kris Longknife shook her head. The *Princess Royal* was back on base course, having just finished the fifth salvo from its aft battery. The battle had been raging for only two and a half minutes. The counter that Nelly was running was appalling.

Of the near 14,000 ships the rebels had begun the fight with, over 3,700 were space dust!

There were as many as a thousand officers and sailors on each of the rebel warships. That thousand was crammed into a ship about the size of one of Kris's ships at Condition Charlie. Well, maybe it was a bit larger. Still, the ship was cramped and the target they presented was nearly twice that of one of Kris's ships at Condition Zed.

And they fought their ships without going to Zed!

Every Iteeche in the fleet knew about the four sizes the human ships used as they cruised the galaxy. The humans that programmed the ships as they grew from a seed to a full, operational warship, showed them the four sizes their ships were capable of.

As one, the Iteeche ordered their fifth configuration. Horribly cramped for their oversize crew, but large for a target.

Thirty-seven hundred ships had been blown to dust or, if they were lucky, limped out of the line. That meant over three and a half million Iteeche had died in the last two and a half minutes.

As Kris watched, her fleet flipped again. While she'd been reflecting on the horror, another 700 ships and 700,000 Iteeche crew had been blasted into whatever their hereafter was.

The admiral across from her had lost over thirty percent of his battle fleet.

She'd had 29 ships blown up. Another 19 had fallen out of the line on the disengaged side and were making repairs. Kris ordered the damaged ships to limp back to the transports. She doubted there would be any fight near them. Still, it let an Iteeche feel that they were serving honorably during the battle.

As far as Kris was concerned every Iteeche, on either side, was serving honorably.

Grand Admiral Kris Longknife, worried her lower lip. This carnage had to stop.

"Comm, send on all circuits monitored on both sides, 'This is Grand Admiral, Her Royal Highness, Kris Longknife, Imperial Admiral of the First Order of Steel and Commander, Imperial Combined Fleets. You have fought honorably. You are being led by senior officers who have poorly prepared you for this battle. You are suffering brutal casualties and are hardly able to strike a blow for your cause. Already, nearly a third of your force has been reduced to dust. Nearly five million of you have been blown to bits in this uneven fight. I call upon you to surrender. I offer terms of surrender that will allow all of you, from your captains on down, to live long and prosperous lives. You do not need to continue to suffer this slaughter. Every thirty seconds, another seven hundred thousand of you will die.

'To show us you are surrendering, turn away from my battle line. Smash the main weapons power busses to your lasers. We can identify a ship with no charge in their capacitors. Do this, and you will live. Refuse, and you will die'."

"Got it, Admiral. I sent it as you spoke it. I'll repeat it on all the channels I know. I've passed it through to Admiral Coth and he'll have his comm people cover anything I missed."

"Well done," Kris answered.

Beneath her, the *Princess Royal* fell out from under her. Once again, for the eighth time, her ships sent salvoes at the confused and ineffective rebel fleet. This time, the casualties were only approximately 650 ships when the aft batteries fell silent.

Nelly's counter showed almost 5,800 battlecruisers destroyed out of the near 14,000 this idiot of a commander had brought to battle. Over forty percent of his force was no more. Surely, he'd have to accept her offer. If for nothing else, to save those serving loyally under his command.

Assuming Iteeche admirals had any loyalty to those they led into battle.

Kris swallowed bile as she waited for some response to her offer.

Admiral Karl of the First Order of Steel, fourth chosen son of the Pasha of the Golden Flying Fish Satrap, stared at the large forward screen on his flag bridge. His eyes were wide. Each breath came to him in small gasps through his wide-open mouth, his jaw hung slack and unnoticed. Though his four eyes were wide, his vision had narrowed. He could see the battle screen, but all around it was a red fog.

Karl, not having been trained in his own biology, could not know that his body was directing most of his blood down, away from his head and brain, to feed the muscles in all four of his legs and arms. All of them would be needed to swim away quickly.

In his gut, something clenched and then released. Clenched and then released. Karl, though an admiral, struggled to keep his sphincter closed. A tiny sack, the vestigial remains of a much larger one, his body was getting ready to shoot black ink out, giving him camouflage, encouraging jet propulsion to speed his flight away from danger.

Admiral Karl wrapped his arms around himself and struggled to hold himself together. As he stared, mouth agape, more of his fleet vanished, as if a huge net had been cast over it and then had been reeled in, thrashing, and fighting, until the fisherman ended their sad fight by slamming a mallet to their head.

He tore his eyes away from his own disaster to measure the effect of his fire on the loyalist fleet. Here and there, a ship might vanish, but they were so few. So very few.

The Longknife human female had devastated four of his five wings. Half of the ships in the vanguard, top, and central wings were gone. Some of the flotillas in the lower wing had also been decimated.

Only the rearguard still existed as a fighting force.

"Comm." Admiral Karl opened his mouth to order the rear guard to move up faster. Then, he saw it on the screen. Something he never thought any Iteeche admiral would ever see. The entire wing of the rearguard had swung around. They were presenting their sterns to the enemy and blasting at two gees away from the fight. Away from the enemy!

"Comm, get me the commander of the rearguard on screen. Now!"

"As you say, it will . . . My Lord Admiral, I am told there is no circuit on net to the rearguard. Every time we try to make a connection, we are told that all circuits are busy."

"I will have his head for this!"

"My Lord Admiral, what are we to do?" pleaded Number 3 Staff Officer.

"Fight! Fight! We fight!" shouted Admiral of the First Order of Steel Karl'sum'Ton'sum'Go qu Chap'sum'We, fourth chosen son of the Pasha of the Golden Flying Fish Satrap.

Then, there was a blinding light. When his eyes let him see again, all he saw were the holes made by two huge 24-inch lasers as they shot through his bridge. His two left arms were cut off, as if by a huge meat cleaver. He looked at the holes in the hull. He could see stars through them.

Then the reactors let loose the wild demons of the ship's own plasma and there were no holes, no ship, no Admiral Karl, nothing but heated gas, cooling rapidly.

∼

Hot gasses from the destruction of Admiral Karl's flagship slammed Captain Sidd back into his restraints as the longboat he and some 23 rational associates were in, fled that disaster. Fate was with them. They survived what few others did.

Still, they were in great danger. At any moment, a stray

laser beam from a loyalist battlecruiser could convert their small craft into nothing.

"Good pilot, get us out of here," he ordered.

"To where, my Captain?"

"There is no place we can reach in this glass jar," his friend, Commander Tarr said. He was a superb virtuoso on sensors. He had brought a complete record of this disaster with him as he raced to the longboat. That needed to live.

"Is there a ship we could land on?" Sidd asked.

Tarr stood in the co-pilot's place. He studied the displays in front of him. Then he stabbed at a screen. "The Emperor Que-Long IV Number 512 is withdrawing from the line. Before it builds up too many gees, can we board it?"

"I will call it," the pilot said, tensely.

A brief exchange and they had permission to board, "If you can catch the hook on the first try. We are not waiting for something out of the deep abyss to bite us on the ass."

It required them to use up just about all the fuel on their small craft, but the pilot was good. He put them aboard their ticket out of the abyss even as the ship passed two gees and kept accelerating.

The Emperor Que-Long IV Number 512 was not the only ship turning its tail to the enemy and fleeing at best speed.

The battle was over. Now all that remained for any warrior was surviving this disaster.

52

Admiral Kris Longknife breathed a sigh of relief as the battle line off of her starboard quarter disintegrated. Unfortunately, it did not disintegrate quite sufficiently to her liking.

The rearguard had suffered few casualties, both because of its place in the back of the line, and the apparent reluctance of its commander to close up when he was, no doubt, ordered to do so. At the moment, he was blasting at 2.4 gees away from Kris's battle line.

If Kris remembered correctly, that was about 3.0 gees to an Iteeche. Someone was in a hurry to get out of here.

Unfortunately, there was no place to go. There were no jumps in that general direction. The rearguard was fleeing, but it was fleeing to nowhere.

Here and there among the other four wings, three of which had suffered well over fifty percent casualties, some ships were drifting, waiting for orders. Others were joining the rear guard in senseless flight at 2.4 gees perpendicular to Kris's course.

Kris needed to set things straight.

"This is Admiral Kris Longknife to all rebel Iteeche ships in this system. The battle is lost. I have promised you, from ship captains to the lowliest seaman, your lives. In order to receive my parole, you must cut all acceleration, empty your capacitors, and smash your main weapons bus bars. If you continue to accelerate away from my forces, I will assume that you are still in rebellion against the Emperor and I will destroy you. This offer will not be repeated. You have fifteen minutes to determine your fate."

"Fifteen minutes?" Jack asked.

"I figure it will be obvious really quick who's willing to slow and who isn't. Then it's up to the crew to persuade those recalcitrant admirals that they really want to surrender."

"Are you going to require that they turn over their admirals to you?" Jack asked.

Kris shook her head. "You've seen what a formal and complete apology involves. Given a choice between that and a long walk out a short airlock, which would you take?"

"Good point."

"Comm, get me Admiral Coth on the screen."

A moment later a very happy Iteeche admiral appeared on a portion of Kris's forward screen. "Sky, sun, and stars, Longknife, how did we win this one with a much desirable and lopsided victory?"

"You remember all the training we did back at Zargoth and on the way here?"

"I heard many a grumble about it, yes."

"Did you see any training cruises while we were in this system?"

"You don't mean?"

"Whoever commanded here was an idiot. He didn't train

his gunners. He didn't train his helmsmen. He didn't train his captains. I know I threw a monkey wrench into our formation by slapping Battle Plan Nelson on us, but at least we had drilled. You saw what happened to his ships when he tried to do anything but maneuver in the standard formation."

"If they had not been under the guns of their enemy, such clowning around would have been funny," Admiral Coth said. "By the way, the idiot who commanded here was fourth chosen son of the Pasha of the Golden Flying Fish Satrap, Karl'sum'Ton'sum'Go qu Chap'sum'We, Admiral of the First Order of Steel."

"A Chap'sum'We?" Kris echoed

"The clans usually have people on both sides of a rebellion. This side of the family lost in the last dynastic change a thousand years ago. I think they want to end up on top this time and have the other wing of the family beholden to them."

"So, clans look after themselves. Who looks out for the average worker?"

"Who would look out for a mere worker," Coth said, bitterly. "I don't believe we have ever seen an admiral, much less and Imperial Admiral of the First Order of Steel concerned about the lower decks. Certainly not one who would end a fight when they had it in their power to completely annihilate their enemy."

"I hope that some of these ships and their crews will fight for us, Coth. However, it appears that some of them are trying to get away."

"Yes, I noticed that."

"Would you kindly take the center and rearguard wings and pursue their rearguard wing? Feel free to pick up any strays that you run across. I have given them fifteen minutes to cut their power and smash their main weapons buses. If they don't, shoot them down."

"All of them?"

Kris frowned. "I gave them fifteen minutes in the hope that any admiral who tried to keep running could be persuaded to take a walk out an airlock, either voluntarily, or with a bit of help. If it appears that some crew has finally gained control of their ship, hold your fire. However, fifteen minutes from now, you decide who dies and who doesn't."

"Knowing the tender heart you human female mothers have, I will fire at a few flagships to get your point across, only after your time has expired and they are still running. I think we can persuade most of the ships left after that to surrender. Do you really think you can, what do you say, rope them and brand them?"

"You have been watching some western videos, Coth."

"They are interesting stories about you humans."

Kris laughed. "Don't think that everything you see on video is true. Some people will say anything to sell a story. Now, about capturing that fleet and getting them to join our ranks. We may need to ship some captains with clan connections back to their clans. We may need to find other jobs for some senior officers, but think of all the promotions we can give to your junior officers. Think of how many admiralty slots this will open up for your captains."

"You make this very appealing, Admiral Longknife. Very appealing. Now, I have orders and a passel of doggies to wrangle up."

"Thank you," Kris said, and a cheerful Coth disappeared from the screen.

"Watching westerns?" Jack muttered.

"The poison from the human race just keeps seeping

deeper and deeper into their blood stream," Megan said, grinning.

Kris had to agree, but she didn't have time for that. "Comm, get me Commanders of the top, bottom and vanguard wings.

A moment later, a human and two Iteeche faces appeared on screen.

"Admiral Kitano, do you have good enough sensor suites on your ships to identify if a rebel battlecruiser has emptied its capacitors and smashed its weapons bus?"

"Every one of our ships can do that, Admiral."

"Good. Under your command, the vanguard and lower wings, minus the First Human Flotilla, will clean up the scattered survivors from the rebel top, center, bottom, and vanguard wings. I've got Admiral Coth, with the rearguard and center wings, chasing the rebel rearguard. They're the most organized force the rebels have left in the system."

"Aye, aye, Admiral," Admiral Kitano said.

Kris turned to the commander of the top wing. "I will add the First Human Flotilla to your command. You will be my main force to escort the attack transports into orbit over Artiecca. Are there any questions?"

There were none. "Then, lady and gentlemen, let us occupy this system as quickly and as mercifully as possible."

53

I t's one thing to say you intend to occupy a system quickly. It was an entirely different process to actually do it.

Between Admirals Coth and Kitano, Kris ended up the proud owner of 8,103 new battlecruisers carrying either twenty or fourteen 24-inch lasers. Each ship brought her a captain to deal with as well as a command structure above them that yielded her 347 admirals of various orders, most with clan connections.

Strangely, 6 battlecruisers managed to slip the net by taking off at three gees for the farthest jump point. Since they were headed off on a tangent from the rest of the rebel fleet, it was easier to let them go than chase them.

Kris hoped that would not come back to bite her on the ass.

The admirals were collected on Admiral Coth's flagship. The eight thousand plus captains were brought aboard whatever loyalist battlecruiser they surrendered to. Prize crews from the Iteeche ships under Coth's command went over, with at least a Marine platoon, and took the ships under their control.

Kris got a call from Coth before the first ship was boarded.

"My Admiral, I need an order from you immediately."

Kris couldn't help but grin at that. "Tell me the order you need from me and I will give it."

"Let me tell you of the two orders you may give and you decide between them. Are you humans familiar with the concept of prize money for captured ships?"

Kris frowned for a moment, then remembered something she found rather arcane when she was reading about naval warfare in the time of sail. "Yes, I believe so."

"It is common for a captain, when another ship surrenders to them, to offer the ship to the Emperor, or central rebel assembly, for purchase. The captain, of course receives the larger sum, maybe half of the entire value. He will pay twenty percent of his prize money to his admirals, with the admiral in your position getting the lion's share of that tithe. The officers get a portion; however, the sailors get a much smaller portion that may well be enough to allow them to buy a small business or apprenticeship when they are discharged."

"I'm not quite sure where you are going with this," Kris said.

"You have given four of your wings orders to pursue and capture a large fortune. Many of our ships will take multiple ships. It is possible that an eager beaver might put a prize crew aboard four or five ships."

Kris began to see a problem here. "Have there ever been fights between ships, or between boarding parties?" Kris asked.

"That is not something that we like to talk about, but yes, it has happened."

"And I have taken one wing totally out of the gold rush, haven't I?"

"Yes, My Admiral."

"So, tell me what my two orders might be."

"You can allow any ship that captures another to take the prize money entirely for that ship. Alternately, you may claim all the ships for yourself and assure every officer and crewman that you will apportion out the total of the ships in accordance with the traditional distribution, and promise each man an equal share in all the ships taken."

"I definitely think that second option is my order, Admiral. Transmit that order to all the fleet, including the wings that I have sailing away from the treasure chest that every officer and sailor will receive a portion, distributed in the traditional way, for all the ships taken today."

"Aye, aye, Admiral. Very good," and a very happy Iteeche killed the circuit.

"Clearly, we're going to have some very happy officers and sailors," Jack said, grinning.

"I wonder what my take will be," Kris muttered.

"And how you might get the money out of the Iteeche Empire," Megan said with an even bigger grin.

"Maybe you could take your money in battlecruisers and ship them to Alwa," Admiral Tosan, Kris's chief of staff offered. "No doubt Admiral Santiago and Granny Rita would be grateful for the extra firepower."

"Not a bad idea, Admiral," Kris said. "Let's see. If I get half of twenty percent of fifty percent, what would that give me, Nelly?"

"Four hundred and five point four-five battlecruisers,

Kris. I would not want to serve on that point four-five battle-cruiser," Nelly said, dryly.

"No doubt, that ship might have a tough time keeping out space vacuum," Jack agreed.

"And how could one and a half reactors keep the plasma contained?" Megan added.

"Enough with the dreaming about our future wealth," Kris said. "I suspect taking this planet will be worth a whole lot more than all those ships."

"Do we get prize money for planets?" Megan asked.

"It will get interesting," Jack agreed.

"Comm, send to the Planetary Overlord, Artiecca 4 and all other senior political leaders in this system: 'From Grand Admiral, Her Royal Highness, Kris Longknife, Imperial Admiral of the First Order of Steel, Commander of the Imperial Combined Fleets and Victorious Admiral over the defeated fleet guarding your system, Greetings. I require you to submit to the proper and fitting worship of your Emperor. Those of you of the highest position will be sent to the Emperor to make your most sincere and complete apologies. Those of you who fill middle clan ranks will be dispatched to your clan households on the Imperial Capital where you will receive reassignments befitting your rank and skills. I require that the planet and all associate production facilities in this system be handed over to me undamaged. No working personnel are to be harmed. I will give you one of your days to submit or I will begin the reduction of your planet by any means I choose.' Comm, attach the video taken in the bunker of the Planetary Overlord on Zargoth. Anyone have any other suggestions?"

Kris was greeted with only shaking heads. "Send."

"Aye, aye, Admiral. It's sent. I'm broadcasting this on all available circuits and nets I have identified. I'm pretty sure everyone down there will have a pretty good idea about this message before the day is out."

"Very good. Now, let's set a course that will get us in orbit around Artiecca 4."

Slowing down to catch the planet turned out to be a bit more difficult than Kris would have liked. The attack transports had done nothing to close the enemy fleet. They managed to catch the planet by only going to 2.0 gees. The battlecruisers, during the battle, were much more out of position and hit 3.0 gees before they fell back to two.

Still, Kris's fleet barely managed to get caught into a high orbit. It took several revolutions before they managed to lower their orbit and sync with that of the planet below.

They were just coming up on the largest station and space elevator serving the system's capital when Kris got a response from the Planetary Overlord.

It was not to her liking.

54

"Know you, human female who styles herself as some sort of Navy officer, you are not wanted here," said a haughty looking Iteeche in an iridescent robe of every color of the rainbow. "This planet will never surrender. If you land forces here, you will confront a wasteland. All the means of production have been mined. We have rigged explosives to everything essential for civilized life: power, water, sewer, and transportation. If you land, you will face a starving people who will have no source of food, water, or health care, but you."

Somehow, the Iteeche Overlord managed to snort. "We know that you do not have a warrior's heart. You are weak. You would never want to place fifty billion dead Iteeche on the blackened soul that you humans claim to have. Be gone. There is nothing here for you."

The message terminated.

"Well, it seems that we will have ourselves a bit of a battle," Kris said.

"I wonder if the space stations are rigged to explode?" Jack asked.

"These space stations are a major investment," Nelly said. "Destroying them, and sending their space elevators crashing to the ground would not only be deadly, but replacing them would likely kill this system. What that overlord is proposing would literally turn a thriving planet back to the stone age."

"And they'd be doing it to themselves," Kris muttered.

"Comm, get me Admiral Coth on the hook."

A moment later, a very happy Iteeche was filling half of Kris's forward screen."

"Are you enjoying yourself?" Kris asked.

"Immensely," the admiral answered. "We have only had to shoot up two ships so far. I think your Admiral Kitano has only destroyed one. You have made all of us wealthy men. Tell, me, Admiral, have you ever thought of establishing your own clan? I think a very large number of admirals and captains under your command would be glad to name you clan chieftain. Chieftain of the Longknife Clan. It has a nice sound to it, don't you think?"

"Yes, but I'm sure there are few clan leaders that would be happy to see a human raised up to be their equal."

"My Admiral, you now command a force of over twelve thousand battlecruisers. Twelve thousand that fight like fifty-thousand. There is no force that can stand against you!"

"While you are probably right that no force of battlecruisers can stand up to us, I fear that the power of conservative tradition and clan prerogatives would be a tough nut to crack."

"If you capture Artiecca and a few more planets like it, you will have a power base to equal or exceed all the clans. Just think about that."

"About capturing this planet. I have a problem. Did you get the message from this Planetary Overlord?"

"Yes, the blowhard. Does he really think the people under him would cut their own throats? Their throats and those of their familiars and chosen? Ha! He does not know what he is talking about."

"However, we must encourage people to step away from him. In order to do that, I need something to demonstrate my strength. Tell me, how do you render a space station uninhabitable? Is there some valve that can be opened that will let all the air out of the station?"

"No. Why would anyone install such a thing?"

"There are always the docking locks that open for ships," Megan piped up.

"Yes, but those are totally controlled," Coth said.

"By whom?" Kris asked.

"The Port Captain's office."

"And how does he order the doors to open? Is it done manually or are they operated by computer net?" asked Kris, again probing.

"Someone in the Port Captain's office flips a switch and the doors slide open."

"Are there any safeguards?"

"You are full of questions, My Admiral."

"I don't want eager Marines perforating my space station. If I'm going to have to kill a lot of Iteeche, I'd rather they were all rebels without a lot of loyalists thrown in."

"I like your attitude. Now let me check."

For a long minute, the sound went down and Admiral Coth spoke to several people on and off screen. When the sound came back up, Coth was barking a laugh.

"Yes, My Imaginative Admiral, the doors are opened remotely. There are not manual controls at the pier. There is no override if the hatches do not seal. A call to the Port Captain's Office is necessary to close it up again. I think we Iteeche reserve too much to those higher up the chain of rank. No doubt, you are going to use this to bite them on the ass."

"I think we can do that," Kris said, then turned away from the screen, "Megan, do I have a job for you."

55

Lieutenant Commander Megan Longknife knew she had nothing to worry about. Kris Longknife herself had told her so. So why was she holding her breath?

For about the thousandth time since the small launch left the *Princess Royal*, Megan forced herself to breathe.

Of course, she might be dead any moment. Certainly, whether she breathed or not would not stop a laser if the search radar on the station suddenly started working.

It wasn't supposed to. Start working, that is. She'd been assured it wouldn't work for at least for the next fifteen minutes.

One of the battlecruisers had been hitting all four of the station's search radars with a high-powered pulse of radio energy every hour or so since around noon the ship's time. Each time they hit it with a pulse, the radars went down. It took exactly thirty minutes to bring the search radar back on line. The first time they took it down, it took thirty minutes to get it back on line, and Iteeche radar crews had gotten neither faster nor slower. Thirty minutes each time, to the second.

Megan, and thirty Marines were crammed into a launch with a boson's mate conning it. A certain Captain Quinn Sung, who didn't seem to know what was good for her, sat in the left-hand seat, monitoring the electronic sensors and countermeasures. Megan had to go on this mission; the captain didn't.

Megan had grown up knowing there was a Longknife legend, knowing she was part of it whether she liked it or not. She could have stayed on Santa Maria where Longknifes did research that usually produced dry holes, but no, she had to not only come back to Wardhaven, but get herself attached to a certain Kris Longknife.

Now she was into the Longknife legend up to her neck. Which might be parted from her head very soon. What was it she'd heard Kris say? Longknifes do what they have to do.

Damn, why did I have to get the brain I've got? With a normal brain, there would be nothing I could do. But I've got this one.

Megan scowled at the captain. She grinned back like she had no good sense. What was it about people when they got around Longknifes? Suddenly they're volunteering.

Then, of course, those were only the ones who made the mistake of getting close. Most people were smart enough to run the other way when they saw a Longknife coming.

Unlike the Marines behind her.

They were all volunteers. Dumb Marines.

The launch gently came to hover above the most extreme arm of the space station. Like all other Iteeche space stations Megan had seen, all one dozen of them, it looked like someone had taken a flat snowflake and pulled it out until it was a stack of the same snowflake. They had picked a place about as far from the command center as they could get.

The station was rotating, so the boson's mate moving this vessel was doing one hell of a job of flying to keep them just a quarter meter above the station's hull. Then she applied just a smidgen more down power, and they settled smoothly onto the station.

There was a hissing sound as the docking collar sealed tight with the station.

One Marine hauled up a hatch that hadn't been in the deck of the launch before this afternoon, and clambered down onto the hull. For a brief moment, the screech of a drill came through Megan's boots, then the Marine hopped out, and Megan hopped in.

She was wearing a belt and bandolier of Smart Metal™, wrapped around her space suit, as was Captain Sung. Quickly, Lily exuded a thin wire of the fine metal and Megan directed it to the hole. It fit perfectly.

On the other side, as yet invisible to Megan, the wire shed tens of thousands of nano scouts, command nanos, and comm relay nanos. Lily dispatched the scouts to get a good look at what lay below them.

Megan saw the picture begin to develop. In a moment, a holograph appeared before her. Below them was a hodge-podge of junk; crates, containers, broken tugs, luggage carts, lift cranes and even what looked like a fire truck.

What Megan didn't see was a single live Iteeche. What she wanted to see was a security camera or an auto cannon. She wanted very much to disable the cannon and suborn the camera.

The scouts searched further afield. They found no cannon. They did find a camera. It wasn't working. One of the cranes had been backed into it, knocking it off the wall.

It dangled by a single wire. Scouts modified themselves, infiltrated the camera and found that no power was getting to it. Further checking showed the network connection to this station was also dead.

Megan considered activating it and using it to infiltrate the station, then discarded the idea. It wouldn't do for some alert Iteeche or observation routine to notice a dead node suddenly going active. It would take Megan a few minutes, maybe more, before she had total control of the station's computer system. Those few or more minutes could ruin this idea of Kris Longknife's and leave Megan and her Marines very dead.

No, Megan needed an active node she could suborn and make nice with.

The Navy lieutenant commander hopped out of the docking collar and stepped away from the hatch on the floor. Two Marines hopped in and went to work.

They took a moment to lay out a long thin line of explosives, slapped an armored cloth over it, and climbed back out.

"Fire in the hole," was called on net, as the two Marines slammed the hatch down and locked it. Aboard the launch, anyone who was still breathing ship air slapped their helmet closed. The boson had been on spacesuit air since they launched. Anyone smart had followed her lead.

They waited. Two seconds later, there was a whoomph. The launch rocked, but both the explosion and the docking collar had been designed to vent the explosion either into the metal they wanted cut, or out into space.

Again, the hatch opened, Smart Metal™ had already converted the docking collar back into a solid seal. Gunny ordered four Marines through the hatch. They dropped one after the other.

Megan had her computer Lily giving her a live stream from the Marines' helmet cameras. Each Marine landed on a crate and immediately hopped from there to the deck. The first turned toward center of the station and checked out that approach, his rifle up, following his eyes. The second jumped off to his right and did the same to that quadrant. The third turned to the left and found himself checking out the nearby station hull. The last jumped to cover their rear. He ran his eye and gun over what Megan and Lily's nano scouts had found unthreatening.

It never ceased to amaze Megan just how paranoid Marines were about having the enemy at their backs. Especially when there might be shooters around them.

Maybe the Marines weren't so bad.

"Clear." "Clear." "Clear." "Clear," followed one after the other on net.

"All clear, go, go, go!" Gunny ordered, and more Marines dropped through the hatch. Gunny jumped about in the middle of the lineup.

Now a staff sergeant took up the call of "Go, go, go!"

Megan, Quinn, and the Marine LT waited until gunny reported that all was safe for the likes of them.

It hadn't taken Megan long around Kris to discover that Gunny was spelled G. O. D.

My momma hadn't raised too many dumb children.

Megan pulled out her service automatic but aimed it at the overhead. The Marines had her surrounded. She wasn't here for a firefight.

Hopefully.

She dropped through the hatch to land with a thud on the crate. Her boots absorbed the shock. It was a short hop down to the deck. She was here to find a data outlet, lean her head against it, and see if the strange tumor in her skull could hitch into the Iteeche net and save a lot of human and Iteeche lives.

Even as Megan came up, automatic ready, Lily was spinning more nano scouts off of the two bandoleers that Megan and Quinn wore. Scouts hurried toward the center of the station, leaving relay nanos behind them to pass what they found to Megan.

For the moment, all they found was an empty station.

Since they'd landed about as far down a pier as they could and not end up breathing vacuum, Megan said, "Lieutenant, can we get moving inward? There's no data link here."

"Yes, ma'am. Gunny, advance us cautiously down this pier."

"Aye aye, sir," Gunny said, and sent his troops forward in waves, about a third moving while two-thirds held, tight against the wall or splayed out on the deck, and kept their guns aimed farther up the wide and spacious deck.

A few Marines still covered their back, as if something might appear behind them.

You could never know.

When the Marines had advanced far enough, Megan and Quinn began moving forward, their backs planted firmly on the bulkhead, their eyes focused down the pier. The only thing moving was in Marine camouflage which, at the moment, looked very much like the pier bulkhead or deck.

"Halt!" Megan whispered forcefully on net. "Drop! Go to ground."

Ahead of her Marines froze where they were. Those exposed dropped slowly and cautiously to a prone position on the deck.

"I've got a surveillance camera up ahead," Megan

reported. "It's aimed this way, but I think it's focused on the short range. Wait one."

Lily worked with Megan to invade the camera and check out its feed. The camera was focused on the space a hundred meters out, or less. Another camera covered the promenade directly across from the pod, and a last one was aimed at the hundred meters toward the center of the station. As nanos slipped into the cameras, both adjusted their focus to sweep the next five hundred meters.

Megan switched back to the camera pointed toward them. If it began to move its focus too far out, enough to capture her lead Marines, she'd have cut it off.

The camera did adjust its lens to sweep further up the passageway. Megan watched, hardly breathing, as it reached maximum extension. The busted camera must have been intended to cover the next five hundred meters. Megan zoomed in tight on the signal. You would have to study it very hard to spot the low lumps on the deck or bulkheads. The camouflage was earning its pay.

The camera slowly pulled back its focus, and Megan breathed a sigh of relief and tried breathing again. It was a very nice addiction her body had to oxygen.

"Stay down. I need five minutes of take before I can create a loop," Megan softly ordered. Strange, there really was no need to whisper, but like a good burglar, she did.

The Marines stayed down. The cameras made a second zoom out and retreat. Megan waited until the third zoom exercise was completed, then switched to her own feed. While Megan had observed the camera take, Lily had been doing some video editing. Any hint of a lump on the deck or bulge on the bulkhead was gone from the feed that now went live.

Nothing here. Nothing to see. Move along and look somewhere else for something to worry about.

Megan wondered how many of these she'd have to suborn before they found a nice data outlet she and Lily could hitch into.

Slowly, they advanced down the corridor. Megan checked out the camera she controlled. It was rather primitive. The data leads into and out of it were tiny, just enough to carry the camera feed and no more.

No, a camera would not offer her a way to infiltrate the network.

Megan remembered an evening with Kris at Nuu house. Grampa and Gramma Trouble had come out for supper and Grampa Trouble had taken to telling stories. It was amazing how he could make life or death situations sound so funny.

Following the Unity War, when the both of them had been involved in chasing pirates, slavers, and drug growers, they'd needed to capture a space station, not at all different from the one in front of Megan. One of Kris's unofficial aunts, Aunt Trudy, had been sent in to get inside the computer but, no matter how hard she tried, she couldn't hack it.

That was very embarrassing and could have led to a lot of dead Marines.

However, Aunt Trudy had chosen to improvise. She'd printed out a handful of job application forms, found her way to the window outside the data center, and offered to hire every one of them there at triple the salary for a five-year contract on Wardhaven.

Ten minutes later, Trudy controlled the station's computer. Thirty minutes later, Marines controlled the entire station without a shot fired.

"Got to love those bloodless ops," Grampa Trouble crowed.

Somehow, Megan doubted she'd be in any position to repeat that bloodless coup.

She did manage to stay two camera pods ahead of the advancing Marines, recording longer surveillance of nothing and turning it into a loop before the Marines came in range. Still, there was no data port and no significant computer net access.

Megan tried slipping nanos into the data conduits. They were tiny things, just large enough for a thin fiber optic thread. Still, nanos had little trouble slipping into them and racing up the line. As more and more threads began to form into a small wire, Megan was still looking for a major outlet.

Six cameras down, some six kilometers into the station, Megan finally discovered a pier. Hopefully, it would have a data port. It was empty at the moment. Most of the ships that had previously swung around this station were now in loyalist hands.

There, Lily finally spotted a data port. Unfortunately, while the pier was empty of ships, it had several armed Iteeche loitering about.

That complicates things.

For a long moment, Megan considered her options. If she advanced, she was going into one hell of a fire fight. If she withdrew, her mission was a bust. That left her standing where she was and wondering how to complete her mission from where she stood.

"Launch, I need the Smart Metal in your hull," she ordered.

"Aye, aye, Commander. Wait one." Half a minute later, the boson was back on net. "I'm in the station, ma'am."

"Keep an eye on the station hull," Megan ordered.

"Nelly, could you move the metal inside, seal the hull, and get us some working luggage cart tugs."

"On it right away," Nelly answered.

"When you have the working carts ready to move, Sailor, bring them up to our rearguard. Also, roll the rest of the Smart Metal with you. We may need it for defensive positions."

"Aye, aye, ma'am."

Megan turned back to her problem. The data port she wanted to access was up there, with a couple of dozen Iteeche workers, guards, malingerers, whatever. If she tried to force her way into that, the fight would be on, and she didn't want that fight.

Megan checked the data conduit beside her. It was too thin to carry much bandwidth. Of course, that was typical Iteeche kludge. She started reeling out more fine filaments from her belt and bandoleer. Hurriedly, fiber optic Smart Metal™ extended itself down the side of the conduit until it reached the data port. At the same time, Lily got ready to cut over the data feed from their Iteeche line to the much smaller human one.

Once that was done, they'd reel out the Iteeche cable and replace it with human cable. That would give them all the bandwidth Megan, Lily, Nelly, and Sal needed to operate deep inside the station and its computer system.

The boson drove a nondescript cargo tug up to the rear of the Marine formation. Trailing behind him were loads of empty cargo bins. Driving along beside her were what looked like the same cargo bins, but was actually their Smart Metal™ supply on wheels.

Megan signaled for one of them to be sent up to her and she used it to cut into the outer wall of the deck. Now she had lots of the nice metal to send down the line to thicken up her bandwidth.

To improve communications with Nelly and Sal back on the *Princess Royal*, Megan had one kilo of Smart Metal™ punch a hole through the outer hull and set up a comm link. Suddenly, Nelly and Sal were much more present in her skull.

"Very good, Megan. Thank you," Nelly said.

"I've got some problems attaching to the network," Megan admitted.

Before, Megan had always had to lean her head against a system she wanted to hack into. Admittedly, there had been times when she was a kid that just being too close to a computer got her nightmares, but those had been basic human systems in her family home.

To hack a fully protected alien system, she needed proximity.

"Let's take a look at the data port ahead of us," Nelly said, and in a moment, an image of one floated in front of Megan's eyes.

"Hmm," Nelly said, as the image rotated in place. "I wonder if you have to be up against an authentic data node, or if it be an exact imitation of one.

"I think we should try that," Sal's voice said. Since, at the moment, all three of the computers were talking through Lily's device at Megan's throat, and each one was sounding exactly like they always did, this interesting conversation was drawing some weird looks from the Marines around her.

Still, they'd volunteered for a Longknife mission. They had to know things like this came with the territory.

"I think we have enough cable between us and the next data port. Let's create our own port," Nelly said, and a data port, exact to the manufacturer's face plate, appeared on the bulkhead next to the hole they'd drilled to feed cable down.

Megan undid her helmet and coughed softly. The humidity in the air was almost enough to swim in and the taste of salt and other things made her throat itch. Still, she leaned her forehead against the port. In a moment, she was racing down the cable toward the next data port. That one was a bit harder to work through.

It took her a moment to make her way past the end block that had been set in place. The port was heavily protected. First, it wasn't mean to work without the physical presence of a work station plugged in to activate the port. Besides that, there were also several passwords and a firewall that needed a key.

While Megan ordered Smart Metal^{TM} to form the necessary physical presence of a communications station to activate the port, Nelly and her kids set about cracking the other security safeguards.

Suddenly, they were through.

Immediately, Megan saw herself as a girl on roller skates zooming through a herd of buffalo.

The lieutenant commander grinned. There had been a song, back on Santa Maria that warned "You can't roller skate in a buffalo herd." On Santa Maria, a horned, six-legged creature of the plains had been named a buffalo. It ate grass and its droppings were huge.

There was no way one could roller skate around all those piles.

Megan, however, had jet packs on her feet, and seemed to be shooting along a good foot above the ground. Soon she was joined by Lily on her right, and Nelly and Sal on her left. Together, they shot up the data stream.

They passed several more data ports. Most were inactive.

A few showed a little sign of life. All told, however, the station seemed quite somnolent.

"Where is everyone?" Lily asked.

"Getting drunk, or whatever you do when your world is about to end," Sal said.

The data stream slowly grew wider with more data flowing toward the center with very little making the trip back. There was no evidence that anything exciting was happening along this pier promenade.

The Iteeche always went for one central computer. They were quite huge compared to human computers. In reality, it had thousands, or tens of thousands of central processors, and massive amounts of data storage. Still, the Iteeche abhorred distributing it out and held onto it tightly in the central information center.

It was there that Megan lead Nelly and her children.

Once again, Megan ran into a solid, black wall just like the one she had encountered when she tried to get into the Iteeche Capital network from the Pink Coral Palace. This time, however, she knew how to handle it. Quickly, the four of them converted themselves to birds, Iteeche data packet birds, and the wall vanished in front of them. Apparently, once you learned to masquerade as an honest, hardworking, Iteeche data packet, fire walls vanished into thin air.

They flew on, deep into the computer. Below them, vast herds of beasts lumbered along, seeming to bounce from their hind legs to their front ones, then back again. They moved in long columns with no room between them for small birds to swoop in and pick at their droppings, to take them off to nearby wetlands and drop them in the ponds to feed eels that somehow converted the data into information to present on monitors as had worked with the Iteeche fire control computers.

Clearly, this was different architecture from what they'd encountered before. Different and bigger.

The Iteeche way of handling data was a slow process. When applied to fire control processes, it was a critically slow process that left them vulnerable with guns that rarely hit anything.

Now, Megan led the flight of human and computers higher up, to give them a better view.

The land below them spread out in multicolored square ponds with brightly colored tracks between them. As they watched, the buffalo type beasts split up and galloped down those paths before splashing into the ponds and immediately dissolving.

"That's not what we saw last time," Megan said.

"No, I don't think it is," Nelly agreed. "This is a much more massive computer, much bigger than a mere ship computer. It may have a significantly different architecture."

"That doesn't sound good," Megan couldn't help but say.

"No doubt, but let's keep flying, children. I see something up ahead.

There was something truly massive ahead of them.

It looked like a large, black cube. As they flew closer to it, it went from large to huge, then to humongous.

When they finally reached it, it proved to be not only immense, but lacking in any openings. Megan handled that problem by just kind of melting her way through the deep black walls.

Inside, she was greeted by a series of open channels with water flowing through them. They were every color of the rainbow, much like the ponds that the buffalo had disappeared into. In each narrow furrow, fish swam, fishes the same color as the water.

That piqued Megan's interest. She dove down and took a

peck at one of the fish. She nipped a scale about in the middle of the fish's back . . . and found herself with a mouth full of data.

"Hey, these fish have more data concentrated in them than anything we've seen," Megan announced.

"But who's it going to?" Nelly asked. "Where's it going?"

The four of them tried pecking several fish with no better idea of where the data was addressed to or from.

Then that changed.

"I nipped the white scale they have on their head between their eyes," Nelly announced. "That's the header file."

Megan pecked at the next fish's white scale and immediately knew it was from the reactor reporting all was well to the central control room.

The four of them began pecking for all they were worth.

However, it was clear to Megan that she, Nelly, and the kids could not search this vast data flow. So, Megan tried something.

She split herself in half. Suddenly, she found herself a disembodied presence above two birds, pecking away at fish. Megan doubled them, then doubled them again and again. Only when she tried to double from sixteen to thirty-two did this bite her on her nonexistent ass.

Sixteen birds continued doing their picking at fish. Sixteen others just stood there, immobile. Megan willed them away and accepted that sixteen was the most she could control.

However, Nelly had spotted Megan's experiment. Moments later, the Navy lieutenant commander found herself surrounded by huge flocks of birds, some on this level, but others dove through the floor and headed for other data streams on other levels.

"I've spotted the data stream on the planet below," Megan announced. "It's not saying much, but that we're still here. There's no message traffic. I'll pinch off the message carrier," she announced and put some of the nano scouts that had infiltrated with them to work.

Very quickly, nothing could go down the data cables of the elevator that didn't get Megan's approval.

While she was at it, she took over control of the ferries on the elevator. The two docked at the station now found alarms going off that sent everyone rushing ashore. The ferries about to depart from the dirtside station were also suddenly full of hooting alarms.

Ferries on the elevator, in the acceleration phase, received warnings that the tracks were warped, their safety was in doubt, and they should turn back. Strangely, those in the deceleration phase got no such warnings, but then, they were few, and, at this time of night, rather empty.

Just as Megan finished isolating the station from visitors, Nelly announced, "I've found the Port Captain's office. It was hard to locate since it's not active. However, I did find a pool of prepared fish; half had ordered the pier hatches open, half ordered them closed."

"Are you sure?" Megan asked. "Can you test it?"

"I think we can. I've got a small crew hatch in the middle of the station. I'll send an open command, then two seconds later, a close command. Let's see what happens."

A few seconds later, the air pressure began to drop. Two seconds after that, it quit dropping.

"Very good," Megan said. "Nelly, tell Kris that we're ready to scare the pants off of a lot of Iteeche."

"Kris says to wait for her to make an announcement."

A moment later, Megan found herself listening to her boss.

"This is Grand Admiral, Her Royal Highness Kris Longknife, Imperial Admiral of the First Order of Steel and Commander of the Combined Fleets of the Empire. Greetings to those of you aboard what you call Artiecca High Station One. We have infiltrated your station and now have control of it. We demand you surrender immediately. If you do not surrender, we will open the hatches on your docks and empty your station of all atmosphere."

Kris paused for a long moment.

"Since I have not received a surrender, it is time for me to show you just how helpless you are. Three large dock hatches will be opened in three, two, one. Open."

Nelly had released three fish with just the right amount of lead time. Just as Kris said "Open," three huge cargo hatches broke their seals and began to roll back on their tracks. Air began to flow out of the station in a hurricane wind.

Nelly had picked three docks with no people around. Still, tugs, cargo wagons and anything not welded to the deck began a hurried departure from the station. Nelly reported to Kris how the air pressure was falling.

On the station, sirens were screaming as commanding voices told everyone to get behind an airtight bulkhead or don a spacesuit.

One of Megan's birds spotted the hastily released fish with every scale devoted totally to, "We surrender! We surrender!" She made sure to let the fish go its way, but advised Kris that the surrender was on its way.

"Close the hatches," came immediately from Kris.

"Fish already on its way," Nelly reported.

A second later, the massive hatches began to roll their way along their heavy tracks. Three seconds later, the loss of pressure ceased.

"We will be boarding you immediately. Do not attempt to resist."

"Kris says for us to check the laser controls and radars," Nelly reported.

"I've got those," Lily reported. "They're blocked. They couldn't fire if they wanted to. I'm feeding the power in the capacitors back into the power supply. No worry here."

Fifteen minutes later, the loyalist battlecruisers began to catch the hooks and be hauled into the station's piers. No sooner were they locked down and their locks opened, than Iteeche Marines marched to occupy the important stations: reactor, Port Captain, Station Manager, communications, and ferry terminal.

Without waiting for further developments, Megan began shipping all the available Smart Metal ^{TM} down the beanstalk. It would take them an hour to get dirtside, but they'd be spreading out, mapping the capital city of the planet, identifying the Planetary Overlord and other important people of power.

Megan already had authority to kill the Planetary Overlord. If she could find him before he could hide away, this might take a lot less time.

56

The assault on Artiecca High Station 1 had an amazing effect on Stations 2, 3, and 4. Within the hour, all three had been quietly occupied.

When you have initiative and momentum behind you, it's amazing how quickly people step out of your way. Hurry out of your way. Throw themselves out of your way.

All this time, Megan, Nelly, and her two kids loitered around in the central computer for Station 1. There wasn't anything they needed to do there to pacify the station. They were just devoting all their time to what the nano scouts were uncovering around the capital city.

Apparently, the quiet standard reports from the stations that Megan and Nelly arranged for, had the intended results. The watch officers continued their naps, games of chance, and quiet visits to the broom closets. Clearly, there was more to Iteeche sexuality than what happened in the breeding ponds.

With no alarms going off, the capital city seemed content to sleep. The first few orbits had created a solid map of the planet and its urban areas, and several Iteeche had identified the Palace of the Satrap. The Palace of the Planetary Overlord was a bit smaller and right next door.

Apparently, if someone needed to borrow a cup of sugar, or a few traitors to torture, they'd be ready at hand.

Within a few minutes of each other, Megan's nanos identified both of the big guys, all asleep, all surrounded by naked females of their species.

Both had taken a sedative.

Megan chose to be a bit more creative in dispatching these two. Nanos entered through the lungs, passed into the blood stream, then created blockages to the heart. Both died quietly of massive heart attacks in their sleep.

Like the angel of death, Megan and her nanos went looking for more victims. There were several palaces around those two massive central showcases of opulence. The minister of security was the next to develop heart problems, followed quickly by the minister of industry and production. The commanders in chief of the Army and Navy had smaller compounds near the palaces, and both quietly turned sleep into a deeper slumber as their hearts betrayed them.

As the sun rose the next morning, most of the officers of the personal guards to both the Planetary Overlord and the Pasha of the Satrap had joined their political masters in death. Around six o'clock, calls to the hospitals sent ambulances screaming across town to Very Important Dead People's houses.

The sirens set a lot of beaks on edge; it didn't get better when the nighttime music was kept on later into the morning. The usual cheery marches that most people awoke to were still soothing sleep music as alarms went off . . . and that was *not* soothing.

Kris Longknife decided it was time to let the people of Artiecca 4 know about the sudden change in management. By now, she had control over all the nets on Artiecca 4 and she put them to use.

Her message was short and to the point. "Surrender and you will continue your life, doing what you have been doing. Some of you high up in the clan structure will need to be reassigned, but no one has to die over this. If, however, you damage any equipment, or attempt to sabotage production, the penalty will be death. For those of you of high clan or government rank who advocated for this system to join the rebels, you may expect to be transported to the Imperial Capital to make your formal and sincere apology directly to the Emperor."

Immediately after that, the invasion began.

By this time, there were 500,000 Iteeche troops standing by on the four stations. Much to the dismay of the dirtside ferry landings, all of the ferries had suddenly hooted hull damage and ordered everyone ashore. Five minutes later, the ferries sealed locks and took off at 2.0 gees for the stations. Now, every ferry was at the station and filling with loyalist Iteeche troops, all with orders as to who to collect and what key locations to secure.

However, they were not the only forces on the move.

As Kris spoke her warning, sonic booms shook the morning silence. Around each of the ferry stations, Iteeche Marines in their own version of Light Assault Craft flipped the tiny landers and completed the rest of their combat jump by chutes. With few exceptions, their parachutes delivered them to the storage lots or parking lots around the elevator stations.

On the ground, the armored Marines quickly took

possession of the station and set up roadblocks on all approaches.

Only two of the stations encountered difficulty. Decapitated like they were, very few of the troops were ordered out of barracks, and a few of those that did get orders balked at carrying them out. The two attacks on the beanstalk stations were weak, poorly coordinated, and quickly repulsed.

An hour after Kris's declaration, tens of thousands of loyal Iteeche troops and their armored vehicles began to move out at high speed from the elevators and take over communications and network nodes. Centers of government administration were also seized. As the bureaucrats showed up at the offices in dribs and drabs, most were waved through to their desks or work benches.

High clan officers in senior management positions tended not to appear for work that day. Once the workday was well underway, a count showed that close to half of the medium to low clan lordlings had been collected when they came to work. Kris went back on the net to invite all other clan leaders to report to collection points. By sunset, they had close to ninety percent of the clan bosses and underlings.

That night, Iteeche Marines went looking for the remaining ten percent. In most cases, they found them already dead by their own hand. In a few cases, they chose to fight.

That didn't last long.

The Iteeche Marines followed Kris's guidelines. Along with the Marines, a member of the clan this official belonged to would go along to offer all the clan guardsmen employment on other planets, both for them and those attached to them.

That was usually enough to get the guards slinking out

of their hiding spot. Sometimes the clan official surrendered. Sometimes they resisted and had to be killed. There
was no attempt to capture them alive.

They knew, as well as Kris, what was waiting for them at
the Imperial Capital.

Next morning, Kris was eating breakfast when she found
herself being joined by Megan.

"That was a good job you did with the station computer,
Commander," Kris said.

"It saved my Marines one hell of a fight," Jack added.

"Glad to be of service, Admiral," Megan said, with a shy
duck of her head. "You think you'll be needing any more of
my unique skills?"

"I hope not," Kris said. "We've got most of the rebel clan
leaders and supervisory team moving up the elevator today
as the new loyal clan leaders and supervisory teams move
down the beanstalk. We cut the clan overhead down pretty
much to where you proved the merit system began to take
over. Frankly, I don't know why we're putting the clan political appointees back over these people. They can run the
place without them."

Megan shrugged. "Who knows. Maybe they will. Heaven
knows, you're dumping an entirely new clan overhead on
these workers. It will be interesting to see how long it takes
these new clan types to figure out how to manage things, or
if they ever will."

Megan paused in her ingestion of what claimed to be
eggs and sausage. "Maybe you're starting something here, as
well as back on Zargoth. You took the time to capture that
asteroid and get their own asteroid mining effort going. A
planet that had been locked in a zero-sum game struggling
with hardly enough resources to feed their fifty-billion

Iteeche now have a chance to turn themselves into a decent place to live."

"Assuming they don't take this as an opportunity to choose a lot more younglings out of the mating ponds," Jack said, not at all optimistically.

"The resources you've got them bringing into their economy won't give them any more food," Megan pointed out. "It will give them a better life for those that are alive. That will mean something. It will mean something for them, and for a majority of Iteeche."

"But if a tree falls in the forest and no one hears?" Jack asked.

"I'm not at all sure that the Iteeche underclass is all that ignorant of what goes on around them. Hell, they know if the clans get too rambunctious, their planet could get gassed."

Kris eyed Megan through a frown. "And you know this, kid, how?"

"Let's just say that throwing a banquet for the hard-working craftsmen that saved our bacon back on Zargoth let me hear some stuff you won't hear in the halls of clan power."

Kris eyed her cousin for a long moment, a thought forming in the back of her head. Was it one she could trust to share with Admiral Coth? It certainly wasn't one she'd share with Ron. He was Imperial Counselor from the top of his bald head to the tip of his toes.

Coth, however, was part of no clan. He'd risen to what rank he had before Kris showed up based on merit, hard work, and the willingness to tackle the messy stuff junior clan lordlings didn't want to get their hands messy with.

She'd have to be careful how she approached Coth, but he'd known what was being said about Kris in the dives and bars outside the Navy piers. Maybe he already had ears that listened here and there.

That was something she definitely needed to check out.

"So," Megan said. "I couldn't help but notice that you didn't land even half of the landing force. Just a quarter. I take it you have something on your mind."

"Yep," Kris said, grinning at Jack. They'd talked it over last night. Megan might as well be the first to learn. "We've picked the next target. We'll spend another week here while Coth goes through the officers on the captured ships and separates those he thinks are questionable from those dependable. We'll also do some training. Next time we do that Nelson Maneuver, I want it to come out cleaner. After that, we're off to add another planet to our merry band of highway men."

"Do we have enough clan boss types to fill the vacancies?" Megan asked. "I like the way things have gone on Artiecca 4 so far. I don't think anyone wants to repeat the problems we had on Zargoth."

"We don't quite have enough for another planet. I'm thinking of sending the *Relentless* out leading a squadron of Iteeche battlecruisers and twenty of the empty fast attack transports. Nelly has a course for them that will keep them well out of rebel space and get them to the capital fast. The transports are taking back all the displaced clan chiefs and their companions. They've also got a freezer full of those that took the quick way out. I don't want anyone thinking we're harboring traitors. I've got enough problems as it is."

"So, they'll come back with more troops and a few of those battleships of state loaded with clan lordlings," Megan said.

"Yep," was Kris's reply.

For a long moment, they thought on that, then Jack

raised his glass of some kind of juice and said, "So, we gut the rebellion."

"We gut the rebellion," two Longknife women repeated, clanging their glasses to his.

"May they be truly grateful for what they are about to receive," Megan added, before she emptied her glass.

ABOUT THE AUTHOR

Mike Shepherd is the National best-selling author of the Kris Longknife saga. Mike Moscoe is the award-nominated short story writer who has also written several novels, most of which were, until recently, out of print. Though the two have never been seen in the same room at the same time, they are reported to be good friends.

Mike Shepherd grew up Navy. It taught him early about change and the chain of command. He's worked as a bartender and cab driver, personnel advisor, and labor negotiator. Now retired from building databases about the endangered critters of the Northwest, he looks forward to some fun reading and writing.

Mike lives in Vancouver, Washington, with his wife Ellen, and not too far from his daughter and grandkids. He enjoys reading, writing, dreaming, watching grandchildren for story ideas and upgrading his computer – all are never ending.

For more information:
www.krislongknife.com
mikeshepherd@krislongknife.com

2018 RELEASES

In 2016, I amicably ended my twenty-year publishing relationship with Ace, part of Penguin Random House.

In 2017, I began publishing through my own independent press, KL & MM Books. We produced six e-books and a short story collection. We also brought the books out in paperback and audio.

In 2018, I intend to keep the novels coming.

We began the year with **Kris Longknife's Successor**. Grand Admiral Santiago still has problems. Granny Rita is on the rampage again, and the cats have gone on strike, refusing to send workers to support the human effort on Alwa. Solving that problem will be tough. The last thing Sandy needs is trouble with the murderess alien space raiders. So, of course, that is what she gets.

May 1 will see **Kris Longknife: Commanding**. Kris has won her first battle, but the way the Iteeche celebrate victory can be hard on the stomach. The rebellion won't quit and now Kris needs to raise a fleet, not only to defend the Iteeche Imperial Capitol, but also take the war to the rebels.

In the second half of 2018, you can look forward to the following:

Vicky Peterwald Dominator on July 1

Rita Longknife: Landing Party on September 1

Kris Longknife Implacable on November 1.

Stay in touch to follow developments by friending Kris Longknife and follow Mike Shepherd on Facebook or check in at my website www.krislongknife.com